PRAISE FOR
WHERE THE FOREST MEETS THE STARS

"Enchanting, insightful, and extraordinary."

—*Novelgossip*

"Though the novel appears to start as a fantasy, it evolves into a domestic drama with murder-mystery elements, all adding up to a satisfying read."

—*Booklist*

"Vanderah's beautifully human story reminds us that sometimes we need to look beyond the treetops at the stars to let some light into our lives."

—New York Journal of Books

"*Where the Forest Meets the Stars* is a magical little gem of a book filled with lots of love and hope."

—HelloGiggles

"A captivating fantasy tale of mystery and intrigue . . ."

—Fresh Fiction

"A skillfully written and thoroughly entertaining novel by an author with a genuine gift for originality and a distinctive narrative-driven storytelling style . . ."

—Midwest Book Review

"*Where the Forest Meets the Stars* by Glendy Vanderah is an enchanting, heartwarming, not-to-be-missed novel that is bursting with love and hope."

—*The Patriot Ledger*

"A heartwarming, magical story about love, loss, and finding family where you least expect it. This touching novel will remind readers of a modern-day *The Snow Child*."

—Christopher Meades, award-winning author of
Hanna Who Fell from the Sky

"*Where the Forest Meets the Stars* is an enchanting novel full of hope and the power of love that will pull at your heartstrings. Perfect for fans of Sarah Addison Allen."

—Karen Katchur, author of *The Sisters of Blue Mountain*

"*Where the Forest Meets the Stars* will grab you from the very first page and surprise you the whole way through. This is an incredibly original, imaginative, and curious story. Glendy Vanderah has managed to create a world that is very real and, yet, entirely out of the ordinary."

—Taylor Jenkins Reid, acclaimed author of
The Seven Husbands of Evelyn Hugo

"In *Where the Forest Meets the Stars*, Glendy Vanderah weaves a deft and poignant story with well-drawn characters, including clever Ursa. With an unexpected and heart-racing climax, readers will wait breathlessly to find out what happens. A beautiful story of love, resilience, and the power of second chances."

—Susie Orman Schnall, award-winning author of *The Subway Girls*

"*Where the Forest Meets the Stars* is a lovely, surprising, and insightful look at the way bonds are formed—both the ones that we choose and the ones that seem to choose us."

—Rebecca Kauffman, author of *The Gunners*

"*Where the Forest Meets the Stars* is an enchanting novel . . . Readers will be taken by Glendy Vanderah's rich and relatable characters and the way in which she weaves their stories together. At its core, *Where the Forest Meets the Stars* is about having faith, nurturing hope, and trusting your heart above your head, because when you do, miracles are possible."

—Janis Thomas, bestselling author of *What Remains True*

"A powerful story of the way in which hearts are mended by love, compassion, and everyday miracles. Cleverly plotted and building to an intense crescendo in the final chapters, *Where the Forest Meets the Stars* is a beautiful and unforgettable debut."

—Julianne MacLean, *USA Today* bestselling author

PRAISE FOR
THE LIGHT THROUGH THE LEAVES

"A memorable story of love's healing power."

—*Publishers Weekly*

"*The Light Through the Leaves* opens with an unspeakable mistake and characters you think at first will never find their way back. Then, with the assured hand of a master storyteller, Vanderah weaves a deeply moving tale of healing and redemption, catapulting the reader toward an ending that will make you believe in nature's magic."

—Steven Rowley, bestselling author of *Lily and the Octopus* and *The Editor*

The

OCEANOGRAPHY

of the

MOON

ALSO BY GLENDY VANDERAH

Where the Forest Meets the Stars
The Light Through the Leaves

The
OCEANOGRAPHY
of the
MOON

a novel

GLENDY VANDERAH

Published by Lake Union Publishing, Seattle

www.apub.com

Amazon, the Amazon logo, and Lake Union Publishing are trademarks of Amazon.com, Inc., or its affiliates.

ISBN-13: 9781542039529 (hardcover)
ISBN-10: 1542039525 (hardcover)

ISBN-13: 9781542026505 (paperback)
ISBN-10: 1542026504 (paperback)

Cover design by Kathleen Lynch / Black Kat Design

Printed in the United States of America

First Edition

For Scott

1
RILEY MAYS

I shouldn't have kept her in this little box all these years. She wouldn't like that. She was what people would call a "force of nature," always lively and laughing and loving. Especially loving. I never met anyone who loved so much.

She was at her best when she was loving things outdoors. Clouds and forsythia and snow, ants carrying crumbs she fed them while we lunched in the park.

Even dirt. She loved dirt. She didn't wear gloves when she gardened. "That ruins the experience," she used to say.

She held a palm of soil out to me. "Do you smell that? Do you feel it?"

I was eight or so and didn't understand what she was asking. I took some of the dirt into my hand and touched my nose to the cool, black crumble.

"That's time," she said, "the actual smell of time, of eroding mountains, and stones pushed by glaciers, and the lives of everything that ever existed on Earth." She held the soil to her nose, inhaling deeply, eyes closed in pleasure. "It's the smell of eternity. There are bits of stars in this soil, Riley. Do you smell them?"

I closed my eyes, as she did, and breathed it in. Yes, I smelled stars. I felt like I was whirling in a swirl of stars in a soil-black universe. The intoxicating aroma nearly made me dizzy.

That's how it was with Aunt Julia. Always magic. Even in dirt.

That's why I have to get her out of the box. She needs to be part of the magic again.

I've been looking for the perfect spot for her ashes since I was twelve. I can't believe it's been nine years and I still haven't set her free.

The perfect place has to be outdoors, but not just any pretty place. I want it to be somewhere she would exclaim, "Look, Riley! Isn't this an enchanting scene!"

I thought I'd found the right spot in September when I last hiked this creek trail. That day, this little rocky waterfall was covered with golden and scarlet leaves. When I first saw it, all the vivid color and silken threads of silver rushing through the mossy stones, the first word that came to mind was *Enchanting!*

It was perfect. And it wasn't far down a trail in a park that's only a forty-minute drive from the house. I could visit Julia at the waterfall anytime I wanted.

But now that I've arrived at the cascade, I'm not sure it's right for her. It looks different in February. No color. Everything is black and brown, and the water is barely trickling. There isn't a cover of snow to make the scene prettier because the weather has been unusually warm. Even the sky is colorless today.

I shouldn't have waited until her birthday to do this. I should have done it right away while I felt good about it. But I could have guessed this would happen when I've backed out of dispersing the ashes several times.

I sit in the cold creek stones and take the white crematory box out of my backpack. I open it and unwrap the inner plastic bag.

"Happy birthday, Julia."

2

I sift my fingers through the rough ashes. At first, I was afraid to touch them. Then one day I realized they looked like moondust, and I had touched the surface of the moon many times. That's when I started to like handling the ashes—and *needing* to touch them.

I suppose that's why I haven't found the perfect place to put them. I don't want to.

I rub the coarse ashes into my left palm. I read the words I penciled on one side of the crematory box when I was thirteen. I can hardly see them, but I know them by heart: *In spite of all, some shape of beauty moves away the pall from our dark spirits.* One of Julia's favorite lines of poetry, from *Endymion* by John Keats.

I study the diminished waterfall in front of me. The creek makes soft licking sounds as it passes over rocks. A downy woodpecker calls. The cascade trickles and drips.

I'm not feeling the magic.

"It's not the perfect place I thought it was," I tell Julia. "I'm not leaving you here." I return her ashes to the box, delicately brushing remnant dust off my hand into the container. "I'm sorry."

I'll take the ashes home and return them to my bookcase. I use the box as a bookend, always with Julia's copy of *Endymion* right next to it.

My bookshelf has been home to the box since it came to me, about six months after Julia died. By then my mother was dead, too, and I'd been living with my cousins, Alec and Sachi, for almost a month. Alec had to go all the way to Chicago from northwestern Wisconsin to get the ashes. That was the same day he picked up my mother's ashes at a different crematory.

Alec hadn't expected me to come into the kitchen and see the boxes he'd brought home. I'd gone downstairs for a glass of water and caught Sachi and him discussing whether they should tell me where he'd been. I stared at the two small cartons on the counter. The white one said "Julia Mays," the brown one, "Nikki Mays." I immediately knew what was inside.

"Riley . . . ," Alec said. "Can I get you something?"

I kept looking at the boxes. How strange it was to see those two women compartmentalized into small containers when only a half year earlier they'd been almost my entire life.

Alec said, "These are . . ." He looked like he'd rather do any awful thing than tell me what was in the boxes. "These are your mother's and aunt's remains. They were cremated. We told you that when you first came to live with us."

I didn't say anything. I rarely did at that time.

"I'm sorry," he said. "Would you rather not . . . we could put them away until you're ready."

I'm still not ready.

"I'm sorry," Alec said again when he saw how I stared at the boxes. "I'll put them somewhere . . ."

As he started to remove the boxes, I took the white one off the counter. I was surprised by how substantial Julia felt when she was only ashes. I hugged her to my chest and walked toward the stairway.

"Riley . . . ," Alec said behind me.

I turned around.

"What about your mother?"

What about your mother? The question of my life. I still see that question in Alec's and Sachi's eyes sometimes. I think they've always known there was more to the story of Nikki, Julia, and me than what the police told them.

Alec offered the box with Nikki's ashes. I could only manage to shake my head before I turned away and continued up the stairs.

To this day I don't know what he did with Nikki's ashes.

~

Sleet starts falling before I return to my car in the trailhead lot. Driving is hazardous, but I still take the long way home and get the groceries on the list Sachi gave me. On the way out of town, I slow down at a house with FOR SALE and SOLD signs on the front lawn.

If not for the clock, I wouldn't have looked twice at the junk piled on the curbside. It's the kind of family history I can't bear to witness: all those broken things that can't be saved. A child's pink bedside table missing a leg. A stained upholstered chair dangling an arm. A doll's head with a vacant stare perched next to its dissociated body. A cheap hollowed-out chest, its drawers stacked on the ground in front of it. Shoes, hats, pants, and shirts too ragged for Goodwill overflowing from cardboard boxes. The sleet that bleeds over the mess somehow makes it seem more miserable.

I avert my eyes from the spectacle of the family's broken possessions as I pull my car to the curb. The mantel clock is vintage, early nineteen hundreds. I imagine it was once cherished, looked to often, setting the rhythm of the house in which it lived. It's been positioned at the heart of the junk pile, in the precise middle of the chest, as if the owner of the house tried to re-create the clock's days of honor. I think they want someone to rescue it, to fix it, to love it as a family did decades ago. But the glass over its face is shattered. Even the junk pickers have left it to the cruelty of the wet weather and the coming trash smasher.

I lift the clock off the chest and take it into the car, propping it against the back of the passenger seat. During the drive out of town, the sleet storm wanes. I'm about ten miles into the countryside when the sun fully emerges from clouds.

I occasionally look at the clock, feeling its presence. As if I have a passenger riding with me. It looks sad to me. Old clocks always do.

"You're lucky I found you," I tell it.

The clock's cracked face stares quizzically at me.

"You were going to a garbage dump. People tell time with cell phones now. Old kinds of clocks don't much matter."

The clock's gaze is melancholy.

"It's okay. You're going to be useful again."

I don't look to see if the clock is relieved by this news. I'm more concerned about how weird it is that I'm talking to a clock.

When I arrive home, Sachi helps me carry the groceries into the house.

"Look what I found in someone's garbage."

She pets the clock as if it's a stray kitten. "What a beauty. He'll love it. He's in his room."

I jog up the stairs. Kiran meets me at the door to his bedroom, as if he knows what I've found and he's waiting to receive it. "Pretty cool, isn't it?" I ask.

"Thank you, Riley."

"You're welcome."

He carries the broken clock across the threshold with care and earnestness, like a war surgeon conveying a wounded patient into an operating room. He gently sets the clock on his worktable, and after a moment of studying it, he sits in the chair at the table. He opens his box of instruments. Following a long prayerlike pause, he selects a tool and begins his work.

I love to watch Kiran with his clocks. The reverence with which he handles each tiny mechanism. After he studies a piece he's removed from the clock, he carefully sets it on the worktable, positioning every cog and wheel in some precise constellation that has significance to him. My heart seems to pause as Kiran leans into the mechanics of time, a river of sunlight washing the color out of his cropped hair. The bright afternoon light has turned his blue dress a glowing white. A dreamy glitter of dust motes drifts around him. He looks like a holy man conducting magical rites with sacred relics.

As unique as Kiran, the space around him is not the realm of a typical eight-year-old. The dormered room with periwinkle walls is more like a shaman's cave. Or a wizard's den. The twin bed with a white coverlet, the only evidence that the space serves as a bedroom, has become lost in a maze of small tables purchased at antique and junk stores.

6

Upon those twelve tables, Kiran has carefully arranged and intermixed hundreds of clock parts and fossils.

Fossils are the other objects Kiran uses in his cryptic communication with the universe. When he's done disassembling the old clock, he'll execute my favorite part of the magic. One by one, he'll place the clock parts in precise positions alongside gears, screws, microchips, and hour hands, and among stones imprinted with ferns, corals, mollusks, and trilobites.

I know it's unscientific, but I like to imagine Kiran's magic is what keeps the universe in order. Maybe he does it with a few other sages who live in obscurity all over the world, and they're all connected in some way the rest of us don't understand. But it's getting more and more difficult for them to keep the order of goodness on Earth, because lately everything is changing too fast.

I look over Kiran's shimmering galaxy of metal and stone. Somewhere on these tables are the pieces of a kitchen clock that measured the last seconds of two lives. Two lives that were in constant opposition to each other—even now, long after they ended. I don't know where that clock's pieces are among the hundreds of parts scattered over these tables, and this comforts me, to know that time has been eviscerated.

Kiran pushes back his chair and stands. He's ready to distribute his newly harvested time into the magic. I hardly breathe so I don't distract him. I've been leaning against his doorway, and I'm not sure if he knows I'm watching. He doesn't mind if I do.

He delicately pinches something tiny in his fingers and lifts it off the table. He looks down at it for a few seconds, then peers around at his tables, at his little objects that look like gleaming stars in the sun's light. He walks to a five-legged oak table we found in an antique store last summer. Its surface is scoured, slashed, and stained, but Kiran doesn't mind. It's only the substrate upon which he puts his universe in order.

He sets the tiny piece I can't see on the oak table among fossils and other clockworks. He studies his decision for a moment before he returns to the mantel clock pieces and chooses another mechanism.

I watch him repeat this process five more times. He's almost in a trance, and I'm quite sure he's not aware of my presence as he places the sixth clock part on a sun-streamed table beneath the west window. But now he looks at me and says, "That one was for you, Riley."

He's never said anything like that when I watched him with his clocks. I want to ask him what he did that has to do with me. But I don't interfere in Kiran's realm. I dare not meddle with the magic when I have all this darkness inside me.

2

VAUGHN ORR

I look up, searching for the moon, one bright star. All I see is a haze of city light reflected from a cover of clouds. Antenna lights wink red eyes at me.

I want to see stars. Lots of stars. Like how it is in some of my books.

But more than stars, I crave darkness. I don't know why. This hunger for darkness has come over me like a sickness. I have to see what a real night is like. The kind you can't find in New York City. I've been trying to hide in all this light for too long.

The WALK sign has been flashing, and I cross before it's too late. It's early February, but the city already smells like spring. Wet concrete and asphalt. Beer. Steaming food-truck grub eaten at leisure on sidewalks.

The balminess unsettles me. As does a young woman walking toward me, staring at me. Possibly she's recognized me, but she walks by as I duck into the dimmed lighting of the tavern where I'll meet Gemma.

I see Gemma across the room, seated at a table next to the brick wall. She has a martini, so I order an IPA at the bar before I go over. She smiles when she sees me coming. "I like the haircut."

I sit across from her, rubbing one hand over the bristled ends of my freshly shorn hair. "Not too short?"

"No, I like it." She leans over a fake candle and kisses my lips. Before she settles back into her chair, she asks, "How'd it go with your agent?"

"Good."

"It's for sure?"

"For sure."

"Oh my god! This is amazing!"

I take a drink of the beer.

"How can you look so calm?"

"I've known for a while. I only signed the papers today."

"Do you know when it will come out?"

"Maybe next year around Christmas."

"Two movies! *Two!*"

The admiration shining in her eyes has got to go. Being looked at like that bothers me more and more.

"Don't get so excited. The movie will probably suck."

"Why?"

I shrug.

"Why do you say that?"

I said it to wipe the giddy look off her face. But my reply is, "Can you imagine that book made into a movie? They'll get it all wrong."

"I *can* imagine it! It will be *a-mazing!*"

Amazing is the main adjective of the few in Gemma's vocabulary. Come to think of it, that was true of my last girlfriend, too. This is no surprise. I choose to hang out with people who don't try to impress me with their vocabulary and knowledge of literature, as many do when they discover I'm an author. Those types usually want to pick my brain about my writing, a topic that's off limits for me. I prefer conversation that has nothing to do with me or my novels, or even with books in general.

With lovers, especially, this is a necessary requirement, and that's why being with Gemma has gotten difficult since she became a fan. When we met, she hadn't read a book in the four years since high school. In the three months we've been together, she's read four novels: the entirety of my life's work. And she's watched the movie created from my second book at least three times, never in my presence.

Gemma is prattling on about what actors should play the characters in the book.

I drink, nodding and inserting an occasional "Do you think so?" but not really listening. I'm replaying my conversation with my agent, Mel, today. I think she noticed my dark mood.

Of course she did. The panic has been getting worse since the last book came out. I feel like I've run out of rope and I'm dangling off a cliffside.

~

"What's wrong?" Mel asked after I signed the contract. "This is a really good deal."

"I know."

"What then?"

"I think . . ." I felt compelled to warn her.

Her green eyes probed mine. "What?"

"I think there might not be any more books."

She leaned back in her desk chair, smiling. "All authors say that at some point in their careers."

"Do they?"

"Yes, and I'm almost relieved you're finally human."

"Am I?"

"You're superhuman, Vaughn. Four bestsellers in eight years—two of them megahits—and now a second movie deal. All at the ripe young age of thirty."

"I don't turn thirty until September."

"Jesus. You deserve a bit of writer's block. Take some time off, a trip or something."

"Now that you mention it, I have been thinking of a trip."

"Where to?" When I didn't immediately answer, she said, "Try Europe. You'll love it."

"No, I'm . . ." Did I dare voice what I'd imagined doing for years?

"What?"

"I'm thinking of buying land somewhere."

"Where?"

"I might look in Wisconsin."

"Wisconsin?" She nearly grimaced. "What city?"

"No more cities. I'm tired of this environment."

"Then what about a beach house? Or a cabin out west in the mountains?" She grinned. "Someplace I'd actually want to visit you."

"Beaches and mountains aren't my thing."

"Right. You're originally from Chicago. I guess that explains Wisconsin."

"I hear there are some nice properties over there. Woods and lakes."

She still looked dubious about the Cheese State. "Would you keep your place in Brooklyn?"

"I don't know. I'm not sure about any of this. I just need a quiet place to think. I need to figure out this writer's block . . . or whatever it is."

I think she finally saw something that might worry her. I studied her eyes. Yes, she saw. I had to look away from her scrutiny. I rubbed my finger over a scratch in the crystal of my Rolex.

"Vaughn . . . it's okay to feel burned out. Anyone would be after the wild ride you've been on."

I looked at her. "I know."

Her usual business expression returned. "When are you going to Wisconsin?"

"Not sure."

"Any chance you'd do me a huge favor if you're near Chicago in the next few months?"

I knew what she was about to ask. She never stopped urging me to do book events. I allow very few signings, only in NYC, and I never do readings or interviews. I was fortunate my first book was a big enough hit that I didn't have to do much to promote it. I'm no good at self-promotion, but what I hate more is the questions: Do you use an outline or write spontaneously? How many hours do you write in a typical day? How fast did you write such and such book? What authors most inspire your work? Who is that person all your books are dedicated to?

"Don't give me that look," she said.

"What look?"

"The pre-no look. You should do this one. It would be a big event. Let Chicago honor their hometown hero."

I squirmed at the thought of it.

"A good friend of mine wants to organize it. We were close in grad school."

"Mel . . ."

"Maybe connecting with your readers will help you break the block. Go out there and get some of their love."

"Love? They're a bunch of window peepers." In a high voice I mimicked two actual questions I've been asked by female fans: "What do you wear when you write, Mr. Orr?" And my all-time favorite: "Do you masturbate when you write your love scenes?"

"Every famous person has that happen," Mel said. "It goes with the territory."

"I know, and that's why I don't do these things."

"Please do this one. For me, if for no other reason." She squinted and pointed a finger at me. "I pulled you out of the slush pile when you were waiting tables. You owe me."

I supposed I did owe her. "When?" I asked.

"*Thank you! And you can choose the date. My friend is Tommi Singh. She has a fantastic art gallery in Chicago, and her husband owns one of my favorite bookstores a couple blocks away. The event would probably be in the bookstore, but if you wanted, it could be in the gallery. That would be a beautiful venue, don't you think?*"

"*Wherever it is, no readings, no speeches. I'm only signing books.*"

"*For god's sake, Vaughn. It's people who buy your books, not a firing squad.*"

"*I wasn't aware there was a difference.*"

She glared like a displeased parent. "*I have authors who would kill to be in your place.*"

I didn't doubt that.

She looked about to say more, maybe remind me that everything had been too easy for me.

I needed no reminder. I looked at my watch again. "*I have to go.*" I got up to leave, though I'd be fifteen minutes early for my appointment if I left right away.

"*Hot date?*"

"*Haircut and manicure.*"

As I turned toward the door, she said, "*You know, if you tell them, they'll stop asking.*"

I turned around. "*Tell them what?*"

"*Anything. Who she is, for starters.*"

"*Who?*"

"*You know who.*"

I knew who. I'd been asked about the person I'd dedicated my books to with increasing frequency as each had been published. But Mel had never asked. It was disappointing that she'd brought it up, especially after I'd just gone off about needing privacy.

She spotted my unease. "*I'm sorry. Is she dead?*" When I didn't answer, she said, "*Only a man with a broken heart could write love like you do.*"

She must have had too many martinis at lunch. The way she was looking at me gave me an uncomfortable flirtatious vibe. To lighten the awkwardness, I said, "How do you know it's a 'she'? The name goes both ways. And maybe he or she was my favorite dog, or the pet hamster I had when I was six."

"Not buying it."

I shrugged.

She focused on a paper on her desk. She was offended. I'd never told her much more about myself than what was written on the jacket covers of my books, yet I knew she came from a blue-collar family in Atlanta, her ex-husband was a bad gambler, and she had a seven-year-old girl with dyslexia.

Without looking up, Mel said, "Let me know your travel plans, and I'll get back to you about Chicago."

~

"Vaughn?" Gemma says.

The bar noise suddenly amplifies. I've lost most of what she said for the last few minutes.

"Are you okay?" she asks.

"A little tired."

She strokes my hand. "Let's go back to your place if you're tired." She caresses up my arm. She's classically beautiful, and the smolder in her cool blue eyes is impossible to deny. I drink down the rest of my beer.

I thud the empty bottle on the table with too much force. As if my hand has taken charge and it's angry with me. The startling bang reminds me why I asked Gemma to meet me tonight. I look at my right hand, still gripped hard on the bottle. *I didn't forget. I actively disremembered. You know I'm a coward.*

I'm talking to my hand. I think this time I'm truly losing my mind.

I need to get away from New York City. I'm really going to do it. And I'll go soon, before I lose my nerve again.

I return my awareness to Gemma, and she's studying me, frowning. "What's wrong?"

I almost tell her nothing is wrong. But if I do, nothing will change. I don't know why I'm suddenly thinking of stars again. Something strange is happening with me tonight.

I gesture to a waitperson, hand her my empty, and ask for another.

Gemma declines my offer of another drink. "I thought we were leaving?"

"I need to tell you something."

She scents trouble. Because I've never given her any reason to feel secure. "What?" she asks warily.

"I'm going on a trip."

"When?"

I almost can't believe it when I answer, "Saturday." As if some outer and maybe nobler power has taken charge of me.

"Where are you going?"

"My agent wants me to do an event in Chicago, and while I'm out there, I'm going to look at properties." I turned it around, but it's a trivial lie compared to the whoppers I've told her.

"Properties? Like to live in?"

"Maybe."

"Where?"

"I don't know yet."

She looks alarmed. "You're moving back to Chicago?"

"No, not Chicago."

"Then where?"

"I told you I don't know." I won't mention Wisconsin again. I made that mistake with Mel.

"Why are you moving?"

"I said I'm *looking*."

16

"But why?"

"I need to get away for a while."

"Get away from what?"

"This city."

"For how long?"

"I don't know." I focus on the waitperson opening my beer. I watch her cross the room and tell her to keep the five I pull from my wallet. I take big swallows of beer, avoiding Gemma's gaze.

We made it to three months, longer than any of my relationships since I moved to New York. It's been making me nervous.

I get up the nerve to look at Gemma, and I can tell she knows it's over. I also sense she's going to cry. I'd rather she curse at me, hit me, throw something at my face. Anything but cry. That hurts the most, but I deserve it.

I wish I could stop doing this.

3

RILEY

Kiran has found a hole in the twisted roots of an old sycamore. He's in the creek bed, pushing his head into the dark burrow, the soles of his black boots pointed skyward.

I imagine an animal jumping out and biting his face. "Come on, Kee," I say.

"This looks like a cool place to hide something secret," he says, thrusting deeper into the hole.

That almost bothers me more than the vulnerability of his face. Because secrets in dark places are best left alone.

"Let's go," I tell him firmly.

He turns around and flashes a grin at me. "Why? Did you put a secret in here you don't want me to find?"

"What would I put in there?"

He considers. "A magic clock that never stops."

Kiran's intuition is really too much sometimes. "We should get going."

"Why?"

Because now I hear the ticking. Aunt Julia's kitchen clock made an audible click for every second it measured. *Click, click, click.* On and on it goes, even after Kiran removed its gears and hands and spread them apart on his tables.

"Can I look for fossils in the creek before we go back?"

"Sure."

I'm relieved when he leaves the black hole. I lie back against the bank with my hands beneath my head.

"Aren't you going to look?" he asks.

"I want to rest for a minute."

Because I need to get the ticking out of my head.

I focus on the soft burble of creek water. I watch Kiran enter one of his favorite realms, that magical place he goes when he's searching for fossils. I know how gratifying his oblivion feels. I had a place like that. I *have* a place like that.

I close my eyes and still see it, every detail, even after all these years. A decade, and not one day without Aunt Julia in my thoughts. I let go of where I am and float into the Sea of Clouds. Julia's ocean.

Kiran's voice drifts through the clouds as if from a great distance. "I found a red rock that's shaped like a heart."

"Did you?" I still have my eyes closed.

"I'm going to give it to Mom."

I think of the day Kiran was born. His heart stopped right after his birth. The doctors said his heart was *defective* and *malformed*, but I don't like to use those words. I think Kiran's heart is beautiful. But it was as distinctive as Kiran is, and it didn't want to follow the usual rules. The doctors resuscitated him and told us he needed immediate surgery. They said his probability of survival was small.

I drift deeper into the Sea of Clouds. I always look for Julia when I'm there, and sometimes I catch glimpses of her, wrapped in shifting shapes of pink and gold clouds, and smiling, as always. I like to imagine Kiran spent the minutes of his "death" with Julia. I see her holding him, watching over him until he returned to Earth. I like to think she put some of her magic in that little baby before she sent him back.

"Riley?"

I open my eyes. Kiran is squatted near, looking intently at me. Sometimes I think he knows when I'm in the Sea of Clouds. Maybe because he's been there with Julia.

I sit up. "Did you find a fossil?"

"No, just the heart." He shows me the little stone in his open palm.

"Sachi will love that."

He smiles, pushing it into his coat pocket.

"Ready to go?"

"Yes. I'm really hungry."

I rub my fingers in his short dark hair. "You're always really hungry."

We continue walking along the trickling creek of the forested ravine. A little snow remains in shadowed nooks and crannies, but it won't last long. The temperature is too warm for February. I try not to think about it. I only want to enjoy the walk with Kiran.

The vintage outfit he chose for me today isn't as bad for hiking as I'd thought it would be. The knee-length dress keeps my legs warm and moves well with my steps. The short, 1950s topper coat is too bulky and warm, but not enough to bother me when I wear it open.

Kiran and I have arrived at the big creek rocks. Now we head south through the forest, cross the old field that used to have horses, and climb over the rail fence that borders our property and Mr. O'Keefe's. Most of our walk was on his property. He's in his eighties, rarely leaves his house, and doesn't mind us hiking on his seventy acres.

When Kiran and I can see our old farmhouse through the trees, I decide to check the mail before we go inside. Alec is in his study writing a research proposal, and Sachi is painting in her barn studio. I'll give them more time to work without being interrupted. That's why I took Kiran for a walk. He'd been hanging out in Sachi's studio, telling her about fossilized dinosaur bones, and I could tell she was having trouble concentrating.

The walk down the gravel driveway that leads to our house is long, almost a quarter of a mile. It separates our apple orchard from the pond near the house, and it's wooded on both sides close to Summerfield Lane, the outer road.

At the last bend before Summerfield, Kiran and I stop short. A man is in our driveway. He looks startled to see us, too, and stops walking. The way he's looking at us makes me nervous, and that surprises me. I trust everyone we know out here in the country, and I have no reason to believe this man will be any different.

The man starts walking again. He's dressed neatly, wearing fitted dark jeans and a brown leather jacket over a navy-and-white-patterned button shirt. His dark brown hair is cut short, and his skin seems a little too pale, as if he stays indoors often. As he gets closer, he says, "I'm sorry to come on your property without asking."

He must not be from around here. If he were, he'd know there's not really any way to ask for permission. You just go up the road to the house if you want to see someone. People who don't want unexpected visitors put gates across their driveways.

The man stops a few yards from us. I still feel like he's staring strangely at me, maybe because of the outfit Kiran chose for me. I must look quite a sight in the muddy boots and vintage dress.

Now the man looks at Kiran for a long while, possibly trying to figure out if he's a boy or a girl because his dress doesn't match his face and short hair. Lots of people do that, and some are mean about it, staring at him or frowning. A woman in a restaurant in Oshkosh once told Alec and Sachi they were wrong to let their son dress like a girl. She said they were confusing him and steering him away from God. Sachi replied, "Haven't you seen pictures of God's son? He wore dresses, and His Father didn't seem to mind." Alec and I still joke about that.

The man returns his gaze to me. He's looking at me oddly again, as if he's trying to figure something out. Maybe he's wondering if I'll order him off our property. His eyes are nice, gray with long dark lashes, and while I'm looking at them, I notice the rest of his face is what most people would consider handsome.

The man gestures backward at the county road. "My car is—" He makes a wry face. "I'm embarrassed to say I've run out of gas, and my cell phone is dead."

"You must be worried about something." I immediately regret the statement.

He looks at me more curiously, for good reason this time. "Why do you say that?"

"Being more absentminded than usual mostly happens when you're worried." Sachi always asks Alec what's upsetting him when he gets forgetful, and usually she's right.

The man nods slightly to acknowledge my supposition. "I think it's more the forgetfulness of travel. I flew into Chicago early this morning."

Chicago is five hours away. I wonder where he's going but decide it's not my business.

The man says, "I'm Vaughn, by the way."

I'm not sure if he said *Vaughn* or *Vonn*, but now that he introduced himself, I suppose he expects the same from me. "I'm Riley. And this is Kiran."

His gaze lingers on me for a few seconds, then abruptly sails over my head and aims down the road. Something is bothering him. Maybe he's in a hurry.

"We might have gas in the shed."

"You don't have to do that. I can call a tow truck from a phone."

"It's no problem if we have some. Come up to the house."

"Thank you."

When we turn around, Kiran says, "What about the mail?"

"We'll get it later."

Kiran looks up at Vaughn as we walk. "Do you like fossils?"

"Well, I don't know much about fossils," Vaughn replies.

"Do you want to know about them?"

"I suppose I could be convinced," he says playfully.

"Is that yes or no?"

"I guess it's yes."

"I have fossils from five states. Do you want to see them?"

"Uh, sure," Vaughn says.

Kiran rattles off names of fossils in his collection. "I have a *Hexagonaria percarinata*—a really cool Devonian coral—and a *Calymene celebra*—that's a species of trilobite—and a *Neuropteris ovata . . .*"

After Kiran names two more, Vaughn says, "You lost me at *Hexagonaria.*"

"You're doing better than most," I say.

Vaughn looks at me questioningly.

"Most people wouldn't remember even one of those names."

He smiles. "Well, I want to see the *Hexagonaria,*" he tells Kiran.

"Okay," Kiran says brightly.

"Nice house," Vaughn says as our Victorian farmhouse and wraparound porch come into view.

"It was built in 1888. The land's been in Alec's family since before that. Alec is my cousin." I shut up because I'm spewing too much information at a total stranger.

"How many acres do you have?" Vaughn asks.

"Twenty-seven. The farm used to be more than a hundred, but they had to sell off a lot during the Great Depression."

"Too bad." He gazes at the bare orchard and pond on either side of the road as we near the house. "This is really beautiful. What a great place to grow up."

"I've only lived here for ten years." I feel stupid again, and I don't know why. Or I don't want to admit why. He's attractive, and he doesn't look that much older than me. I'm guessing he's in his upper twenties.

"Warm for February," Vaughn says. He opens his coat all the way.

"That's because people are killing our planet with carbon dioxide," Kiran says.

Maybe I should tell Alec to cut back on the global-warming discussions in Kiran's presence. Kiran talks about it too much lately.

"Do you know about climate change?" Kiran asks Vaughn.

Vaughn grins. "Is there anyone left who doesn't know about it?"

Kiran remains serious. "Do you think we can stop it in time?"

"Well, some people think the warming could be part of a natural cycle. Maybe it can't be stopped."

"Those people are wrong. We have to do something about it!"

Vaughn looks surprised by Kiran's outburst.

I hug my arm around Kiran's shoulders. "People will figure it out, Kee."

"Dad said it's too warm today. It scares me."

"I know, but we'll be okay." I kiss his cheek.

Alec steps onto the front porch. He looks curious, not at all worried by the unfamiliar man with us.

"This is Vaughn," I tell him, pronouncing it between *Vaughn* and *Vonn*. "His car is out of gas. Do we have any in the shed?"

"We do." He comes down the porch steps and extends his hand. "Alec Mays."

Vaughn grips his hand. "Vaughn Orr," he says. "I'm sorry to bother you, but I got caught without a charge on my phone when I ran out of gas. I must be more tired than I realized."

Alec takes in his crisp haircut and snappy clothes. "You from around here?"

"New York City. I don't own a car, and I guess I forgot my rental requires fuel to run."

Alec smiles. "I can see how that would happen. What brings you to these parts?"

"I'm looking at properties."

Alec appears a little worried. "To live in yourself or develop?"

"Live in," Vaughn says. "I was driving around to see how I like the area."

"Pretty quiet around here. And Chicago is a good five hours away."

"I just came from there. I flew into O'Hare this morning."

"I'm surprised you got this far on one tank of gas. Is this the only area you're looking at?"

"No. It could be anywhere out in the country."

"Why Wisconsin?" Alec asks.

"Why does everyone ask that?" Vaughn says.

Alec smiles again. "Because we aren't the classy Martha Stewart kind of country living. I'm surprised you aren't looking in upstate New York. It's a lot closer to home."

"I grew up in Chicago," Vaughn says. "This feels more like home than out there."

"I thought I heard Chicago in your accent. I grew up there, too. What neighborhood are you from?"

"Here and there," Vaughn says. "Riley tells me this house was built in 1888. It's beautiful."

"It's a never-ending project, but we like it."

"Come look at my fossils," Kiran urges Vaughn from the porch.

Vaughn looks at Alec and me, uncertain of what to do.

"You're welcome to go in while I get the gas," Alec says. "But I warn you—people who get pulled into Kiran's vortex sometimes never come out."

"He wants to see the *Hexagonaria*," Kiran says.

"I don't want to impose," Vaughn says. He looks torn between granting Kiran's request and getting the gasoline with Alec.

To help, I say, "I'll take you up with Kiran. I know how to escape the vortex."

Vaughn politely wipes his shoes on the doormat, but when he sees Kiran and me removing our boots, he starts to grab his right shoe.

"You can leave them on. Ours are muddy because we were hiking in the woods."

Kiran and I hang our coats on the hall tree bench, but Vaughn keeps his on. He comments on how pretty the house is, especially the old fieldstone fireplace.

Kiran hurries up the stairs, Vaughn behind him, and me last. It's not until we're near the top that I realize my bedroom door is open, and it's the first thing Vaughn will see at the landing. I can't let him see what's in there. What would he think of me?

I'm almost as upset by my shame as I am about him seeing what's in my room. I've never thought of it as embarrassing before. It used to be more important to me than food, or even air.

Suddenly I'm angry at Vaughn for intruding on our privacy. I look at his nice ass in his ridiculous tight jeans, and I hate him more. At the top of the staircase, I shove past him, rush to my bedroom door, and jerk it closed.

Vaughn stares at me.

"This room is private," I explain.

"The moon is in there," Kiran says. "It's really cool."

I glare at Kiran, but he doesn't notice the reprimand.

Vaughn is looking in my eyes, trying to figure out why I'm upset.

I don't know why I am either. I shouldn't have brought him up here. We need to show him the fossil, get his gas, and be done with him.

4

VAUGHN

I don't understand Riley's sudden mood change. She's looking at me like a young teen who's mad that I almost saw her messy room. As if I give a damn about her unmade bed or clothes on the floor.

Speaking of clothes, I see all kinds in NYC, but Riley and Kiran might stand out even there. Their outfits make them look like children of a cult. Riley's hair is plaited into two braids tied with ribbons, and she's wearing an old-fashioned purple dress, insulated rubber boots, and a frayed, burned-orange button coat that would have been new in her grandmother's youth. She had that on to hike in the woods.

Kiran's outfit is as unusual, a blue-flowered dress with long sleeves and a hem down to his knees. Despite his short hair, I'd thought he was a girl until Riley referred to him as *he*. He's a striking kid: rangy, with dark, cropped hair, huge cheekbones that dominate his thin face, and large eyes that are nearly black.

Alec is mostly ordinary looking, dressed in a pilled blue sweater, baggy pleated khakis, and old open-heel slippers. He has no idea who I am. I risked giving my full name, and neither he nor Riley blinked an eye. How have they not heard the name *Vaughn Orr*?

No one here knows me. I keep telling myself this is good. It's what I wanted. But it still feels strange.

I pause at the threshold of Kiran's room, at first too astonished to enter. It's like a portal into an alien marketplace on another world. The room has unusual angles with two dormer windows on different sides of the room, and the walls have been painted an eerie twilight color. There are old tables everywhere, and each is covered with all kinds of stuff. I lean close to one table to see better.

"Clocks and fossils," Riley says from the doorway.

I look at her, assuming I'll get more explanation.

"His two favorite things to collect," she says. "It's the machinery of clocks and watches. He likes to take them apart."

Kiran is getting impatient. "Come look at the *Hexagonaria percarinata*," he says.

I walk over as he lifts a large fossil off a table and launches into a lecture about it. He knows a lot about fossils. That could be a typical hobby for a kid his age, but the clock parts are bizarre.

Riley comes to my side as Kiran concludes his spiel.

I gesture at the fossils and clock pieces. "What's it all about?"

She frowns slightly. "It's about whatever you see in it."

"What do you see?"

She gazes at the tables. "It's art. It's beauty and science and time." She looks at me as if challenging me to disagree. "It's a kind of magic most people can't see."

Kiran grins. "Riley always says that. She thinks I can make things happen with my magic."

"Can you?" I ask him.

He shrugs with one shoulder. "I'm hungry," he tells Riley.

"We'll have lunch soon," she says.

"Can I have a cookie?"

"Sure."

He hurries down the stairs, leaving Riley and me alone in his room. My heart seems to rise and pound in my throat.

Why do I feel like this? What's wrong with me?

I know what's wrong, but I can't let her see that she has this effect on me. I'm about to pick up a clock gear to pretend interest, but she says, "Don't. You'll mess up his . . ."

"Magic?"

She doesn't answer.

"What would have happened?"

She still doesn't respond, but I can tell she's serious about me not touching the *magic*.

Resentment glitters in her eyes when she sees how I'm looking at her. I can only imagine how it looks—this fascination, fixation, whatever it is that keeps my gaze on hers.

But now I feel the intensity in her gaze as more than anger. It's scrutiny. Same as I'm doing with her, she's trying to figure me out. I feel exposed, as if she's found a peephole in the wobbly fence propped around me, and she can see all the damage behind it.

The chaotic room full of rocks and clockworks is suddenly spinning. I'm dizzy, sick to my stomach, and I have to get out.

5

RILEY

Vaughn left in a hurry. I shouldn't have mentioned the magic, but I wanted to smack him with more than magic when I saw how he looked at the tables, as if he thought Kiran's art was strange. Only a few of our friends have seen Kiran's room—mostly biologists, artists, and homeschool families—and they enjoy the beauty of the clockworks and fossils. But once two boys who live down the road came over to have a playdate, and they said the tables were *weird*. One of the boys even asked Kiran if he was *crazy*. We never had them over again.

I follow Vaughn downstairs.

As we arrive in the living room, Sachi comes in with Alec. She's taken off her painting apron to meet our visitor. She's a little breathless, staring wide-eyed at him. "I don't believe this," she says. "It's really you."

"It's really me." His smile looks phony, like someone else's grin pasted onto his face.

"You know Vaughn?" I ask Sachi.

"Yes, and so do you!"

"I do?"

"He wrote *The Sound of Absence* and *When Leaves Let Go*. And *The Feather and the Heart* and *A Box of Broken Stars*. He's *Vaughn Orr*!"

Vaughn isn't denying it. It must be true. My face flushes. I suddenly regret almost everything I've said to him. I wish I weren't such a socially awkward person—but I have no one to blame but myself.

Sachi offers Vaughn her hand. "I'm Sachika Jain-Bell. Everyone calls me Sachi."

Vaughn takes her hand and holds it. "Very happy to meet you, Sachi."

Sachi is the only one in the family who's read all his novels, but still, I should have recognized the name. I've read only his second book, *When Leaves Let Go*, and I liked the movie they made of it.

"Is it true you're looking at properties around here?" Sachi asks.

"Not just here. In Wisconsin in general."

"Well, we'll have to convince you to settle here!"

Sachi is like this with everyone, an extrovert and super friendly, but I'm surprised she said that when we know nothing about him other than that he wrote a few books. He could be a terrible person for all we know.

I don't know why I'm thinking this. Maybe because I've never met anyone famous. Or maybe I don't trust him because I saw how he changed when Sachi recognized him. Now he seems so full of himself.

But he rattled me before I knew who he was. And it's not only that he ran off while I was talking magic upstairs, because I probably deserved that. I don't know what it is that makes me feel shaky in his presence. I think it's the way he looks at me, as if I'm a curious little animal he has in his palm.

"Where are you staying?" Sachi asks him.

"I have no plans. I'll let the sun setting over the road make that decision."

"Isn't that romantic?" She looks at Alec, and they have a wordless exchange through their eyes. They do that all the time, and Sachi is brilliant at reading people, especially Alec. "Would you like to stay here?" Alec apparently gave his consent to ask. Before Vaughn can answer, she adds, "You would have lots of privacy. We have a room and full bath in the barn above my studio."

"You're an artist?" he asks.

I think he's stalling. Sachi's offer is awkward, and he's trying to think of a polite way to decline.

"I'm a mixed-media painter," she replies.

"Do you sell your paintings?"

"I do, in galleries in several counties. I also sell online."

"Is it a good market?"

He's definitely stalling. He still hasn't settled on what excuse to give her.

"It's decent," she says, "especially in the bigger tourist areas."

"Her market is much more than *decent*," Alec chimes in. "She's very talented and well known among painters in the Midwest."

Vaughn looks impressed. "I'd like to see your work."

"You will. Look all you like when you pass my studio to get to the apartment. You can come and go as you like, by the way. You won't bother my work at all."

"But it's okay if you don't want to," I add.

Vaughn, Sachi, and Alec look at me. I hope it's not obvious I'd rather the famous author not stay. He upset Kiran when he said climate change can't be stopped. Wait till Alec finds out about that. And he's wearing a dead-animal coat. I'm surprised Sachi can be so close to him and bear the smell of it.

Vaughn says, "I'd like to stay. You've all been very welcoming."

I see something false in his eyes, and I think he knows, because he quickly looks away from me. He's up to something. But what?

I want to tell Alec and Sachi they shouldn't trust him. But Sachi is the most intuitive person I've ever known, and she invited him. I must be imagining all this.

But now Vaughn is staring at me again. Why does he keep doing that?

6

VAUGHN

Why did I say I'll stay here? I feel like my actions have been beyond my control since the day I told Mel about this trip. As if I've been trapped in a house that's madly spinning inside a tornado, and now I've fallen into this surreal land. Riley with her childish braids and dress, and the strangeness of this place, feels like *The Wizard of Oz*. I have to remind myself that I can tap the heels of my magic ruby slippers and get out anytime.

While Sachi gets the guest room ready, Riley and Alec take me to put gas in my rental car. I discover Alec is a lepidopterist who teaches at a small college I've never heard of. Riley is a student there. Alec says she started a major in biology in the fall, but she seems too old to be a freshman. I'm not surprised she's behind in school, considering the weird clothes and *magic* and everything.

I also learn Alec studies the effects of global warming on moths. He said Riley inspired that research when she first came to live with them when she was eleven. Neither of them explains why she had to live with cousins, or what happened to her parents, and of course I don't ask.

I try to engage Riley, asking how she inspired Alec's climate research. She replies, "I worried about it a lot when I was little. Alec wanted me to see that people are working on it—because kids need to feel hopeful about the future."

She says this in a pointed way that makes me feel bad about what I said about climate change to Kiran. I don't think she likes me. She was friendly at first—I thought she might even be flirting with me—but she changed after she found out who I am. Some people are like that. They don't know how to behave around a famous person.

I won't hold that against her. I don't know how to behave around me either.

Alec pours a generous five gallons of gas into my car. I offer him money, but he refuses. He says I've made Sachi's day, and maybe more than a few years of days.

Riley looks peeved by this adulation. And I have to respect her wisdom. Maybe she isn't as immature as I first thought.

Now that I've gotten used to the braids, eccentric clothing, and lack of makeup, I can see she's attractive. She has an appealing tanned, pink-cheeked, outdoorsy glow to her skin; long, bronze hair streaked by the sun; and generous cheekbones and lips. But it's her eyes that really stand out. They're large and feline, tawny brown and fringed in long, dark lashes. I like the wildcat wariness I see in them, but every so often, when she lets down her guard, I glimpse something that intrigues me. I think I would call it *tenacity*. She's holding on to a ledge with her claws, some sort of inner strength that keeps her from falling.

I wonder if she suspects my claws, also, are slipping off the ledge.

Why am I thinking these things? It's like I feel some kind of connection. I have to stop doing this.

I look at her silhouette as the truck disappears down their road. I slow the rental car, tempted to accelerate past the driveway. I should drive on and stay away from her.

I can't. They're waiting for me. I spin the steering wheel and drive back into Oz. The family is standing in front of the porch steps when I arrive.

"We thought we'd lost you," Alec says as I get out of the car.

"Just enjoying the scenery."

Riley narrows her wildcat eyes at me.

"Let's take a look at the loft," Sachi says.

Sachi always seems to be smiling, someone people would describe as "sunny." When she looks at you, you feel warm and bright, as if she's radiating energy, and I'm pretty sure she makes everyone, not just famous authors, feel that way.

Since I met her, I'm not worried about a cult. Her cropped hair is hip, and she wears the kind of artsy glasses I see in NYC every day. She and Kiran look very alike, her light brown skin a little darker than his. She's dressed in a blue button shirt and calf-high boots with faded jeans that look too realistically frayed to have been mocked up in a factory. I don't know why her son and Riley are dressed peculiarly, but it's none of my business. Maybe Sachi feels that way about how they dress, too.

"Do you like Indian cuisine?" she asks.

"Love it."

"Good. You'll have dinner with us. I want to fete our eminent visitor."

Few people have the vocabulary—or pluck—to use a word like *fete*. But I don't get the feeling she did it to show off because I'm a writer. She seems too genuine to be like that.

"That's not necessary," I say.

"Of course it is!"

I hoist my leather messenger bag and duffel out of the car. She leads me to the barn, which is moderate in size and made of unpainted boards that are weathered but in good condition. The tall modern windows must have been added when it was turned into a studio and guesthouse.

We step into a charming space with light filtering through the windows. Riley and Kiran enter behind us. An open-tread wooden staircase ascends into the barn attic on our left, and Sachi's large studio is on the right. The studio is furnished with two worktables, supply cabinets, a small couch, and numerous paintings.

"Alec and I started converting this barn into my art studio almost as soon as we moved in. Just a year before, his grandmother still had a cow and a few horses in here."

I set down my bags and walk farther into the studio. "You did all this yourself?"

"Everything but plumbing and electricity. We had no money to pay contractors, and we enjoyed the challenge."

"You both know carpentry?"

"I knew more than Alec when we first got together. I was raised in communes where everyone had to work and learn how to build things like chicken coops and cabins."

Maybe I was wrong to discard the cult idea. "What kind of communes?"

"I was born in a Hare Krishna community. Later we moved to a farm commune—a hippie kind of thing—then to another when I was twelve. My parents split a few years after that because my father returned to his Baptist roots."

"From Hare Krishna to Baptist? That's quite a leap."

"Not if you know he'd grown up with Southern Baptists who took their church life very seriously. He rebelled in his teen years, especially after he met my mother. She'd been raised by Hindus and also tossed her parents' religion. That was the early seventies, when young people were searching for new kinds of meaning in their lives. But it was just a phase. If you can believe it, my father is a deacon of a Baptist church now, and my mother is an atheist."

"And where did you land?"

"Well . . . nowhere and everywhere. My parents flew me through Hare Krishna, Buddhism, goddess worship, and eventually atheism and Christianity. I've had no solid ground to land on." Smiling, she adds, "I prefer to stand on shifting ground when it comes to spirituality."

"You should write a book."

"I have no talent with words. Riley is the writer in the family."

This news jolts me. "You write?" I ask Riley.

"No," she says.

She's lying. She said it too defiantly. I look at Sachi. She knows I want confirmation, but she appears uncomfortable, unwilling to speak for Riley. She looks at Riley apologetically for bringing up the topic.

Kiran breaks the tension. The green ribbon on Riley's left braid is falling off, and he stands in front of her to tie it.

"Very pretty," Sachi tells him when he finishes. "I love the outfit you created for Riley today. The colors combine quite poetically. I should make a painting of her."

"I like the colors, too," he says proudly.

"Kiran is our budding fashion mogul," Sachi explains. "Every Saturday he delights us with his art when he designs an outfit for his sister."

Well, that explains Riley's bizarre outfit. But not his, and Sachi says no more.

"Your paintings are really beautiful," I say—because that would be expected. "Do you mind if I look around?"

"Not at all."

I know little about visual art. My decorator chose everything for my home in Brooklyn, and most are modernistic oils. I walk around the studio and view the watercolors. But they aren't really watercolors. Most have ink or other kinds of paint mixed in, and a few have bits of paper, sometimes printed, that give them texture. I guess this is what *mixed-media* painting is.

Some paintings are quite large; others are small and frameless, unfinished studies pushpinned into the wall and supporting barn beams. She paints surreal images, mixing landscapes with natural and human-made objects, animals, nondescript swirls of color, and people or parts of people—hands, eyes, ears, and naked torsos. Looking at her art is like entering her dreams. They remind me of some of Chagall's paintings, and they really *are* quite beautiful.

My favorite so far is of a city at night. The moonlit urban landscape has a wondrous white-gold luminosity that feels eerily real. I wonder how she did that. Above the shadowed city is a naked man curled in a fetal position. His skin is cyanotic blue, as if he hasn't been born yet. He's floating in a moon-bright sky above buildings, and my heart beats faster when I notice the vaporous faces peering out of the dark high-rise windows beneath his gliding body. Incongruous objects appear in some windows: a trumpet, a gun, an animal that looks like a wolf. When I look closer, I find one of Kiran's clock gears, then the coiled white shape of a fossil snail. A moth flutters against the panes of another window. Subtle texture and brushstrokes in the building walls suddenly take shape into mysterious forests, as if embedded in a Magic Eye illusion.

"I finished this painting a few days ago."

Sachi's voice startles me. I didn't realize she was standing close to me.

"It's called *Man, Asleep*. The vision came to me during the last full moon. I had to run out here and start it right away. I sketched the underpainting in moonlight."

"It's magnificent." The word doesn't come close to describing how the painting makes me feel. "Magical," I add, but that sounds ridiculous.

"Thank you."

"How did you get the texture?"

"In that one I mostly used crinkled rice paper. In others I use something else to get texture—watercolor, gouache, acrylic, and ink with various kinds of papers and gesso. I don't like to limit myself when it comes to inspiration."

"Like your spirituality."

"Exactly."

I consider asking if I can buy *Man, Asleep*, but I'm afraid that will sound patronizing. Another downfall of being famous.

I walk on and stop at a collection of mostly unframed watercolor studies of nude bodies, pinned to a back wall of the studio. I recognize Alec and Riley. A few are self-portraits of Sachi's naked body. My face is warm; my whole body is. I feel like a voyeur peering through the windows at this family. I *am* really, and I'm almost as light-headed as I was in Kiran's room.

I look at Riley, naked, sensuously posed in a field of grass and flowers. Her tanned legs stretch toward me. She's leaning back in golden sunlight, propped on her hands and arms, and she looks directly at me with her tenacious wildcat gaze. She's simultaneously relaxed and tense, as if she might spring and rake me with her claws. When I look closer, she seems defiant, almost angry.

"These are private," Riley says behind me.

She has her arms crossed tightly over her chest, as if to cover what's bare in the painting, and she *is* angry.

Sachi is just behind her, and she obviously doesn't care about my study of the painting. In fact, she looks amused by my predicament. "Oh come on, Riley," she says. "The naked body is nothing to be ashamed of. It's art, made by the greatest master of all time."

"What master?" I ask, assuming her answer will be *God*.

"Change," she says.

I'm not getting her answer.

"All life on Earth was created by tiny changes in molecules. An inestimable number of changes. Our bodies are miracles of transformation."

Riley's eyes are still clawing me. To escape, I turn around and look at the miraculous works of transformation.

"Most of these are only studies," Sachi says. "Practice in painting the human figure."

Studies or not, the paintings are some of the best nudes I've seen. She has a talent for bringing tremendous emotion into her subjects' eyes.

"Hey, I meant it. Private," Riley snaps.

I turn to her, want to explain I was only appreciating Sachi's technique, but the breathtaking fury in her tawny and black eyes makes me speechless.

"Sachi needs models," she says. "Would you be willing to volunteer?"

Sachi presses her hand over her mouth, stifling her urge to laugh.

"Seriously," Riley challenges. "Paint him now. Do it and I'll watch."

Sachi is seized by laughter.

"Need help with your clothes?" Riley asks me. "Take them off, and you can lie on that couch over there."

I say to Sachi, "Maybe you could get good money for a nude of Vaughn Orr."

She laughs harder.

"I bet the Cheese State tourists would eat that up."

"Oh god, stop," she says breathlessly. "Or I'll make you do it."

"We'd better not. I think my agent wouldn't like it. At the least, she'd want a cut of your profits."

"No, we'll sell it by auction, and the proceeds will go to charity," Riley says. "Or would you prefer a foundation that funds climate-change research?"

This shift in topic saps the last of our levity.

"Let's get your bags to your room while you still have some time to look at properties," Sachi says.

I'd forgotten I was looking at properties.

"I'll fix you a bit of lunch before you go," she says.

"No, you won't. I've already imposed too much."

I need to get away from Riley for a while—before my agitation becomes noticeable. But I think it's too late, at least with her. She saw it as soon as we met.

Alec enters and hands me a flashlight. "I'm sure you have a light in your phone, but keep this in your room just in case. It's very dark out here at night, and you'll need a light to walk over to the house."

"We don't use outside lights," Sachi says. "They confuse nocturnal moths."

"They confuse me, too," I confess. "I'm hoping to find a place where I can see good stars."

"Then you'll love it here!" she says. "How does it go . . . ? *The sky was a deep drink of black cola, an effervescence of stars that tingled all the way down.*"

Now why did she have to go and do that? She's quoting from one of my damn books.

7

RILEY

Vaughn has been gone for more than four hours. I'd like to say my house has returned to normal, but it hasn't. Alec had to run over to the market to get ingredients, and even before he returned, Sachi had started working her butt off preparing her favorite dishes. All the way upstairs the house smells like a restaurant steaming with scents of cardamom, cumin, ginger, fenugreek, and turmeric. Everyone is cleaning and straightening, and I was asked to bring in a big stack of firewood. We rarely light fires, but tonight we will because Vaughn said he loves our fieldstone fireplace.

Yes, let's put some more carbon into the atmosphere for the guy who told Kiran climate change can't be stopped.

Kiran is the only one in the house who seems untouched by the author's questionable charms. I've been studying in his room while he sits at a table rearranging his fossils and clock parts. "When do you think Vaughnorr will come back?" he asks, joining the name he's heard too often in the last few hours.

"I don't know."

"Do you like him?"

"He's interesting."

Kiran studies me, as if trying to interpret my reply.

I've lost my last refuge. I lay my physics book on his bed, head downstairs, and hear a new voice in the kitchen. I look in, see a familiar thatch of copper hair. Colton has come for dinner. Sachi must have invited him because of Vaughn Orr.

Colton is helping cook. And getting his Sachi fix. He adores her, as everyone does, but his bond with her is much deeper than that. Sachi is the mom Colton always wanted. When he was a baby, he was left with a grandmother who lived in a tiny house in remote wooded country. She was more strict than maternal with him, pushing him in school and whatever jobs he could get. When he turned eighteen, Colton thought he should get a full-time job to help his grandmother, but she insisted he enroll at the small college where Alec teaches. Colton and Alec connected when Colton took Alec's entomology course. Alec was impressed with him from the start. He says he never met anyone who knows more about the wildlife of Wisconsin.

Since the entomology class, Alec's been both adviser and dad to Colton, and thanks to his help, Colton got into a graduate biology program at the University of Wisconsin. Colton studies mammal ecology and conservation, and Alec is on his graduate committee.

When Colton sees me, he grins and comes over to view my Saturday outfit. "Kiran has outdone himself. The braids are a good look."

"But you missed the vintage coat that made it genius."

"The socks are genius."

I wiggle my exposed toe in the striped sock. "Especially the hole, right?"

"Especially."

I sit on the couch, and he settles into his favorite soft chair.

"Please tell me you didn't drive four hours to eat Saturday dinner with the famous author."

Colton frowns. "Why do you say that?"

"Did you?"

"I sort of did. Sachi called and told me to come over for a big dinner with Vaughn Orr. But you know her cooking is the main reason I'm here." He looks embarrassed, adding, "And all of you."

"I knew it was a joke, for god's sake." I could never doubt he's here to see us. His grandmother died when he was nineteen, and he's got no one to love and love him but us. He helped Alec and Sachi create the upstairs apartment in our barn and lived in it for two years. He's part of our family, though we don't see as much of him since he moved to Madison this autumn.

"Don't you like Vaughn Orr?" he asks.

"He's pretty full of himself."

"How could you not be when you're that famous?"

"Don't you think it's strange that he agreed to stay with us?"

"Not really. Sachi could get the pope to stay if she asked him to."

"I think it's odd. And how could he drive all the way up here from Chicago without knowing his car needed gas?"

He narrows his eyes, apparently in agreement that it's suspicious.

"And now he's staying in our barn instead of at some five-star hotel."

"Are there any of those around here?" he asks with a smile.

"No, and that's the point."

"What is?"

"That he's up to something."

Colton trusts things I say, and he looks worried. "Up to what?"

"I don't know. He looks at me weird. And you should have seen him gawking at Sachi's nude of me. I was about to bust him in the chops."

Bust him in the chops is a favorite Colton phrase. But Colton doesn't smile. He's simmering, his cheeks pink beneath his freckles. He leans close. "You think he's after you, like in a bad way?"

"I don't know."

"Have you told Sachi and Alec?"

"No, because I'm probably imagining it." I gesture at my outfit. "I mean, look at me. Not exactly up to the standards of New York City rich people."

Colton's blue eyes gleam. "Rich or poor, he'd be after you, Riley. You're—"

"What?"

He considers what to say. "Very good looking. And maybe he likes how innocent you are."

Innocent. The word unsettles me.

He notices and looks worried. "I don't mean that to sound bad. I meant . . . you're different from most of the women I meet at school. You don't care about all that stuff they do. You're the best woman I ever met." Now he really colors, most likely regretting the last sentence.

He's had a crush on me for years. But he's figured out that can't work when we're nearly sister and brother. Alec says someday he'll find the right woman among the wildlife biologists he meets, but so far living on campus has been miserable for the humble bear whisperer.

"I'd think Sachi is the best woman you ever met."

He's relieved I'm joking. "You're the best *young* woman I ever met."

"And Sachi is the best old woman you ever met?"

"You know what I mean."

"I know. I just like to make you turn red."

He rubs his hair. "Ain't enough up here for ya?"

"How many times do I have to tell you your hair is copper, not red?" I put my fingers in its perpetual disarray to smooth down a patch. Colton stills like a wild creature that's found the joy of being caressed. "It's the most beautiful color of hair I've ever seen."

Three hard knocks rap on the front door.

I drop my hand from Colton's hair. "Shoot, there he is, and Cinderella was supposed to have a roaring fire going for him."

Colton grins. "Go let him in, and I'll be Cinderella."

"To be authentic, you'll have to wear one of Kiran's dresses."

"Sorry, but no."

I open the front door. Vaughn is standing there with a shopping bag and a big bouquet of flowers. My stomach rolls at the thought he might have brought them for me.

"It smells great in here!" he says.

"You can hang your coat there." I point at the free hooks on the sides of the hall tree bench. "How'd it go? Did you see anything you liked?"

"I saw a lot I liked. It's beautiful around here."

He notices Colton, who already has a fire going.

"That's Colton Reed. He's having dinner with us."

Colton dusts off his palms and comes over to shake hands with Vaughn.

"Colton, this is Vaughn Orr."

"Good to meet you," Vaughn says. I think he expects Colton to say his books are wonderful, but he'll get none of that. Colton's favorite reads are the *Farmers' Almanac* and the *Journal of Wildlife Management*.

Colton has an intent gaze on Vaughn's eyes. "I hear you're looking at properties around here."

"All around Wisconsin," Vaughn says.

"You have a real estate agent then?" Colton asks.

"Not yet. Not until I narrow the field."

"How long will you be staying?"

Vaughn glances at me, and Colton takes note. "I don't know," Vaughn replies.

"Did you see that pretty property for sale over on Fanning Road?" Colton asks.

"Not sure," Vaughn says. "Where's Sachi?" he asks me.

I point, and he heads to the kitchen with the shopping bag and flowers, which thankfully aren't for me.

Colton comes close. "Did you hear that? He already thinks he's staying more than one night."

"Sachi and Alec might have told him he could."

"How long was he out looking at properties?"

"More than four hours. Why?"

"The place on Fanning Road is only twenty miles away. He for sure would have seen it in four hours. And it has a blue barn he'd never have missed."

"Maybe he saw by its description it's not what he's looking for."

"It's forty acres of woods and fields with a house and barn. I'd buy it in a heartbeat if I had the money." He watches Vaughn pull bottles of wine out of the bag as he talks with Sachi in the kitchen. "Where'd he find all that fancy wine?"

"How do you know it's fancy?"

Colton gives me a look, and I see his point. Doubtful a famous big-city author would drink the cheap wine they sell at the local store.

"Looks like he did more shopping than looking at properties," Colton says. His gaze still on Vaughn, he adds, "I'm staying over."

"I know." He usually stays one night when he visits now that he lives more than four hours away.

"I'll sleep on the pullout in your room since he's got the barn," Colton says.

To propose something as bold as that is very unlike him. "What, to protect me?"

"You're the one who said he's up to something. And I'm pretty sure you're right."

8
VAUGHN

Colton is in love with Riley. It's obvious in the way he looks at her. From the little I know about Riley so far, I wouldn't think he's her type. She seems like a woman who would want a more complex partner, someone who would challenge her opinions rather than go along with everything she says, as Colton does. But before I arrived at the front door, I saw her stroking his hair when I looked in the porch windows.

Alec and Sachi may be pushing them together. They seem very taken with the ginger man of the woods. I don't understand why they would encourage her to settle when she should find someone who better suits her. But she doesn't know she can do better, because she lives in this isolated little world of theirs. I can't imagine why Alec, a college professor, didn't encourage her to move to a big university and see more of the world.

Money may be the problem. They grow their own vegetables, buy secondhand clothing, drive old cars, and need new furniture. From what I can tell, Alec's position at the small college doesn't pay well, and though Sachi's paintings are brilliant, her sales to tourists can hardly add enough to support a family of four. Apparently, Colton used to live here, too.

Alec has returned to the world of modern clothing. For the author fete, he's changed into fitted slate-colored pants and a blue-and-gray shirt made of light flannel. In this outfit, I better see how he matches with Sachi. I saw that in the nude paintings in the art studio, too. He looked good in those paintings, strong and lithe, his tousled tan hair boyish, his sun-bronzed body at ease with his nakedness. I saw in his eyes and smile that he liked to pose for his wife.

Rather than eat right away, we have wine and kachori appetizers in front of the fire. I had to scour Google and drive quite far to find good wine. I can tell the family has no idea how expensive it is, and I won't be so boorish as to tell them. Colton won't touch it. He's drinking beer.

I ask Alec and Sachi how they met. The answer is more surprising than I expected.

"My aura brought us together," Alec says.

He's smiling, but I can tell he's serious. Sachi also smiles, rubbing one hand on his back as he continues the story. "I was in my senior year at the University of Wisconsin, and I'd found a cool rare moth near the lake where the students hang out. The moth wasn't doing too well, and I nudged it into my palm to get a better look."

"He handled it so gently," Sachi says, "with such wonder and compassion."

"I didn't know she was watching me," he says. "She was with the other students, doing a painting of the lake. After I captured the moth and sat in the grass to look at it, this beautiful woman comes over and says, 'I have to know what you're looking at. Your aura is so beautiful.'"

"You see auras around people?" I ask Sachi.

"Sometimes," she replies.

I want to ask Alec, a scientist, if he believes this, but the question would be crass during their meet-cute story.

"So he showed me the moth," Sachi says, "and he told me about its life cycle, habitat, host plants, and everything. I loved how he talked about this small creature that not one other person in that crowd would have noticed. I immediately felt kinship with him."

"She asked if I would hold the moth while she did a quick painting of it." Alec caresses Sachi's bare nape. "Nothing would have been more of a turn-on. And watching her while she painted that moth . . . Jesus, I wanted to throw her down into the grass and love her right there."

"We both did," Sachi says, laughing. "But we held out a few hours more, didn't we?"

They kiss passionately. My face warms. I feel like a voyeur again. But they opened the curtains willingly.

"Would you like to see the painting?" Alec asks.

"Wow, you still have it?" I don't want to see the painting, but Alec gestures me down the hallway to his office.

As he flicks on a few lamps, I'm caught up in another vortex, a whirling cloud of moths of every imaginable—and unimaginable—shape, color, and pattern. Framed moth paintings in a variety of sizes cover almost all the space on the dark green walls of his office.

"Sachi has given me a moth painting for my birthday every year since we've been together. At first, she only did Wisconsin moths, but now she paints whatever strikes her fancy." He points to a colorful moth that looks too exotic to be real. "This one is the Madagascan sunset moth. And here's the one she painted that day at the lake."

"This collection is stunning," I say in all truth. "She's very talented, isn't she?"

"She's pure magic." He touches his finger to the moth she painted the day they met. "I thank our moth every day for bringing us together. Even the lives of the smallest creatures can change the world, you know?"

"Yes." Interesting idea, but I think he's had too much wine.

We leave his office and enter the dining room. Someone has decorated the table with pine greens mixed with dried leaves, grasses, and flower seed heads collected from the outdoors. It's simple but charming—created by Kiran, they tell me.

"We eat a plant-based diet," Sachi says as we sit down. "I hope that won't bother you."

"Of course not."

I'm disappointed that the tantalizing dishes on the table won't include meat, but my worries are unwarranted. The food is very tasty. I miss the flavor of meat only a little, and the wine I brought helps make up for that. As the dinner gets underway, I'm surprised no one brings up my books. Most of the conversation centers on what Colton is doing in graduate school. And while Alec and Colton talk about their science, climate change comes up. Again. This family is obsessed with the topic.

I pour another glass of wine and savor it while they talk.

Colton interrupts my reverie. "Mr. Orr, I hear you believe climate change is a natural cycle that can't be stopped."

I glance at Kiran, who has an intent gaze on me. "I was only offering an alternate opinion."

"Which opinion do you believe?" Riley asks.

"You should study the science before you tell Kiran something like that," Colton says.

"All right, let's not all pile on Vaughn," Sachi says.

Damn right.

"Are you working on a new book?" she asks.

I appreciate her changing the topic for my benefit, but I'd rather hear more about how I shattered Kiran's hope than talk about the status of my writing. They're all waiting for my answer, and I suddenly realize I can use the situation to my advantage.

"I'm . . ." I take a sip of wine. "I'm having a little trouble with that right now. That's why I'm here."

"Do you mean writer's block?" Sachi asks. "Is that what you mean by *trouble*?"

"Yes. Absurd after all those books, isn't it? I thought getting away from the city and the pressure might help. That's why I'm looking for properties in the country. But I don't know if doing that is right. What if I buy some acreage and I'm still stuck—or it gets worse?"

The four adults look at me sympathetically.

"So, I'll make a little confession. I didn't look at properties today. I drove around. I moped. And I found wine. I truthfully have no idea what I'm doing out here."

Riley and Colton exchange a look. I know Colton's earlier questions were aimed at finding me out, and now he and Riley will think they have nothing to discover.

"I'm very sorry," Sachi says. "I may be the only one at this table who understands the pain of a creative impasse."

"Riley and I know more than you think," Alec says to his wife. "When you can't paint . . . well, let's just say you aren't exactly easy to live with."

"It's real torment for an artist," Sachi says. "Do you have the insomnia that goes with it?"

I nod. A slight lie. I've had insomnia for years.

Sachi leans in and looks at me earnestly. "Stay here as long as you like. Don't worry about looking at properties. See if you like country living before you make a big decision like that. The last thing you need is more pressure."

"Thank you. Happening upon this place—and all of you—today has been the best I've felt in a long time." This is mostly true, but Riley is searching me for lies again.

"Then stay awhile," Alec says.

"I wouldn't feel right unless I pay for the rental of the barn loft. I planned on doing that even if I stayed one night."

"That's not necessary," Alec says.

He's only being polite. Getting rental income would be a nice boon for the family. Serendipity. That's what I want this to be.

"It is necessary, and we'll work out a price later." I pick up my glass. "But now I'd like to toast Sachi and this delicious meal she prepared."

They lift their drinks, even Kiran.

"To Sachi, the kindest, most welcoming person I've met in a very long time. And no hyperbole when I add that she's a brilliant artist and cook as well."

Everyone drinks and Sachi says, "Thank you, Vaughn. I'm glad you've found tranquility in our home. We'll leave you to explore and work on that peace of mind as independently as you wish. But please feel free to depend on us if the need arises."

I thank her and we continue to eat. We drink quite a lot of wine, and beer in Colton's case. Everyone is warm. No one talks about my writing or climate change. And now I have carte blanche to be here without guilt. My confession has been a win-win-win.

During dessert, Colton asks Kiran if he'd like to look for fossils the next day.

"Can we go to the good place?" Kiran asks.

"Sally Run Creek?" Colton asks.

Kiran vigorously bobs his head, eyes alight.

"Okay," Colton says. "What about you, Riley?"

"Sure," she says.

"Do you mind if I join?" I ask.

"It'll be cold, and the hiking gets your feet wet," Riley says.

"Sounds like New York City in winter," I say, and everyone laughs.

"This is a great idea," Sachi says. "Immersion in nature is essential for a healthy soul." She pushes out her chair. "Now how about those stars? The moon hasn't risen yet."

While everyone puts on coats and shoes, I hear Sachi talking to Alec in his study. A minute later, he's standing at the door, holding a trumpet.

"Is this the annunciation of a lesser god whose birth I don't know about?" I ask.

Riley and Alec grin. Colton looks at me as if I spoke in Kurdish.

"You never know," Sachi says, as she shrugs on a coat. "But for Alec the divine spirit is in the music, specifically trumpet music. He's played most of his life."

"He plays outside?"

"It's been a ritual in this house since Kiran was born. Kiran was a poor sleeper, so sometimes Alec would play far from the house if the baby was sleeping." She smiles. "It was stirring to hear the trumpet from a distance during a perfect summer sunset. Ever since, the woods and fields are our favorite trumpet venues."

"Not so much in winter, though," Alec says. He waggles his fingers, half-bared in fingerless gloves. "Cold air is tough on flexibility."

"But tonight the temperature is in the forties," Sachi says. "And we thought you might enjoy hearing the music."

"The annunciation of Vaughn Orr," Riley says drolly.

"I like that," I say. "Shall I descend from my usual cloud?"

"I think you already did."

Clever riposte, and true in more ways than she knows.

Sachi distributes flashlights, and we set out for the pond, the family's usual stargazing spot. Alec walks in a different direction to distance himself from us. The silence of the surrounding woods feels strange to me. But I like that it does. The constant verve of NYC became boring for me years ago.

The darkness beyond our flashlights is almost solid. Despite several relaxing glasses of wine, my light-habituated senses become edgy and hesitant. I wouldn't know if I were walking off a cliff. I stay in the middle of the flashlight beams.

After a few minutes, we arrive at a pond that's almost big enough to call a small lake.

"I've never seen it this thawed in early February," Sachi says. Her light illuminates a shining layer of water over the ice. "Colton, would you hold Kiran's hand?"

"Got it," he says.

Sachi takes me by the shoulders from behind. "Vaughn gets the best spot." She guides me out onto the wooden pier. It's unsettling to walk toward that watery blackness as if impelled down a gangplank to my death. She positions me at the end of the pier and has everyone turn off our flashlights. She tells me it takes a while for retinas to acclimate to darkness.

As my eyes adjust, I'm standing in millions of stars. They're above me, and imperfectly reflected in the watery ice below. I try to find a solid reference point in the star-filled void, but I can't. I'm floating in the universe. The sensation is so disorienting I stumble backward and grab for anything that might have substance. I clutch Riley's arm, knocking her off balance.

"Don't push me in, Vaughn!" she yelps out of the starry darkness.

Colton sniggers, but the thought of her falling through the ice is horrifying. Riley unclasps my hand from her arm and slips her hand into mine. I feel silly, like a child, but I suppose she does this to keep me from bumping into her again. She understands how dangerous it is if either of us falls in.

Riley and I aren't wearing gloves, and I'm acutely aware of the warmth of her palm and fingers as I venture another look at the stars and their reflections in the black ice. I've never felt anything like this, as if my body is spreading out into the blackness and stars. My only connection to myself is Riley's warm hand.

In a high, sweet timbre, the trumpet declares its first long note from across the water. Another note streams out into the darkness, and another, and now a deeply affecting melody winds its wavering spell around us and into infinity.

Sachi is right. The trumpet is much more stirring out here. I've been to many concerts, heard the best trumpet players in the world, but the music of those fancy halls never made me cry.

I don't know why these hot tears are on my face. It's an entirely new sensation. I try to remember the last time I wept. Probably when I was little, before I learned how to shut down my emotions when my father raged at me.

Riley presses my hand. "Hey—are you okay?"

I wonder why she asks, what she feels in my silence that worries her.

She presses my hand again to get an answer.

"I'm okay."

This is the biggest lie I've told all day.

9
RILEY

To find a fossil in a galaxy of rocks, you have to see in a different way. It's called having a *search image*, a biological term Alec taught me. A search image is simply a picture an animal has in its mind as it looks for food or habitat. When an animal finds something that helps it survive, it fixes the visual characteristics of that thing in its mind. If it finds it again, the sharpness of the image improves, as does the animal's chance of survival. Humans got where they are today with the help of search images, and we still use them every day. It's how we quickly find our favorite cereal in a vast landscape of boxes.

Colton, Kiran, and I have good search images for rocks that contain fossils. Vaughn does not. I think he's just wandering around in the creek bed. When I glance at him, he's often not looking down. He's watching us or staring out into the bare forest like a shipwrecked sailor searching for a boat.

My feelings about Vaughn keep changing. Today I feel sorry for him. I'm even a little worried about him. I'm afraid he might be more depressed than he's letting on.

Last night on the pier I sensed something in him. I don't know what. But I do know he was afraid of the ice. That was obvious when he jumped back from the dock edge and grabbed on to me. He had no idea how much I understood his panic. I had to hold his hand. And when I did, after a while, I felt something more in him, some kind of sorrow I'm certain I understood.

But it's possible I projected my own darkness onto him. Stargazing on the dock always submerges me in the murkiest of moods. But I never let on because Alec and Sachi have loved that ritual since before I came to live with them.

I move farther up the creek and continue searching for a glimpse of something unordinary among the browns, grays, and tans of the rocks under my boots: the spiral swirl of a cephalopod or the radiating rays of a brachiopod. I think about Vaughn's confession at dinner last night. It surprised me. And it made me feel guilty about turning Colton against Vaughn. Colton still doesn't like him, and I feel responsible.

But it's not only what I said. Sometimes Vaughn acts as though he doesn't like Colton, and Colton is a perceptive person who picks up on that. Last night I thought Vaughn might even be jealous of him. When we went back to the house from the dock, he asked me where Colton was sleeping when he saw him going upstairs. Before I could answer, Colton said, "I'm sleeping in Riley's room."

"I'm sorry I took your usual room," Vaughn said.

"No reason to be sorry," Colton said, and he continued up the stairs.

"I feel like I've caused a problem," Vaughn said. "I can sleep on the couch and give Colton the loft."

I was glad Colton didn't hear. Or see the question in Vaughn's gaze. He was fishing to find out if Colton and I were sleeping together. And though I felt kindlier toward him by then, I just said, "It's really no problem. Have a good rest."

I could have told him the bed in my room has a trundle mattress, and that Colton would sleep on it. But I didn't. Because what Colton and I do is none of Vaughn's business.

Colton and Kiran have wandered upstream. They're talking loudly as they look at something in Kiran's hand. Vaughn is behind me.

"Let's go see what they have," I say, inviting Vaughn to walk with me. "I guess this has been pretty boring for you."

"A little," he admits.

"I'm sorry I didn't warn you."

"Don't be. I deal with boredom very well."

"I can see that. All those stories running through your head."

He looks at me, his expression melancholy. I regret mentioning his writing when he's upset about his creative gridlock.

But it's not remorse that keeps my eyes on his. I'm aware of how compelling his sad gray eyes are in this moment. They mirror the low somber clouds and the gloomy mood they've cast over our outing.

He isn't hiding anything. That's why I have to keep looking. Everything around me vanishes, swallowed into the grief I see in his leaden eyes. Now I know I wasn't wrong about what I felt in him on the dock last night. But I don't understand why. What I see seems so much bigger than his desire to write a story. What I see in his ashy eyes *is* a story, some tragedy that snakes dark and deep all through him.

Vaughn looks away from me. The creek returns to my senses so quickly I feel giddy. I gaze ahead to orient myself. Colton is only yards away, and he's staring at me. At us. He saw Vaughn and me looking into each other's eyes.

My cheeks flush with a heat of guilt that confuses me more. How has Vaughn done this to me in the span of one day? And what, exactly, has he done?

"Look, Riley!" Kiran says. On the palm of his black glove is the coil of a fossil snail. I've always thought their spiral shapes look especially poetic when placed among his clock gears.

Kiran enlightens me about the creature in his hand, but I'm still thinking about Vaughn and registering little of Kiran's lecture. I tell Kiran the fossil is beautiful and he's found the best of the day. He pockets the stone and walks off with Colton to find more. When I finally have the courage to look at Vaughn, he's seated on a log, his forearms rested on his thighs as he stares down at the ground.

"You look like a man who needs some blood sugar." I draw a veggie wrap out of my bag. "Want one?"

"Sure, thanks."

I sit next to him and take out a wrap for myself. We eat in silence except for the trickle of the creek and a few birdcalls.

"Can I ask you something?" He's looking at the last of the wrap in his hand, not at me.

"Depends," I say through chewing.

"Yesterday, why did Sachi say you write, and you said you don't?"

I suppose he's revealed enough about his writer's block that it would be unfair to deny him an answer. It's no big deal anyway.

"I thought I wanted to study writing when I first started college, but I dropped out in my second year."

"Why?"

"I didn't like it once I started doing it."

"What about it didn't you like?"

Now he's getting into difficult territory.

When I don't answer, he asks, "Was it fiction or nonfiction?"

"Both. You must know how those beginning classes are—expository essays and short stories and poetry and all that."

"Which did you like best?"

"None of it."

"I don't understand why you studied it then."

"I guess I don't either."

Through my peripheral vision I can see he's studying me. I turn to him, and our eyes meet for the first time since what happened while we were walking. This time I see only curiosity in his gaze, the attentive kind, not prying. I suppose he's interested because he's an author.

Maybe he can understand what happened with my writing more than I can.

"Do you know how they say people go into psychology to heal themselves?"

He nods.

"I think I tried writing for the same reason, to heal myself."

He appears fascinated. Maybe he understands.

I look out at the forest. "The professors told us we had to be honest with our emotions to write well—but I couldn't be truthful. There are all these things I keep behind a wall and don't let myself think about. And if I can't be honest with my emotions inside myself, how can I write them, let alone have some professor I don't know read them?"

Vaughn looks down at the ground again. "What do you wall off?"

"If I wall it off, do you think I'd tell you?"

He emits a soft laugh. "I guess not." He turns to me. "I'd love to read anything you've got and give you an opinion. Maybe you were being too hard on yourself. Lots of people quit writing when their first attempts don't meet their expectations."

I suppose he's trying to be a mentor. Maybe he thinks he can help me get published, a repayment for my family's hospitality.

"Do you have anything I can read?" he asks.

"I threw out almost everything."

"What didn't you throw out?"

"It's nothing. A journal I kept for my last writing class."

"Can I read that?"

Why did I mention the journal? What is this power it has over me?

"Can I?" he presses with unseemly urgency.

Doesn't the word *journal* imply intimate thoughts? Why would he want to read that? I don't care if he's a bestselling author and he wants to help me—he shouldn't ask.

He's waiting for an answer. I stand and look down at him. "Do you know why it was the last writing class I ever took?"

"Why?"

"Because of that journal. We were studying memoir, and I was supposed to write about an important event from my life. I tried to break through the wall while I was writing, but all I did was crash into it. I quit school and couldn't go back for a long time. It all made me feel like a total failure—that's why I'm so far behind in college. This fall Alec persuaded me to try biology classes."

He stands, looking into my eyes. "Why didn't you throw out the journal if it was so painful?"

"I don't know."

"I do."

"Oh really? Tell me."

"You'd finally broken through to real emotions, and they scared the crap out of you. That journal may be your most honest expression of yourself, and there's no way a writer could toss that into the fire. It would be like burning a part of your soul you'd finally gotten back."

I can't believe he said that. He looks smug, aware that he's hit on the truth, and I want to yell at him, tell him how much misery he's stirring up. But of course I don't. Keeping it all inside has been the hardest work of my life. That's why the journal hurt so much; it was more like bleeding than writing.

"Maybe you're right," I admit. "But I can burn it—and I will."

He looks alarmed. "Please don't. At least let me read it first."

Is he really so desperate to impart his great wisdom onto a novice writer? I think the success of his books has inflated his ego.

I walk away and he follows. I'm grateful for his silence. After the next bend in the creek, we find Kiran bent over, looking for fossils. Colton is up on the bank, studying something at the edge of an aspen swamp. When he sees we've arrived to keep an eye on Kiran, he heads off into the underbrush. I think he's tracking an animal.

Colton experiences field and forest as both predator and prey. He admires both. When he was growing up with his grandmother, before he was old enough to get a job, he had to hunt and fish to keep them fed. A neighbor taught him the basics before he could legally hunt, and from there Colton essentially became an animal of the woods himself. The inside of the tiny house was grim, Colton once told me, and he said he spent most of his time outdoors. That was his true home, even in winter. He knows how to survive outside for any length of time in any weather. What he perceives in a particular spot in the forest is more than what's in the present. It's also what was in the past, and what could happen in the future of that place.

Vaughn and I watch Colton disappear into the brush. "I guess he has to use the outhouse—so to speak," Vaughn says.

I continue looking for fossils. Vaughn sits down again. He pulls out his phone and sighs when he can't get a signal.

After ten minutes or so, I find a rock with a partial coral in it. Kiran happily adds it to his pocket. I see Colton coming. And that's the funny contradiction of him. There he is, at one with the woods, yet his copper hair and bright-blue eyes immediately draw my gaze.

Colton steps into the creek bed and walks over to Vaughn. "I want to show you something, Mr. Orr."

"You can call me Vaughn."

"Come on, get up," Colton says. He says to me, "I need your help, and bring Kiran."

"What are we tracking? Sasquatch?"

"Come on, Riley. Before it leaves."

We follow him into the brush at the edge of the swamp. He frowns at us and puts his finger to his lips because we can't walk as quietly as he does. I see the trail we're following, a narrow chute in the brown grasses, and I think I might know what animal we're tracking.

At a fallen tree, Colton directs me to walk in a certain direction with Kiran and instructs Vaughn to stay where he is. "We're going to flush it toward Vaughn," he says to me. "If you see it, keep it going in his direction."

"Hold on," Vaughn says. "What are you flushing at me? I'm not liking the sound of this."

"Be quiet," Colton whispers.

"Jesus," Vaughn mutters.

I do as best as I can without knowing the exact plan. Kiran follows me without complaint. He's used to exploring wild places with Colton and me.

I keep my eyes on Colton as we get farther apart in the undergrowth and saplings. He waves a finger to the right, and I adjust my course. Shortly after, he points at some dense shrubs between us. I slowly walk toward the bushes. I can see it. I couldn't miss it. The poor thing stands out like a sod house in a subdivision.

As I near, the snowshoe hare darts toward Colton. Colton lunges right, turning it toward Vaughn. "Vaughn!" he shouts. "It's coming!"

"What? Where?" Vaughn calls back.

That's what Colton wanted him to do. The sound of Vaughn's voice stops the hare. It freezes, sniffing the air, unsure of where to go when it's surrounded by four people.

"You see it, Vaughn?" Colton says in a gentle voice.

The hare doesn't move. I swear animals hear something in Colton's voice that calms them.

"I see it," Vaughn says. "It's a white rabbit."

"Snowshoe hare," Colton corrects. "If there was snow on the ground, which there should be right now, you would have trouble seeing it. It doesn't know we can see it so well because it's programmed by evolution to think it's invisible. And that's how the lynx or the hawk gets it. It's easy prey in this new warm world."

Vaughn stares at the exposed white hare. I wonder what he's thinking, if he understands why Colton has shown him the snowshoe.

"I don't want it to die," Kiran says despondently. His words seem to make the hare remember it should run. It dashes between Vaughn and Colton, disappearing in the direction of the swamp.

Colton, Kiran, and I walk to Vaughn.

"That was lucky," Colton says. "I hardly see any now. In my lifetime, they've disappeared from the southern two-thirds of Wisconsin. They evolved to survive in a winter that has snow into March and April."

Vaughn doesn't say anything. I can't tell if he's irritated with Colton's climate-change exercise, or if the plight of the snowshoe hare has affected him. His face is oddly devoid of expression.

On our way back to the creek, I say to Vaughn, "It's a beautiful animal, isn't it?"

"Yes," he replies distractedly. "Riley . . ."

"What?"

"Please don't burn your journal. Don't do that because of me."

This is getting too strange. As if the journal that made me quit writing is a disease that has infected him. I need to get rid of it.

I walk past Vaughn and say to Colton, "Let's go home and warm up with a big fire."

10

VAUGHN

I doubt Riley is serious about the fire. If the journal caused her enough pain to quit school, her bond with it, however anguished, would be difficult to break. I only hope I haven't pushed her into doing it. I shouldn't have kept asking to read it after she said it made her quit writing. But who wouldn't be intrigued by a piece of writing with that much power?

She doesn't light a fire when we arrive at the house. Colton packs his bag to return to Madison, and the family affectionately says goodbye. Riley and Colton embrace but don't kiss. That verifies what I decided during our outing: they're close, but they aren't romantically involved.

Last night, when I assumed they were sleeping together, I had trouble falling asleep. And that bothered me. I keep promising myself I won't get emotionally involved, but I can't seem to stop myself. Is the connection I feel with her real, or is it a phantom of things I've done in the past?

Even if it's real, I should go and leave her alone.

After Colton departs, Riley shuts herself in her room to study for a quiz. Kiran tinkers with his new fossils, and Alec returns to his den of moths. Sachi tries to plan my dinner and generally fusses over me. I can tell she feels obligated to entertain me when she'd rather be painting on a quiet Sunday afternoon. I tell her I'm going out for dinner. Of course I don't mention I'm craving a cheeseburger.

I stay out a long time, well past dinner hours, to make sure Sachi doesn't try to feed me. Also to give Riley and me some breathing space. We need to move on from our debate about the journal.

As I return to the house, following a blue-white flow of headlights into the darkness, I almost can't remember what I've been doing since I left. I recall a long time in a dark tavern, browsing a blur of topics on my phone. The only ones I remember clearly are several articles about snowshoe hares. Riley thinks I was unaffected by the white creature in a brown world, but she is much mistaken.

The cozy gold of the quaint home's windows entices me. I decide to go inside before retiring to the barn loft. I should have a reason, though, and a gift I bought will be just the ticket to get me in. I intended to give Kiran the old alarm clock tomorrow, but an impulse drives me onto the porch.

I knock and Sachi opens the door. She's already wearing pajamas and a robe.

"I'm sorry. I shouldn't have knocked this late."

"Nonsense, come in. Would you like to join me in the kitchen for an herbal tea? My mix is great for insomnia."

"No, I don't want to bother you."

She looks at the windup clock in my hand and smiles. "I bet I know who that's for."

"I found it in an old gas station store. Has he ever taken apart one of these? I thought the bells on top might be interesting for him."

"I don't know. He finds his clocks in junk and antique shops with Riley and Alec."

"Is he awake? Would it be okay if I gave it to him?"

"I'm sure he's awake. Go on. Riley is up there, too—doing homework."

I don't know if she said this to suggest I leave her alone or to imply I should say hello. I decide to interpret it as the latter. "Enjoy your tea. I'll let myself out after I give Kiran the clock."

Smiling, she pats my arm before I walk to the stairs. The gesture warms me, almost makes me feel as if I belong in this house.

Kiran's door is open and the lamp is on. Riley's door is closed, but I see light at the threshold. I'll go to Riley first. She should come with me to see Kiran because he doesn't know me very well. I knock lightly on her door.

"Yes?" she says.

This is an occasion when I'd rather ask forgiveness than permission. I turn the knob. As I poke my head in her room, she throws down the book she was reading in bed and hurtles at me. Afraid she'll decapitate me, I quickly thrust the rest of my body into the room.

"What are you doing?" she hisses.

I don't know what I'm doing. I haven't for a long time. If I did, I wouldn't be in her room, looking at her in snowflake-pattern leggings, fuzzy pink socks, and a shirt that says I'M WITH HER below a picture of Earth.

Her fury intensifies when I don't answer. "You have no right—"

I don't hear the rest. The walls of her room have me spellbound. It's like nothing I've ever seen, as strange and provocative as Kiran's gallimaufry of time. Now I understand why she didn't want me to see her room.

I want to see it better, but she's blocking me, arms crossed over her chest.

I hold up the clock. "Sachi told me I could give this to Kiran, and she said you were up here. I thought you should come with me. He doesn't really know me."

She stares at the clock, some of the redness draining from her cheeks.

"I'm sorry I bothered you."

"I'll come with you to give it to him, but you shouldn't have burst in here."

"I'm sorry," I repeat.

She tries to push me toward the door, but I stay where I am.

"What are these drawings?" I ask, gesturing at the mural painted on the papered walls.

"It's the seas of the moon," she says tersely.

"Really!" That's a better answer than I imagined, even if it's peculiar. I look around at the many seas. "Which one is Mare Nubium?"

Her eyes widen, her arms dropping to her sides. "You know the Sea of Clouds?"

"It's in my last book."

She looks more stunned. "It is?"

I smile. "Apparently you aren't a fan of my books."

"I've only read *When Leaves Let Go*. And I saw the movie."

She's read one of the books. I try to hide how this news affects me. I'm too agitated to ask her opinion of the book, but the film is safe territory. "What did you think of the movie?"

"I thought they got Lydia wrong. I think she was too fragile or something."

I'm nodding. She's more perceptive than most readers. Usually they say they loved Lydia in the movie.

She adds, "But it's not like that ruined the movie. It was good."

"I have another coming out. They're doing *A Box of Broken Stars*."

"Really? The one with the Sea of Clouds?"

"That could get cut. You never know how they're going to hack up the story."

"You aren't writing the screenplay?"

"That's not my skill." I point at a blue sea barely visible beneath a cover of fluffy pastel-colored clouds. "That's got to be the Sea of Clouds."

"You found it. Not too difficult, I guess."

"It's beautiful." I look around the room. "It all is."

It really is very well done. The seas cover all the walls, painted on a panoramic canvas of art paper. "Did Sachi help you paint this?"

"No, but Kiran did."

"He drew some of this?"

"I drew it all. But I sketched it the way it is on the moon, without any color. For years these walls were only shades of gray; then one day I walked in here and discovered Kiran—he was only three and a half at the time—had colored blue crayon all over that sea over there. You can still see the crayon marks through the watercolor."

I note the waxy scribbles that couldn't be covered by the watercolor paint. "I like it. It adds a bit of wildness to the sea."

"I know. And that's funny because that's Mare Tranquillitatis, the Sea of Tranquility."

"Way to go, Kiran. Were you angry?"

"I was, and I still feel bad that I reprimanded him for scribbling on my art. But he didn't get upset. He said he colored it because seas are supposed to be blue. I reminded him that the first astronomers who named the dark areas of the moon had thought they were oceans, but in reality they were only gray dirt. His response convinced me to color the whole mural."

"What did he say?"

"He looked at one of the colorless seas and said, 'I see blue.' I assumed he meant he saw blue *in his mind* when he looked at the seas. Then I remembered I had, too, when I was little. I learned the moon seas at age five. When I saw them through the telescope, they were gray, but when I thought about them, I often imagined them full of water. And sometimes I saw magical colors, because it was the moon, and anything could happen out there, far from Earth." She points to one of the seas. "Mare Nectaris, the Sea of Nectar, was the most magical. It was my favorite when I was little."

The water in the Sea of Nectar is colored in pastel hues similar to the tints in the clouds over the Sea of Clouds, but the color is mostly golds and oranges that reflect off the blue water.

I'm intrigued that viewing the moon through a telescope inspired the art. More than intrigued. When she first mentioned it, I was afraid she'd see my astonishment, but she was talking enthusiastically about the moon seas and didn't seem to notice.

I like how she changed when I asked about the mural. She's as unguarded as I've ever seen her, and I find this lively new Riley, possibly the real Riley, very appealing. But I dare not let that show.

To redirect my thoughts, I look over more of the oceans. There's a cloudless sea dotted with blue-gray islands. Another is swept with curls of whitecaps. One is misted with wisps of cloud or fog. The one that stops my gaze is the darkest of the seas. It's positioned up high in a corner. When I look closer, I notice the sinuous shape of a long serpentlike creature roiling in the sea's murky water. "What is that one?"

"Mare Anguis, the Serpent Sea."

"Looks ominous."

I continue looking at it, but she doesn't.

"It's the only one that has a creature in it. Why aren't there other animals in the lands around these seas?"

"It's the moon. Nothing can live there."

"That doesn't make sense. How can there be water and atmosphere?"

"That was just how I imagined it. It was only me and water and rock and dust. It was never meant to make sense."

"Nothing living but you and a big-ass serpent." I grin at her. "There's some interesting symbolism going on there. Biblical? Freudian?"

She doesn't get my jests. Her expression becomes impassive, but deep in her wildcat eyes, I see an emotion that could be anger. "Let's give the clock to Kiran. He's supposed to go to bed soon."

She walks out the door. I suppose she did get the joke about symbolism, and it bothered her for some reason.

My gaze is pulled back to the sea serpent in the corner. Its snake mouth smirks at me. I don't know why I see it as female. I almost hear the sea hag's derisive cartoon cackle. I sense she knows what I'm up to and finds it amusing. I wonder why.

"What are you doing?"

I turn around. Riley has caught me staring at the serpent.

"You did a really good job with that thing. It's so realistic it grabbed me and almost dragged me under the water."

She stares at me. The phrase "as if she'd seen a ghost" comes to mind. I've said something that's sent her into shock. Something to do with the sea monster. I wonder what it means to her and why she painted it on her wall.

I wish I could read her journal. These tantalizing glimpses into her life make me hungry for more. But how much will be enough?

11

RILEY

I can't face Alec. We usually meet on campus for lunch on Thursdays, but I canceled to avoid talking about my disastrous physics exam this morning. I'm probably too wiped out to think rationally, but I've decided I can't survive the math, chemistry, and physics required to major in biology. I don't know what to do, and I can't talk to Alec and Sachi. They've been worried about me since I quit school after the writing fiasco.

I arrive home around three, noting Vaughn's car is gone. I wonder what he does during the day when Alec and I are at college and Sachi is homeschooling Kiran or painting. When I got home on Monday, his car was here, but he left an hour later and came back at about ten. On Tuesday and Wednesday he wasn't here when I got home, and he still hadn't returned when I went to bed.

He's been keeping to himself. He hasn't come over to the house since Sunday night, when he burst into my room. I was afraid he would make a habit of it. And at first I thought the clock for Kiran was just an excuse to ask me about the journal again, but he didn't.

I think his appreciation of my moon seas was genuine. He didn't seem to think it was weird that I would have them on my walls. Maybe

I was wrong to be so nervous about him seeing them. But what he said about the serpent still makes my heart race every time I think of it. How could he have come so close to the truth?

Kiran is absorbed in schoolwork at the dining room table.

"How's it going, Kee? Need any help?"

"No," he says distractedly. "This math is easy."

"More like you're really good at it."

He flashes a sweet smile, and I kiss the top of his head.

He turns sideways in his chair and studies my face. "What's wrong?"

"Why do you think something's wrong?"

"Because I can tell."

Of course he can. Just like his mom.

"Are you sad that you never see Vaughn anymore?"

"What? No! Where did you get that idea?"

He doesn't answer, just continues looking into my eyes.

"Vaughn likes to keep to himself. He's trying to work out some problems."

"I think he's sad. I think you should talk to him."

"Yes, he's sad—because he wants to write and he can't. But there's nothing I can do to help him with that."

"I still think you should talk to him."

"Why?"

"Because."

I smile. "Good thing Sachi didn't hear you say that. Remember what she said about answering 'Because'? It's always better to try to put your feelings into words."

He considers for a few seconds. "Sometimes 'Because' is the best answer."

"So I should talk to Vaughn just . . . *because*?"

He nods.

"Because the sky is blue? Because you're good at math? Because a man on the other side of the world sneezed?"

74

"Yes! And because lots of snow is coming tonight."

"Is it?"

"Mom said it is."

I ruffle his hair. "If you want to play in it, you better get that math done."

"It's not happening until after I'm in my pajamas."

"When has that ever stopped us?"

He grins and turns back to his math.

I'm relieved he stops talking about Vaughn. I can't imagine why he went off on that tangent when we've seen so little of our resident author lately.

I eat a muffin Kiran baked with Sachi. She uses cooking to teach him about measurement, fractions, and volume. Sometimes cooking becomes a social studies lesson when she talks about where a spice or dish comes from, or a science lesson about why yeast rises. She homeschooled me, too, and time in the kitchen was one of my favorite ways to have lessons.

I can't get the physics test off my mind. It'll be the worst of several bad test scores in that class. I curl up in my bed under the flying-geese quilt Aunt Julia gave me. It's tattered now, but it always makes me feel better.

I lie on my side and look at the moon seas. I feel the serpent in Mare Anguis watching me.

Why am I in bed in the middle of the day? Nikki used to do that. I jump up and leave the room.

I cross the yard to Sachi's studio. She's bent over her worktable. "How was your day, love?" she asks. "Come give your opinion on this frame."

She turns around and peers at me over her purple-and-red glasses. "Want to talk about it?"

She's already picked up that the test didn't go well. "Not really," I reply.

She pulls me into the kind of all-encompassing warmth only Sachi can create. In her embrace, I think I can feel more, my aura brightening from the center outward.

She touches my cheek. "You have so many gifts to offer the world, Riley, and one day you'll know how to use them."

I try to smile, but there's no fooling Sachi. "Show me the frame you wanted an opinion on."

She displays the choices for a painting of a forest of bare white birches with pale spirit-like people and natural and human-made objects mixed in. As always, her art speaks straight to my soul. I could immerse myself in that forest for days and never learn all its secrets.

"I like the rustic wood for this one. The darker finish to contrast the white in the birch trunks and ghosty people."

She smiles at how I describe them. She picks up the wood I chose and pushes back the others. "Did you see the muffins?"

"I had one. Really good."

She nods as she works.

"Do you see much of Vaughn?" I ask.

"If I'm out here when he comes and goes, he says hello. But not much else. I'm a little worried about him, but I don't want him to feel obligated to spend time with me."

I decide not to tell her I think Vaughn might be badly depressed. But knowing Sachi, she's figured that out, too.

"I've offered to teach him yoga and meditation."

I smile.

"What's so funny?"

"He doesn't strike me as a bendy, mantra kind of guy."

"No one is until they try it."

"But you have to want to."

"Yes, and he clearly does not. But he may be isolating himself too much."

"Maybe that's what he needs after New York City."

"Maybe."

I flop onto the couch to watch her work. And I might nap, though I told myself I wouldn't.

I'm drifting into sleep when Vaughn comes in. "What are you working on?" he asks.

"I'm matting and framing a few paintings to sell. Want to see?"

I hear his footsteps coming and sit up. He stops walking and stares at me. He didn't know I was here.

"How's it going?" I ask him.

"Not bad," he says.

I easily see that's a lie. He looks like he hasn't slept for days.

"How about you?" he asks.

Maybe because I'm groggy, I reply, "I'm as *not bad* as you are."

Sachi shoots me a glance, sort of a reprimand. But Vaughn looks like he appreciates that I noticed. "What's put you in a *not bad* mood?"

"Nothing much, other than being a failure at everything."

"Wow. To fail at *everything* would be quite an accomplishment."

Sachi smiles and turns back to her work.

Vaughn walks to her table and looks at the three paintings she's framing. "You're going to sell these?"

"Once I frame them."

"Too bad," he says.

"Why?"

"I was thinking of buying this one." He points to the painting of a man floating over a city, the one Sachi said she began in moonlight.

"You can still buy it. I'd love for you to have one of my paintings."

"Not *have*," he says. "I'll pay whatever you charge."

"You will," she says, smiling. "The price depends on the frame. I'll let you choose it."

"He wants the one that's gilded in twenty-four-karat gold," I say.

"Absolutely," Vaughn says.

Sachi pulls out the boxes of frames she has in the studio and gives him catalogs in case he doesn't like those choices.

While they talk over the frame, I return to the house. I find Kiran in his room looking at a book about dinosaurs, his latest interest.

"Done with your homework?"

He nods, his gaze on the book. "I wish I could find a dinosaur fossil."

"Maybe you will someday."

I notice the two bells from Vaughn's old alarm clock are still on his worktable. I wonder why. I've never seen him leave pieces outside his universe after he's taken them out of a clock.

As darkness falls, I start dinner, and Sachi comes back to the house to help.

"Did Vaughn find a frame he liked?"

"He did. He has an artistic eye."

"I assume you invited him to dinner? Should I make extra?"

"I invited him, but he declined, as he always does."

He accepted the first night. I wonder what has changed since then.

"I think I may try to be more forceful tomorrow," she says. "He said he isn't sleeping, and he looks unwell."

When Alec returns and we sit down to dinner, I wish Vaughn were eating with us. Maybe it's only that I miss Colton. During the two years he lived here, I got used to five at the table. Or maybe I think Alec would be too distracted to ask me about the physics test if Vaughn were here.

Possibly I simply crave distraction. I like how Vaughn changes my opinion of him every few minutes. Egotistical, humorous, irritating, mournful—I never know what I'm going to get with him.

Only a few bites into the meal, the inevitable question arrives.

"How'd the physics test go?" Alec asks.

"I don't want to talk about it," I respond.

"Okay."

Everyone eats in silence for a minute.

"It's one test grade in your college career—in your whole life," Alec says. "Don't make it into more than it is."

He can say that, but he didn't experience the panic and tears after realizing I hadn't studied right for the exam. And to somehow keep trying despite my brain being sucked into a cold spinning blizzard. Sure, it was only one test in my life, but I'll remember that awful hour for its duration.

I'm aware of the tension among us, and of the subtle conversation Alec and Sachi have with their eyes. They're worried I'm going to quit school again. And they're wondering what will happen if I do. They're probably afraid I'm going to turn out like my mother.

But they don't really know what Nikki was like. I've never told them, and the only other person who knew was Aunt Julia.

Kiran looks like he feels the tension, too. Sweet kid that he is, he tries to lighten the atmosphere. "Dad, there's a big storm coming tonight."

"So I hear," Alec says.

They talk about the storm while I pick at the food on my plate.

After dinner, I go upstairs to my bedroom window to look at the barn. One pale light that must be the bedside lamp glows in the loft window. Though it's early, I imagine Vaughn in bed, reading. I wonder what a famous author reads.

But my eyes are drawn to another light, a flashlight beam moving from the barn to the trail beyond. Where is Vaughn going? The night is black with the storm moving in and no moon or stars.

I watch the light slowly recede into the distance. Sachi said leaving him alone might not be good. Kiran said I should talk to him. Maybe I should go out there.

I want to escape the claustrophobic feeling of the house anyway. I hurry down the stairs and grab my coat and flashlight off the hall tree bench. I'm quite sure everyone is too far back in the kitchen to see me slip out the door.

The temperature is much colder than it was when we stargazed on Saturday. I walk down the dirt trail to the pond, pulling on gloves I had in my pocket. I see no light on the dock, but he must be out there. I would see his flashlight if he'd walked on down the trail.

As I get close to the pier, I keep my light pointed downward. If he's out there, I'll pretend I was taking a walk. I can't admit I was worried about him.

"Riley?" he calls out of the darkness.

I pretend to jump. "You scared me!" I shine my beam onto him but drop it when he holds up his hand to block its glare. He's seated cross-legged at the very end of the pier, facing the frozen pond.

"What are you doing out here?" I ask.

"Looking at stars," he says. "Except there aren't any."

"I'd think you could have figured that out before you walked this far."

"I did. But I came anyway."

I stand at the edge of the dock. I can't think what to say or do. I don't want to leave him alone until I make sure he's all right.

"Why are you out here?" he asks.

"Just needed some fresh air. I like to sit on the dock at night, too."

This is a big lie. I have never sought this dock at night. Or any other place with black water that brings back the nightmare.

"Sorry I took your spot," he says.

"It's okay."

"You're welcome to sit with me."

"Are you sure?"

"It's your dock." He quickly adds, "And I don't mind company."

I shine my light on the planks as I walk to the end. When I sit on the cold wood, he repositions himself to face me. "Light on or off?" I ask.

"Off, if you don't mind."

He's been drinking. I smell it on him. I switch off my flashlight and lay it inside my folded legs.

"I came to the country to see darkness like this," he says. "I've described it in a few books but never experienced it."

"I hadn't either until I came to live here." I expect him to ask where I used to live, but he doesn't pry. "I used to live in Chicago."

"Did you?" He doesn't sound especially interested that I'm from his hometown.

"I remember how bright the streetlights were. Nights were nothing like this."

Rather than comment, he asks, "What was all that about being a failure today?"

Something—his irrelevance to my life, the anonymity of the darkness, or maybe both—compels me to answer honestly. "I think I failed a physics exam today."

He makes a wry sound. "That doesn't mean you're a failure. It just means you're in the ninety-eight percent of the population that would fail a college physics exam."

"When you're majoring in biology, you have to be in the two percent of the population that doesn't fail them."

"Maybe biology isn't your thing. When we talked about your writing, you said Alec persuaded you to try biology classes. If you really love something, you don't need to be talked into it."

"You need to be talked into anything if you keep failing."

"It doesn't sound like you failed at writing. You quit."

"Quitting is another way of failing."

"Jesus, your inferiority complex is the size of Manhattan."

"Maybe bigger."

It's strange to have this weighty exchange without seeing him. But also liberating.

"You're only twenty-one," he says. "Give yourself a break."

"How old were you when you published your first book?"

After a hesitation, he says in a quiet voice, "Twenty-three."

"Not that much older than me, and I bet you started writing the book when you were my age."

"Few people succeed at writing—or at anything—as early as I did. It was a total fluke. Don't compare yourself to me, or to anyone."

I do compare myself to someone, but not in the way he thinks. I relentlessly compare myself to Nikki, that person I would rather not call "my mother."

After a long silence, he says, "No reply?"

No reply. Nikki has brought this topic to its inescapable dead end.

"Are you all right?" he asks.

Funny, I came out here to make sure he was.

"Riley?"

"I'm okay. I just don't want to talk about this anymore."

"I understand." After a pause he adds, "I'm sorry. You came out here to erase it, didn't you?"

I hear the soft chafe of his clothing on the rough wood planks. "I love this," he says, "how dense this darkness is. As if I could climb into it." I can tell by the sound of his voice that he's facing the frozen pond again.

"Climb to where?"

After a few seconds, he replies, "Into deeper darkness. Oblivion."

He has no idea how well I understand this fantasy. The desire for oblivion is a perplexing contradiction. Oblivion sounds like death, but that's not really what you want. You want all that anguish inside you to die. You try to imagine how it would feel to walk the earth if you were insensible to whatever caused the pain. I guess the fantasy is mostly about wanting to forget.

I wonder what Vaughn wants to forget. Maybe whatever is causing his inability to write. It must be something big if he craves the solace of this dark abyss. Again, I contemplate what has changed. Last Saturday

I sensed the darkness frightened him. Even in the light of the stars, he was jumpy.

My silence must be worrying him, because he says, "Forgive me for talking bullshit. I'm somewhat drunk."

"It's not bullshit. I get it."

I hear him move. He's facing me again.

"Do you want a sip of whiskey?"

"You brought a bottle of whiskey out here?"

"A flask. It's premium whiskey."

"I've never even had bad whiskey."

"Try it. It'll help you stay warm."

Normally I'd say no. Because of Nikki. I refuse to need alcohol and drugs like she did. But I'm tired of her slithering over my every decision. Maybe this darkness really does help erase things. I reach out. "Where is it?"

"Here." One of his searching hands, the empty one, bumps into mine. His hand is bare, and even through my gloves, I can feel the heat of his fingers. He must have had his hands in his pockets. He places the flask against my palm, and I curl my fingers around it. He keeps his hands on mine, asking, "Got it?" though he can feel I've secured the flask.

"Got it."

I withdraw my hand from his and unscrew the cap. The whiskey jolts my taste buds like a fist in the mouth. Then it burns all the way down.

"What do you think?" he asks.

"It's awful."

He laughs. A real laugh, not the fake one he uses with Alec and Sachi. "Have more. Learn how to savor it."

"Is that possible?"

"I'm proof that it is."

I take another drink, but *savor* is not happening. I drink more because I'm determined not to quit as I do with everything. I'm twenty-one. I should know how to drink whiskey, especially expensive whiskey.

I get used to it after a while. And I'm starting to feel it in my head. I like the way it warms me inside and how it connects me to Vaughn. I want to feel what it's like to climb into his darkness. I wonder if his feels the same as mine.

"Pass it here," he says.

Our hands immediately connect this time, as if a golden aura of whiskey ties them together.

"You drank a lot," he says.

"Did I?"

"You'd better stop. Sachi and Alec will think I'm a bad influence if you come stumbling home."

"I'm old enough to drink."

"But not experienced enough. You have to work up to it."

I listen to him uncap the flask and drink. I hear the subtle sounds of him sliding the flask into one of his jacket pockets, then pushing his hands into them.

A warm veil falls over my mind. I begin to see why Nikki liked this. And why Vaughn does. It's a kind of oblivion.

"Vaughn . . . ?"

"Yes?"

"Are you going back to New York soon?"

"Funny you ask that."

"Why?"

"I came out here to sort that out."

"Did you?"

"I think I've decided I should leave."

The disappointment feels almost like a stab in my chest. It startles me.

"Why?" I ask.

He doesn't answer.

"You're welcome to stay."

"I know, but I shouldn't take advantage of your family's kindness."

"You aren't."

"You sound like you want me to stay."

I'm not sure what to say. I didn't want him to stay. Then I didn't mind so much. And now I don't want him to go. Maybe I only like that he's a distraction. From the moment I set eyes on him, I felt lifted from this place that's become increasingly oppressive. He's been a glimpse over the trees.

"It's not every day a famous person comes to stay." I realize this was a stupid thing to say before I finish.

"That's the problem," he says.

"What is?"

"If I were some nobody who was careless enough to run out of gas, would Sachi have invited me to stay?"

I doubt she would have. She would want the loft room vacant for Colton's visits.

"You see?" he says when I don't answer. "Can you imagine how this makes me feel?"

"I can." I understand more than he knows. I felt like "Poor Orphan Riley" when I first came to live here, and I hated the smothering attention. At the time, I believed my cousins had taken me in because I had nowhere else to go—mostly because they pitied me. Maybe Vaughn feels a similar kind of insecurity about his celebrity.

"I guess I should go," he says.

"Don't go for that reason. What difference does it make now that you're here? Who you are doesn't much matter to Alec and Sachi now. They like you."

"I notice you didn't include yourself in that last comment."

"Quit fishing."

He snorts. "I hear ice fishing is an interesting sport."

"But you have to cut a hole in the ice first. Would you give me that whiskey?"

His loud laughter reverberates off the ice so hard I think it might crack. We exchange the whiskey with ease, and I drink its heat into my belly. I relish the feel of my mouth on the flask where his mouth touched.

"Is the whiskey melting a hole in the ice?" he asks.

"Maybe."

I incline my head to drink more fire. A strange sensation pricks all over my face, like little hot needles. After a few seconds I realize the stings are cold and wet.

"It's snowing!" he says.

I keep my face tilted skyward, enjoying the tingle of snow on my skin. "You say that like you're as excited as someone from Florida."

"I've never seen a snow come on so fast," he says.

I sense he also has his face turned upward. "You didn't see it. That's what made it so much better."

"It was better. I never felt a snow like this. It's—"

"It's like it might not be real because you swear you can see its whiteness in the dark."

He's staring at me. I feel that he is. I don't need light to know everything he's doing. It's as if the darkness has connected our bodies.

"Will you have a drink with me tomorrow night?"

I look toward him but see only darkness. "I'm having a drink with you tonight."

"Another drink. At a place I found that I like. I'd invite you to dinner, but the only plant-based eateries I've found around here are loaded with cows and manure."

I laugh loudly. I think I might be getting drunk. "Are you asking me on a date?"

"What answer should I give to make sure you accept?"

"Say, 'I'll leave tomorrow if you don't have a drink with me.'"

12

VAUGHN

Riley, Riley, Riley.

This is how I've been thinking of her today. Riley tripled. Riley cubed. One declaration of her name is not enough, and three times is a charm. I've had only three conversations alone with her: at Sally Run Creek, in her room the night I gave Kiran the clock, and on the pier last night. How is it possible this is happening?

I never expected or wanted this. I should go back to New York. I was going to leave today, but now I can't because she wants me to stay.

Riley, Riley, Riley has put some kind of magic on me.

By afternoon I'm quite certain it's all in my head. I'm imagining I have a date with her. I didn't really drink whiskey with her on the dock last night. We didn't run back to the house sliding and falling and laughing in a sudden snowstorm. I didn't walk her onto the porch and want to kiss her. As she went in the door, she didn't say, "Tomorrow night sounds fun. You won't forget, will you?"

I assured her I wouldn't forget. But I almost wish I could. The complications of going out with her are beyond imagining.

Complications be damned. If she still wants to go, we will.

I drive to the nearest Laundromat. I'm nearly out of clean laundry and don't want to bother Sachi with a request to use her washer and dryer. I'm also afraid to get into a sticky conversation if she noticed Riley was somewhat drunk last night.

The Laundromat reminds me of when I first arrived in NYC, broke and homeless. I slept at a ghastly hotel until a friend of a friend of a friend let me share his studio apartment. I slept on a saggy, dirty couch but still paid 50 percent of the rent when I got a job as a dishwasher.

Remembering those days doesn't make me grateful for where I am now. The memories are nostalgic. My life was so much easier in those days. Back then I was a brown rabbit in a brown world. Now I'm a white rabbit in a brown world.

After the laundry is done, I stay out for dinner to avoid eating with the family. Dinner conversation would be awkward if we discuss the date. I imagine I'd feel as uncomfortable as a teenager having dinner with his girlfriend for the first time.

I don't know why I'm having these thoughts. I'm twenty-nine, not some giddy teen going on a first date.

I eat a salad and drink only one beer. I don't want to be bloated on salt and alcohol tonight.

I return at six thirty, past sunset and dinner hour. I change into the dark jeans and shirt I wore the day I met Riley. The shirt is one of my favorites, navy with flying white swallows. Gemma picked it out when we went shopping a few months ago. I roll the sleeves to just below my elbows, looking at myself in the mirror. Is the guilt I see in my eyes more about breaking up with Gemma or going out with Riley? I guess I don't have to choose. I have enough self-reproach for every occasion.

It's six fifty. Last night Riley and I were too tipsy to discuss when we would meet. It's a little early for a drink, but she doesn't know we have a forty-minute drive. I hope she's ready.

I don't see anyone in the living room when I step onto the front porch. The lights are turned low. I knock and no one answers. I hate to rouse the whole house, but I have to. I ring the bell.

Like Sunday, Sachi opens the door, wearing a robe over pajamas. "Vaughn, come in!" she says brightly.

Riley comes down the stairs. She's wearing pajamas. I guess the date wasn't real. Maybe the connection I felt with her wasn't either. I try to conceal my disappointment, but it must be obvious.

Riley has a questioning look, and I don't know what to say.

"Are we going?" she says at last.

"I thought we were."

"I . . ." She looks at Sachi.

"I'll go finish my tea," Sachi says.

"I thought you forgot," Riley says as Sachi leaves the room.

"Why would you think that?"

"You were gone. And it's late."

"It's early for a drink."

"I guess I don't know the city rules."

"And I didn't know bedtime in the country is seven o'clock."

"It's winter. Darkness and pajamas come early."

"You'll have to change. Even for this country pub."

"So we're going?"

"Do you want to?"

"I did . . . I do."

My heart stammers like I'm thirteen years old. "I'll wait in the living room while you get ready."

"I'll be quick," she says, trotting up the stairs.

Kiran came downstairs during our conversation, and he stays. He's wearing an old purple robe over blue-and-pink pajamas. His gaze is oddly penetrating for a kid his age.

"How's it going?" I ask him.

"Okay."

"I hope I didn't wake you up when I rang the bell?"

"No."

I sit on the couch, and he sits across from me. "Do you like Riley?" he asks.

"Yes," I reply.

"Do you like her a lot?"

I'm relieved I won't have to answer when Alec and Sachi come out of the kitchen.

"How are you, Vaughn?" Alec asks.

"Good. How about you?"

"No complaints. Are you and Riley going out?"

"For a drink." I'm squirming because I've just admitted I'll be drinking and driving with his daughter.

"Be careful. The roads are slippery after that storm."

"Where are you going?" Sachi asks.

"A place called the Blind Wolf." Hoping they'll think it's the reason I'm taking Riley, I add, "They have live music."

Alec nods. "I know that tavern. Tolly Duff owns it. His grandmother Lena used to be close with my grandmother. She visited this farm often."

"Small world," I say.

"It was back then. I thought nothing of riding my bike eight miles to see Lena Duff."

"To see Lena or Tolly?" I'm not especially interested in his history with the Duff family, but I'd rather talk about that than drinking and driving with Riley.

"To see Lena," he replies. "She was one of my favorite people on Earth. She knew everything about plants and their remedies. She took a liking to me because I was fearless about hiking into the marshes and woods around here, despite my Chicago upbringing. She considered it her duty to tutor the clueless city kid in the backwoods wisdom few know these days."

"You came here often when you were young?"

"Very often. And I usually spent my summers up here. This place was actual heaven for a city kid who loved nature. This farm is the reason I became a biologist."

"Then it's perfect that you ended up owning it."

"It's a dream come true to be the custodian of this land. Gram left it to me because she knew I'd protect its nature. We've never cut and sold the timber on this land. And since Sachi and I took it over, we've let the cow and horse pastures revert to grasslands that support lepidoptera and other wildlife."

I enjoy that Alec inserted the word *lepidoptera* with natural ease into his conversation. I've never met anyone who could do that.

Riley arrives. She may have patterned her clothing on mine. She's wearing slim dark jeans and a fitted button-down shirt in autumnal colors.

"I assume this is okay for a bar?" she asks.

"It surpasses *okay*, but your toes might get a little cold."

She gives me a look. "Can I borrow your brown boots?" she asks Sachi.

"Of course," Sachi says.

As Riley disappears upstairs again, I walk toward the front door.

"The Blind Wolf is a long drive," Sachi says.

"Everything is a long drive from here."

"I guess it is, but please be careful on those slick roads."

She's forgotten that Alec already warned me about the snowy roads, or maybe she just wants to reinforce the point. The parental concern in their eyes is entirely new for me. Never in my life has anyone looked at me like that.

Riley arrives in Sachi's knee-high brown boots. She looks great. Very different from the fairy-tale girl in braids, rubber boots, and colorful garments.

Outside, I ask, "Would you prefer to drive us in your car? They're worried that we're having a drink and driving."

"Are you kidding? After how I got on a few sips last night?"

"You had more than a few sips. And you weren't so drunk that I noticed."

"What about when I fell on my butt?"

I sense she's been fretting about last night, and I enjoy the possibility that I've been on her mind as much as she's been on mine. "Have you forgotten that I fell, too?"

"Only because you tried to catch me."

"The snow was slippery. That had nothing to do with the whiskey."

"When I went to bed, I felt like the room was spinning."

"Yep, that was the whiskey. I hope you didn't . . ."

She shakes her head. "But no whiskey tonight, okay? I'm not up for another ride on the Tilt-A-Whirl."

"No whiskey, I promise."

We head out, the high beams of my rental car illuminating a newly white-and-black world. Snow in the country is different from city snow. It remains white and smooth and sparkly in sunlight.

Since morning I've been thinking about the snowshoe hare Colton showed me. From the moment I looked out the loft window and saw the snow, I was comforted to know the hare was back in its protective white world. This thought has brightened my mood all day.

These are not typical feelings for me. Being with Riley, Riley, Riley is doing curious things to me.

Our conversation during the drive remains in the present, unusual for a first date. Typically it's an archaeological dig, an exchange of questions about where you grew up, what your parents did for a living, where you went to school, and on and on. But if there's one thing I could guess about a person who was orphaned at age eleven, it's that she'll evade the past as much as I will.

She tells me she received a D on yesterday's physics test.

I hold up my hand for five, but she doesn't hit me. "Come on, you said you failed, and you didn't."

"It's not funny."

I drop my hand. "You're taking it too seriously."

"That's what Alec says. It's easy to say that when you succeed at everything."

"You succeed at plenty."

"You don't know that," she says. "We just met."

"And you don't know me. You don't know anything about my failures."

"You can forgo the pep talk. You were famous by age twenty-three. You obviously have good genes. Mine are programmed for failure."

I glance at her as I drive. "I really hope we're talking about our pants, but I don't think we are."

"Ha ha ha," she says.

"I think living with a biologist has skewed your view of the world."

"It has. Since I've lived here, Alec's taught me about evolution and natural selection anytime we're out looking at plants and animals. He really can't help it."

I laugh a little at that, but she didn't intend it to be funny.

"He didn't know he was helping me understand my problem."

"Which is what? You think you inherited bad genetics from your parents?"

"Just forget it," she says.

The conversation has swerved too close to the past. I wonder why she thinks her genetics are messed up when it clearly isn't true.

We don't talk for the next ten miles or so, but it's a comfortable silence.

"Where are we going, anyway?" she finally asks.

"The Blind Wolf."

"Oh, the place Tolly Duff owns."

"You've been there?"

"I just know of it. I've never been in a bar."

"Really?"

"I only turned legal drinking age in January," she says a little defensively.

"They have music most nights. Kind of indie folksy stuff. You'd better tell me now if that will make you gag."

"It won't."

"What do you usually listen to?"

"Nothing."

"Nothing?"

"Alec's trumpet . . . obviously."

What a peculiar little island she lives on. "He's really good."

"Yes," she says.

We sink into silence again. The quiet feels awkward this time. I try to think of something to say that won't lead to dangerous ground. I suppose Kiran is a safe topic.

"Has Kiran always been homeschooled?"

"He went to public school for kindergarten and part of first grade." After a pause she says, "Sachi and Alec took him out because he was getting bullied."

"Because of his clothing?"

"Yes, but not at first. In kindergarten, he wore what we called his 'school clothes,' outfits most people see as 'male.' We got him used to that idea because we knew he'd get teased if he wore dresses. But as he got older, he wanted to wear his usual clothes sometimes, and we didn't think it was right to tell him he couldn't. Then the school said he had to wear 'regular boys' clothing' because his supposed 'girl' clothes were causing too much trouble and distraction."

"I bet that pissed off Sachi and Alec."

"It did, and me too. Sachi told the teachers and principal they should use the opportunity to teach the students about compassion and tolerance, but the teasing only got worse."

"Poor kid. Why does he wear girls' clothing?"

"Why do you wear what you wear?"

"Okay, so he likes those clothes. But does he know boys usually—"

"Of course he knows. He goes out into the world. He reads books. We've talked about it, and he says his pronoun is *he*, but he might want to change it someday."

"How old was he when he started wearing those clothes?"

"When he was around four."

"He just suddenly asked Alec and Sachi to buy him dresses?"

"His first dresses came from me—from the boxes of clothes I moved from Chicago."

We're back in dangerous territory. I'll return the conversation to Kiran, away from her pre-Wisconsin life. I want to ask a question that's been on my mind since I arrived. I'll spend the next few hours alone with her, and I need to know what I've gotten myself into.

"How long has he been making magic with clocks and fossils?"

She's looking at me. Even in the faint glow of dashboard lights, I can see the irritation in her gaze. "Is that still bothering you?" she says.

"When did I say it bothered me?"

"When you ran out of Kiran's room like I was too weird to stand next to."

I did run out. But my reasons for leaving had nothing to do with Kiran's supposed magic.

"I like to imagine things that are beyond our understanding," she says. "And I don't care if you think that's strange. If you knew Kiran like I do, you'd see the magic. You'd *feel* it."

"I'd like to." I'm not lying. Who doesn't want to experience magic?

"His heart stopped shortly after he was born," she says. "He's been to the other side. Maybe he experienced something beautiful we can't imagine."

"Why did his heart stop?"

Glendy Vanderah

"The doctors called it *congenital defects*. They resuscitated him, but he needed immediate surgery."

"Jesus."

"He's had three surgeries on his heart since he was born."

"Will he need more?"

"The doctors can't say for sure."

Now I understand more about the family dynamics. When you think your child might die young, you probably let them do whatever makes them happy. You would encourage their every whim. That would explain Riley letting him dress her in the strange outfit, and the family giving him clocks to take apart and hunting for fossils with him.

This might also explain why Riley believes Kiran can perform magic. Fear can make people superstitious. Maybe she thinks those clock parts and fossils are keeping him alive. Maybe that's why she wouldn't let me touch the clock gear.

The Blind Wolf parking lot is more crowded than I've ever seen it. Inside, musicians are setting up on the small stage. Riley stakes out one of the last free tables while I get us glasses of beer. She wants lager; I get an IPA.

I hold up my glass for a toast. "To your first experience in a tavern."

We tap glasses and drink. She looks around at the rustic tavern. It's moderate in size, and the walls are brick on the sides it shares with other buildings. The floor, bar, tables, and beams are an unpainted timeworn wood. The ceiling is made of decorative tin, probably original.

"How many times have you been here?" she asks.

"Twice before tonight."

"I always wonder where you disappear to."

This warms me, but I make sure I don't show it.

"I spent a fair amount of that time looking for a tavern I like," I admit. "It's an important refuge for me."

"Why?"

"A good tavern is dark, full of generally happy strangers I don't have to talk to, and it gets me high." I lift the glass and drink to demonstrate the last. "And this is the particular kind of drinking establishment I like, rustic with decent music."

"Are there places like this in New York City?"

"Yes, but this has an authentic rural flavor. I like the name, too."

"Do you? I've always thought the blind, white-eyed wolf on the sign is sad."

"During Prohibition, some places that illegally sold liquor were called Blind Pig or Blind Tiger. Supposedly they were charging to see a curious animal, but once inside you could drink."

"Was there a blind pig or tiger?"

"I doubt it. Lots of bars are still called the Blind Pig or the Blind Tiger. I'm only guessing, but I think the owner of this place used his own version of the speakeasy name."

"Is that research you did for one of your books?"

"No. I like to look up random things on the internet."

We turn our attention to the singers. The woman sits on a stool, holding her guitar, and the man remains standing with his. I like that they'll play their own songs rather than cover known musicians. The singer says they'll open with a fitting ballad for the Blind Wolf, and several people applaud, apparently familiar with the song.

The ballad is about a woman whose soul is only half-human. The other half is divided into pieces among a pack of wolves. The woman has lived alone in the wilderness with her young daughter since her lover was killed by the wolves. She gave them half her soul in exchange for the promise that they wouldn't also kill her little girl. One of the wolves, feeling her humanity in the piece of soul he shares with her, begins to understand her pain and fears. He falls in love with her.

The way the lyrics describe the split souls of the wolf and woman is affecting, as is the harmony of the duet. I look at Riley. Tears drip down her cheeks, twinkling like little stars in the dim light. She sees that I'm looking at her, and for a few seconds she smiles as she wipes one hand across her cheek.

I am, quite literally, stabbed by an emotion I cannot describe or understand. I have to look away from her. I'm not hearing lyrics.

The song ends. I compose myself and look at her. She's dabbing her face with her sleeve. A few people watch her, smiling. I wonder how I would have felt if one of my past girlfriends had cried openly at a song in a tavern. I think it would have bothered me, especially when she wasn't close to tipsy yet. Maybe I would have assumed she was pretending the tears to look adorable.

Riley leans over the table, whispering, "Wasn't that a beautiful song?"

"It was. Is Alec's trumpet getting some competition?"

"Definitely." She focuses back on the singers.

The following songs aren't quite as affecting as the first, but they're good. Too good. The music has Riley rapt, and I'd hoped we would talk while we drank.

As a song ends, I'm about to ask Riley if she wants the same kind of beer when the woman singer says, "This is the last one before we take a little break, and I want to see some fires gettin' kindled on this cold night. Grab your partner and get on up here. Come make me warm with some close rubbin'!"

Couples migrate to the dance floor, clearing my path to the bar. As I rise, Riley gets up with me, assuming I stood to go dance. Noting my hesitation, she asks, "Are we going up there?"

I have the impression she didn't understand what the singer asked of the audience. She wouldn't if she's never been to a club or bar.

"It's a slow dance," I reply.

"Oh." She watches the dancers embrace as the music starts.

We're locked in an awkward moment. I hate for her to feel this distress, but I can't move. The thought of our bodies pressed together has me as alarmed as I've yet been in her presence.

Smiling sheepishly, she says, "I have no idea how to slow dance."
She sits down.

What the hell is wrong with me?

I know what's wrong. I never expected this. I have to reorder every
thought I've ever had about her.

I extend my hand down to her. "I don't know how to, either, but
let's give it a try."

She takes my hand. If only Sachi were here to tell me what my aura
looks like. But maybe I wouldn't want her to see the powerful effect
Riley has on me.

We insert ourselves among the slowly rotating couples. We quickly
assess the others. After a few clumsy tries that make us laugh, I hold her
hand at shoulder height and encircle her waist with my other arm. She
puts her other hand on my shoulder. Our heights work well together.
She's a few inches shorter than me, maybe about five eight. I'm five ten,
though my father was a huge son of a bitch. I don't know how tall my
mother was, but I've always assumed drinking and smoking in my teens
stunted my growth.

I'm irritated that my father and mother and their delinquent son
intrude on this moment. I shove them into the dark, webbed cellar of
my brain, where I usually keep them. Riley Mays is in my arms, and I
will live in every second in the present to make the most of it. Future
complications be damned.

There is no future. There's nothing before me but Riley's big
tawny-brown eyes. I'm so close I can see flecks of color in her irises
anytime she turns toward the stage lights. I keep my hand loose on
her waist, but I'm very aware of the warmth and firmness of her body
through her shirt.

"What do you think of your first tavern experience so far?"

"I love it," she replies.

"Mostly the music?"

"The music is my favorite part. I loved that first song. Its ending was so sad."

"I missed the ending," I admit.

"What! How could you miss it?"

"My mind drifted."

"The wolf gave the woman back her soul even though he knew the other wolves would kill him for doing it. He died in her arms."

"That's sad."

"Yes, and now I'm missing this song because I had to tell you what you missed in that one."

"All right, let's listen." I use this as an opportunity to bundle her closer. My body is pressed on hers, and the side of my face rests against her hair. It's soft and smells faintly of flowers.

She's relaxed against me, her head rested on my shoulder. I try to listen to the lyrics in case she questions me, but I'm in a sensory over-load of Riley Mays. Every receptor in my body is occupied by her.

When the song ends, we break apart and applaud with the other dancers. "I think we did that pretty well for not knowing how to do it."

She looks at me playfully. "There's no way you never slow danced before."

"This is the first slow dance I've *enjoyed*. The other two times I was dragged against my will."

"Who dragged you?"

"I can't remember their names. That was back in the days when I was draggable."

"You aren't now?"

"I've learned how to say no and mean it. You have to when you're famous."

Her smile is wry. "Is being Vaughn Orr really so difficult?"

It's nearly sucked the soul out of me. But now Riley is smiling and flirting with me. I don't want to talk about being famous.

"I'd better hurry over to the bar. The line will get long while the singers take a break. How about a pitcher of your brand so we don't have to get up during the music?"

She agrees and heads to the bathroom. I'm still waiting to get the bartender's attention at the crowded bar when she returns. She notices a white cat sleeping on the bar, and when she traces her fingers on the cat's head, the creature seems oblivious to her touch.

"Riley?" a middle-aged man behind the bar says. "What are you doing in this dive?"

Riley grins at him. "I'm drinking. And dancing," she says in a way that makes me smile.

"Hold on," the man says. "How old are you now?"

"Twenty-one," she says.

"Thank god. I thought I'd have to throw you out." He finishes tapping a pitcher and hands it to a young man. "Who are you here with?"

"My friend," Riley says, gesturing at me.

The man looks at me. "What are you drinking?"

I tell him, and he immediately starts filling a pitcher. The female singer walks up to the bar and pets the cat with Riley.

"Neither of you tattle to public health that you saw her up there," the bartender says. "We rescued her from our garbage dumpster and discovered she's deaf."

"No wonder she's so calm in all this chaos," the singer says.

"What'll you have, Thea?" the man asks.

"Water, no ice," the singer says.

He nods and turns off the spigot to my pitcher. He fills the water, hands it to Thea, and brings the pitcher of beer from behind the bar. "On the house," he says, handing the beer to me. "Alec and me go way back."

"Thank you."

He extends his hand toward me. "I'm Tolly Duff. I own Blind Wolf."

I shake his hand and say, "Vaughn."

He curls his hand by his ear, unable to hear over the crowd. "What was it?"

"Vaughn," I repeat.

Like many people, he looks perplexed by the odd name.

"Vaughn Orr," Riley says in a loud voice.

Damn. I wish she hadn't said my last name. Tolly didn't recognize it, but I think the singer did. She's in her thirties and female, a prime demographic for my books.

"Vaughn Orr?" she says. "As in Vaughn Orr, the writer?"

Why didn't I choose "John Brown" when I legally changed my name?

"Are you?" Thea asks.

"Guilty," I say, employing a precious reply I overuse.

"Holy shit." She wipes her palm on her skirt and introduces herself as she shakes my hand. The other musician is drinking a beer with a group of patrons nearby. "Jason," she calls to him, "come meet Vaughn Orr."

"What?" Jason says.

"No . . ." I try to stop her from saying my name again. If she does, I know what's going to happen.

"Vaughn Orr. The writer," Thea says. "Come meet him."

Jason comes over to shake hands. Then Sheila and Joe and Suzie and on and on. They want to know why I'm here. They praise my books. A woman asks when the movie of *A Box of Broken Stars* will arrive in theaters, news that must have hit the internet in recent days. I'm handed napkins and pens for autographs. Tolly takes the pitcher out of my hand so I can sign them on the bar. I think many of them don't know who I am. They only want to be near someone famous.

I'm engulfed in the circus and can't see Riley. Tolly insists I have a photograph taken with him. When people keep asking why I'm in their town, I have to say I'm looking at properties. I make no mention of

Riley or her family. I don't want anyone to know where I am. My life in the city has been a study in tedium—with meticulous prudence—to keep the hounds off me. I've never once made a mistake in seven years. But that's only made my fans hungrier for juicy bits like what's happening right now.

Tolly asks where I'm staying.

I pretend I don't hear as I sign another napkin.

"Do you know Alec and Sachi?" he asks.

"How about we give the stage back to Thea and Jason?" I say to him.

"That's a good idea," Riley says behind me.

I turn on the barstool to face her.

She takes my hand. "Are you draggable right now?"

"Very."

She faces the crowd and hauls me behind her like a little mule pulling a wagon. I hear people in the crowd ask, "Who is she? Is that his girlfriend? Does she live around here?"

As we arrive at our table and empty glasses, I want to grab our coats and haul ass for the door. "I think we should go," I say into Riley's ear.

"You can't. Not now. It would be too rude."

I sit down. Since when do I care about being rude?

Since Riley. She's looking at me in a bemused sort of way.

"You shouldn't have said my full name."

"I didn't know. I had no idea . . ."

"That it would be the annunciation of a lesser god?"

"Lesser?"

"I'm pretty sure the Bible is still more popular than my books in the Cheese State."

She looks around. Many continue to stare. "This is what your life is like?"

"Not when I can help it. And being a bestselling novelist in New York isn't a big deal like it is here. There are stars that far outshine me in that city."

Tolly arrives with our beer and fresh glasses. "I tapped you a new one," he says. "The other got warm."

"It would have been fine."

"Nope. I won't have you saying you got warm beer at Blind Wolf."

As he walks away, I whisper to Riley, "Who does he think I would tell?"

"Other famous people."

"Other famous people who will drive to the middle of nowhere in Wisconsin to drink beer on my recommendation?"

"Stop it. Tolly is nice."

"Yes, he is," I say, as I pour free cold beer into shiny, clean glasses.

Thea and Jason strap on their guitars. Thea sits on her stool, leans into the microphone, and says, "This was inspired by a writer I met when I was living in Scotland. This one's for you, Vaughn."

Everyone turns toward me. Thea and Jason smile at me as they start to play. It's intrusive. Why can't they see that?

I can never come back. My perfect tavern is ruined. The whole night with Riley is, because now our every move will be monitored. I try to pretend I'm enjoying the song, but I'm simmering, very aware of people looking at me to see my reaction to Thea's song. Riley seems anxious. I think she knows I'm angry.

When the song ends, I lean over to Riley and whisper, "Can we go now?"

"No. Hold on a little longer. And we can't leave all this beer or Tolly will be offended."

I fill my glass and drink it down while keeping her gaze. Her eyes go wide when she sees how fast I can empty the glass, an easy trick I learned as a teenager with my old buddy Kaz. I fill the glass again, and as I drain it, she whispers, "I didn't mean drink it in two minutes! I'm driving, by the way."

Before the song ends, the pitcher is empty, and I'm a little light-headed from drinking so fast. I lift my eyebrows at Riley during the applause between songs. She shakes her head. Another song begins.

I decide to take matters in hand. I pretend I'm leaning back in my chair to watch the singers and knock my elbow into her half-full glass of beer. I'd intended most of it to spill on the table while a small amount hit her lap, giving us an excuse to leave. But the glass slides toward her before it clunks onto the table, and all the beer pours onto her shirt and jeans.

Riley gives me an I-can't-believe-you-did-that look. I cringe when I see how much spilled on her. Many, including Thea, watch me dab at her wet shirt with two cocktail napkins. The paper is instantly soaked. I throw a hefty tip on the table, grab our jackets, and lead Riley to the tavern door. We burst outside into the frigid night air, laughing billows of white vapor.

"You're so bad!" she says when she can catch her breath.

"I'm so smart. It was the perfect out. Admit it."

"If you don't mind looking like an idiot."

"I don't give a rat's ass what they think—but I only meant a small amount to get on you. I'm sorry it was the whole glass, but I couldn't take another minute of their stares. I felt like a baby panda at the zoo."

"You're nowhere near that adorable."

"Thank you for your refreshing honesty."

"You're welcome." She looks down at her wet shirt and pants. "This is really cold."

"A necessary sacrifice." I help her put on her coat. "I'm truly sorry, and I owe you one."

She treads backward in front of me as we walk along the shoveled sidewalk. "What sacrifice will you make for me?"

"You can choose the act as you see fit."

"You should be glad they love your books."

"I am."

"You didn't look glad."

"Of course not. I'm out with an enchanting woman at my favorite bar, enjoying a slow dance for the first time, and *blam!* I'm up to my elbows in cocktail napkins I have to autograph. Talk about an evening killer."

She stops walking backward, which means I have to stop moving forward. "Enchanting?"

"It's not PC to call a woman 'beautiful,' and if I say 'smart' I'm suspected of condescension. I think 'enchanting' captures both, don't you?"

"I see. You use this word on lots of women."

"Believe me, I don't. It only sounded premeditated because you made me explain."

"I bet you know lots of enchanting women in New York City."

"If this is a circuitous route to asking if I'm with someone, the answer is no."

She steps closer to me, studying my eyes in the luster of a streetlamp. "How could you not be?"

"Am I so desirable it can't be true?"

"You'd only have to be as famous as you are for it to be unlikely."

"What are you implying? My appeal exceeds my fame?"

She emits an incredulous laugh.

"Am I an adorable panda after all?"

A grin spreads across her cold-blushed cheeks. "I'm not going to feed more candy to your ego. I think it's too fat already." She turns away and walks toward the car. "And I'm freezing thanks to your beer."

I'd been soaring on our banter, but now I lose the updraft. At the car, she holds out her hand. "Give me the key."

"I'm not drunk."

"Give it."

"The car doesn't need a key to start. But here, take it." I assist her with the unfamiliar dashboard controls, dialing up the heat and turning on her seat warmer. "Where are we going?"

"Home." She looks at me. "Where did you think we were going?"

Five minutes ago, I thought we might be headed for a kiss, at the least. Now, returned to reality by her pragmatism, I'm relieved nothing happened. I don't know why I keep ignoring the risks of getting involved with her.

"Home sounds good," I reply.

13

RILEY

The moon is almost full. I wonder if Vaughn even notices its gloss on the snow. Some people don't see the beauty of things like that even when they're looking right at them.

He may be asleep. He hasn't said anything since we got in the car. Or he's angry and doesn't want to talk to me. I shouldn't have said that about his ego. And I think he's disappointed that the night is already over. We'd still be at the Blind Wolf if I hadn't bullhorned his name to everyone. I guess I did it on purpose, hoping Tolly and everyone else would know who he was and be impressed that I was with him. Talk about problematic egos. Mine's so small it needs an injection of famous-author steroids to be seen in a microscope.

But I honestly had no idea people would react like that. I didn't know writing novels could cause such a hullabaloo, to use a word Colton likes. I thought Sachi's enthusiasm when she first met Vaughn was only her typical extroversion. I didn't know it meant Vaughn was an actual celebrity.

I'm going to find his last book and start reading it tonight. I want to see the part where he mentions the Sea of Clouds.

I look up at the moon through the front windshield. There it is, the Sea of Clouds, a pool of darkness I know well.

"Riley . . . ," Vaughn says.

"I thought you were asleep."

"No. Do you think you could pull over for a minute?"

All that beer he tossed down must have him uncomfortable by now. I stop on the one-lane road. We're surrounded by open, rolling fields, but no one will see him. There's not a house or car in sight.

As soon as I put the car in park, he hurries outside. I keep my eyes on the moonlit road to give him privacy. He returns and opens the passenger door but doesn't get in. "Come out and listen to this."

I step outside. "Those are coyotes."

"I thought so."

I turn off the motor so he can hear better. He stares out at the snowy field beyond the wood-and-wire fence. The coyotes' raucous conversation ends, but he doesn't move.

"I've never seen a moon this bright," he says.

"It'll be full day after tomorrow."

He's very still, looking out at the moon-washed snow. The white vapor of his exhalations is soft and slow, as if he's relaxed in meditation. I step away from the car to get closer to him.

A coyote starts again, calling a rowdy *yip, yip, yip!* Vaughn turns to me, his smile wide with wonder, his gray eyes lit in the lunar light. I like how the moon silvers his hair and burnishes the high curve of his cheekbone. He looks like he poured down from the moonlight, here just for me.

He's staring at me. I'm afraid he can see what I'm thinking about him. I have to say something to distract him.

"That might be a female trying to find a male." Before I finish, I realize how awkward that statement is in this moment. I add, "Coyotes breed at this time of year. Colton taught me a lot about them."

Mentioning Colton helps ground me, but only for a few seconds. Vaughn is still looking into my eyes, straight into my mind, it feels like.

"I think a male was calling back to the female," he says. "I heard more than one before."

The road seems to sway beneath my feet. "Yes, it was two."

He comes closer. He's terribly beautiful. And he knows I see it.

"I hope she isn't scared off by his gargantuan ego," he says.

"I'm sorry I said that."

"Why be sorry when it's true?"

"It's not."

"Isn't it?"

"I don't think so. You asked if your appeal exceeds your fame because you want it to. You don't want people to like you just because you're famous."

He puts his hand, warm despite the cold, on the side of my neck. "Would you like me if I were just a clumsy guy who spilled a drink on you?"

I try to think of a clever answer, something a New York City woman would say. But I'm afraid anything I say will stop what's about to happen. The coyote quiets abruptly, as if she agrees silence is best.

He puts his lips on mine. The alcohol on his breath makes me giddy. His face is cold and smooth. His skin is still fragrant from a recent shave.

I'm glad I know a little about how to do it. Last spring Colton and I kissed when we were in the woods watching a pair of vireos build their nest. I let it go on for a little while, but only to satisfy my curiosity. Colton started acting like I was his girlfriend afterward. I had to tell him I didn't think of him that way and that the kiss was a mistake. He stopped talking to me for a whole week. It was torture, and I was so relieved when he finally forgave me for leading him on.

What's happening with Vaughn doesn't feel like a mistake. It doesn't feel anything like what I did with Colton. I hardly know where I'm standing. I'm on solid ground but I'm not. It reminds me of sailing on a moon sea.

When the kiss ends, Vaughn pulls me against his body. His warmth feels good. Everything about him does, same as when we slow danced.

"Are we really doing this in the middle of a road?" he says.

"We are."

"Don't try this where I live."

I laugh a little. Then I kiss him, the first I've ever initiated. I can tell he likes this. He holds me tighter and everything changes. The first kiss was only wading into shallow water. Now we're going deeper. And deeper. It's better than the moon seas. We're floating in a whole new world we created. It's much more satisfying than sailing on a moon sea, because I'm not alone.

After a while, we're too cold to stay outside. Neither of us is wearing gloves. We walk back to the car, and Vaughn turns up the heat when I start the motor. I almost wish I didn't have to drive. I wasn't drunk before, but now I am. Everything feels off kilter. I'm uncertain about what Vaughn and I have started.

"Are you okay?" He takes my hand in both of his and rubs warmth into it.

"Yes."

He leans over and kisses my cheek, his lips warmer than my face.

I put the car in gear and somehow get home; I hardly remember the process of getting here. We didn't speak, but I thought only of him. How does this strange new present connect to our future? I truly can't fathom it. I'm sure it's easier for him because he's been through this with many women.

I stop his rental car closer to the barn than to the house, where he usually parks it. I wonder what he expects. Does he think I'll go to the loft and sleep with him? I'm so dazed I don't even know if I want to.

I'm glad he comes straight toward me when we get out of the car. He wraps his arms around me and holds me. Maybe he senses I need security.

"Thank you for coming out with me tonight," he says.

"I had fun."

"Good."

We know these bland words don't come close to expressing what we want to say. I thought he'd be smoother with a woman, but I think he's as uncertain as I am.

"I should go." I pull out of his arms. "I won't be surprised if Alec and Sachi stayed up. They aren't used to me going out at night."

Why did I say that? I know why. I did it to warn him away. If I scare him off now, he'll never find out the truth about me.

"I'd think you got asked out quite often in high school," he says.

He's given me the perfect opportunity to sabotage what we started tonight. And being Nikki's daughter, I can't pass up a chance to wreck something that feels good.

"I didn't go to school after I came here. Sachi homeschooled me, and I did most of high school online." To make sure he realizes how peculiar I am, I add, "Other than this, Colton's the closest thing to a date I've ever had."

"You used to date him?"

"No, unless hiking counts."

"It does if you were more than friends."

"We weren't."

I assume Vaughn's silence means he's reflecting on the implications of all this. Namely, that I've never been with a man. I'd think that would be enough to scare off a famous author who can have any woman he wants.

But he caresses my cheek. "I understand," he says with unexpected emotion.

Maybe Colton was right, and Vaughn has been drawn to my naivete from the start. I've noticed he rarely asks anything about my past. It's been as surprising as it is a relief.

My suspicions about Vaughn don't bother me as they should. I'd honestly rather he be attracted to me for some reason other than myself. If it's only a virgin he wants, he can have that.

I like the idea of him being my first—especially if sleeping with him is even a little like what I experienced on the road. And after he got what he wanted, I imagine he'd go back to New York. He'd never really know me, and I wouldn't know him. It would all be clean, easy. We would both just move on.

"I'll walk you to the porch," he says.

I consider asking if I can go to the loft with him. But I'm not ready. I need to think about this a little longer.

"Do you want to do something tomorrow?" he asks, as we walk to the house.

"What?"

"You can choose since I chose tonight's destination."

Tomorrow Kiran will create my outfit, and he usually likes to dress me in vintage clothing. Doubtful it will be appropriate for a date. But why worry about that when I can't even think of a place I'd like to go with Vaughn?

He's waiting for an answer.

"Okay, but I'm not sure where yet."

"It can be anywhere. No big deal."

We kiss again on the front porch, and it feels as intense as on the road. I never knew I had this hunger for a man inside me—but only for him. Maybe I am ready.

But when I catch a whiff of the damp beer on my clothes, I decide I'd like to smell better when I sleep with him.

"Sleep well," he says.

"You too."

Inside, I find Sachi seated at the kitchen table, sketching. "You're home early," she says.

"The night didn't go as expected."

"What happened?"

"This, for one thing." I point at my partly dried jeans.

She wrinkles her nose. "Is that beer I smell?"

"Yes."

"How did that happen?"

"Vaughn knocked it over." I don't tell her the whole story. I like that only he and I know the truth about how the beer spilled, though a bar full of people saw it happen.

"Poor Vaughn," Sachi says. "Is he embarrassed?"

"Not especially."

She looks worried. "Was he drunk when that happened?"

"No, he's fine."

She gets up and kisses my forehead. "I'm glad you're home safe. I'm going to bed."

"You didn't have to wait up."

"I know. But a heart that loves can't be reasoned with."

We turn out the kitchen lights and head for the stairs.

"Will it bother you if I run a bath?" I ask.

"Of course not."

"I'm going to read while I soak. Do you know where Vaughn's last book is, the one called *A Box of Broken Stars*?"

A sly grin spreads over her face. "I think maybe this outing didn't go as badly as you implied."

"Do you have it?"

"I'll get it."

While I'm running water into the tub, she knocks on the door and hands me the book. The cover art looks like a child's drawing of two people holding hands, the lines connecting stars in a night sky. The constellation is Gemini, the twins.

I undress and slip into the hot water. I settle the book onto the bookrest Sachi and Alec gave me for my sixteenth birthday. I look at the cover image again. I open the book to the title page, my gaze lingering on "Vaughn Orr," the man who kissed me on a snowy road less than an hour ago.

I turn to the dedication page and stare at it for a long time. I almost think I'm imagining it.

14

VAUGHN

Why did I kiss her?

I've pondered that question too many times tonight. It's nearly three in the morning. I'm whacked out and I need sleep.

I kissed her because I'm attracted to her. It's that simple.

Except it's not simple. I've created a complicated mess. It had to be the beer. I wasn't thinking straight. But why did I kiss her again on the porch?

This attraction, or whatever it is, is making me too reckless. I don't want to corner myself into a situation where I have to hurt her. If I don't stop what's happening, my life will be over. I know I won't escape the punishment I deserve a second time. I need to get away from her. I'll make an excuse and go in the morning.

What's funny is, I've made this promise every night since I've been here, and every night it eventually mollified me into sleep. Then I stayed another day. And another.

But now the situation has escalated. I'll leave as soon as I get some sleep.

~

"Vaughn . . . Vaughn?" Riley says softly.

At first, I think this is part of my dream. I pick up my phone. It's 4:50. I've been asleep for only two hours, and the sun won't rise for several more. Why the hell am I awake?

But then I smell her. A sweet floral scent. She's standing next to the bed.

"Riley?"

"Yes."

I prop on my elbow to see her better. She's holding a small flashlight, its beam aimed at the floor. Her hair looks freshly washed, its glossy bronze sleekness tumbling down her shoulders. She's wearing an open flannel shirt over a snug pink tank top and gray leggings that leave very little to the imagination. She's staring at my bare chest. When she looks into my eyes, I easily see why she's here. "Can I be with you for a little while?" she asks.

I sit up, pulling the blanket to my belly. "Are you all right?"

"I couldn't stop thinking about you. I had to come over." She removes the flannel shirt, turns off the flashlight, and lays both on the floor. She stands before me in her tight clothing, shoulders bare. "Can I come in?"

Riley, Riley, Riley. What am I going to do now? Her tawny wildcat eyes question. Her lithe body invites. I can't remember ever wanting a woman as much as I want her. And she has me too stirred up to care about the complications.

"I sleep naked," I say, to make certain we're on the same page.

She smiles. "Is that supposed to make me run away?"

I move back to give her room. She gets in and curls her body onto the bed, facing me. Before my phone darkens, I look into her eyes once more. There's no trepidation, though this must be the first time she's been in bed with a naked man.

We're wrapped in darkness. I take her loosely into my arms. Her hand brushes my cheek. She presses it there to help find my mouth before she kisses me. She's much bolder than she was a few hours ago. I can't keep my hands off her body. When she does the same, I have to decide whether to slow her down or go full on. Assuming she's never done this before, I can choose only one of those options.

I take her hands off me and hold them. "What were you thinking when you couldn't stop thinking about me?"

She gently bites my lower lip. "You, obviously."

"What about me?"

"I've been reading *A Box of Broken Stars*. I haven't slept."

I lie back on the bed. As bled of desire as a grasshopper drained by a spider.

"I'm more than halfway through it," she says.

"You read a lot."

"I couldn't stop reading. It's so beautiful. I love Joey."

"Everyone loves Joey."

"But it was mean of you to kill off her twin." When I don't respond, she says, "But I guess there's not much story unless that happens. When I was little, I had one of those old cigar boxes like Joey has. I kept all my treasures in it."

How could I not have known this would happen?

She climbs on top of me. "I looked you up on the internet. They say you refuse to give interviews. All the articles used words like *mysterious* and *enigmatic* and *reclusive*."

She waits for me to say something. I'm glad the moon isn't still shining in the window. She can't see how wrecked I am.

"I don't care if you don't tell anybody else," she says, "but you're going to tell me. Who is 'Riley'?"

I can't speak. The weight of her body suddenly feels like a mound of stones. One stone for every lie I've told. Just the burden of the ones I've told in the last week is enough to crush the life out of me.

She puts her hands on my cheeks. "Tell me! Who is she?"

"How do you know it's a she?"

"Isn't it?"

"The name goes both ways."

"I think it's a she."

"Even if it's a she, what species is she? Maybe I dedicated my books to my favorite dog. Or the pet hamster I had when I was six."

I can't even lie inventively. These are the same diversions I used in Mel's office a week and a half ago, the day I decided to come to Wisconsin. I've been here one week. Seven days. I don't understand how it's possible that Riley Mays is stretched over my naked body.

I must be imagining this. All of it. The perfect little farm with its pond, orchard, and woods. Riley and her realm of lunar oceans. Sachi and her dream paintings. Kiran and his altars of time. Moons that shine much too brightly to be real.

Yes, maybe I'm more inventive than I realize. Riley's appearance in my bedroom makes more sense if it's happening in my mind. Only I could be this cruel to myself. To bring a siren version of Riley to my bed, then have her kick me in the balls with her adoration of my book. If Vaughn Orr is finally going off the deep end, this is exactly how he would lose his mind.

"Are you really not going to tell me?"

"I'm not." I maneuver her off me and get out of bed. I feel around in the darkness for my sweatpants and pull them on. After more fumbling, I turn on the bedside lamp.

She's propped up on the bed by her arms, her body curled in an S. She looks like a snake in her slithery clothes. I shudder, envisioning the serpent in her murky Mare Anguis. She's worse than a sea siren or serpent; she's me, this monster I've created that won't rest until it pulls me under.

"Vaughn . . . what's wrong?"

I feel too exposed. I grab a T-shirt and yank it over my bare chest and belly.

"Why are you so upset?"

"You shouldn't be here."

"You were fine with me being here before I mentioned the book."
She climbs out of the bed. "It's not what you're thinking."

"What am I thinking?"

"That all I care about is you being famous."

"That's not what I'm thinking."

She lifts her shirt off the floor, and I'm relieved when she covers her body. She slips on her slipper boots and picks up her flashlight.

"You're right," she says. "I shouldn't have come here. I got caught up in the book, and I haven't slept. And I was thrown off by everything that happened before that. I wasn't being rational."

She looks so hurt, so ashamed. But all the shame is mine. Only mine. I feel almost too sick to remain standing.

"Vaughn . . . are you okay?"

She has to leave before I give in to this reckless urge to tell her the truth about the book dedication. I've never been so scared in my life. Not even that night when all this started.

She walks toward me as if trying not to scare a wild animal. "Maybe you'd better sit down. You don't look good. Let's talk about what's going on."

I really feel like a trapped animal. I need her to get away from me. "I don't look good because I've only slept two hours and you woke me up!"

My god . . . my voice, that snarl. It's as if my father is standing here in my place.

My harsh tone nearly makes her cry, but she blinks back the tears. "You didn't mind when I first came in. It's something else. Something to do with me talking about the book." Her eyes light with sudden insight. "Is it Riley? Did something happen to her?"

"Yes."

My reply stuns me. I've been asked that question several times, and I never answer truthfully.

"I'm so sorry," she says. "What happened to her?"

I start grabbing clothes and shoving them into my bag.

"Please don't leave."

"I have to." I throw my toiletries into their zipper bag.

"Vaughn . . ."

I turn around. She's standing in the bathroom doorway. "I don't think you should leave right now. Not like this. Maybe you could talk to Sachi if you don't want to talk to me."

"Why would I talk to her?"

"She's good at helping people see things."

"What will Sachi help me see? An aura? A goddess emerging from a cloud? Will she wave a crystal over my head and fix my life?"

Her eyes contract into fiery sparks. "Is this the real you? This is what you've been thinking about her all along, that she's a ridiculous person you laugh at behind her back? How could you when she's been so kind to you!"

Is this the real me? Have I become my abuser? I wonder if this is how it started with my father, self-hatred filling him to such a volume that his body couldn't contain it. And once he released it onto other people, the relief felt too good to stop.

I need to get out of here. I push past her and toss the toiletries into my duffel bag.

"Answer me!" she demands.

I face her. "You should have trusted your first opinion of me."

I can tell this jolts her, which means it's on the mark.

"I saw that you didn't like me. You didn't want me to stay. You knew there was something wrong, didn't you?"

She looks alarmed. "Why did you stay? What's the truth?"

I turn my back to her as I stuff the rest of my clothes into the bag. "I'm a bad person. That's the only truth you need to know."

She grabs my arm and makes me face her. "I don't believe that."

"You did."

"I changed my mind about you."

"Only because I worked on you. And on Sachi and Alec. The gifts of wine and flowers. Bringing the clock to Kiran so I could talk with you . . ."

She's shaking her head, but in her eyes I see she knows it's true. To discover you shouldn't have trusted a person you've let into your life is one of the bitterest medicines to swallow.

"I don't know why you're lying about being a bad person," she says, "but I know it's a lie. I've seen you when you're being real. And Sachi has. She sees things other people don't—"

"My aura?"

"Yes. And other things. She wouldn't have let you stay here if you were bad."

"Jesus, Riley, when will you grow up and figure out there is no magic?"

Tears brighten her eyes. "Why are you being like this?"

"I shouldn't, right? If I were the person you hope I am, I wouldn't be like this."

My mocking tone makes her clench her jaw. "You're only doing these things to make me think badly of you."

I sit on a chair to put on my shoes. She'll never be convinced. Maybe that's proof that she's nothing but a hallucination. Deep down no one wants to believe they're bad. She's the part of me that still fights my conviction that I'm broken beyond repair.

When I stand, she says, "Do you know what's interesting?"

"What?"

"You never did tell me why you decided to stay here. You started all that talk about being a bad person to avoid answering."

Perceptive of her to see that. But she'll never be shrewd enough for this world if she thinks bad people can be easily sorted from the good.

"I think you stayed here because you found a refuge that helps with your troubles—like you said that first night at dinner."

I throw on my jacket and hoist my bags over my arms. "Why are you so determined to think well of me?"

She stares at me, almost daring me to walk out of the room. When I start to move, she says, "Because I've never felt the way you made me feel."

"I see. Did you think you were in love with me?"

"I don't know. And if you leave, I'll always wonder."

That won't do. I will not have Riley Mays martyred by Vaughn Orr's unrequited love for the rest of her days.

I set my bags on the floor. "You won't wonder. You'll never want to think of me again. And I guarantee you won't read the rest of that book."

"Why?"

"Because I'm going to tell you why I stayed here."

She sees something in my eyes that unsettles her. As it should.

"Like I said, something bad happened to Riley. And I did it to her. I can't tell you what because I'd be arrested if I did."

Her eyes widen, and I find her dismay perversely satisfying.

"So . . . I stopped here to get gas, and here is this beautiful woman named Riley. I know you saw how I stared at you. You brought it all back to me—what I'd done years ago."

She looks alarmed—but that isn't enough. I want her to hate me as much as I detest myself.

"I thought I'd stay one night, but I couldn't leave. I don't know why. Maybe I thought I could save Riley from myself this time. Maybe I only wanted to hurt her again. I knew how wrong it was to be attracted to you—to this new version of Riley—but I couldn't stop myself. That's why I kept pushing about the journal—I wanted to read it to feel closer to you."

Her look of outrage fills me with a shameful kind of joy.

I gesture at the tangled covers on the bed that nearly trapped me in the second biggest mistake of my life. "If you hadn't mentioned Riley, we'd still be in that bed. And what we'd be doing *would* be wrong, but you wouldn't have known it."

She turns around and walks away. I hear her feet thud down the wooden stairs. The outer barn door opens and closes.

Her departure feels like if I'd kept a desperate bird trapped, and I've finally done what's right and let it go. But its escape feels more like my heart leaving my body. I can't move.

As I recover, I lift my bags and walk to the door. I can't look back at the loft. She was right. This place has been a refuge. But it didn't help with my troubles. Staying here has made them much worse.

Leaned against the wall at the bottom of the stairs is the painting I bought from Sachi. *Man, Asleep.* We decided it was too large and fragile to take on the airplane, so Sachi is going to ship it to me. I don't want the painting now, but I've already paid for it and its shipping.

But I haven't yet paid for renting the loft. I sit on a lower stair to find the stash of cash in my bag. We never discussed payment for renting the loft, and without much thought, I pull out $2,500.

I write my address on a scrap of art paper and beneath it scrawl, *Please send the painting to this address. Thank you for your hospitality.*

I can't write more. Anything I think of sounds insincere at best.

I'm looking for a prominent place to leave the money and note when Sachi comes in. She's often up at this hour. She stares at me anxiously, not her usual radiant self. I wonder what my aura looks like, if she can see the darkness pouring out of me.

"Vaughn . . . what's going on?"

"Did you talk to Riley?"

"She's upset and went to her room. She wouldn't say anything."

"I have to leave." I give her the money and note. "This is for renting the room. Thank you for everything, Sachi."

I sling on my bags. As I'm going out, she says, "This is way too much money!"

It could never be enough to pay for what I've done. I step into the cold darkness and close the door.

15

RILEY

Colton moved into the loft yesterday. He's done with classes like I am, but he can stay with us for only a week. He'll spend the rest of the summer in Madison teaching.

I'm trying to feel as happy as I should about Colton being back. And about him having a girlfriend. We met Leigh for the first time yesterday, and she'll stay here with Colton all week. She's a good match for him, an easygoing Earth lover who wears old work boots, T-shirts, and jeans. Like Colton, she just finished her first year of graduate school. Her thesis project will have to do with declining pollinators.

Last night Sachi made a big dinner of Indian food to welcome Leigh and Colton, and all I could think about was Vaughn and the same dinner we had with him. Then everyone sat out on the porch with beers, and Colton, Alec, and Leigh got into a deep scientific discussion about how climate change is affecting insect populations. I tried to get into it with them, but I ended up brooding again.

And all the while Colton and Leigh were wrapped around each other and exchanging little secret smiles. I hate to admit I was jealous, but I was. And I am. Colton has stopped paying attention to everything I do. I should be glad he isn't in love with me anymore, but it hurts more than I'd have expected to watch Leigh pet his copper hair while he stares into her big hazel eyes. I think it's mostly that I need his attention right now. I need something to fill the big trench Vaughn dug in me.

Last week Sachi told me it's about time I was done with Vaughn. She said three months is long enough. The problem is, she thinks I was only in love with him and he ran out on me. She doesn't know what he said. What he did. Or what I almost did.

What Vaughn did isn't something you get over easily. That's why I'm wishing I were Leigh, cuddled up on the living room couch with Colton, the sweetest, most trustworthy man in all the world. Why couldn't I love Colton back? If I had, Vaughn could never have burrowed into me like he did. And maybe I'd be a happy, stable person if I loved a happy, stable man like Colton.

But I never will. Because now I know without doubt that I have a lot of Nikki in me. I'll always go for guys like Vaughn. It's genetic. I could be blindfolded with ten men, and I'd sniff out the one who's abusive or a sociopath. Or a murderer.

Sometimes I wonder if Vaughn was hinting that he'd killed Riley. I understand why he would nearly admit it. When you have a terrible secret poisoning you for years, you want to leak some of it out. Just a little, without all the gory details, to lessen how much it hurts.

Maybe I'm confusing Nikki with Vaughn. And I'm mixing up my secret with Vaughn's secret. It's all tangled inside me.

And Sachi doesn't know. And Alec and Colton don't. That's why they look at me the way they're looking at me right now. As if to say, "Get over it, Riley. Everyone gets jilted at some point in their lives." Like I jilted Colton. He must be at least a little satisfied to think I'm pining for Vaughn like he did for me.

But I'm not pining. They don't know the half of what Vaughn did to me. And they don't know what happened with Julia, Nikki, and me. I haven't leaked one tiny drop of all that poison for ten years.

Colton leaves Leigh talking to Alec and Sachi about the research she's doing this summer. He sits next to me on the floor and rests his back against the big chair. "Are you okay?" he asks quietly.

"Yes."

"If you are, how come you didn't say anything when I said I might be doing research in Alaska next summer?"

"I didn't hear that."

"You've always wanted to go to Alaska. Maybe you could come visit."

"That would be great."

"I'm not feeling the excitement," he says.

"I'm tired."

"Yeah? You look as wound up as a chipmunk trapped in a mason jar."

I am a chipmunk trapped in a mason jar. I've been in there since Julia died. Looking through thick glass at the rest of the world. Tormented by what I see outside, those many incomprehensible beings who live free and contented lives.

Colton glances at everyone else to make sure they aren't listening. He quietly says, "I wish that guy never came here. I hate to see you like this. He was a lone wolf looking for prey, and you aren't prey, Riley. You're the wolf."

I remember the song about the woman and wolf who fell in love. It was one of the most beautiful songs I'd ever heard, and Vaughn wasn't even listening. I should have known there was something strange about that. I did know, and it bothered me. But I ignored all those clues. Because I'd sniffed out that he was as damaged as I am, and I hungered for that.

"I've always seen you like that," Colton says.

"As a wolf?"

"Not a wolf. More of a mountain lion. Because of your eyes."

"A mountain lion? I wish."

He clasps my hand. "You are," he says. "You're stronger than him."

"A mountain lion beats a wolf?"

He lifts one gold-red eyebrow. "Well . . . maybe it was a bad comparison."

"The wolf wins?"

"It would if it had any of its pack to help. But a lone wolf and a puma would be in a close battle."

Vaughn is definitely a lone wolf. Everything I read about him on the internet verifies that. I like this image of us engaged in a raw battle of teeth and claws. No games, just a clean evolutionary fight.

But I didn't fight. The night he left, I turned tail and ran. I guess he won, but I'm not sure what he got out of our encounter. He easily could have had his way with me. I was ready to lose my virginity to him, an impulsive decision I made while reading one of his love scenes. But he stopped it from happening. I was ready, starting to take off my clothes, when he grabbed my hands and began talking to me. I remember I was surprised—and a little irritated—that he stopped me. Then I mentioned the book and dedication to Riley and he sprang out of the bed as if it were on fire.

These scenes play in my mind again and again. If he'd really stayed at our house to be close to me, why did he quit when he easily had me? The lone wolf had the puma by the throat, and he let her go. It just doesn't add up.

Colton squeezes my hand. "Forget him. He's not good enough to be a wolf. He's a tick on a hairy boar's butt."

I smile, and he smiles back. I look into his cerulean eyes. I want to touch his hair. I want to be healed by his goodness.

He says with sudden seriousness, "I want you to be happy, Riley."

I can't be, Colton. I'm no puma. I'm a chipmunk in a jar.

He can't understand, of course. He knows nothing about Nikki. He can't see the venomous helix of her DNA wrapped around me like a strangling snake.

But it's more like being locked up with a snake. I've always thought the barred structure of DNA looks like a cage. Because that's exactly what it is. All of us are trapped inside the good or bad DNA we got from our parents, and I'm sure the helical prison I inherited from Nikki and my neglectful father must be especially bad and inescapable.

I'm so tired of Nikki. It's been ten years, and I still think of her every day. Of course, Julia is right there with her. The two of them in my brain are like the puma and wolf engaged in a long, gritty battle. But neither will ever win the territory of my memory banks. Julia versus Nikki is the age-old battle of good versus evil, and that's a fight that will continue to the end of time.

I want to see Kiran. He's the only one in the house who doesn't look at me anxiously. Even Leigh does. I'm sure Colton told her I fell for the famous author Vaughn Orr and he kicked me in the teeth. Maybe he told her I need special attention because I'm heartsick. I suppose that's why Leigh is smiling at me this very moment, though Colton is holding my hand.

I pull my hand away. "I'm going to see what Kiran is up to."

Colton accepts my departure without comment. Upstairs I find Kiran seated on his bed, reading a book.

"How's it going, Kee?"

He's so engrossed in the story he can't take his eyes off the page. "They found a dragon egg."

"Cool." I shouldn't bother him when he's at a good part in the story. I know how that feels.

I look at his little worktable, the one surface that's free of objects unless he's dismantling a clock or wristwatch. But the table's surface isn't clear. The two half-orb bells from the alarm clock Vaughn gave him are still there. They rest close but not touching, cup side down, like two humped creatures protecting their underbellies.

I'm too obsessed with these bells. I check Kiran's room every day, usually more than once, to see if he's integrated them into his galaxy of fossils and clockworks. He's never left clock parts on his worktable. It's been three months.

I normally don't interfere in Kiran's realm, but today, for whatever reason, I have to ask. "Hey, Kiran . . . ?"

He looks up from the book.

"Why are these two bells still on your worktable?"

He studies the bells for a moment. I think he's troubled by them, or maybe I'm reading that into his expression. "I don't know where they fit."

That makes sense. He's never taken apart a clock with bells before.

But maybe he doesn't know where they fit because they don't fit the beauty of his cosmos. I want to grab them off the table and throw them far from here. But I dare not touch his magic. I know I can't be trusted after what I did to Julia's magic.

I cringe when Kiran looks at me with that same concerned expression as everyone else in the family. I hate that I'm leaking my poison into everyone in this house.

"I'm sorry," he says.

"Sorry about what?"

"I'm sorry the magic got messed up and you're sad. I'm going to fix it."

My god, the poor kid. He thinks he's responsible for my crappy mood these last months. I look at the bells on his worktable and burn with rage. At Nikki, and Vaughn. And myself.

"You should throw out those stupid bells."

His eyes widen. "But, Riley, you always say the magic—"

"I was wrong! There is no magic. Just throw them away."

I didn't mean to say it so bluntly. But Vaughn was right. He has to get with reality, and better now than when he's twenty-one.

Tears fill Kiran's eyes.

I want to tell him it isn't true. Except it is. I won't lie to him anymore.

He just stares at me. He wipes his sleeve under his eye.

I want to cuddle him. But if I do, I'll take back what I said, and I can't do that. I've been hurting him with all the ridiculous talk of magic. It's selfish of me. I have to let him grow up. Isn't he the age when parents finally tell kids there is no Santa Claus?

Kiran looks so small and lonely without his magic. I can't bear it.

I have to get my poison away from him. I dash into my room and head for the box of Julia's ashes on my bookshelf. I need to touch her, remember her goodness.

But before I reach the ashes, my gaze is drawn to the serpent in her tumultuous sea. I always see Nikki's face on the serpent in Mare Anguis. I rarely looked at it in recent years, but now Nikki haunts my thoughts almost as much as when I first came to live here. Because of Vaughn.

The night he left, he said, "You brought it all back to me—what I'd done years ago." I have no idea what he's done, but he's made the same thing happen to me. He's brought back what I did years ago. All those lies I told. Julia's death. Nikki's death. Why is it all rushing around me like a big black ocean again? I don't understand this terrible connection between Vaughn, Nikki, Julia, and me.

Obsessing over negative events is a tendency that surely came from Nikki. She used to harp on incidents with loathsome repetition. I broke Aunt Julia's favorite vase at age eight, and Nikki would remind me every time I touched another vase. "Don't break that one, too," she would say. Or, "Don't be a klutz with that, Riley." Or, "Maybe you'd better let Julia do that before you drop it."

And I did let Julia do it. I stopped putting flowers in water, almost hated flowers, though Julia brought them in from her garden often and insisted she trusted me with her vases.

I hated mirrors because of Nikki, too. When I was in fourth grade, she caught me with my face close to the bathroom mirror. I was looking at my eyes, trying to decide what color they were. A boy at school said they were orange, and other people usually said they were light brown.

Nikki laughed and told me I was a narcissist like my father. She'd never told me anything about my father, other than that he was an asshole who ditched her when she got pregnant. That day I learned my father was a narcissist in addition to being an asshole.

After she said I was a narcissist, she added, "Don't fall too in love with that face. It'll be a wreck all too soon." And from that day on, anytime she saw me look in a mirror, she would criticize me with similar comments. I stopped looking in mirrors in her presence, even felt uncomfortable using mirrors when I was alone. And as I got older, the comments turned more and more to how I looked.

"I suppose you spent hours in front of a mirror to look like that," she would say when I came downstairs in a nice outfit. Or, "How long did that weird look take to put together?" Or, "How can you live with being so adorable?"

Julia always stood up for me. She would tell her not to talk to me like that. And Nikki would retort that she was my mother and she could talk to me any way she wanted. Then the usual argument would ensue as I hurried out the door.

I look at Mare Nubium. The sweet, soft Sea of Clouds. Julia's place.

I'm sorry, Julia. I'm sorry I made your life living hell for six and a half years. I'm sorry for what I let her do to you.

I remember Vaughn standing in my room the night he was looking at the serpent. "You did a really good job with that thing," he said. "It's so realistic it grabbed me and almost dragged me under the water."

Why did he say that? How did he know?

My brain goes numb, like it's frozen in outer space. I can't take a normal breath.

It's all happening again.

I won't let it.

I feel like someone else's hand is dragging my desk chair to the corner. I stand on the seat and start ripping at Mare Anguis. Big pieces of the dark sea tear off beneath my clawing nails. But I can't reach the serpent. I painted her too high. Why have I given her this refuge? For ten years. She's been in my life for too long.

I stack books on the seat. Holding the back of the chair, I carefully step up onto the books. I can reach her. "Goodbye, Nikki! You're gone! You're gone forever!"

I tear her body in half. I grab her tail and rip it out of her murky ocean. I reach for her head. "You're gone! I hate you!" I yell at her. Her head peels off the wall with a satisfying ripping sound. I dig my nails at the rest of the Serpent Sea, shredding it into brittle paper scraps.

The whole mural is garbage. It's got to go. All of it. Why didn't I see that long ago?

"Stop!" Kiran shouts from my doorway. "Riley, no! Stop! Stop . . . !"

I twist around to look at him and lose my balance, falling into a maelstrom of moon seas and Kiran's screams. I've never heard him scream like that. I think I've broken his universe. Maybe my moon was connected to his galaxies. Maybe there really was magic and I've wrecked it.

My head cracks on the side of the desk. A black shadow falls over the moon.

16

VAUGHN

I wedge my fingers under the tractor tire and flip it over. I lift the tire and push it over again. I can barely lift it on the eighth attempt. Or is this the ninth? My muscles are running out of glycogen. I stumble backward as I flip the tire again.

"That's enough," my trainer says.

Two hours of physical agony is not enough. I have to be near total collapse so I can sleep tonight. I put all my remaining power into trying to flip the tire again.

Cedric pats my back. "You're done, Vaughn."

I lean over with my hands on my thighs, watching drops of sweat plop onto the black rubber mat. "I can go longer."

"Nope, time's up. If you want to torture yourself more, you'll have to do it somewhere else."

I certainly will.

As I recover enough to stand, Cedric says, "Man, this has gotta be a girl." It's at least the third time he's said that in recent weeks. "She must be really hot to get you into this state. I've never seen you like this."

"You are aware that people work out for other reasons than to attract partners?"

He grins. "Whatever you say. See you tomorrow?"

"Yeah."

Difficult to imagine my body will be recovered enough by then, but it always is. Cedric is a good trainer who mixes up the workouts to make sure I don't overwork any muscle group.

At first, even his easy, one-hour workouts were brutal. When I returned from Wisconsin, I spent nearly every day wasted, either on my couch or in a club. After more than five weeks, I was as physically ill as depressed, and that prevented me from sleeping. I was desperate for at least a short-term way of achieving oblivion.

I don't know how I pulled myself out of that dismal cycle. I guess it had to do with Riley. The day before I went back to my gym, I thought about contacting her to try to fix what I did. But I still can't figure out how to do that.

As I leave the club, the new woman who works behind the desk is waiting for me. She has my latest book clutched against her chest. "Mr. Orr . . . ?" she says quietly.

"Sign it?"

"If you would. I'm sorry to bother you, but my mom is—"

"It's fine. What's her name?"

She replies, "Kathy." I ask if it's spelled with a *K* or *C*. I sign the book on the title page the way I always do: *For Kathy* and beneath my name, *Best wishes, Vaughn Orr*. Boring, but I'm too tired to get creative.

"I heard it's going to be made into a movie," the woman says.

"Yes."

"We're looking forward to it."

"Me too," I lie. Because short answers that don't lead to more questions are best.

"When is your next novel coming out?"

"I'm not sure." I return the book to her.

"Well, keep up the good work." She smiles. "I can't believe you find time to get in here every day. I don't exercise every day, and I work here."

She's flirting with me. She's attractive, but not my type. Vaughn Orr fans never are.

"I'd better go. I have an appointment," I say, though this is unlikely at four thirty on a Friday.

"Oh. Sorry. Thank you for signing it."

"No problem."

Signing the woman's book makes me think about the Blind Wolf and all those napkins I autographed. And of Riley.

Too much makes me think of her. Every time I see the moon, or even a picture of it. The word *magic*. Clocks. Rabbits. Snow. Stars. The phrase *climate change*. And you can't go anywhere these days without hearing about climate change. The bartender was talking about it the last time I went out.

Not that I didn't think of Riley a whole hell of a lot before I went to Wisconsin. But that Riley, the first Riley, wasn't real. She was an amalgamation of thoughts and ideas I had in my mind. She was a fantasy. A fairy. A unicorn.

But the more I think of it, the living, breathing Riley—the "new" Riley, as I think of her—has become a fantasy, too. All of it has. Riley mapped the seas of the moon, actual oceans with vivid waters. Sachi saw me in a vision called *Man, Asleep* just weeks before I arrived. Alec attracted her with his aura when he appreciated the beauty of a moth. Colton is like a woodland pixie who can make snowshoe rabbits do as he bids, and Kiran uses clock parts and fossils in his mysterious sorcery.

I miss the magic. And this is odd because I don't believe in magic. But I believe it exists in Riley's realm.

I plod with weak legs up the stairway to my house, the kind of Brooklyn brownstone you see in movies. I bought it four years ago, after my second book hit big and was made into a movie. I never dreamed I would live in a place like this. But since the magic of the farm on Summerfield Lane, looking at it doesn't fill me with the same pride and wonder.

I unlock my front door and enter a scent cloud of bleach and furniture polish. The cleaning crew was here today. I have them come on Friday so the house is neat for any women I might entertain over the weekend.

There haven't been any since Riley. I tried a while back with a woman I met in a bar, but I called her a taxi before anything happened. I told her I thought I was getting sick.

Propped against the foyer wall is a package the maids must have taken in for me. The box is big and flat. My heart beats wildly. The parcel is a size and shape I think I recognize. It reminds me of the brown paper package I last saw as I departed the barn loft.

Months ago, Sachi returned the money I'd paid for the painting on PayPal. At the time, I assumed she was too angry about what I did to Riley to sell me the painting, and I had a feeling she was offended by the $2,500 I gave her for renting the loft. I never thought I'd see *Man, Asleep* again. If this is it, why did she wait three months?

My phone pings. An email from my agent. Mel wants to know what's going on in Wisconsin, if I bought a place. She asks if I'm still up for the Chicago book event with her friend. She sent a similar email two months ago, but I didn't answer it. I can't bring myself to tell her Wisconsin is forever dead to me.

Yet here is this box, the word *Fragile* written all over it.

I lift the parcel to look at the return address. Summerfield Lane, Wisconsin. No name. I assume the printing is Sachi's, but I wonder if it could be Riley's.

I take the package to the kitchen to get a glass of wine. I normally want nothing to do with alcohol after a long workout, but I can't open this box without taking some of the edge off. And after a workout like I had today, a glass of wine will hit me like a shot of whiskey.

I pop the cork on a good chardonnay I have in the refrigerator. I pour a glass of the cold wine and hold it out to the box. "To you, Riley, if you're in there." I tap my glass on the box. "Welcome to New York City."

After I've downed half the glass of wine, I slice open the box. The painting is wrapped in cardboard and Bubble Wrap to protect the glass frame. Beneath all the layers, a large manila envelope is taped to the glass. There's a sheet of white paper folded in half and paper-clipped to the top of it.

Why couldn't Sachi send the painting and nothing more? I don't want to read a letter from her or Riley. I crumple the envelope and letter, open the trash, and toss it in.

I sit on a stool at the kitchen island and sip the wine, looking down at Sachi's painting. I watch the fetal man float above his luminous night city. I know how it feels to live in his cold blue skin, to be trapped in an endless hover, unable to join the ordinary lives of all those people I see down there on Earth.

I look below the man, scanning high-rise windows for objects I associate with the Summerfield Lane farm. A trumpet. A snail fossil. A clock gear. A ghostly, greenish luna moth tries to escape one of the windows. Since I first saw the painting, I've learned luna moths are one of the species Alec studies.

My gaze drifts to the murky shape of a wolf in a lower window, a reminder of my date with Riley at the Blind Wolf. Near the wolf is a window with a gun. Now that I know Sachi, I'm surprised she would put a gun in one of her paintings.

I guess there's good reason. But Sachi couldn't have known that.

My gaze drifts from the gun to a shape I didn't notice before. I pull the painting closer and stare into the first-floor window. Hairs raise on the back of my neck. What an odd coincidence.

I jog upstairs, open a drawer, and remove the small silver box. I take out the antique key on a thin silver chain I found in my drawer when I was very young, just tall enough to open the drawer by myself. The silver box was hidden inside a pair of toddler socks and pushed to the back of the drawer. When I was a boy, I liked to take the key out of the box and look at it, but I had no idea whose or what it was until I was seven.

"Dad . . . ?"

"What?" he asked irritably.

"What is this?"

He stared at the necklace. He looked stunned.

"Where did you get that?" he asked.

"It was in my drawer."

His expression turned to anger. It scared me, but I hoped he wasn't drunk enough to hit me.

"What is it?" I asked.

"It's an old key."

I looked at the strange thing, trying to equate it with the keys I'd seen.

"It's a piece of junk that belonged to your mother. Just throw it away."

My mother! There weren't even photographs of her in the house. My father had purged everything that reminded him of her. I couldn't even picture her face.

"I said throw it away!" he said.

"But if it's a key . . . does it open anything?"

He made a scornful sound. "The only thing I ever saw it open was your mouth. When you were a baby, you sucked on that thing whenever she held you. Always sucking on it. You weren't a smart one, didn't even know how to suck a tit the right way. She gave up and put you on bottled milk. But you always liked that damn key in your mouth . . . better than a tit." He grunted a laugh. "No, not so smart."

I imagined the sound of a mother shushing me, could almost feel a metallic tang on my tongue. I'd been looking at the thing for years, and now I had an image, almost like a memory, attached to it.

I think my father didn't like the reverent way I looked at it. "It was because you couldn't suck right she started to go crazy, you know."

I looked at him.

"You couldn't suck right, and you were always crying. She couldn't take it. Doctors said she got something called 'postpartum depression.'"

He saw I didn't understand.

"Postpartum means after a woman has a baby and depression *is sickness in the mind. You were the one who made her sick. She was always crying and putting that damn key in your mouth to quiet you. That's when all her crazy stuff started. You were too much for her—that's why she took all those pills and killed herself."*

I can still feel those words. Coldness. A penetrating chill, as if my mother's ghost had passed through my body. That day her sadness became a permanent part of me.

As I got older, I realized what I felt was more guilt than sadness. And that made me angry. Angrier and angrier. I hated my father for blaming her death on me. And sometimes I hated my mother for leaving me alone with the monster she'd married. Early on, I figured out it was him, not me, she'd needed to escape.

My father rose from his chair. "Did you hear me? I said throw it away!"

I had learned I was in danger if he got out of his chair to reprimand me. But I felt attachment to the key and didn't want to throw it away— especially now that I knew it was all I had of my mother.

He stepped toward me.

"I will! I'll throw it away!" Even back then, I hated that supplicating sound in my voice.

The kitchen garbage was near to overflowing, and I was afraid to put the necklace on top, where he'd see it as he continued to drink into the evening. He followed me to the back door, watching as I tossed the necklace into the outside trash can. I doubted he'd suffer maggots and putrid garbage to dig it out of there.

He cuffed my head as I returned to the house. "I shouldn't have to tell you to do something three times!"

"I'm sorry."

I wasn't sorry. I already knew I'd rescue the necklace when he drank himself into oblivion. Planning the rebellion filled me with a giddiness I came to know well during the years I lived with him.

I bring the necklace downstairs and lay my mother's key next to the antique key in the painting. My mother's has a slightly different top, and the knobs on the shaft are different, but the similarity still feels uncanny.

For years, I worked hard to keep the key hidden from my father, frequently moving it to new hiding places in my room. I've always hoped it was a parting gift from my mother. My father hadn't known I had it the day I showed it to him, and that had to mean she hid it in my drawer before she took the pills.

I've often wondered what it opened, imagining ornate boxes and mysterious attic doors. But what would I see when I unlocked the box or door? If my mother wore the key around her neck, it must have opened something important.

My mother was rarely in my thoughts before the day my father told me about the key, but after that, I felt her presence with it. And when I really needed her, when my father had hurt me bad, I'd take her out of the box and sometimes speak quietly to her. "Mom, should I run away like you did?" I often asked. I knew she couldn't answer, but talking to her made me feel less alone. The key inspired and comforted me with its steely coldness, silence, and unbreakability. From my metal mother, I learned those were the essentials of enduring my father's brutality.

The key warms as I take it into my hand. I haven't looked at it, or thought much about my mother, since I moved here four years ago and put it in the drawer. I can't shake the feeling there's a reason the painting made me look at the key—something right in front of me I'm not seeing.

My gaze is drawn to Riley's dusky seas on the moon in the painting.

The letter I threw in the garbage. That's it. That's what's bothering me.

I down the last wine in my glass and retrieve the crumpled papers from the trash. I hesitate with my hand hovered over the can. I should throw them back in. I don't need more guilt.

The metal knobs on the key's shaft press into my skin. I open my fist and look at it. I've been wanting it to open something for twenty-two years. Maybe it's meant to make me open this letter. Face what I've done. All of it. Maybe it's time for Man Asleep to wake up.

I sit on the stool, open the crumpled sheet of paper, and smooth it out on top of the manila envelope. I pour another glass of wine, take a big drink, and start reading.

17

THE LETTER

Hi Vaughn.

    Here is your painting finally.

    I doubt you expected a letter from me. I didn't expect to write to you either. But Sachi thought it would be a good idea for me to have closure with what happened between us.

    The problem is, I'm not sure what happened. Are you?

    Don't worry, I never told Sachi or anyone else about it. But bottling it up wasn't good. I did something stupid and ended up in the hospital. I got a concussion and a small fracture in my skull. Then the doctors said I was depressed because I didn't want to eat and refused to talk to the psychologist they sent to my room. They tried to put me on antidepressants, but Sachi wouldn't let them. She said my depression was situational, not clinical, and she wanted to try other therapies before I was given drugs. It was a bit *of a fight with the doctors, but you might imagine Sachi never gives in when she's certain she's right.*

So here I am, back home, and Sachi is making me write this letter. I also have to take a walk every day, and work in the garden for at least an hour. And paint my room.

I tore down the drawings. Kiran is upset about that. But I think it was good for me to move past the moon seas.

You'll understand what that means when you read what's in this envelope. Except you won't really understand because the journal isn't the whole truth. Remember I told you that the day we went to Sally Run Creek?

I don't know why I decided to send the journal. And sometimes I think you didn't tell the truth about why you wanted to read it.

I've figured out that you lied about some things. You said you got interested in me when you found out my name was Riley. But I remembered you looked at me in a strange way even before I'd introduced myself. And if you stayed on the farm because you were attracted to the new version of Riley, why would you leave when you had me in your bed?

I don't know what to believe. Was there really another Riley you hurt? If not, who is the Riley in your book dedications? None of it makes any sense to me.

I hope Sachi is right and writing some of this down helps me let it go. But I sent the journal more for your closure than for mine.

Sachi and Alec don't know I sent it. They don't even know it exists. I'd appreciate it if you would get rid of it after you read it. It's a very burnable bit of nothing.

One last thing. I didn't tell you these things to make you feel guilty. You'll see by the journal that I had problems long before I met you. I inherited my issues from my parents. I tried to tell you that a few times. I wanted to warn you that I'm a very messed-up person. But I suppose I didn't because I liked you and I wanted you to like me.

I hope you are well,
Riley

18

VAUGHN

I lay the wrinkled letter on the island and reread a few passages.

Fracture in my skull. The doctors said I was depressed. I don't know what to believe. I'm a very messed-up person. I liked you and I wanted you to like me.

The moon seas are gone. Kiran is upset. Sachi is spending her days monitoring the activities of her depressed twenty-one-year-old daughter. Maybe she's too troubled to paint. I'm sure Alec and Colton are trying to help Riley, too.

I've obsessed about the repercussions of my stay, but now I know without any doubt: I killed the magic of that unusual place. I really and truly did.

I ball up the letter and throw it on the floor. With a swipe, my wineglass follows with a splintering crash.

This sound brings me back. Glasses and plates and beer bottles broken in fits of anger. I would hurry to my room, assuming I was next. Sometimes he'd let me go. Sometimes he'd make me clean it up because it was my fault he got angry. And sometimes I was next.

I'm not in my kitchen. I'm in the cold void, the dissociative refuge I created for myself before I can even remember. I like this place. There is no pain here.

But it can't erase Riley's. I see her words: *I had problems long before I met you. I inherited my issues from my parents.*

What problems? What did her parents do to her? I hear my father's ruthless tirades, feel his huge hands seize me, hurt me, and I can't bear to think of Riley being treated like that—or even worse.

I start to notice another void, as if a cavity has painfully opened inside my chest. I know what it is. It's an empty space where Riley Mays used to be. I thought I knew everything. I had meticulously fabricated the whole of her life, moving her around like a little plastic figure in a dollhouse I'd created for her.

I had no right. From now on, Riley will always speak for herself.

I pull the sheath of printer paper from the envelope. I hear Riley's voice as I start to read.

19

RILEY'S JOURNAL

One

After Julia died, I lived on the moon. There wasn't anywhere else to go. Earth was uninhabitable without her.

I was eleven, and I don't remember much about the first weeks after. Only that I was often at sea. Sometimes I walked the rugged shores of parched seabeds, a lone cartographer meticulously exploring and mapping the bleak landscape of my new, lifeless world. Other times the lunar seas would be miraculously full, and I would toss on their waves in a ship that looked like the HMS *Beagle* of Darwin's voyages. Except without a crew—or any other kind of life. Not a seagull, dolphin, or tree in sight. Because no living thing can exist without oxygen.

No living thing but me. I was a singular creature, uniquely adapted to lunar life. I didn't need to wear a space suit. I didn't eat or drink. But I often slept. Usually on the ship's deck, curled in a ball beneath the stars.

At night, I'd sometimes lie on my back, the moon's sea heaving the creaking ship up, down, up, down, and I would look at the distant Earth. I saw it as a pale orb, as desolate as people on Earth saw the moon. I was only in sixth grade, but I'd seen enough to understand the inevitability of our planet's future. We would never fix problems like war and pollution, because most human beings were treacherous and selfish. They would kill the most precious life in the universe just to get a few minutes of whatever it was they wanted.

That was why Earth looked like the moon to me. It was never blue. It wasn't beautiful.

But it was when Julia was alive. She made everything beautiful. She was one of those people who sees beauty in gasoline-slicked city puddles. At first, I thought she was simply peculiar. In the puddle I saw only filthy water, broken asphalt, browned cigarette butts, and a sad little blackened toddler's sock. I eventually learned Julia saw those things, too, and it made the rainbow of gasoline all the more poetic to her. With Julia, I started seeing all kinds of things I'd never noticed before. Impish faces in tree bark. The mystical wink of a crow when it opened and closed its third eyelid. A rose miraculously unfurled in our dormant garden in November.

At least one magical thing happened every day of my life with Julia.

She'd insisted I call her Julia from the start. My mother and I came to live with her when I was five years old. Nikki, my mother, told me I should call her Auntie or Aunt Julia, but Julia kept saying, "Please call me Julia, sweetheart."

No one had ever called me "sweetheart" before. Or "honey" or "darling."

A lot of people think aunts are secondary kinds of people. They think a mother is more important. But that wasn't how it was with Julia, Nikki, and me. By the time I was six, Julia was everything—my earth, my sun, my stars—and that was why I lost those things when she died. But I didn't lose the moon, because Julia gave it to me.

Julia had the most marvelous contraption, a telescope called a *Celestron*. One night, she asked me if I wanted to look at the moon with her. Before that night, I'd been shy around her, hardly saying a word. I had no idea how to live in a nice house with a nice lady. All I'd known before Julia was weird people and dirty apartments. There were even a few nights when my mother and I slept outside in bushes.

That first month, I tiptoed around my aunt and her pretty house like I was walking on a fragile veneer of candy glaze. I supposed Julia must be faking her kindness for some terrible reason I'd soon discover, or, more likely, my mother would ruin everything, as she always did.

Every morning, when I woke beneath the blanket pattern Julia called flying geese—in a sweet baby blue room I had all to myself—I'd prepare myself to leave Julia's house. I'd go downstairs to breakfast expecting my mother or Julia to tell me we were leaving. And as every morning passed, I dreaded that news more and more.

The first time Julia showed me her telescope, she told me the moon was one of the only things we could see well in the night sky of a big city. She explained what light pollution is, and I still remember how sad I was when she said we would be seeing a magical river of stars called the Milky Way right there above us if people hadn't ruined the night with lights.

Julia took me on my first tour of the moon, telling me the names of moon places and how they got them. She said astronomers in the sixteen hundreds mistook the dark areas of the moon for oceans. That topography looked dark because of deposits of volcanic rock called "basalt," but people didn't know that yet. The scientists called those regions the "maria," the Latin word for "seas," and they gave them Latin names that sounded like magical incantations to a five-year-old.

Mare Insularum, the Sea of Islands. Mare Undarum, the Sea of Waves. Julia's favorite was Mare Nubium, the Sea of Clouds. That was a favorite of mine, too, but I liked Mare Nectaris a little bit more. How could a girl not love a place called the Sea of Nectar? Imagining how that ocean would smell and taste always put me in a dreamy state. Once I painted a watercolor of the nectar sea for Julia. I drew flowers all around its shore and swirled the sky and water with pastel colors that looked like the spun softness of cotton candy. Julia loved it and hung it on her kitchen wall in a pretty frame. My mother said I was as much a lunatic about the moon as Julia, because everyone knew the lunar landscape was as colorless and dry as dust.

I never visited the Sea of Nectar in the months after Julia's death. Only dark waters could express my grief. Mare Frigoris, the Sea of Cold, or Oceanus Procellarum, the Ocean of Storms. And the darkest of them all, Mare Anguis, the Serpent Sea, the terrifying sea that always made me think about my mother.

Two

There was only a week left until Christmas vacation when my home-room teacher told me to take my lunch to Mrs. Wozniak's office. I'd been asked to have lunch with the school counselor twice since Julia died. That was after they noticed I was asking my teachers to use the bathroom and not coming out. I was found on the cold tile, just sitting there, I guess. I don't remember much about it.

"Riley, come in," Mrs. Wozniak said when I stood at the threshold to her office. Almost all I can recall of her is that she had warm brown eyes and glasses frames that were the color of a deep-blue sea. She gave me a cupcake and Santa Claus napkin—from someone's birthday in the main office, she said.

"You can open your lunch," she said. "Mine's right here." She gestured at a salad and metal fork in an open Tupperware container. She must have thought inviting a student to eat lunch with her would feel like a buddy kind of thing, maybe help ease me through whatever uncomfortable topic she had to discuss.

"Go ahead." She picked up her salad and ate a few forkfuls.

The counselor frowned as I opened the bag and took out a granola bar and a battered spring water bottle I'd been refilling for weeks. "That's it?"

In my mind I walked the shore of Mare Marginis, the lunar Sea of the Edge. I measured its shape with my steps: turn to the left, straight for a while, turn right, then left again . . .

The Sea of the Edge was almost as scary as the Serpent Sea. It bordered a dark abyss that fell away into nothingness. One wrong step and I'd slip off the edge.

"Riley?"

I looked at her.

"I asked if your mother packed that lunch."

If she reported my mother for neglect, the authorities would start digging and might discover the truth. They'd take me away from Julia's house. I quit walking the shore of Mare Marginis to concentrate on my answer. "She did. There was a sandwich with ham, cheese, and lettuce, but I ate it on the bus this morning."

"Didn't you have breakfast?"

"I had two eggs, bacon, a banana muffin, and orange juice." I hadn't, but I might have if Julia were still alive.

"Why did you eat your lunch on the bus?"

"I was still hungry." I'd never done that, but I'd seen kids dig into their lunches on the morning bus.

"It's hard to believe you have such a big appetite. You've lost weight, haven't you?"

"That happens when you have a growth spurt." I opened the granola bar and bit off almost half of it to demonstrate.

Mrs. Wozniak didn't look especially convinced but moved on. "How are you doing these days?"

"Okay," I said through the granola.

"And your mother?"

I shrugged.

"I know losing your aunt was a terrible loss for both of you."

I was mapping the Sea of the Edge with my steps again.

In a soft voice, she said, "Riley, she died four months ago, and your teachers say you aren't getting better. They say you've gotten much worse."

I walked a narrow little curve between mare and chasm.

"I hear you're not doing your work."

I looked out into the seabed, deep and dry. For some reason I'd never seen Mare Marginis with water. It was a treacherous deep crater surrounded by cliffs.

"Your teachers say you hardly talk to anyone. Are any of your friends from grade school here?"

I'd had two best friends in grade school. One moved away in fourth grade and the other went to the middle school with advanced programs. Julia wanted me to apply for that program, but my mother wouldn't let me. She said she wanted me in the middle school I was zoned for because the bus ride to the magnet school was too long. Julia said the bus ride should have nothing to do with it, and the magnet program was a great opportunity for me. But my mother wouldn't relent. It had been a nasty fight—many fights, actually—and when my mother got like that, she usually won. I went to the nearby school, and my one best friend went to the far school and made new friends. I wouldn't have wanted to see her after Julia died anyway.

"Riley? Would you please answer?"

"No."

"No?"

"I mean, no, I don't have friends at this school."

I ignored her sympathetic look and imagined the color of her glasses in one of my seas. Maybe Mare Insularum, the Sea of Islands. I'd once drawn it for Julia as a pretty blue sea dotted with verdant tropical islands.

"Your teachers say you don't pay attention in class." When I didn't respond, she said, "Just like you're not paying attention to me right now."

I was back at the Sea of the Edge.

"Riley, look at me."

I looked at her.

"Where are you? You look a million miles away."

She wasn't even close. I was 252,000 miles away, the approximate distance of the moon at its apogee, the farthest it ever gets from Earth. Most people don't know the moon's distance from Earth changes because the moon has an irregular orbit, a wobble I sometimes felt beneath my feet after Julia died.

Mrs. Wozniak leaned toward me. "What's on your mind when you look like that? Are you thinking about anything specific?"

I was, but not if I could help it. That was the whole point.

"Riley?"

I knew she'd needle me until I answered. "I'm thinking about our earth dying."

She leaned back, looking astonished.

"The polar caps melting and seas rising and everything turning into a desert. One day Earth will look like the moon."

"Who told you that?"

"Everyone talks about it."

"Riley . . ."

"Don't try to tell me it's not happening." To further distract her, I said, "I'm scared all the time. All of us are."

She frowned. "Did Mrs. Robertson teach you this?"

The distraction was a grand success, but I didn't want to get my science teacher in trouble. Mrs. Robertson was funny and kind, and her class was better than any science I'd had in grade school. And she *had* talked to us about climate change, though she didn't say anything I hadn't already known.

"It's not Mrs. Robertson," I said. "Kids hear about climate change all over. It's on the news and internet, and their parents and everyone talk about it."

That was the truth. And I hadn't lied when I told her I was scared about our planet dying. I'd been preoccupied with climate change since the night Julia told me the lunar sea Mare Humboldtianum was named for Alexander von Humboldt. She said he was a brilliant scientist, the first to describe how industrial gases and cutting forests leads to climate change. He'd already understood that two centuries ago.

My aunt, a librarian, was ecologically conscious. She only wanted to educate me when she talked about climate change. She didn't realize how it was to be eight years old and feel powerless over an unstoppable fate. Add in images from futuristic books and movies to make it more real, and I'd bet more kids than me were anxious about the coming catastrophe.

But my preoccupation got much worse after Julia died. By the time I was called to Mrs. Wozniak's office that day, I'd been living on a lifeless moon for four months. I knew what it was like to live on a dead planet. To be a lonely survivor in a wasteland.

"Riley . . . Riley, please listen to me," Mrs. Wozniak said. "You don't have to worry about climate change. You're too young to tackle a big issue like that. Don't you think? Right now you should be focused on school and friends and your mom." She smiled. "And Christmas presents. Winter vacation is just six days away. I guess that's what most kids are thinking about right now."

I certainly was thinking about winter vacation. Dreading all those days at home alone with Nikki. The moon was the only way I would survive it.

"Are you going to the school dance tomorrow?"

She had no idea how absurd the question was. As if I could go to a middle school dance when I lived on the moon.

"Riley?"

"No."

"Why not?"

I tried to think of a normal reason for not going to the dance. "My mom doesn't let me go to dances yet."

Mrs. Wozniak frowned skeptically, but this might have been true. The girls I'd heard blathering about the dance had all been asked by boys. I could imagine Nikki's reaction if I told her a boy had asked me: "Let's save grinding on boys for high school, shall we?" Or a cruder version: "If you think I'll let you start poking around at boys' dicks at age eleven, you're very much mistaken." Even if she let me go, she would have said something like, "You have a date before you even have your period or tits?"

Mrs. Wozniak said the words I most dreaded. "I think I'd better call your mother. The three of us will talk." When she saw the look on my face, she added, "You aren't in trouble. Not at all. I just want to make sure you're getting what you need right now. I'm going to call her today and arrange a meeting. Okay? Is that all right, Riley?"

"She's pretty busy since my aunt died—taking care of everything by herself."

This was a huge lie. I couldn't even look at her as I said it. Released from Julia's restrictions, Nikki had spent the last four months stoned, on the computer, or with one of the many men she invited over to the house. *I* was the one who was trying to take care of everything. Cooking dinner, doing laundry, cleaning up after Nikki, getting the trash out on garbage day. Until the lawyers and banks released Julia's money to Nikki, we wouldn't have a car because Julia's got wrecked in the accident. I had to walk to the grocery store, fortunately only a few blocks away. And I opened the mail and made sure Nikki paid the electric and other important bills. I had no choice but to leave the moon to do these many things, but as every day went by, remembering to come back to Earth to take care of Julia's house became more and more difficult.

"I understand that she's busy," Mrs. Wozniak said sympathetically. "But I think she'll see how important this is. Because you're important to her. She loves you, and she'll want to know things have been rough for you at school. We'll talk about it and think of a way to get you on a better path during winter break."

Anyone at my elementary school would have known none of that was true. They knew Julia was more like my mom. By the time I was in second grade, they'd figured out my aunt was the one they should contact about things like school open house, play rehearsals, and permission slips for field trips. In fact, if the staff at my former school knew I was now solely in Nikki's care, they might have had someone check on me by now.

"I don't want to take up your whole lunch period," Mrs. Wozniak said. "Why don't you see what's going on in the lunchroom?"

I cleaned my trash off her desk and stood to go.

"Don't forget this delicious cupcake!" Mrs. Wozniak said.

The cupcake with gooey red and green icing made my stomach feel even sicker. I wrapped it in the Santa napkin and threw it in the garbage on my way down the hall.

Three

I thought I might vomit when I rode the bus home. And I felt worse as I walked the last block to the house. Nikki would be livid about the school calling her. She would remind me of how dangerous it was to get anyone involved. She'd say I'd risked everything. If the lawyers saw her as an unfit mother, she wouldn't get Julia's money. She would lose the house because she'd have no money to pay property taxes or anything else. We would be back to the life we lived before she found out her father had left her half the house in his will. Or maybe DCFS would put me in a foster home. Or I'd go to an orphanage because no one wanted kids as old as eleven.

Nikki thought the threat of being taken away from her would scare me, but it didn't. I sometimes fantasized versions of her removal from my life, but in mine, I didn't have to leave home. Julia's house was all that was holding me together.

I repeatedly told myself everything would be okay. Nikki probably hadn't answered Mrs. Wozniak's phone call. She'd have ignored it when she saw it came from the school.

By the time the house came into view, I was charting the shore-line of Mare Crisium, the Sea of Crises. The Sea of Crises is loosely connected to Mare Anguis, the Serpent Sea, and I was about to see the serpent any minute.

I tried the front door. It was still locked from when I left for school. Julia had taught me to lock doors from a young age, but Nikki usually didn't remember or care. Finding the door locked probably meant Nikki was home. But she could have gone out the back door. I put my key in the lock, hoping she had.

The front door opened onto a sweet little sunporch with a wall of windows that faced south. It was one of my favorite rooms, especially in winter, when it was full of light. Julia kept her collection of potted succulents and cacti in that room.

Of course, Nikki had ruined the sunporch, and in the cruelest way possible. She'd crammed it with boxes of Julia's belongings that she supposedly would sell on Craigslist. She said she needed to sell things to support us until the money came through, but I knew the truth. She was jealous that Julia became my mom. She had been for years, and Nikki was showing me those days were over.

The nastiest of her purging was the Celestron. Nikki said the tele-scope was worth good money, and we had to sell it to keep food on the table. When she wasn't around, I carried it off the porch up to my room. Julia used to keep it in her room next to a small balcony that looked out over the backyard. But I couldn't put the telescope where it belonged because my mother had taken over the main bedroom. She'd often complained that Julia had the best bedroom when the house was half hers. Julia would reply that if she wanted to contribute a full 50 percent to the house in salary and labor she could have the biggest bedroom.

My mother brought the telescope back to the porch while I was at school. I carried it upstairs when I got home. She returned it to the porch the next day. This happened numerous times until I'd finally given up.

And now it was gone.

With that telescope, Julia had given me the moon. And knowledge. And magic. And love.

I stood on the porch staring at the emptiness where the Celestron had been. I was not on the moon. For the first time in months, I was fully on Earth, in that hateful underworld Nikki had created. I'd never hated my mother more.

My gaze dropped to the baseball bat and two gloves Julia had used to play ball with her dad. My grandfather, a man I never met, was Nikki's father, but she had a different mother. Sometimes Nikki used to rage because her father had loved Julia more, and Julia would try to soothe her, reminding her that their father had left Nikki half of everything. But Nikki couldn't be pacified. Because there could be no doubt that my grandfather loved Julia more. As I did. As anyone who lived with the two of them would.

And that's why Julia's treasured baseball bat and gloves were on the porch, though I begged Nikki to keep them. My mother hated what they represented.

As had the telescope. It was really gone.

I wanted to pick up the bat and go find Nikki. I wanted to kill her.

The thought scared me back to the moon. I flew those 252,000 miles straight to Mare Frigoris, the Sea of Cold, the most frigid of all the seas. I became a solid wave, a once-animate thing that was frozen away from its power. I'd been stuck in the same place since Julia died. I would never find my way back to shore.

Somehow, I walked into the house. I stopped between the kitchen doorway and stairs, trying to determine where the best refuge would be. Wherever Nikki was not. I looked farther into the kitchen.

And there was Nikki. Facedown on the kitchen floor. A pool of congealed blood spread like a devil's halo around her head.

I could only assume it was a hallucination from my rage. I glided to her like a frozen wave slowly melting into slush. I shook with cold and slumped to the ground next to her. She had a big wound on the back of her head. I touched the blood on the floor to see if it was real. Then I placed my whole hand in, palm down. It was cold and gluey.

I lifted my hand and looked at it. I rubbed it over my other palm to be sure it wasn't a trick she was playing on me. It smelled irony and foul. The stink of a dead serpent's blood.

I sat there for a long time, looking at my bloody hands. The tick of the kitchen clock sounded louder than usual. *Click, click, click . . .*

I had killed her. Between the porch and the kitchen, when I felt frozen, I must have taken the baseball bat and hit her in the back of the head. I had killed my mother.

20

VAUGHN

I drop Riley's journal onto the kitchen island and spin my mother's key with my thumb and finger. The chain winds, enclosing it in a silver circle. I watch the key go round and round like the hands on a clock.

I understand why Riley couldn't write more entries. She must know by now that she didn't kill her mother. Maybe that's why she said the journal isn't the truth.

But what if she still thinks she did?

She hated her mother. Her mother was emotionally abusive. Maybe she hit Riley, too.

I stop spinning the key.

This is important. This changes everything.

I look at the clock on my kitchen wall. Time and place blur. I see Riley, age eleven, listening to the tick of a kitchen clock as she stares at her bloody hands.

I look at the clock. The hour and minute hands stand in perfect opposition to each other. Like Riley and me. But our lives will cross again, and uncross, and come together again. We're trapped in a little box of time, connected by mechanisms beyond our control, spinning around each other.

I have to make it stop. Not with brutal workouts or getting wasted or having sex with women who don't know who I am. Short-term oblivion just makes me keep circling this wretched clock. I have to make it stop forever. Smash the damn clock with a hammer.

I look at my kitchen clock. I make myself see the numbers. It's six o'clock, plenty of time to catch a flight to Chicago.

I pull the chain of my mother's necklace over my head and settle the key against my chest. I've never worn it. Maybe I think it'll be like a talisman to give me courage.

I'm going back. I really am. And this time I'll tell Riley everything.

~

When I arrive at the farm, Riley's old sedan is parked in front of the house. Sachi's car is next to it. I loudly close my car door to announce myself.

Sachi appears at the side of the house. She's wearing a straw hat and muddy gardening clothes. She doesn't look especially pleased to see me, but she isn't overtly angry either.

"Vaughn, how are you?" she asks, arriving at my car.

"I could be better. How've you been?"

"Same," she responds.

The apparent evidence of the damage I caused feels like a fist to the stomach. This is not the radiant Sachi of my last visit.

"I guess you're here because you got the painting and letter," she says.

I nod. "Riley said she fractured her skull. Is she okay?"

"The fracture is minor, but she'll have ongoing treatment for the concussion."

"It was that bad?"

"She could have died that night."

"What happened?"

"I'll let Riley tell you if she wants to."

I look at the house. "Is she here?"

"She went into town with Alec and Kiran for groceries."

Neither of us knows what to say next.

"If you think I should leave before Riley gets back, I will."

She smiles slightly. "That's what you want me to say, isn't it? Losing your nerve?"

"I don't think I have any to lose."

"Come inside. I'll make us tea."

Being in the house with Sachi feels awkward. I'm not the person she saw the night of my author's fete, and she's not the person I remember. Even the house feels different.

She invites me to take a seat at the little antique table in the kitchen, but I prefer to stand after the long drive. She puts the kettle on the stove and leans against a counter with her arms folded over her soil-stained shirt. "Are you writing?" she asks.

"No."

"I'm sorry to hear that."

"As would be my agent and publisher, if they knew."

She studies me for long enough that I feel nervous. "You don't know why you're here, do you?"

"No." I look at the front door. "I keep thinking I should leave."

"Please stay. Riley will want to see you."

She doesn't know what a relief this is. I feel like someone cut a tight wrap of rope from around my chest.

She's looking at me shrewdly again.

"Do you see an aura around me?" I ask.

"Why does everyone ask that?"

"Because it's damn intimidating to think someone sees into your soul."

"It's not like that."

"Do you see something that worries you when you look at me?"

"Yes. I see a man who's confused and unhappy."

"In my aura?"

Rather than answer, she says, "If you trust me, I'd like to help."

"I trust you, but you can't help."

"I'm sorry," is all she says. She opens a cupboard. "What kind of tea would you like? Calming, invigorating? Something spicy like chai?"

"Do you have one with nerve in it?"

"I have just the thing." She opens a small blue-and-white tin and fills a tea strainer with the dried leaves. She opens a green tin and adds something else. For her own tea, she scoops out of an orange container.

We sweeten our tea with honey and bring the cups to the table. The tea has a floral flavor that makes me think of the blooming trees I saw in the orchard as I drove in.

We sip in silence. It's calming not to feel pressure to talk. The peacefulness of Sachi's nature must have been good for Riley after everything she'd been through.

"Do you know much about Riley's mother and aunt?"

Sachi looks astonished, setting down her cup. "She told you about her mother and aunt?"

"A little." I won't say more because Riley asked me not to mention the journal. "She hasn't said much about them?"

"Never. We gently probed, and we tried to get her to see a child psychologist, but she refused to talk about her mother and aunt. We know nothing about her life in Chicago. Alec hadn't seen Nikki and Julia since he was a boy, and we didn't meet Riley until we found out she needed guardians. We were only told what the police knew about Nikki and Julia's deaths."

An icy sensation seizes me. I don't want to be the only person who knows about her life with Nikki and Julia. I have no right to be that person.

Warmth cocoons my left hand. Sachi has wrapped her hand around mine. She doesn't say anything, only looks at me reassuringly.

"You don't know why she put the moon seas on her walls?" I ask.
"No."

I'm stunned again.

"We assumed it had to do with her mother and aunt, but we didn't know specifics. Drawing the moon seas was an important turning point for her."

"In what way?"

She takes her hand off mine and studies me for a few seconds. "Did Riley tell you how her mother died?"

"Yes."

"I suppose I can tell you a few things if she's trusted you this much."

I want to say Riley shouldn't have trusted me. And confess that I abandoned her in the nastiest way possible. I want to get up, drive away, and hear no more. But I can't move.

"When Riley came here, she lived in a shell she'd made to protect herself. Alec and I were completely unprepared for how broken her spirit was."

"How shut down was she?"

"She could take care of herself. But she rarely talked, and she avoided us as much as possible. It was like she was here but not here."

She was on the moon. Alone. Charting the shapes of dry seabeds, tossing on lifeless waters in a ship that had no pilot.

"Her first turning point came a few months after she arrived, when she started drawing the moon seas on art paper I'd given her. Alec and I had no idea what it was all about, but we encouraged it because it was her first sign of expression. I gave her a supply of charcoal pencils she wore down to a nub. And as the seas began to fill her walls, she started trying to make them bigger, connecting them with taped pieces of paper. I understood her vision, and together we put up the art paper that became the mural in her room."

Sachi sips her tea. "I found out I was pregnant during that time. Alec and I had been trying for years and had given up on it ever happening. I thought the timing couldn't be worse. I had this child who needed everything I could give her, and now I was distracted by the experience of growing a baby inside me."

Her eyes shine. "But how could I not be grateful for the miracle of having *two* beautiful beings to nurture? How could I be afraid when I had these children who needed me?"

"How did Riley respond to your pregnancy?"

"It was difficult to tell. As I said, she didn't speak much. Alec made some progress when he started teaching her about moths. But even then, she remained aloof. But, my god, when that baby was born . . . how she loved him. Kiran's birth was the real turning point for her."

"She told me he nearly died."

She nods. "It was a terrible time for us. But something about it made Riley stronger. And that helped Alec and me during that time when we thought Kiran might die. When Kiran could finally come home, she really changed. It was like he opened a door in her. And after a few years with Kiran, one day her gray moon seas were bright with color. The morning I walked into her room and saw Kiran chattering away and telling her which sea to paint next . . . that was one of the most miraculous moments of my life."

"Is that when she painted the monster into the Serpent Sea?"

"It was. Alec and I have always assumed it had some deep meaning for her."

I can't betray Riley's trust and tell her Riley specifically named her mother as the serpent in her journal. Maybe when she'd healed enough to paint water and clouds into the seas, she was also well enough to confront her feelings about Nikki. Except she discovered she still couldn't handle that much grief and anger. Instead, she painted the monster in the corner up high, where it couldn't reach her.

"I hear she tore down the mural."

"She did. At the time, I didn't know if that was a good or bad development. But now I have to think it's good if she's been opening up to you."

"Nothing I did when I came here was good."

She rests back in her chair. "You know, back when Riley came to us, many of our friends and family pitied us. They could only see her as broken. Some see only bad; I see only good. It's very often a matter of perspective."

"Some things are unequivocally bad."

"Of course. The deaths of Riley's aunt and mother obviously were bad. But those events brought Riley to us and us to Riley. And Kiran without Riley? I can't even imagine that. Their bond is a huge part of who they are." She smiles. "Do you know what I think?"

"What?"

"I think Kiran was waiting to be born until Riley arrived."

If she'd said this to me last February, I would have scoffed. Now the remark nearly brings tears. I don't understand what this family has done to me.

"We didn't know Kiran feels happiest in girls' clothing until Riley unpacked her boxes," Sachi says. "She wouldn't look in them for years. She was afraid of them, of all the emotions they would stir up. But Kiran wanted into those boxes. 'What's in the boxes?' he'd ask. 'Riley, show me what's in your boxes.' So one day she opened a few. Kiran is innately a collector, and the appearance of all that intriguing stuff really got his attention. He had a four-month birthday party going through Riley's boxes with us."

"Four months of unpacking?"

"It was the whole house. We had movers bring it all because Riley was in no shape to tell us which things were important to her. We stored it all over—shed, barn, attic—but I think seeing them overwhelmed her. Sometimes I'd catch her looking at them as if they were actual ghosts."

I can imagine. If someone told me I had to go through boxes of belongings from my father's house, I'd have set them aflame first chance I got.

"But Kiran's excitement helped her unpack them all. She'd say, 'Look at this, Kiran. This is a necklace I wore for Halloween when I was Cleopatra.' And she'd put the necklace on him and dig around until she found the dress that went with the costume. Kiran's closet is full of Riley's clothing. Much of what you see him wear was hers when she was little."

I recall the fuzzy purple robe Kiran likes to wear. Talk about ghosts. It must be painful for Riley when the clothing stirs up memories.

"Kiran's first clock came out of the boxes, too."

"Really? He took it apart?"

"Not at first. He was only four. Riley had given him a kitchen clock when she saw how it fascinated him. It was a few years later, during Kiran's take-everything-apart stage, that he disassembled it. And after that, all he wanted to take apart was clocks."

A kitchen clock. It has to be the same clock that was ticking when Riley found her mother. A chill ripples my skin. That clock inspired Kiran's art. Its mechanisms are part of the magic on his tables. No wonder Riley didn't want me to touch the clock gear.

"Did Riley tell you why we decided to homeschool Kiran?"

"Yes, the teasing."

"First grade was a really tough time for Kiran—for all of us. We tried to focus on subjects he liked, and on the students who treated him kindly. But there were few, and many teachers weren't supportive of us letting him wear what he wanted. More and more, Kiran would come home crying or in a gloom, and that is so unlike him. Taking him out of school—the realization that those children and teachers would never accept him—was almost as bad for our family as when he was in school. That was when he started putting the clock parts and fossils together. The arrangements are deeply comforting for him, as are fossil hunting and scouring antique stores for clocks with Alec and Riley. Collecting helped ground him—and they brought my family closer together when Kiran most needed us."

"Now that I know all of you, I see how Kiran's tables evolved: your art, Alec and Colton's science, Riley's love of antiques . . ."

"Yes, Kiran's collection is beautiful, an artistic metaphor for the bonds in our family."

"And don't forget the magic."

"The magic is the best part. I'm surprised Riley told you about that."

"She told me the day I arrived, and I have to admit, I thought it was really out there." I look into my cup at a scatter of tea-leaf fragments. "But when I went back to New York, I would think about Kiran's tables. I thought about those gears and fossils a lot. I don't know why."

When I look up, Sachi seems fascinated by my confession. "Everything connects in ways we can't comprehend," she says. "Don't tell me no good came of your time with Riley until we see how it all works out."

I press my hand on the antique key hidden inside my shirt, a new habit since I put it on. I consider asking Sachi about the key in the painting, but she stands and peers out the window. "I hope that tea has given you some nerve," she says. "They're home."

21

RILEY

"Cool Porsche," Alec says, pulling in next to the black car.

"A Porsche?" Kiran says. "What is that?"

"A brand of sports car," Alec says.

Kiran rises in his seat to see it better. Alec casts a nervous look at me over Kiran's head. We don't know anyone who would drive a sporty car but Vaughn.

I feel like the oxygen has been sucked out of the truck cab. I fumble with the door handle, and when I get out, I have an urge to hide somewhere before Vaughn sees me.

Too late. He and Sachi have come out the front door.

"Let me help," Vaughn says from the porch. He walks over, his gray eyes fixed on me. He looks good in fitted tan pants and a white, long-sleeved shirt rolled up his forearms. I don't remember him being that muscular. And his hair is longer, wavy and attractive.

He pulls two bags of groceries out of the back of the pickup. "How are you?" he asks quietly.

He's standing so close I can smell whatever soap he used this morning. It's too much. Too sudden. I'm going to cry or say something stupid. Then I remember I already have said something stupid. I sent him the journal. He knows what I did that day.

I can't stop the tears. I run up the porch stairs.

"Riley . . . ," Sachi says, reaching for me.

I push past her and run to my room. My room that doesn't feel like my room. It doesn't even smell the same since I painted it. Sometimes my need for the seas is a terrible ache in my whole body; other times I'm glad they're gone. Right now, I need them. I curl up in bed and pull Julia's flying-geese quilt over me. My tears wet the pillow fast.

When I finally process that Vaughn is here, my first thought is that he might leave, and I don't want him to. But I've made such an ass of myself, I don't know how to face him. I wish I could act like a regular person. I'm twenty-one and hiding in my room from a man.

A man who said terrible things before he ran out on me. And now here he is acting like he's Mr. Nice in front of Alec and Sachi. Of course I'm crying and hiding.

Someone knocks on my door.

"May I come in?" Sachi asks.

I open the door. She's alone.

"Are you okay?"

"Yeah." I wipe my hands down my face.

"Do you want him to leave? He says he's going."

If he does, I'll never see him again. I'd gotten used to the idea, but now that he's here, I can't let it happen. I have no idea why.

"I look awful."

"You're beautiful. Hurry before he leaves."

Alec is at the bottom of the stairs. "He left."

Every cell in my body screams, *No!* And how irrational is that when Vaughn was so nasty to me? But I run out the door. This must be how Nikki was with my father. Whoever that bad man was, she just had to have him.

Vaughn is seated in his car, but the door is open, and he's talking to Kiran. I think Kiran stopped him from leaving. Kiran is wearing the purple capri pants I wore in third grade. The right back pocket has a unicorn embroidered on it, and on the left is a rainbow. I called them my lucky pants because I won a spelling bee wearing them. Julia, of course, let me keep them when they got too small and I didn't want to give them to Goodwill.

"Hey, sorry about that," I say to Vaughn.

"You don't have to apologize."

"It was just a surprise."

"I should have called first. But I wasn't really thinking when I left New York."

Kiran says to me, "Porsches are made in Germany. This one has a turbocharged engine."

"Is it yours?" I ask Vaughn.

He shakes his head. "My rental car company gave me a good upgrade deal on it. I'd never driven a Porsche and wanted to see if it lived up to its hype."

"Kiran has been interested in how cars work lately."

"Are you taking them apart yet?" he asks Kiran.

Kiran shakes his head, smiling. "Can I see the turbocharged engine?"

"Sure." Vaughn opens the engine cover.

When Kiran leans in to look, Vaughn says quietly, "I'll go if you want me to."

"I don't."

He looks at my jeans and button shirt. "Is this your Saturday fashion-mogul outfit?"

"No." I motion for him to walk away so Kiran can't hear.

"Should I not have said that?" he asks when we get some distance.

"It's okay. But Kiran hasn't wanted to do that since my accident. It might be because I was in the hospital on a Saturday, and missing one week messed up the ritual. Or maybe he's still mad at me for taking down the moon seas."

"I'm mad at you for taking down the moon seas. They were beautiful."

I study his eyes to see if he's only humoring me.

"What color did you paint your room?" he asks.

"Blue."

"Same color as your room in Julia's house?"

"No, gray-blue. I can't believe you remember that little detail."

He looks away for a few seconds, taking a deep breath. "I'm afraid anything I say about the journal will come out wrong. But it really affected me, Riley. It's a big part of why I'm here. I also have to say you were wrong about it not being truthful. The emotions you wrote were incredibly real."

"You can't understand why it isn't truthful."

"Do you still think you killed your mother?"

"I was in shock when I thought that. She was murdered by someone who robbed our house that day."

"Did they catch the person who did it?"

"No."

He studies my eyes. "Does that make you angry?"

"It doesn't make me anything. Just getting through it all was more than enough for me."

I'm saying these words, but it doesn't feel like me. It's like a machine inside me is saying them. I don't know how I'm talking about this. The journal was the closest I ever got to expressing anything about what happened, and I had a near breakdown after I wrote it.

"I'm sorry about how your mother treated you," he says.

The only person who ever said that to me was Julia.

"I understand," he says. "My father . . ."

I can see the anguish in his gray eyes. "He was like that?"

Vaughn swallows hard. "He hit me. He was verbally abusive, too."

"What about your mom?"

"She died when I was fifteen months old. She overdosed on pills."

"I'm sorry."

He nods.

"Do you have siblings?"

"Just me."

"Then it was a lot worse for you. At least I had Julia for six years."

He stares down at his feet for a few seconds. "Riley . . . I'm sorry about how I treated you. I know it's not a valid excuse, but I was a mess when I came here."

And I've been a mess since he left.

"You were right," he says. "That night I was only saying awful things because I thought it would make leaving easier."

"Why did you leave?"

"It's complicated. It's . . ." He looks around, as if suddenly aware of where he is.

"It's what?"

"I can't explain. Not right now."

I don't know why this is enough for me. Maybe because of what he told me about his father. Or because I'm not telling him the whole truth either. He apologized and admitted he'd treated me badly to make leaving easier. I don't want him to leave, but I'm afraid he will now that he's apologized. I don't care if it's Nikki's DNA that makes me want him so bad. I have to make him stay.

"How long will you be here?"

"I haven't thought that out yet."

"You can stay in our loft."

"No. Not after what I did."

"Please stay."

He looks at the barn. "It would feel all wrong."

I can see why. His last hour in that place was awful, with me jumping into his bed and all. "Blackberry Inn is only about twenty minutes away. It's a bed-and-breakfast next to a lake."

"Why do you want me to stay?"

"Don't you want to?"

He smiles. "Not fair. I asked first."

"Let's just say you're staying one night at Blackberry Inn and go from there. You can't drive all the way back to Chicago now."

"I could in a nice Porsche."

He's teasing. He's going to stay. I forgot how attractive he is. My body feels like it's in some kind of overload, and I have to stop looking at him. "Come on, I'll take you over to Blackberry."

Kiran is seated behind the wheel of the car, touching the dashboard gadgets.

"Can Kiran come with us?" Vaughn asks.

"He'd like that. I'll tell Alec and Sachi where we're going."

Alec and Sachi are nervously waiting just inside the door.

"He's going to stay at Blackberry Inn," I tell them. "I'm taking him over. He invited Kiran to come with if that's okay."

"That was nice of him," Sachi says. She looks much more positive about Vaughn being here than Alec. I guess he's just being a protective dad.

Vaughn and Kiran mostly talk during the drive to the bed-and-breakfast, first about Porsches, then fossils, then dinosaurs. Kiran is talkative. He seems happy Vaughn has returned, but I could be imagining he is because I am.

"Wow," Vaughn says when he sees the log lodge overlooking the lake. But he's worried they won't have a room when he notes how many cars are parked in the front lot.

"You can use those canoes and rowboats if you're staying here," I tell him. "And swim off the dock or beach."

He's staring at the lake. It reminds me of the way he looked at the moon the night we listened to the coyotes. "It looks like a dream."

"I guess it would when you're used to a big city. It's called Loonsong Lake."

"There are loons? I've always wanted to hear that sound."

"Let's see if they have a room."

I'm glad to see sweet, hippieish Marnie behind the front desk. She and her husband own the inn, and she's known Alec since their teenage years. I've always suspected they had a fling one summer when Alec was staying with his grandmother—something about the way they look at each other whenever they meet.

"Riley, Kiran! How wonderful!" she says. She slides the familiar bowl of Dum Dums suckers closer to Kiran. "They've been waiting for you, honey."

"Is there Blu Raspberry?" he asks.

"If you find one, it's yours." She's looking curiously at Vaughn, and I hope she doesn't know who he is. People in the area might have talked about him showing up at the Blind Wolf with me.

"This is my friend Mr. Orr."

She extends a hand. "Good to meet you, Mr. Orr."

Vaughn and I exchange little smiles of relief.

"He's hoping you have a room."

"Well, shoot, I don't," she says with genuine disappointment.

"Too bad," he says.

"He lives in New York City, and he's never heard loons."

"Well, we can't have that." She studies Vaughn, drumming her fingers on the desk. "How long are you staying?"

"I'm not sure," he says.

"Are you a shower or a bath person?"

"Shower . . . usually."

"Most men are," Marnie says to me with a wink. Turning back to Vaughn, she says, "If you don't mind the mess in the bathroom, you could take the boathouse cabin. We were replacing the old tub with a spa bath, and it leaked. We're waiting for another to be delivered."

"Oh . . . no, I don't mind," he says.

"The bathroom is a real mess," she warns. "Big hole where the tub was, construction dust everywhere. I wouldn't offer it to anyone but a friend." She laughs. "Not that I rent awful rooms to friends! I'd rather you stay in one of our best."

"I really am fine with it," he says.

"Good! And I won't charge you since I couldn't have rented it anyway."

"That's much too generous," he says. "I insist on paying."

"Wait till you see it before you say that."

She asks a woman in the kitchen to watch the front desk and takes us to the cabin. She drives down the dirt road in her pickup, and we follow in the rental car. Old Boathouse is the most private of the four cabins. It has its own dock and canoe.

Vaughn loves the rustic cabin that was constructed out of a 1930s boathouse. Marnie is pleased to see that one of the housekeepers has cleaned the bathroom since the plumbers left. "You would have cleaned in here even if I hadn't asked you," Marnie says to me.

"You worked here?" Vaughn asks.

"For three years."

"Best worker ever," Marnie says. "So what do you think? Can you live with the hole in the bathroom?"

"I've lived in far worse conditions," he says.

"Oh really?" Marnie says. "I guess that was before you bought the Porsche?"

"It's a rental."

"Were they out of economy cars?"

"Yep, all they had."

"Poor you," she says, winking at me.

"Porsches are made in Germany," Kiran tells Marnie. His tongue is bright blue from the raspberry Dum Dum. He points out the cabin window with the sucker. "That one has a turbocharged engine."

"Now don't you get all sweet on fancy cars," Marnie says. "I think you should stick with the clocks and fossils."

"I will," he says.

"Good. Lots cheaper. I'd better get back to the desk," she says to me. "You can give the spiel about breakfast hours and checkout." She hands Vaughn keys to the boathouse. "Come up to the lodge after you unpack, and we'll do the paperwork. I hope you hear your first loon very soon."

"I look forward to it."

After Marnie leaves, Vaughn steps through the double doors onto the dock. "This is really great! Right on the water."

I stay where I am. I never liked how the boathouse cabin hangs over deep water. Kiran follows Vaughn onto the dock.

"Aren't you coming out?" Vaughn asks.

"No. We should get Kiran inside. Marnie doesn't let people with kids younger than twelve rent this cabin—because of the deep water."

He leads Kiran into the cabin. I close the door behind them and lock it.

"He can't swim?" Vaughn asks.

"He can. Alec taught him because of the pond."

"I swim really good," Kiran says. "But not ever with Riley. She doesn't like the pond."

How did he know that when I've never said it?

Vaughn frowns. He remembers me saying I like the pond.

"We should get you checked in," I tell him to change the subject.

"She'll see what my full name is."

"I know. How about you write a *V* and your middle name instead of *Vaughn*?"

"I have no middle name."

"Really? Neither do I. What's your excuse?"

"Mine's a pen name that I made into my legal name. I saw no point to a middle name when I knew I wouldn't use it. What's *your* excuse?"

"Nikki. She said *Riley* was all she could think of."

It's strange to say things like that and know he'll understand now that he's read the journal. Maybe it's not so bad that I sent it to him. I kind of like that he's the only person in the world who knows a little about Julia, Nikki, and me.

"What name were you born with?" I ask.

His face clouds. "A name I dislike."

"Because it was your father's name?"

"Partly. I'll get my luggage."

He evaded. I'm probably right that he doesn't want to use his father's name.

He lifts his duffel bag out of the car. Just watching him engage in this simple task makes me giddy. My body doesn't feel wholly mine. It's as if every cell of my being is a tiny nocturnal insect that wants to fly into his dangerous halo. Collectively, those little wings have a strong pull, but something counterbalances their attraction, stops me from making a first move.

This prudence must come from the bit of DNA I share with Julia. I hear her voice in my head. Calm and reasonable. Loving, protective. She's telling me to be wary of this man. She reminds me I don't know why he's returned, or why he stayed with us in the first place. He was cruel to me the night he left. He said he hurt someone named Riley, and he'd be arrested if the police knew what he did.

Vaughn beams at me as he walks up the gravel path with his bag. His gray eyes pull at my heart. I never knew caring for a man would hurt this much.

"Ready," he says after he puts his bag in one of the bedrooms.

"I'll need you to drive Kiran and me home after you register. I'm leaving soon to help Alec with his research for two days."

Vaughn looks confused. I'd told him to make a reservation for one night, and now I've informed him that I'll be gone for that night and the next. It makes no sense. But nothing I'm doing makes any sense. That's why I should go on the trip with Alec.

"Sounds fun," he says.

I can tell he's disappointed. I feel the same, and I don't like that his arrival has diminished my excitement about the trip. Research trips with Alec are the best part of my summers. We camp, kayak, and browse out-of-the-way antique shops. We discuss scientific ideas and stop at farm stands and cafés we discover along the way. Spending time in nature with Alec is like going on a meditation retreat. I always come home revitalized.

But the Nikki in me is pushing to cancel the trip.

Julia disagrees. She tells me time away from Vaughn will be a perfect test. If he doesn't wait, he's not worth the risk of getting involved again.

"But what if he doesn't wait?" Nikki shouts.

Julia grabs me by the arm and drags me away from Vaughn and his sad gray eyes.

22

VAUGHN

I shouldn't have come here spontaneously. Riley will be away with Alec Saturday afternoon through late Sunday night. Monday she has medical appointments for concussion treatment. The earliest I'll see her is Monday evening.

I should leave. But when I drop off Riley and Kiran at the farm, Riley says, "I'm glad you came back."

"Are you sure about that?"

"If I'd known, I wouldn't have planned this trip with Alec. Please stick around until I get back."

"I will," I promise, which means I'm stuck with nothing to do for two days.

I go back to the boathouse and the plastic-covered hole in the bathroom. The cabin isn't as inviting without Riley. Nothing is familiar. I feel like a bird that's migrated to the wrong continent.

I have to get out. I drive to one of my old haunts for dinner, then out for a drink to a place I don't like nearly as much as the Blind Wolf. I'm finishing my second drink when two women in their midtwenties sit down with beers at the table next to mine. The one with long dark hair reminds me of a woman I was with a few years ago. She has a full mouth and a bold look in her dark eyes. Her blonde friend is attractive, too.

They keep looking at me, smiling. I'm worried they know who I am. I smile back, then try to look elsewhere, but they're in my sight line.

The waitress brings my third whiskey. As she leaves, the two women raise their beers in salute. I tip my glass at them and drink.

"Looks like you're doing some serious drinking," the dark-haired woman says.

I smile but don't reply.

"Everything okay?" she asks.

"Seems to be," I reply.

"Then why are you drinking by yourself?" When I don't answer, she comes to my table. "Do you mind if we sit with you?"

I almost tell her I want to be alone, but I'm not in the mood for conflict. The whole point of being here is to relax. "Go ahead," I reply.

My table is a two-seater, so they pull over one of their chairs. The dark-haired woman holds out her hand. "Claire," she says.

I clasp her hand. "Tyler."

She doesn't react to the name. I guess I was being paranoid about them knowing who I am.

Claire's friend offers her hand. "I'm Miranda."

"Great name. Did you know Shakespeare invented it?"

"Seriously?"

"He created the name Miranda for a character in *The Tempest*. It's from the Latin word that means 'worthy of admiration.'"

"No way."

"It's true."

Claire looks a little jealous that her friend is getting my attention. "So tell us about yourself," she says.

"Not much to tell," I respond.

"What do you do?"

"I'm in sales."

"Selling what?" Miranda asks.

"Whatever people will buy, which is pretty much anything."

They laugh.

"I thought maybe you were an English professor or something," Claire says.

I finish my whiskey. "Sorry to disappoint."

She grins. "I hated English. Especially Shakespeare."

She's the type I ask out. But I feel no attraction. All I feel is the absence of Riley.

Claire finishes her beer. "Is that Porsche outside yours?"

I reply, "Yes," but don't mention it's a rental to avoid more questions.

"It's gorgeous," she says.

The car stands out in this tiny town. If they noticed it and she's asking, I suppose the car is most of the reason they're talking to me. I'm too used to people being interested in my money and fame to care. And I'm glad they mentioned the car. They've reminded me I'd better not have a fourth whiskey.

A waitperson arrives to refill our empties. "What would you like?" I ask Claire and Miranda.

They order martinis.

"Put it on my tab and close out the bill," I tell the waitperson.

She nods, casting a wry look at the women.

"You're leaving?" Claire asks.

"I'm meeting my girlfriend."

"Why were you drinking alone if you have a girlfriend?"

"Long story."

"Did you fight?" Miranda asks. "You looked upset when we came in."

More like the guy who owned the Porsche. My clothes probably gave me away. Too polished for this remote little pub.

Claire studies my eyes. "Aha, you did fight."

"Did I?"

"Yes. And who wants to deal with that on a Saturday night? Miranda and I will be a lot more fun."

She's right. They would be a lot more fun than Riley. No complications, no doubts about why I'm with them, no regrets when it's over. But I can have that in NYC. I have had it, and it's never fulfilled me as much as one slow dance with Riley.

The waitperson brings my bill. I pocket my credit card before Claire and Miranda see the name *Vaughn Orr*. I write in a generous tip and stand. "It's been a pleasure. Enjoy your drinks."

"Are you sure you want to go?" Miranda asks.

"I'm sure. Have a good one."

I return to my hole-in-the-floor cabin and immediately sink into bed and sleep.

I'm pissed at myself for the whiskeys when I feel crappy in the morning. I rarely drink that much since I started the extreme workouts with Cedric. To punish myself, I go for a run around the lake in a misty rain. I hear a weird sound that might be my first loon call. It's an affecting wolflike cry that reminds me of the night Riley and I listened to the coyotes. At breakfast, Marnie tells me there are different kinds of loon calls, and what I heard was called a *wail*. I wish I hadn't heard it without Riley and knowing what it was.

The chilly rainy day and my constant worries about how to fix things with Riley immerse me in a gloomy mood. I drive around and visit more spots where I wasted time last February. I stay out late, and drink several beers at a different tavern. When I return to the boathouse, Marnie has left a note on my door. It says Riley called. Her doctors' appointments will take up all of Monday, but would I like to come over for lunch with the family on Tuesday? There's a number to text back my answer. I text Riley saying I would like lunch and ask what I should bring. Though it's past midnight, Riley replies right away: Just bring yourself. Come at noon.

Another whole day to kill.

Early Monday morning I run and do calisthenics on the lake trail. In the clear day and with the promise of seeing Riley tomorrow, I notice things I didn't in the gray mist the day before. The woods are vivid with spring flowers. I find a clump of orange mushrooms, the spiraled heads of baby ferns, and a bee with bulges of pollen stuck to its legs. I even notice the smell of the air: pine trees still wet with rain mixed with the sultry aroma of the lake.

My mood plunges when I spot Colton in front of Old Boathouse. He takes in my jogging pants and sweaty T-shirt with a penetrating blue gaze. "Looks like you had a good workout."

"Really good," I reply. "Is everything okay with Riley?"

A critical look flashes in his eyes. "Yeah, she and Alec got home last night."

"I know. So what's up?"

"I'm on my way back to Madison and decided to stop in for breakfast. Have you had the B&B Stack yet?"

"I'm not much of a pancake person."

"You will be if you try it. Go shower, and I'll drive us up to the inn."

We both know this isn't the friendly visit he's making it out to be. I'd rather eat breakfast alone without the stress of whatever he's come to say, but I'll do it because Riley and her family adore the guy.

During the short drive to the inn, Colton tells me he stayed at the house Saturday night and Sunday. "I don't like them to be alone while Alec is away," he says, leveling a pointed look at me.

I hope he's not saying what I think he is. "Did you know I was in town?"

"Yes."

"Who told you?"

"Sachi. We talk all the time."

Heat rises in me. He's saying he came to protect Sachi and Kiran *from me.* The depth of the insult astounds me.

"You know, if you told Sachi you came to protect her, she'd probably kick you in the nuts."

Colton laughs rather than get defensive. "I guess she would. So would Riley. But so what? They're my family." He gives me another of his looks.

What a pain in the ass. I regret coming to breakfast with him.

Marnie hugs Colton as if he's her son. She has us wait until a table is cleared so she can give us a view of the lake. "Are you having your usual?" she asks Colton.

"You know I am. It's been too long."

"It sure has. What about you, Mr. Orr?"

"You want the same, don't you?" Colton urges. "You can't leave here without having the B&B."

I sense his mention of me leaving isn't meant to be an offhand remark. But I go along with the stack in a false show of camaraderie.

Colton and I sip our coffee, looking at the lake. I wait for the coming lecture or warning or whatever it is he's brought me here to say.

"Do you have a return flight?" he asks.

"No."

"How long do you plan to stay?"

I'm already tired of waiting for him to get to the point. "Why did you come here, Colton?"

He pins my eyes with his gaze. "To ask you that same question."

I left New York in a haze after reading Riley's journal. I thought I was coming here to tell her the truth. But I can't divulge any of that.

"She was messed up by you," he says. "She could have died the night she fell."

"Fell?"

"She didn't tell you?"

"No."

"I guess she wouldn't. But I know it had to do with you."

"What had to do with me?"

186

"She got all wild and started tearing the moon seas off her walls. She was trying to reach that serpent thing in the corner and fell."

In her letter Riley said, "I did something stupid and ended up in the hospital." I've imagined many scenarios, including suicide attempts. I'm greatly relieved to hear the truth.

"Why would you assume that was my fault?"

"She hasn't been the same since you ditched her. Three months she's been upset." Unconcealed rage floods his gaze. "It had to be something big to make her like that for so long. What did you do to her in February? Did you—"

I grab his shirt at the neck. "I swear you'll be eating your teeth for breakfast if you say more!"

My fury stuns him. It surprises me even more. I always backed down from fights growing up. If there's a gene for courage, I didn't get it. Of course I didn't. Half my genetics come from a man who beat a defenseless child.

"Everything okay here, guys?" Marnie hovers behind Colton, her stare fixed on me.

I unclench Colton's shirt.

"We're good," Colton says. But he locks eyes with me to show he's not afraid to take our argument outside.

"Your food will be up soon." Marnie clasps the coffeepot to her chest. "And no more coffee for you two. You're too riled up as it is." Her mouth quirks as she adds, "Or should I say, too *Rileyed* up?"

Colton and I can't help but grin. Marnie looks relieved and walks away.

Colton has been an insulting dolt, but I want to smooth things over. I know he's truly concerned for Riley. "She was tearing down the moon seas for another reason," I tell him.

He's taken aback. "You know why?"

"I think I do."

"Why?"

"It's not my place to talk about it. She asked me not to."

He slumps against his chair. "She's talked to you about things—about when she lived in Chicago?"

"Some."

He stares at me as if seeing what happened between Riley and me in a new light. But his anger snaps back. "That's even worse! She opened up to you and you ghosted her?"

I can't tell him she didn't open up until I got the package in the mail, and that's why I came back.

When I don't respond, Colton leans toward me. "Her mother was murdered—I'm sure you know that by now—and Alec told me Riley was the one who found her body. And just a few months before that, her aunt died in an accident."

He waits for me to acknowledge that I knew these things, but I don't.

"She has a lot of pain inside her, Vaughn. And for some reason she just goes it alone and doesn't let it out. You have to be careful with her. She's fragile."

Fragile? I think not. I saw the tenacity in her from the start. But *tenacious* doesn't define her any more than *fragile*. Colton has made the mistake I did. He's constructed his own version of Riley Mays in his mind, and his version is as biased as mine was.

"Colton . . . I can't say much to explain what's going on with Riley and me. I haven't even had a chance to talk to her yet. Whatever happens, I didn't intend to come here and hurt her."

He studies me. "Are you in love with her?"

Good question. When I was little, I used to wonder if my father could love me even though he repeatedly hurt me. I decided early on that it wasn't possible. I think this powerful connection I feel with Riley must come mostly from guilt.

"Are you?" Colton presses.

"I've spent one week with her."

"One week with Riley is long enough for it to happen. One day would be."

"So . . . you're still in love with her?"

He drinks the rest of his coffee in a gulp. "I have a girlfriend now."

"That's not an answer."

"I will always love Riley. But she wants me to love her like a brother, so I do."

Honesty. I like that about Colton. He's one to cut through the bullshit.

Marnie arrives with our food. "Two Blackberry and Bacon Stacks. Extra whipped cream for Colton."

"Thank you, ma'am," Colton says.

The B&B is three fluffy pancakes crisscrossed with two thick slices of bacon and slathered with blackberry preserve syrup. Crowning the decadent pile is a dollop of whipped cream.

Colton digs in without waiting for me.

"I thought you ate a plant-based diet?"

He snorts. "Only when I'm with Sachi," he says through a mouthful of pancake. "I was born a hunter, and I'll die one. Sachi is the only person in the world who can make me eat a bunch of plants for dinner." He points his fork at me. "That family is the love of my life, Vaughn. Don't mess with them."

Suddenly, I'm sick to my stomach. I make the excuse that my appetite was diminished by my workout, and Marnie puts most of my stack in a to-go box.

Before Colton and I part in the parking lot, I ask him if he knows of good hiking trails nearby. This morning I'd felt almost euphoric until he popped my bubble, and I want to see if more nature can bring me back to where I was.

"I don't see you as the hiking type," Colton says.

"I hike all over the city. I don't even have a car."

"I meant in nature."

"First time for everything."

He shows me the location of a scenic trail on his phone. "Stay on the main path. Don't get lost out there and make us come looking for you."

"Would you?"

He studies me for a few seconds. "I guess I would. Riley is real excited to see you tomorrow." He gets in his car and pulls out.

Riley is real excited to see you. Colton's words alternately elevate and burden me throughout my hike. The trail winds past two lakes and through woods and fields. I take pictures of things I see along the way, intending to show them to Riley.

I go to bed unusually early. I've never known darkness and a soft bed to be comforting. The night restlessness started when I was a boy, when I dreaded my father bursting into my room. Because I left my shoes out or my bike in the driveway. To this day, I compulsively put things away for fear of repercussion. But often my father entered my room at night for no reason other than to spread his rage. He'd usually been drinking when he did that.

I don't know why I've been thinking about my father so much lately. He's typically as far from my thoughts as I can push him. To distract myself, I get up and open all windows despite the chill. I fall asleep to the sounds of loons, a hooting owl, and the lap of water on the dock and canoe. I wonder if that might be how it is for a child to fall asleep in a gentle mother's arms.

~

My stomach flutters with a peculiar combination of dread and anticipation when I leave for the farm. I don't know what I want to happen. When I left New York, I imagined I would tell Riley everything. But now that I'm here, I don't know if that's the right thing to do. She's recovering from a fractured skull and depression, even burst into tears when she first saw me. I have to wait for the right moment, give her more time to recover.

As I near the house, I see Kiran ahead and slow down. He's seated in a lawn chair next to the blossoming orchard. When he spots me, he looks at his wristwatch. I find this unsettling. I've never seen him conscious of actual clock time.

I stop and lean out the window. "Hi, Kiran. Is everything okay?"

"I'm the *official guide*," he says, probably using Riley's words.

"Okay. Where are we going?"

"To the picnic."

"Where's the picnic?"

"In the orchard. Park there," he says, pointing.

We walk into fragrant clouds of apple blossoms. He's barefoot, wearing a pale-green dress with a pattern of pink roses. I think he must like the feel of the loose fabric, because he occasionally stops walking and spins in a circle to let the dress swirl around him.

"I like your dress."

"Thank you. We got it at Save the Last Dance."

"Is that a vintage clothing store?"

"It's my *favorite* vintage store."

We're sprinkled with white confetti as we follow the grassy path between the blooming fruit trees. Kiran crosses into another row of trees.

"You know what?" he says to me as we walk.

"What?"

"I knew you would come back to Wisconsin to see Riley."

He knew before I did. I suppose Riley would say that's part of his magic.

Ahead Riley and Sachi are arranging dishes on a table. I expected a blanket. Riley smiles when she sees me, but I sense she's as nervous as I am.

The blue-and-white tablecloth looks vintage, as do the dishes and teapots overflowing with wildflowers. Each of four porcelain plates with a floral design is unique in size, shape, and pattern. Everything is strewn with petals, and the high-noon sun filters through arching branches. The tableau is dappled with the kind of dreamlike light I expect of this place. I can almost feel the magic of the farm trying to come back.

Especially when I look at Riley. She's barefoot, wearing a silky sky-blue-and-white dress that clings to her curves and plunges between her breasts.

"My excellent guide has delivered me out of the wilds into civilization," I announce.

"Good job, Kiran," Riley says.

"He was eleven minutes late," Kiran says.

"Forgive me."

"We'll let it slide this time," Sachi says. Smiling, she takes my hands and looks into my eyes. If anyone but Sachi did this, I would be put off. I don't know why I welcome her touch readily. "You're looking good," she says.

"I feel good. I've been sleeping well in the boathouse cabin. Last night I heard loons. And an owl."

She squeezes my hands and says, "Marvelous!"

She's also barefoot and wearing a high-tea kind of dress. Hers is longer than Riley's and Kiran's and made of fabric printed with soft green leaves against a buttery yellow background.

"I think I'm underdressed."

"You're perfect," Sachi says. "Riley, Kiran, and I like to have an excuse to wear our vintage dresses now and then. It's a ritual with our orchard picnics."

"You do this often?"

"At least once when the trees are blooming," Sachi says. "Also at harvesttime."

I'm relieved they didn't set out the orchard picnic just for my visit. Even so, I feel unworthy of its beauty.

"I'm really hungry," Kiran says to interrupt our small talk.

"Good. Let's eat," Sachi says. "Alec sends his greetings," she says as I take the chair across from Riley. "He's busy with his research and couldn't be here."

I wonder if he's avoiding me. He was cordial the day I arrived, but not as warm as he was during my February visit. He may blame me for Riley's fall, too.

"How was the doctor yesterday?" I ask Riley.

"Okay. Have some fruit salad."

I take the bowl and decide not to pry. I don't want to talk about the doctor either.

Lunch is simple, elegantly served from antique porcelain. Sweet-potato-and-black-bean enchiladas, fruit salad, and apple cake. Also, warm green tea and ice water flavored with slices of lime and watermelon. Everything is lightly sprinkled with apple blossom petals, and I'm instructed to eat and drink them as Gaia's seasoning to the dishes.

Sachi takes charge of the conversation. Not an easy task. She steers clear of Riley's troubles and my reasons for leaving—and returning. We talk about vegan food, then current political issues. When our foray into politics gets heavy, I ask Sachi what art she's working on. This is a mistake. She says she's been too busy to paint lately. I take *lately* to mean since Riley's accident. Everyone goes silent.

Before I killed the conversation, Riley had been animated, often looking into my eyes. Now she's silent, staring down at her plate.

I take out the three packets I constructed that morning. "I almost forgot. I brought everyone a gift."

"I told you not to bring anything," Riley says.

"Then you'll be glad to hear it isn't anything. This one is for you, Kiran."

He takes the lump of moss into his hand.

"The moss is like wrapping paper. You have to open it."

He unfolds the moss to reveal a small stone with a fossil in it.

"Do you know what kind it is?"

"It's some kind of coral." He looks at Sachi. "Can I go?"

"To look it up?"

He nods.

"Go ahead. But first maybe say something to Vaughn?"

"Thank you, Vaughn."

"You're very welcome."

He disappears into the rows of blooming trees.

"I found it in the parking lot at Blackberry Inn, and who knows where that gravel came from. It might be hard to identify."

"That makes it all the better," Sachi says. "Collectors love challenges."

I give Sachi her package, wrapped in leaves held together with a piece of vine.

"How beautiful!"

"The leaves have wilted."

"Softening leaves are a lovely expression of impermanence," she says. "And look at this! Impermanence indeed." She holds the bird skull in her palm.

"Crow?" Riley says.

"I think so. Where did you find it?" Sachi asks.

"During a hike yesterday. I thought you might want to add it into one of your paintings."

"I certainly will." She clasps my hand. "This is a very touching gift, Vaughn. Thank you."

I hold up a folded paper towel wrapped with vine. "This is an odd-looking moth I brought for Alec to identify. I found it dead on my doorstep the day before yesterday. I hope it didn't get too bashed up in my pocket."

"That won't matter," Riley says. "He can tell a species from a piece of wing." She leans over the table and looks at my pockets. "Don't I get anything?"

I take the rock out of my pocket and hold its cold angular shape in my fist. I'm not sure if I should give it to her. I'm afraid it's too sentimental—especially considering how I left her the morning after we kissed in the snowy road.

Sachi senses the tension and stands. "I'll go check on Kiran."

As she walks away, I hold my closed hand above the table. Riley hovers her flat palm beneath, and I drop the rock into it. My attempt to wrap it in birch bark failed, but I decide not to tell her that. "Do you see what I wrapped it in?"

"Yeah, I see it . . ." She slants her eyes at me, asking for a hint.

"Moonlight?"

"Obviously." She holds the stone up for inspection.

My stomach is as cold and hard as the rock. "Maybe you won't see what I do. I see an almost full moon in black sky and a snow-covered landscape below it. The black line is a country road."

She stares at the flat side of the rock. "I see it." She bows her head over it to view it closer. "The moon is perfect. Waxing, not quite full."

"Two days from being full."

She smiles because I remembered.

"I heard coyotes. Do you?"

She presses the rock lightly to her ear, as if listening for the sea in a shell. A breeze scatters white petals over her loose dark hair and azure dress. "I hear them."

"How many?"

"Two."

She looks into my eyes, and I see what she wants. But the span of the table with its landscape of porcelain feels like miles of rocky terrain between us. To cross over from this pure moment of white petals and dappled light is to enter the certainty of a polluted future with her. I can't accept her invitation.

She gives up, looks down at the rock in her hand.

"Do you like it?"

She looks at me again, and the strength of her gaze catches my breath. "Why did you come back?"

"Colton asked me that same question."

"Colton? When did you see him?"

"Yesterday morning. He came to Blackberry Inn to have breakfast with me—or to beat me to a pulp. I'm not certain what his original intention was."

"What did he say?"

"You can imagine. He takes being your big brother very seriously."

"I know. I bet he told you to leave me alone and go home."

"Something like that."

"Are you going to listen to him?"

I should. He warned me not to *mess* with his family, and if I follow through with what I came here to do, I'll create a mess of incalculable proportion. But I don't want to leave. Not now, not while I'm looking at Riley through drifts of apple blossom petals.

When I don't answer, she walks around the side of the table. She still has the rock in her hand, and I read determination in her eyes. For all I know she's come over to crack the rock on my head. I rise from my chair to meet whatever fate she wants to deliver.

"I'm not letting Colton come between us," she says. "He has no right to interfere."

"Doesn't he? He told me you fell and nearly died. He says it's my fault."

"I fell because I was trying to balance on a chair to tear down the moon seas. I fell because I was so desperate to get them out of my sight."

"Why, when they'd been on your walls for ten years?"

"Because I saw what they were."

196

"What were they?"

She considers for a few seconds. "They were like a cage that trapped me in the past, what you read about in my journal. And it was you who helped me see that."

"How did I do that?"

"I don't know. I guess what happened between us made me see there's a bigger world beyond my walls."

"Then it *was* my fault that you fell."

She shakes her head. "All you did was help me get out of the cage."

I try to wrap my mind around this. Had I actually done something good for her when I came here?

"And now that I'm out"—her gaze drops from my eyes to my mouth—"I want to feel the freedom. This is my life and my decision." She softly kisses my lips, then looks in my eyes to see my response.

What I perceive in hers is strength, certainty, passion. There's not a wisp of the fragility Colton sees in her. She looks about to devour me. And I want her to.

We press into a desperate embrace and kiss. I rake my hands into her thick, soft hair, and she throws her arms around me, the rock in her hand pressed hard into my back. We push closer, kissing yet more fiercely, and it's like the night she held my hand on the pier, that moment when I was engulfed in stars and lost all sense of myself and everything around me—except for the warmth of her skin on mine.

We pull apart as suddenly as we kissed. I'm dizzy, as if abruptly deprived of oxygen. Riley looks in the direction Sachi went, clearly worried she saw us. She then catches sight of the rock in her hand. We both look at it for a few seconds, as if to go back to where we were, that stable ground we stood on before the kiss.

"What do you think of it?" My voice sounds as shaky as I feel.

"It's strange how perfect the picture is," she says.

"I found it yesterday at a lake, but it was more like it found me. It stood out from all those thousands of rocks. It was like some kind of magic drew me to it."

She looks into my eyes. "The night you left, you said magic isn't real."

"I'm sorry I said that."

"Why? I know I'm just being weird when I imagine all that stuff."

So it's true. I killed the magic. Maybe that's why Kiran now follows clock time rather than the magic of his tables. And why Sachi isn't painting. Maybe this is why Alec avoids me. I turned his magical land into a common domicile of miserable people.

"It's not just you being weird. I never saw anything like the magic I found in this place. I think that's part of the reason I left. It scared me."

She grins. "Okay, imposter, what have you done with the cynical Vaughn I know?"

"I've imprisoned him in that rock. Until he learns to behave."

Her eyes light up. "I like that! And who's the imposter who kissed me?"

"I don't know. I came out of the rock."

"Maybe you were trapped in there until *you* learned to behave. You trade places with the next person who goes in. It's a curse that's been going on since the first humans came to North America."

"Maybe not North America. The rock could have been carried here from an African country, or somewhere in Asia or the Amazon."

"Maybe it's not from Earth," she says.

"You're right. I bet it isn't. It's ancient magic of the universe. Did you know you can even smell the snow?"

She lifts the rock and breathes in its mineral scent—as I did when I found it. "It does smell like snow!"

"Put it against your cheek. Feel the winter."

She presses the smooth side of the rock to her face. "Freezing!" She looks at the snowy night. "Poor Vaughn. He must be cold in there."

"He deserves to be cold."

"He's not such a bad guy, is he?"

The ultimate question. When will I answer it? Not now. Not when the magic is inching its way back.

"He was bad enough that the curse worked on him, right? We'll have to see how he is after his period of exile."

She pets her index finger over the snowy road in the rock. I can't seem to breathe for the few seconds she touches her lips to the rock, kissing Vaughn.

"Hey, you're making me jealous."

She kisses me. "I'm sorry, imposter."

That name won't do. Too real for this fantasy.

"You have to call me Vaughn. No one can know about the curse, or it will be broken."

"I don't want it to be broken." She seals our secret with another kiss.

23

RILEY

My first summer in Wisconsin, Alec took me into the woods one night. I didn't want to leave my room and the moon seas, but he encouraged me, in a kind but firm way, and wouldn't say why. I decided to go, but I remember how my heart thudded. I'd only ever been in the woods with Julia, in Chicago forest preserves, and never at night.

Alec and I walked in the dim light of his flashlight until we stopped at a place that was eerily bright. The distant bulb shone from behind a white sheet strung between two trees. I was scared and got ready to run. I supposed the sheet was there to wrap my corpse after Alec murdered me, and maybe the light was to see by when he cut my body into pieces.

Though I'd lived in his house for almost six months, I didn't know Alec because I spent most of my time in my room. He seemed a steady, soft-spoken man, but I supposed lots of killers appeared that way on the outside. When he and Sachi came to get me from Chicago, Alec explained that he was family, the son of a younger brother of my grandfather. But to me, he and Sachi were strangers. They were the ones who made me leave Julia's house. I wanted nothing to do with them, and I was certain they hadn't wanted anything to do with me. The police and family services people had forced them to take me.

Alec came toward me, but I countered with backward steps. He stopped and said, "Are you afraid of me? Please don't be."

I wanted to ask him what girl wouldn't be afraid of being taken into a dark forest and seeing that creepy glowing sheet. But I didn't ask, because I hadn't seen the point of talking—or of anything, really—since the day Nikki died and the police made me leave Julia's house. I spoke only to say something important, such as telling Sachi the flying-geese quilt must remain on my bed, and no, she may not wash it. I didn't tell her why, that it still smelled like Julia's house.

Alec tried once more to come near me, but I backed up again, trying to remember which way the house was. But I wasn't certain if that was where I should go if Alec attacked me. I thought of Nikki, her gunshot head haloed in blood. Julia's house was the trap that killed her. I'd overheard a policeman say she was almost out the back door when the burglar shot her.

Alec stood still and started talking. He reminded me that he was a biologist who studied moths. He explained that the sheet and mercury vapor light were one way lepidopterists attract nocturnal moths. He said most navigate in darkness by positioning themselves at a fixed angle relative to the moon and stars. They evolved that behavior long before humans came along with their fires and artificial lights. Our lights muddle their ability to orient themselves, and they end up whirling in confusion around the trap of light.

He went silent. I sensed he was deciding whether to say something. Cricket song filled the quiet. At last he said, "You remind me of a moth caught in a trap, Riley."

Now this was really something. I certainly felt like a moth trapped in a light. I'd been whirling and bashing against a sham afterglow of Julia's light for almost a year, since the August night she'd died.

"I don't know what the moon seas mean to you," Alec continued, "and I won't ask. I understand they somehow connect you to the life you lost, to your mother and aunt, and to the home and city you loved.

But the moon in your room isn't your loved ones or that home. The moon you drew on your walls is a false light that has you trapped. It's time you learn how to step away from it. Find the real light, Riley. Find the dependable light of your new home, and of the two people who love you."

The two people who love you. I doubted that. Why would they love me? I'd never given them any reason. I made sure of that. Though I knew it was an impossible dream, I hoped they might give up on me and let me go back to Julia's house.

"I'm going to show you something," he said. "Come over to the light."

I followed him, hanging back enough to escape. When we neared the brightly lit sheet, I saw the moths that covered its glowing surface. I thought of Julia, and how she would love this strange spectacle.

"We have two," Alec said. "This is always a good spot for them."

On the sheet were moths and other insects that ranged from teeny to large, but the two huge green ones entranced me.

Alec pointed at one. "Do you know what this is?"

"A luna moth," I said.

"Right. Come look. Don't mind the other insects. They won't hurt you."

The insects fluttered and landed all over both of us, but I'd never been squeamish about insects. Julia and I had looked for them in her yard or on nature walks, identifying them with insect books.

Alec somehow got one of the luna moths onto his finger and gently transferred it to mine. Julia was always impressed with people who had kinship with animals. She would have said he was a "moth whisperer." I enjoyed that thought, and the surprising feel of the winged creature on my index finger.

"*Actias luna,*" Alec said. "It's named *luna* for the moonlike eye spots on its hind wings. Its family name, *Saturniidae,* is a reference to the planet Saturn. Do you see why: the concentric rings around the spots?"

I saw it. Moon and Saturn right there on my hand. The wings were a luminous bluish green, the lower ones extended by long, slightly twisted tails. The four white eyes were hypnotic, ringed with crescents of white, blue, yellow, pink, and black. The moth's chubby, pale body covered in fur made it look like a baby white mouse, and the legs attached to my finger were as pink as Julia's favorite garden rose. The antennae were beautiful, like tawny fern fronds.

"That's a male," he said. "Both of these are. Do you know how you can tell?"

"How?"

"Males have bigger, bushier antennae than females. They use them to track the pheromones released by females. You've heard of pheromones?"

"Yes."

"Luna moths have been one of my favorite animals since I was a boy running around these woods. I would even say they're the reason I got interested in the study of moths."

"You lived here when you were little?" I asked.

"I often wished I did. I lived with my parents in Chicago but visited my grandmother on her farm whenever I could. I spent most of my school vacations up here. I made friends and knew all the neighbors, and later held jobs and even had girlfriends in this place. It was difficult to leave every time my vacation ended—like losing the half of my life I loved the most."

I looked at him, the first time I'd made real eye contact. I realized how very like Julia's his eyes were, the same shape, and the irises colored with a similar mix of green and brown. But the more important similarity was their depth of kindness. Perhaps their eyes and gentleness were a family trait they shared with Julia's beloved father, the man who connected Alec to me, the one relative other than Julia I knew to be a good person.

I had family. Real family. Bringing me into this forest to see a moth was so like Julia. I felt as if she were speaking to me through Alec's soft eyes, and I saw without a doubt that I could trust him.

"While his wings are open, do you see how they look like two elephants facing each other?"

I saw it, two darling pachyderms touching trunks, the moth's upper wings forming their ears and the long tails their trunks. I wished Julia were there to see it. It was the kind of imaginative game she'd loved. She was always seeing faces in tree bark and clouds.

"Shall we look at some of the other moths we've lured before we turn the light off?" he asked.

There were hundreds, big and small. They clung to the white sheet, flitted over my arms and cheeks, crawled in my hair. I had to gently brush one off my lips before I spoke. "Do you know them all?"

"Moth nerd that I am, I do."

I smiled, maybe my first since Julia died.

That night I felt the magic of Alec and Sachi's farm for the first time. Like Vaughn, I was frightened by it, but I didn't have to run away from the powerful sway it had on my soul, because I was used to that feeling from Julia. And though I was afraid to let someone else's magic in, I was also entranced by the wonders the farm had to offer me.

After Kiran was born, I let go of my remaining fears and embraced my new family and home. That was when I started helping Alec with his research. I can identify most moth species found in Wisconsin. I love the ones with weird or poetic names: joker, implicit arches moth, blinded sphinx, venerable dart, bold medicine moth.

Alec taught me the secret language of moth scientists, words like *instar*, *imago*, and *crepuscular*, and Latin nomenclature every bit as enchanting as the moon sea names. *Autographa precationis*, the common looper. *Manduca quinquemaculata*, the five-spotted hawk moth.

Moths aren't the drab creatures many people think they are. Some are colored vivid emerald, scarlet, blue, or gold; others are lacy, furry, or shimmery, or display wing patterns that look like modern-art paintings. Some flash astonishing hidden "eyes" at predators; others make clicking sounds to confuse bats. But of all the moths, *Actias luna*, the moth that helped me learn how to trust again, will always be my favorite.

A few years ago, when we were talking next to a campfire, Alec told me the truth about why he brought me to see a luna moth that night. He and Sachi had concluded that my spirit was too distant for them to reach. Almost a half year had passed since I'd come to live with them, and I hadn't shown interest in anything but my moon seas. Surprisingly, it was Alec's idea, not Sachi's, to introduce me to an animal that might guide my spirit back to Earth. Peoples of Earth had connected with animals as spirit guides since humans themselves felt part of the animal world, Alec said. And what better bridge between the moon where my spirit lived and the earth where my body lived than the ethereal, winged luna?

I know everything about my spirit guide: how to identify its eggs, the host plants the caterpillar eats, and the way the pupa wriggles vigorously inside its silk cocoon. The last stage of its life cycle, the moth, is called an *imago*. A luna imago lives for less than a week on the nutrition it stored as a caterpillar. It has no mouth or digestive system. It can't eat.

This bothered me when Alec told me. I saw it as a cruel trick evolution had played on the luna, to let it eat voraciously when it was a caterpillar and take away that pleasure when it became the creature that shared its name with a moon goddess. Why not let the goddess eat and live a longer life?

Alec said a luna's life, from egg to caterpillar to pupa to moth, has one goal: to find a mate and pass on its genetic material. It has no need for a digestive system because it achieves this purpose in just one week, then dies. I asked Alec if he thought the luna remembered eating and missed it, and he replied, "Let's hope not."

I never came to terms with the idea that a luna moth is trapped in a body without a mouth. Until today. Finally, I understand the luna imago's ephemeral life. It isn't torment. It's ecstasy. This anticipation, this heavenly cloud of pheromones growing stronger and closer.

Twilight arrives at last. As the sun disappears into the trees, Vaughn takes my hand and squeezes it. Seated next to us on the porch, Alec and Sachi don't notice as they kiss. Vaughn and I are near bursting to do the same. At least I am. We haven't been alone once since we kissed in the orchard, and we've hardly touched all day.

"Want to take a walk and watch the moon rise?" I ask Vaughn.

"I'd love to," he says.

Kiran stands, assuming he's coming with us.

Sachi knows we want to be alone. "I was going to dish up the sorbet we made," she tells him. "Are you going to help?"

"Yes!" he says.

"Will you have some before your walk?" Sachi asks Vaughn and me.

"Maybe later. If you're okay with that," I say to Vaughn.

"Later sounds good. But don't eat it all, Kiran."

"I won't," Kiran says. "It's blueberry. I made it."

"Then I definitely have to try it." As we leave the porch, Vaughn asks, "Where to?"

"The hill in the south field has a good view of the rising moon."

He keeps his hand on mine as we walk. We don't talk. I can't say why he's silent, but I know why I am. I'm afraid to disturb the precise balance of the universe right now. I sense this equilibrium between Vaughn and me is precarious, hovering between now and what will be.

Even where we walk is a fine line, the exact boundary between spring and summer. I'm aware of petals raining down from the orchard trees, as if I can hear them fall from this distance. Microscopic apples are already growing in the ovaries of the pollinated flowers. I refuse to imagine what will have become of Vaughn and me when those apples are big and sweet.

The low hill in the south field is one of my favorite places on the farm. It overlooks the soft swells of the meadow and the surrounding forest. On its crest is a large lone oak that used to provide shade for the cows and horses. The tree is a favorite summer reading spot for my family, and Sachi likes to paint portraits on the hill.

Sachi painted the nude of me on this hill last May. Taking off my clothes was unusual for me, a reaction to the warm sun, fragrant grass, and billowing clouds. I wanted to feel the springtide on every inch of my skin, absorb its freshness into my very bones.

More than that, I wanted Sachi to document my youth before it was gone. After I turned twenty, I started to feel trapped in my life on the farm, like a moth that couldn't escape the cocoon it had spun around itself. I was afraid my body had bloomed for no reason. I still lived at home, and I'd never even been on a date. I'd met friendly guys at college, but I hadn't felt attracted to any of them, same as what happened with Colton. As if the pheromones were all wrong. I felt like an oddity that couldn't find another of its kind.

Until Vaughn. A creature as anomalous as me. I believe he is. I scented our likeness almost from the moment I met him.

We ascend the gentle slope of the hill in the final shades of dusk. Crepuscular light, the precise balance between day and night. This is when hummingbird moths feed on flower nectar. Evolution let them keep their mouth.

I celebrate the human mouth, kissing Vaughn as we reach the hill's apex. He pulls me in and hungrily receives my lips. We lie down on the hill. He presses over me, and my skin shivers as his lips drift from my mouth to my neck to the cleft between my breasts. He stops there and looks down at me. "Riley . . . I—"

He rolls off me and sits up. In the last light of dusk, I see him push his fingers through his hair. I can't believe it's happening again. He's gone cold like he did that night he left.

"Before this goes any further, we should talk," he says.

I had a feeling this was why he'd been quiet. He's going to ruin it. He thinks he has to confess things I don't want to know. And if he does, I'll be expected to confess what he doesn't want to know about me. I want nothing to do with a clean soul. If I wanted that, I'd be with Colton.

I push closer and stroke my hand on his chest. "Had I given you the impression I wanted to talk?"

"No. But I—"

"I don't need to know any more about you than I do."

This clearly surprises him. "You don't know anything about me."

"I know, because you're the guy who came out of the rock." I kiss him. "It's kind of a turn-on to be with a mysterious guy who was cursed because he did something bad."

"Don't you care about the bad thing he did?"

"Why should I when he's atoned for his sins?"

"Has he?"

"Obviously he has if he was released from the curse." I kiss him again. "I could see how different you are when you brought those nature gifts. Vaughn would never have done that. He brought expensive wine and a clock for Kiran that was a trick to get in my room."

"What a jerk."

"He was," I say against his lips.

He kisses back. Soon we're lying down again, but this time I'm on top. I have no doubts about where we're heading. And only in the very best of my fantasies did it happen like this, on my beloved grassy hill beneath the stars.

"We're being watched," Vaughn says.

"What?" I peer around, afraid Alec, Sachi, or Kiran is coming.

"I meant the man in the moon," he says.

I sit up and look at the rising moon, edging over the treetops. He's using the moon, *my* moon, to rein us in. He's using the journal, that sharp little piece of my soul, like a weapon against me. This is the problem with letting people in; you give them everything they need to manipulate you. Nikki was a master at that.

But I can't be too angry with Vaughn. I know he wants what I want. I feel it as plainly as the grass prickling my bare legs. He's just afraid I'll have regrets. He doesn't understand how much I've examined my feelings for him. He doesn't know I left him on Saturday to make myself wait—and I thought of nothing but him during my trip. He doesn't know how relieved I was when I called Marnie late Sunday and she told me he was still at the inn. And how could he ever guess that I stayed up half that night contemplating whether I'd sleep with him if today's reunion went well?

It couldn't have gone better. I already knew I'd let myself have him when he brought out his gifts. Fossil, skull, moth, rock. I recognized him as my kind with certainty. He and I have to be, even if just for a few hours. Why else did he come back?

He sits up and contemplates the moon with me. "I see the face clearly tonight. I suppose you see only the seas."

Yes, he's speaking to me in subtext.

"I mostly see the seas, but I can see the face and other shapes."

"What other shapes?"

"In some Asian countries, people see a rabbit. Other cultures see a person carrying sticks, a woman, a toad, a dragon, and other things."

"Did Julia tell you about that?"

"Yes, she knew all the moon stories."

"I guess that isn't surprising if she was a librarian."

"She'd have been like that no matter what she did. She was a curious, clever person—what I'd call an intellectual."

"You said in the journal her car was wrecked. Is that how she died?"

I look up at the dark hollow of the Sea of Clouds. "Yes."

"She was never married?"

"She was with her soul mate for six years. When she was thirty-three, about a month before they were going to marry, he died in an accident at work. He was a construction engineer."

"Sad."

"It devastated her. She couldn't even stay in Chicago."

"Where did she go?"

"New York City. She took a librarian job at Columbia."

"Prestigious. I'm surprised she came back to Chicago."

"She came back because her dad was sick and needed help. She took care of him in his house until he died. It was a few months after he died that Nikki and I went to see her. Nikki wanted the money for her half of the house, but Julia refused to sell."

"What did Nikki do for a living?"

"Nothing, really. Unless extortion counts."

"Extortion?"

"When she realized how attached Julia and I were, she started threatening to leave and take me with her. Julia couldn't bear the thought of me going back to Nikki's unstable druggie life, so she let her sister sponge off her to keep me safe."

"Julia bought her drugs?"

"She gave her a monthly allowance, knowing some of it went to drugs and alcohol. But she set as many limits as she could. Keeping Nikki in line was a constant battle for her."

"And you were stuck in the middle of all that."

"Yes, but it was far better than my life before we went to Julia's."

I've never talked about these things. Not to Sachi, Alec, or Colton, three people I trust without question. And here I am telling this man who's not yet proved himself trustworthy. But he came back, even after he read the journal.

I kiss him, letting him feel how much I want him. I sense his surprise. He didn't expect renewed passion after our solemn discussion. But he gives in to it.

I pull down one shoulder of his flannel shirt.

"Riley . . . what are we doing?"

I slide the other arm down and take off his outer shirt. I lift the bottom of his T-shirt up his chest.

"Riley . . . ," he protests weakly but lets me remove the shirt.

I sit back and stare at his chest and arms. "What have you been doing to get so strong?"

"Breaking rocks on a chain gang."

I look into his eyes. "Penance?"

He smiles, but in a forlorn way. "I guess it was self-punishment. I've been beating myself up at the gym every day."

His chest and arms, his cheeks and jaw—all of him is sculpted in lunar light. His eyes look like they did the night we kissed in the snowy road, his gray irises almost transparent in the pure light. Even his dark hair has changed, silvered like the moonlit flow of a black river. He's as perfect as anything I could imagine.

I've been too distracted to pay much attention to his necklace. The only jewelry I've seen on him is the expensive watch he always wears. I lean closer to better see the pendant in the moonlight. It's a key, the old kind I see in antique stores. Sachi has always liked them. Sometimes Kiran and I bring her an especially pretty one we find.

Vaughn watches me study the key. I sense his mood change since I started looking at it, as if he's waiting to hear what I'll say about it. I wonder why he's wearing the old key, what it means to him. I take it in my fingers. The outer side is cool; the side that was touching his body is warm. Like Vaughn: one minute passionate, the next cold.

"Why are you wearing an antique key?"

When he doesn't answer, I look into his eyes. Even in darkness, I can see there's something complicated there.

"I'm not sure why I'm wearing it," he says at last.

"Where did you get it?"

"It belonged to my mother."

Now I understand. He said his mother overdosed when he was only fifteen months old. He has no memories of her. I rub my thumb over the key's bit, the teeth at the end. "What does it open?"

"I don't know."

I rest the key in the cleft between the contours of his pecs. "It's beautiful."

He smiles and caresses my cheek. I love the roughness of his hand. Maybe that's from lifting weights, too.

I run my hands over his chest. "I want you to undress me."

He searches my eyes, unable or unwilling to speak.

"Then I will." I take off the denim shirt I had over my dress. Then I untie my hiking boots, which he called the *pièce de résistance* of my high-tea fashion.

"We can't," he says. "I don't have . . . protection."

"I've got that covered."

He looks surprised. "You do?"

"Of course." I reach for the button on his jeans.

"You've never done it," he says.

"What kind of an argument is that? Should nestling birds not fly because they've never done it?" I unzip his jeans but can't remove them without his help.

He keeps his butt firmly planted on the ground.

"Are you always so difficult to bed, or only with me?"

"Only with you."

"I want to take that as a compliment."

"You should."

I tug the top of his pants. "Come on, lift up. This is too much like undressing a stubborn two-year-old, and that's not exactly a turn-on."

"Give me one good reason why we would do this."

I contemplate the good reasons: Because we both want to. Because he's beautiful. Because there's us and this grassy hill and the rising moon.

Then there's the matter of the clock bells. They've finally found their place in the universe. Kiran made the two half spheres into an orb and put them on his biggest table next to one of his favorite fossils. I'd been bitter about the magic since the night I fell, but when I saw how perfect that shiny little moon looked in its galaxy, I felt as if something important had happened. Something good.

That was Friday morning.

"When did you fly into Chicago?" I ask.

"Friday night." He seems puzzled by the topic change. "Why do you ask?"

"When did you read my journal?"

"It arrived Friday afternoon."

"So you read the journal and got on a plane right after?"

"Of course I got on a plane when you said you had a skull fracture. I was worried about you."

"Is that the only reason you came back?"

"I don't think so . . . no."

"What other reason was there?"

"It's complicated."

"It didn't feel complicated when we kissed in the orchard."

He smiles. "I know."

"Then let's find our way back to uncomplicated. Did you come here because you feel attracted to me?"

"I think that's obvious."

"How did the journal push you to act on those feelings?"

"I feel like I'm in therapy."

"You are. Answer the question."

He considers what to say. "The journal made me feel connected to you. Maybe . . . I think because of what I'd been through with my father."

I take his cold hand in mine.

"That's not a good kind of connection, Riley. It's sad and dark. I think I shouldn't have come back. I have things to say that will . . ."

He gets up and stares at the moon.

I stand and go to him. "What?"

He still won't say. But I think I know how the sentence ends.

"You have things to say that will probably break us apart?"

"Yes."

I understand. I battle it, too, this constant urge to sabotage good feelings because I don't think I deserve them. His father made him fear happiness same as Nikki did to me. As he said, this is not a good kind of connection. I think that's why we're drawn to each other: we feel more comfortable in darkness than in the light. But isn't the night sky as beautiful as the one we see in daylight? Doesn't he see how perfectly matched we are?

I look at the moon with him. At Julia's Sea of Clouds. "Have you ever heard of *Endymion?*"

"He was a shepherd, the mortal lover of the moon goddess Selene."

"Right, but I meant the poem."

He looks at me strangely. "John Keats wrote it."

"Julia liked the opening of that poem, especially a long line that begins, *Therefore, on every morrow, are we wreathing a flowery band to bind us to earth—*"

"I know the line," he says. "It ends, *Yes, in spite of all, some shape of beauty moves away the pall from our dark spirits.*"

I can't believe he knows it by heart. That's Julia's favorite part, the words I wrote on the box containing her ashes.

I think he has tears in his eyes. Or is it a trick of the moonlight?

I hold his hand. "Keats explains it better than I can. Why focus on what's sad and dark when you have all this beauty around you? Julia showed me how to do that. And today you did."

"What did I do?"

"You know what. You felt it when we kissed in the orchard. It felt like a miracle, didn't it? Together we had the power to wipe away everything that was sad and dark."

"But for how long?"

"Stop thinking that way. What's happening with us really is like some kind of magic, and you said you believe in magic."

He caresses my cheek in a sad way that makes my chest hurt. "If only I felt I deserved your magic."

"You do. Let me show you." I kiss him, relieved when he holds me tight. His warmth returns. I whisper in his ear, "Undress me, Endymion."

"I dare not say no to a goddess."

"You dare not."

He lifts my dress over my head and lays it in the grass. Even in moonlight I can see how his eyes change when he looks at me, as if my desire reflects in his gaze.

He wraps his arms around me, the open zipper of his pants cold against my belly. "You're so beautiful, Riley. You nearly stop my heart."

I know the feeling.

He kisses my neck beneath my ear and whispers, "Are you sure?"

"I'm sure. Get that cold zipper off me."

"I don't think a zipper ever came between Selene and Endymion."

"Exactly." I unclasp my bra and slip off my panties. I stand before him like the gift he gave me today, wrapped in nothing but moonlight.

His eyes have the beautiful hunger again. "My god, you *are* Selene."

"I promise I won't let Zeus put you into eternal sleep. I want you fully awake."

He doesn't take his gaze off me as he slides off his jeans and undershorts. "You don't have to worry about me falling asleep." He pulls me into his arms. "But why do I always feel like I'm in a dream when I'm with you?"

"All that matters is that the dream is good." I pull him down to the grass, still warm from the heat of the sun.

24

VAUGHN

I'm worse than I ever knew. I've made love to her. Every day for a week. And still I haven't told her the truth.

And since the night we talked on the hill, I know the truth will be harder for her than I thought. That conversation was shocking, life-changing—for both of us. I think that's part of the reason I kept silent. How could I be honest with her when I discovered my version of the truth was wrong only minutes before we made love?

But what about the next morning? I should have told her then. But again, I couldn't. What is this curse she silences me with? As if she's truly Selene, who put me into slumber so she could enjoy me as her subdued mortal for eternity.

I shift the Porsche into high gear, and hit ninety on an open stretch of one-lane country road. Riley laughs and leans her head out the window, her hair whipped wildly around her face. "This day is so beautiful!" she shouts into the airstream.

She certainly is. I shift down for a curve—and up again on another straight stretch. I climb a hill fast, slowing down in just enough time to see if there's a car ahead.

She pulls her head back in. "You're going to get a ticket. The cops around here love to take down guys like you."

"What kind of guy am I?"

"A big-city rich boy who likes to show off in his fancy car."

"I can't help it. These roads are too fun."

"I don't think the sheriff will let you off because the roads made you do it."

"The car does. Do you want to see? Do you know manual?"

"Alec taught me on that old truck of his grandmother's in the shed."

"Do you want to drive the rest of the way home?"

"No."

"I'll help you."

"It's not that. I'm just not turned on by a car. I'd rather watch you play with your joystick."

I look at her. "Meaning, I'm turned on by it or you are?"

"Both. That's the point of this kind of car, isn't it?"

"That's the usual cliché, along with a midlife crisis, which I can also claim as an excuse for enjoying it."

"Twenty-nine isn't a midlife crisis."

"It is when you're with a hot twenty-one-year-old."

"Your thirtieth birthday is still four months away."

"How do you know my birthday?"

"Wikipedia."

"Damn, a person can't hide anything these days."

We glance at each other, and I wonder if she's thinking what I am. Not once since we became lovers has she asked me about the Riley in the book dedications. I find it as perplexing as it is a relief.

"Late September is a nice time to have a birthday," she says. "The colors are nice up here at that time."

This is a first. My birthday is the only future date that's been mentioned. *Future* is the F-word. Not to be spoken, or even imagined. I guess we both know remaining in the present is how we stay in the dream.

Yet I see Riley and me on a driving tour to view fall foliage. We joke about the conventionality of our trip: rooms in quaint bed-and-breakfasts, photographs on covered bridges, hot cider in apple orchards, picnics in piles of fallen leaves. My thirtieth is the best birthday of my life.

But what happens a week after our trip? A month after? I know the day will come when she'll ask about the other Riley. If I tell her, the dream will burst apart. If I don't tell her, the dream will end in a slower, more tortured way. She'll keep asking about the book dedications, and I'll forbid her to mention it again. But that will only increase her curiosity. She'll read all my books. Then will come the questions, tunneling deeper and deeper into the dirt of my past.

It's been the same pattern with every woman since I became a published author. And so it will be with Riley. I'll have to leave her, too.

My mind returns to the present. I have no idea where I am, not good when I'm driving eighty on a narrow rural road. I gear down for an intersection ahead.

I look at Riley. She's been watching me. She saw how distant I became but doesn't ask what I was thinking, as most of my past girlfriends would. She knows how it is to leave the present, and even Earth, for a while.

I take my hand off the gearshift to caress her thigh. To reassure her. Though I have no right to.

This is my life now. There are two of me. Miserable, guilt-ridden Vaughn trapped in the frozen night of the stone, and the Vaughn imposter who lives out here, enjoying balmy spring days with Riley. Every time I touch her, I know the cold Vaughn feels, the pain of wanting to be the one who touches her warmth but can't.

I turn the car onto the curves of Riley's wooded driveway. Already the trees are greener than a week ago, and the apple trees have lost most of their petals. I want to ask Kiran to slow down time for Riley and me, hold back the clock gears a little longer before we fall apart. Before I have to let Vaughn out of the stone.

Sachi comes outside to help us carry in the groceries. "This car must be expensive to rent for so long," she says.

"It will be. I got a good deal on it, but they've told me I can't extend the rental at the same rate. I didn't know I'd be staying for so long."

"Can you exchange it for something cheaper?"

"I'd have to go back to Chicago."

"No worries," Riley says to Sachi. "Vaughn has money to burn. Look what he bought." She holds up the bottle of scotch I found at a liquor store. "Two hundred fifty dollars."

"For a bottle of whiskey?"

"For twenty-one-year-old, single-malt Scottish whiskey that's finished in rum barrels." I take the bottle out of Riley's hand. "It's a gift for Alec."

I discovered he likes scotch, and I suppose I'm trying to improve his opinion of me. He's still not as friendly as he was in February, though he's been forced to treat me more amicably since Riley and I got together. I'm aware that trying to sweeten his opinion of me with an expensive gift is foolish, especially when he isn't the kind of man who can be influenced by money.

After the groceries are put away, Riley and I do our chores in the big organic garden behind the house. I cultivate rows of vegetables while she plants marigolds. The pungent flowers are used as natural insect repellant in the garden, and the family uses the flowers in recipes.

Riley walks over and tucks a marigold behind each of my ears. I drop the hoe, probably crushing some of the baby plants. I take the remaining flower from her hand and push it deep into her cleavage. "You said it's edible, didn't you?" I put my mouth between her breasts and eat the flower. Its spicy flavor excites me, and I press my mouth to her skin.

She sighs, leaning into me. "If only the sweet corn was tall enough to hide us from the windows."

"If only."

"Future goals."

I wish I could fully believe it will happen. Riley and me making love in a sweet-corn field on a hot August day. More and more, I want to believe in that future.

But right now we're too exposed in the garden. We return to the house to help Sachi and Kiran make dinner. This has become a ritual. At first, I felt awkward, but now I look forward to cooking with the family. Sachi and Riley teach me how to prepare their favorite dishes, and Kiran chatters about fossils and dinosaurs and how to use a whisk the right way.

As I sauté or chop, Sachi often wraps her arm around me and chats. It's just how she is. I'm as nourished by her as I am by the food we make.

Alec arrives when the meal is nearly ready. He doesn't plop onto the couch and let his wife and kids cook for him. He always takes up a task without asking what needs to be done. I never knew a family could be anything but angry, indifferent, or spiteful. Those were the attitudes of all the families I visited growing up. I seemed to choose friends and girlfriends who came from families like mine.

But I didn't have a family. I didn't even have a place I would call *home*. For me, home was a rock upon which I was chained, and my family—my father—was the eagle that tore out my liver every day. From the moment I read that story in high school, I felt a kinship with Prometheus. Our freshman English teacher told us the liver was understood to be the source of human emotion in ancient Greece, which meant the eagle was tearing out what we now refer to as the heart or soul of a person.

When your heart is torn out daily year after year, you learn how to stop feeling pain. In fact, you come to enjoy the pain in a perverse sort of way. It's all you know of love. It *is* love, you begin to believe. And when you're finally unchained from the rock, you continue to need that feeling. You have to batter yourself, rip your own heart out.

I give Alec the bottle of scotch before we eat. I'm relieved no one mentions how much it cost. Alec thanks me, genuinely, patting me on the shoulder. He pours small amounts over ice into four glasses. Kiran wants some until Alec lets him sip from his glass. He winces and says, "I hate whiskey."

Laughing, we tap glasses for Alec's toast: "To the warmth of whiskey and love."

I imagine the heat of whiskey spreading through my body is real love. This family's. Riley's. Why can't it be? I want to stop ripping my heart out every day. All I have to do is tell Riley. I think she's the kind of person who would forgive me.

Inside the stone, Vaughn sits in the middle of the snowy road and laughs at his imposter's naivete. Recently his bitterness is really getting on my nerves. But I know why he's like that. He's cold and hungry and trapped.

After dinner cleanup, Riley asks if I'd like to take a walk. I've learned this is code for "I want to make love." I think Sachi and Alec know this, too, because I catch them exchanging grins.

Outside everything is burnished coppery red by the last light of the sun. "Let's stay out until the moon rises," Riley says.

We quickly put house and barn behind us. Daylight wanes as we cross a small field and copse of birch trees. On the other side of the trees is the field with the hill.

I've never cared about any piece of earth as I do for this hill. Its low, oblong rise out of the surrounding field is unexpected. Riley says it's a natural formation, though it looks like something out of a fairy tale, perhaps the burial mound of a giant. And the inviting tree on the hill's crest is the best part of its magic.

Tonight the hill is backlit with cloudy streaks of pink and orange overlaid on violet. Above the tree, a few bright stars already glitter. A party of chimney swifts swoops and circles as we climb to the hilltop. Their twittering calls sound jubilant, as if they've come to welcome us.

We lie down in the patch of grass where we made love a week ago, just beyond the reach of the old oak's branches. There is no Vaughn. No curse, no stone. There is only us and this patch of grassy earth.

The first notes of the melody weave into our lovemaking as naturally as the surrounding cricket song. Riley turns her head toward the music, smiling. I recognize the song Alec is playing: "Hallelujah."

"Is this really happening?"

"It is. He's playing one of my favorite songs."

The trumpet music makes the summit of our passion feel almost too blissful to be real. But I know it is. That's the magic of this place.

The last notes of the trumpet fade into insect song. Riley and I hold each other.

After a few minutes, Alec begins a classical piece. "Sachi told him to play that," Riley says. "It's her favorite."

The moment is exquisite. Tears wet my eyes, like that first night I was enveloped in stars on the dock.

She touches her lips to mine. "You're very quiet. What are you thinking?"

She's not once asked me that. I usually shut down when women ask me that question.

Alec's trumpet pauses between phrases in the melody. The silence is heartbreaking, as if all the universe is waiting for more. Then the next note comes, prolonged, high, and sweet.

She asked what I'm thinking, and for once I want to answer. "I was thinking about you and your family."

"What about us?"

"How beautiful it is to be with you on this hill and listen to Alec play." I prop on my elbow and caress her face. "Sometimes I feel like I'm really in a dream created by a goddess."

The silence that follows is like the heartbreaking pause in the trumpet music. Except we don't move on to the next sweet high note. Most couples talk about their future at this stage. Or at least hint at it. She's the first woman I've known who wants to stay in the pause with me.

The trumpet song ends. "Will he play more?" I ask.

"Probably. He's resting. Playing a trumpet is a workout."

We nestle close, waiting for another song. She smells of grass and earth. Of moon seas. I swear I smell stars in her hair.

The trumpet begins again. Riley sits up. "Not that one. Not now . . ."

"What's wrong?"

"Nothing," she says, but I think she's crying.

I find her shirt in our pile of clothes and pull it onto her. I put on mine and hold her against my chest. I recognize the song. It's "Strawberry Fields Forever."

She pulls out of my arms and wipes her hands over her face. "I'm okay."

"It has to do with Julia?" I know it can't be anything else.

"Yes. She loved this song."

"Does Alec know?"

"He wouldn't play it if he knew it hurt me. It's just a song he plays now and then." The stars are bright enough that I can see her lift the bottom of her shirt and wipe her running nose. "Julia liked the Beatles. She had all their albums. They were her dad's."

I think of my friend Kaz. He's flipping through crates full of albums. The Beatles, the Rolling Stones, the Who. *These are original. I think they might be worth something.*

"We had her dad's old turntable," Riley says. "He loved rock and roll. My grandfather was a cool guy. I never met him, but Julia told me everything about him."

How do I fix this? Is it possible? I think it's more repairable than I understood all those years. Because I didn't truly know anything about Riley Mays. Or about Julia.

The final notes of "Strawberry Fields Forever" fade into the night.

Riley says, "I don't know why, but I miss Julia's house more than usual lately. I wish I could see it again. Even if it's different now, I just want to see it. The last time I was there was the day Nikki died. Alec picked me up from the family services people and brought me here. I never had a chance to say goodbye . . . but I guess I was in no shape."

Has she answered my question? I look toward the house. I want to study Kiran's gears and fossils. Maybe they'll help me see what will happen if I follow through with this idea.

Riley sees me looking away. I think she assumes I'm indifferent, because she puts her hand on my thigh to get my attention. "I'm sorry I'm blathering."

"You aren't. Don't apologize." If I say the next words, I have to let Vaughn out of the stone. Except he isn't Vaughn. His name is Tyler Webb.

"What if . . . ?"

This time the pause feels ominous, like the silence that precedes disastrous weather.

"What?" she asks.

"What if we went to Chicago to see Julia's house?"

She doesn't answer. Did she feel every cog and wheel on Kiran's tables shift when I said that? Is she as terrified as I am?

"I should go to Chicago to get a cheaper car if I'm going to stay longer."

"I didn't think you cared about the cost."

"Whether I do or not, they want their car back. I told them a week."

Another long pause. This time I welcome it. I don't think she likes the idea.

"If you don't want to, that's okay."

"I want to," she says.

"You probably can only see the house from the outside."

"I know. But I still want to see it."

"Are you sure?"

"Yes."

Getting away from her family and farm—from all this overpowering magic—might be the only way I can talk honestly with her. And if I predictably back out, we'll just make a fun trip of it.

A nice hotel. Maybe she'd like the Drake, a more vintage atmosphere than the usual luxury hotel. Great restaurants. But I'll have to research where we can get vegan dishes. We'll walk on the lakefront and go to the Field Museum. She'd like the Art Institute, too.

I remember my agent mentioning an art gallery.

"There's another reason I have to go to Chicago. My agent wants me to do a book event for a friend of hers."

"What happens at a book event?"

"What happened at the Blind Wolf. Except without beer and music."

She laughs. "Could you bear that?"

"Only if you were there to help me."

"I see. You're going to spill a drink on me to make a quick exit."

"If you agree to go, I promise we'll exit in a distinguished manner."

"Can you get it organized that fast?"

"I'm not organizing it. And I'd rather my agent and her friend have little time to plan. I'd prefer to keep it small."

"That's Vaughn talking. Will you let him out of the stone to sign the books, or will you forge his signature?"

How did she know to ask that?

"I guess I'll have to forge it. Do you want to go?"

"I do. I want to see you trying hard to pretend you're Vaughn Orr."

Sometimes the magic of this farm is too much.

"You know what you are?"

"What?" she asks.

"A conniving goddess who likes to see a mortal squirm."

"I'm glad you finally get our relationship, Endymion." She strips the T-shirt off me. "Why did you put this on? We have hours to go until the moon rises."

25

RILEY

Ten years and five months since I left Chicago. I'm not sure about the number of days because I don't know the date I arrived at Alec and Sachi's. I was mostly living on the moon at the time.

When Vaughn programmed my Chicago address into the car's navigation system, I became aware of how sequestered my life with Alec and Sachi has been. As if I've truly been on the moon, and now I'm in a spaceship returning to Earth. The world has changed since I left it, but I feel like I haven't. I thought my relationship with Vaughn matured me, but here I am in this little rocket, hurtling toward my beloved home, and I'm still a wounded eleven-year-old who lost everything.

I don't know why I'm doing this. What animal returns to the scene of its greatest hurt? Even more evidence of my maladaptive DNA.

I think Alec and Sachi are worried. They didn't tell me not to go, but Alec reminded me, in his soft-spoken way, that I'm still recovering from the fall. He said this might not be the best time to revisit old wounds. I told him I felt great and I was ready, that the trip was mostly to have fun in the city.

I have felt great. Of course. I'm immersed in a dizzying cloud of pheromones. But I'm aware that this makes me vulnerable.

"Do you want music?" Vaughn asks. "You can look through my playlist and put something on Bluetooth."

I know what Bluetooth is, but I have no idea how it's used to play a song in a car. We've only been on the road for thirty minutes, and already it's as if I'm in a bewildering futuristic world.

I crave Kiran's easy warmth and innocence. When Alec and Sachi hugged me goodbye on the porch, Kiran was in an uncharacteristically gloomy mood. "I want you to stay here," he said.

"I know, but I'll be home soon. Keep the magic going."

"I don't know if I can," he said.

I'd never heard him say anything like that. It gave me a prickle. I kissed his cheek. "I love you, Kee. I'll bring you back something cool, okay?"

Vaughn is waiting for my answer.

"If you want music, go ahead."

"Maybe in a while," he says.

His jaw is tight. All of him is, and I'm not imagining he's tense just because I am. I've sensed a change in him since we set our departure day. He seems detached, even depressed, more like he was in February. I don't know why, but I keep thinking this trip could be the end of us. But I don't understand why he'd take me to Chicago to break up with me. That seems too harsh even for the old Vaughn, especially when he knows how difficult seeing Julia's house will be.

No, he wouldn't do that. I have to believe something else about this trip troubles him. He's not keen on doing the book event, but that's not enough reason for his mood swing. Maybe Chicago stirs memories of his father. He told me February was the first time he'd returned to the city since he left at nineteen. He flew into O'Hare again for this trip but immediately left, as he did the last time. This will be the first time he stays in the city for more than a few hours.

He puts his hand on my thigh and looks at me. "Everything okay?"

227

He knows everything isn't okay. We both do. I think he asked to soothe himself.

"I'm a little nervous," I reply.

"Are you sure you want to go straight to the house? Maybe we should check in to the hotel and have a fun night in the city first."

He's proposed this plan before. He doesn't want to start the trip with Julia's house. Maybe he thinks it'll be more traumatic than expected, and I'll want to go home.

I hate that I'm viewed as so delicate. Since my fall, I've sensed this attitude in Alec and Colton and sometimes in Sachi and Vaughn. If they only knew the strength I've exerted every moment for the last decade to hold it all down. It's not easy to keep a secret this big for years. How could I be delicate when I've stomached this foul thing inside me for so long?

Vaughn rubs my thigh and looks at me because I still haven't answered.

"I'd rather see the house first. Otherwise I'll be thinking about it, wondering how it will feel to see it again." I put my hand on top of his. "I don't want to be distracted from enjoying the city with you."

He looks in my eyes. His mouth curves upward, but he's not smiling. He looks almost terrified beneath that fake smile.

I can't help thinking his distress has something to do with the other Riley, the one I'd rather believe is fiction. But she must be real because his novels are dedicated to her. I checked in Sachi's copies, and each of the four dedications is the same: *With love to Riley.*

Vaughn confessed that he told me lies to make leaving easier in February. For a while I believed he lied about doing something to another Riley that could get him arrested. But now I'm not sure. I swear I can feel something he's hiding. It's almost tangible, a presence that lurks between us. I think I recognize the feel of it because I have a dark secret that haunts me, too. But I keep mine better hidden than Vaughn does. I haven't let him get even a whiff.

I don't understand why Vaughn can't be content with us as we are. If something bad happened to someone named Riley, why does he think he has to tell me about it? Why not, as Keats said, wreath our heads in flowery bands when we've found this beauty that can move away the pall from our dark spirits?

I think of Julia, her arms open to the sky, reciting the Keats line. I watched her say it in snowfalls, beneath stars, in the rain, to the setting sun. After her lover died, I think every moment of beauty became an equal measure of pain for her. When she wished he was there in the twirling snow with her, she spoke the line to remind herself that humans innately can be healed by beauty, especially the splendors of the natural world. She said the words like a prayer to beauty, invoking its power to lift her spirits.

But I eventually understood she was also saying the line to me. She'd seen how damaged I was when I arrived at her house, and she worked hard to undo, or at least balance, as much of that darkness as she could with her light. She gave me Keats as a reminder that I could always count on small beauties to pull back the darkness. The magical iridescence of a beetle carapace. Afternoon sun on a jar of roses. The softness of the blue mittens she knitted for me. The song of a migrating white-throated sparrow. All I had to do was notice these beauties to feel their sway.

I unzip the bag at my feet and pull out my water bottle.

"You slept for almost an hour," Vaughn says.

I don't tell him I only had my eyes closed. I've been thinking, mostly about Julia. I'm glad I'm going to see her house. I miss it more now that I've brought her to life in my thoughts.

"Do you still know people in Chicago?" I ask. "If you want to visit someone, I don't mind."

"There's no one."

"Does your father still live there?"

"I found out he died two years ago."

"What do you mean you *found out?*"

"With my name change and move to Brooklyn, they had trouble finding me. Four months after he died, I got a letter from his sister. She lives in Arizona. She must have hated my father as much as I did. She never once visited us."

"What happened to your father?"

"She said it was a stroke."

"Did he still live in the house you grew up in?"

"Yes."

"What happened to it when he died?"

"I don't know and I don't care." He glances at me, sees I'm surprised by his coldness. "I moved out of that house when I was sixteen. Other than getting my stuff, I never set foot in it again."

"Where did you go?"

"My friend Kaz's."

"Kaz?"

"John Kazmirski. Everyone called him Kaz."

"His parents let you move in?"

"Kaz did. I went to his house one night with a swollen lip and shiner, and he told me I could stay. His mother had left his father by then, and his father didn't care about much of anything. He hardly saw us, anyway. We lived in the basement and came and went from the entrance down there."

"Where is Kaz now?"

"Last I heard, he's in prison."

"That's too bad."

"I think it was inevitable."

"What did he do?"

"Not sure."

"Have you seen him since you moved to New York?"

"Not once."

"Really? You must have been close if you lived with him."

230

"We were. We became friends in third grade. I almost revered him back then. I was drawn to his confidence—I guess because I felt like I didn't have any—and hanging out with him was an escape from my father. But I think we were attracted to each other for the wrong reasons. As we got older, I realized he was mean and controlling. He's part of the reason I left Chicago when I was nineteen. I had to get away from his influence."

"Is that when you changed your name?"

"I changed it later when I signed with my agent."

"How did you pick *Vaughn Orr*?"

"My favorite teacher was Mr. Orr in fifth grade. He once took me aside and told me I was one of the brightest students he'd ever had. He said I could do anything I wanted with my life. I think he sensed my life was a mess, and he was trying to encourage me."

"Are you still in touch with him?"

"He died from cancer when I was in high school. Taking his name was sort of a memorial to him."

"I like that. And where did *Vaughn* come from?"

"It's an aeronautical engineering college. I saw a sign for it one day and decided it would make a good first name. It has a sort of lofty sound to it."

"It does. And it goes well with *Orr*. Simple but distinctive."

"I thought so."

"Were you writing books yet when you moved to New York?"

"No," he replies. "Do you mind if I pull over for a coffee stop?"

"Of course not." He changed the subject. He always does to keep conversation off his writing. Alec, Sachi, and I quit bringing it up.

I start to recognize landmarks. An Italian restaurant Julia loved. The gas station she used most often. The intersection near my grammar school.

"Here's the street," Vaughn says, turning the corner.

"Everything looks different."

231

"It's been ten years."

The houses look smaller. And I didn't remember how close together they are. The huge spruce that used to be in the Mendezes' front yard is gone. The Ramseys' lawn and flower garden, once the neatest on the block, are a chaos of weeds. They were in their upper seventies, and I suppose they moved or died.

Vaughn slows the car. I stare at the Walshes' front door as we roll past. I wonder if Jim and Mary still live there. The last time I stood on their porch, I smeared Nikki's blood on the doorbell. Jim was the nicest man I knew, and I went to him for help that day when I finally came out of shock. He was the one who called the police.

When we get to the house, Vaughn puts the car in park but leaves the motor on. I decide not to get out. I don't want any neighbors I knew to see me. I'm not in the mood for their questions.

I roll down the window to better see the two-story brick house. Whoever owns it takes decent care of the property, but not as well as Julia. The decorative shutters used to be forest green but now are light blue. I can see only a little of the backyard, but I think Julia's beloved flower garden is mostly gone. It required lots of tender care, especially the roses. I can still see her peonies and forsythia bushes at the side of the garage, and the front garden has been replaced by low bushes. I'm glad the river birch Julia and her father planted is still at the corner of the house, now grown beyond the roof.

Through the windows of the sunporch, I see a rocking chair, a side table, and not much else. I think of Julia's cacti and succulent collection. The plants weren't moved to the farm, though Alec was careful to bring everything that could be packed. I hope they weren't thrown away. Studying their unusual shapes and textures used to be like a way of meditating for me.

I look through the glass front door to where the Celestron telescope and boxes of Julia's possessions were the morning I went to middle school for the last time. Those belongings came back to me at the farm. Except the telescope and everything else that was stolen.

"Are you okay?" Vaughn asks.

"I'm more okay than I thought I would be. I feel detached from it now. I think that's the saddest part of seeing it again."

"I guess that's better than still feeling too attached."

"I guess so."

I wish I could see the balcony off Julia's bedroom. She taught me the moon seas there. We rarely looked at stars because of light pollution, but she showed me other miracles in the night sky. That was Julia.

"In a way, being forced to leave was the best thing that could have happened after Julia died."

I'm more thinking aloud than speaking to Vaughn.

"Nikki was wrecking the house. It would have been agonizing to keep trying to stop her. I'm glad my memories of this place are still more about Julia than Nikki. But that wouldn't have lasted much longer."

I look at Vaughn. "That must sound awful. I'm not *glad* Nikki was murdered. What happened to her was terrible. No one, not even a cruel person like her, deserves to die like that."

"I understood what you meant," he says.

I turn back to the house, looking at the kitchen window. The back door opens off the kitchen onto a porch around the corner from the driveway. "The police said she was trying to get out the back door when she was killed. They thought whoever did it panicked and hadn't meant to kill anyone."

"I'm sure that's true," he says.

I face him. "But why rob this house of all houses? I wonder if one of Nikki's friends cased the house when he came over to get high with her. The telescope alone was worth decent money. And Julia had some nice jewelry."

He doesn't say anything. He's looking at me strangely.

"What's wrong?"

"I think we should go," he says.

"Why?"

"We should check into the hotel."

"You said we didn't have to do that until closer to our dinner reservation."

"I want to walk around the city." He looks away, out his side window, as if staring at the house across the street, but I know he isn't.

Why am I certain he's lying? And why would he? I think it has something to do with the burglary.

"Did you talk to Alec and Sachi about the burglary? Do you know something I don't?"

"Riley . . ." He presses one hand on his forehead. "Damn it!" he says. "Damn it!"

"What? Tell me!"

He finally looks at me. His eyes are dark and strange, as if glazed with ice. They remind me of the snowshoe hare's when we had it trapped.

"I could lie to you," he says. "I want to. But I can't anymore."

No, not this. He's going to spew his mucky secret right here in front of Julia's house. That's the only thing that could make him look like this. The first night we talked on the hill, he said he had something to say that would break us apart. I feel sick and dizzy.

"I want you to know I didn't plan to tell you here," he says in a shaking voice. "I was going to do it at the hotel. Or somewhere else. Not here. I know how much this place already hurts."

I'm so frozen with dread I can barely make my mouth work. "Tell me what?"

He turns his gaze to Julia's house. "I used to live near this neighborhood. And Kaz's house was just around the next block."

What he said sinks in. I'd been expecting something else. "You lived here?"

He nods, looking into my eyes as if he expects me to understand why he told me this.

I look at the car's navigation screen, still marking the endpoint of our route. "Did you realize that when we got here?"

"No, I knew we were from the same neighborhood."

A scrabbling, sharp-clawed creature seems to climb up my stomach into my chest. I look at Julia's porch, at the last place I saw the telescope. But in my mind I see Vaughn walking up the farm's driveway. He says, "I'm embarrassed to say I've run out of gas, and my cell phone is dead." He's looking at me in a peculiar way. Almost as if he knows me.

I throw open the car door, leap out, and slam the door behind me.

He jumps out without turning off the car. "Riley!" he calls.

I hurry down the sidewalk. He comes after me. "I never thought I'd be able to tell you. You've changed me. I've—"

I press my hands over my ears, shouting, "No!"

He circles in front of me and grabs my arms to pull my hands down.

My heart hammers all the way into my head. "You killed my mother?"

"Kaz did."

"Were you there?"

"No, I had no idea until I saw the stuff he stole from you in his room—I told you we lived together in his basement back then."

"Why didn't you report it?"

"Because he said he would implicate me if I did."

"I thought you weren't there?"

"I wasn't. It was the telescope . . ."

"What do you mean?"

"I saw it on your porch one night, and I told Kaz I'd like to have a telescope someday. He gave it to me as a gift a week later."

He's speaking, but the words aren't making sense. Vaughn was given Julia's telescope as *a gift*? Could it get any weirder?

"I was furious," he says. "I told him I didn't want it and threatened to report the crime. Then he got so angry, I was afraid he'd kill me. He had a gun and told me he had to get rid of it. That was how I found out someone had been killed during the burglary."

"He had no proof to implicate you. You just don't want to admit you were afraid to turn him in."

"I was afraid of him. I fully admit that. But even if I turned him in, I was afraid his friends might kill me. I didn't realize until that night how much Kaz was terrorizing me. First my father, then him. I wasn't in my right mind when I ran away from Chicago that night."

I understand, but only the part about being terrorized by someone.

"You've been stalking me? All these years?"

"Not stalking. I only knew where you lived."

"How did you know?"

"The friend who drove me to the bus station that night was close with the daughter of one of your neighbors. She found out where you were moving to from her parents."

"Why did you come to see me after all these years?"

He doesn't answer.

"Out of guilt?"

After a few seconds he says, "Yes. But there was more to it than that. If you'll let me explain . . ."

I walk away from him. There's nothing but this between us. He's only with me out of guilt, or to somehow make himself feel better about his involvement in my mother's murder. He was too selfish to bear the burden alone. He had to pass it on to me. He really is another Nikki.

He hurries to my side. "I knew you'd turned twenty-one, and I had to make sure the murder hadn't wrecked your life." He grabs my arm to stop my charge down the sidewalk. "But that's not the reason I came to Wisconsin."

"I know. You were looking at properties."

"Kaz stole a laptop from your house."

"What about it?"

"He told me to wipe it clean. But when I opened it . . . I saw pictures of you . . ."

My god. That night in February when he left so abruptly: *I knew how wrong it was to be attracted to you—to this new version of Riley—but I couldn't stop myself.*

"You looked at the laptop? I thought you said you ran?"

"I did. I took the laptop with me."

"Why?"

"For you. I took it for you."

"What are you talking about?"

He grips my upper arm harder, as if to keep me from running away. The clasp of his hand on my biceps must hurt, but I'm aware of nothing but the darkness in his eyes. They don't even look gray anymore.

"Everything on the computer said Nikki Mays. All these years I assumed the computer belonged to your mother."

"It was Julia's. Nikki took it when she died. She took everything."

"I know. You said that in your journal. That's when I started to question some assumptions I'd made."

"I don't understand."

"Do you remember the line from *Endymion* you said to me that night on the hill?"

"Of course. Julia said it often."

"You've never read *The Sound of Absence*," he says.

His first novel.

"That quote is in the book, Riley."

A chill ripples over my arm skin, up my nape.

He sees I'm beginning to understand. "Julia wrote books?"

Oh yes, Julia wrote books. She had to write. And write and write. It didn't take me long to understand that her writing was like a demon that had taken possession of her soul after her lover died. She had stacks of bound journals that didn't survive Nikki's purges. The journals dated back to the year Julia's fiancé died, but she stopped writing in them not long after I arrived. That was when she bought a laptop. She typed away on it, writing stories, she said, whenever she had a chance.

"Can I read your stories?" I asked her when I was nine.

"One day you will," she said. "But not now. You're a little too young."

"I can read grown-up books."

"I know you can. But there are some parts in my stories that are for older readers."

"Sex?"

She grinned. "Yes, sex. And things you'll better understand later."

"I thought your mother wrote the books," Vaughn says. "The folder they were in was called Nikki's Books. But I don't think your mother changed the book dedications. It was the same in every book: *With love to Riley.*"

I'm falling. I'm falling. What happened to the ground beneath my feet? I used to draw hopscotch squares on this sidewalk with Julia. How is it possible it feels like a chasm that grows wider and deeper with every word Vaughn speaks? How is it possible I've cared about this man, this devil who crawled out of this awful crater he's opened?

He keeps me standing, taking my other arm into his hand to make me face him. "From the dates on her research for the first book, I figured out all four were written in a span of six years—the time you lived with her."

"You stole her books?"

"I took them to keep them safe from Kaz. I was going to send them to you in the mail when you were old enough to read them. But later I decided you'd benefit more if I could get at least one published. I thought if it made any money, I'd send it to you anonymously."

"I don't recall getting a check," I say bitterly.

"It got complicated when the first book became a huge bestseller. Suddenly everyone was scrutinizing my life, and I was afraid to make any move in your direction. I was trapped in the book's success. Then my agent and publisher started hounding me for another book. So I put out another: for you. This will sound strange, but the more money the books made, the more I thought it would compensate for what Kaz did—for what I did when I drew his attention to the telescope."

"I guess you buy the most expensive brands of whiskey to feel better about my mother's murder, too?"

He says nothing.

He didn't report the man who killed my mother. Then he stole all that was left of Julia. He took her words and made them his, and he became rich and famous. But that hadn't been enough. He had to make me feel attracted to him to feel better about himself. He made me want the sad man with writer's block. With his whiskey and close dancing and magical rock. How dare he make me like him!

I feel like I have no body. No brain. I'm on fire. My body is pure hot energy. Like the night I ripped the Nikki serpent off the wall.

I don't need him to hold me up. I jerk my arms out of his hands with so much strength I stumble backward. Away from him. This steaming piece of shit I thought was my lover.

I need him out of my sight.

He hurries after me. "I'm sorry it took so long. I couldn't figure out how to send the money. If I sent cash, how much? And I was afraid it might get traced to me if your family went public about it. It all got so confusing. Then I thought maybe I could anonymously invest in your future—if you had a business or something like that. That was the reason I came to the farm, to see what you and your family needed."

"We didn't need you or your goddamn money!" I scream. "We didn't need your lies!"

I walk faster.

He catches up. "I know how awful all of this sounds, but I want you to know my feelings for you are real. But at first that confused me. I was afraid it had to do with the guilt. That's why I left . . ."

I can't listen to one more word of his bullshit rationalization. I break into a run. It feels good to use all that fiery rage to put space between me and him.

"Riley!" he shouts.

"Stay away from me!"

I want nothing to do with him. What he's done is not something we can discuss. What he's done will take me another decade to get over.

I can think of no way to escape other than using the car. I jump into the Porsche's driver seat and slam the door. I have to go before he reaches the car. The car is running, and I quickly put all of Alec's manual driving lessons into motion.

I pull the car out from Julia's driveway. My chest is heaving like explosions lit by the fire inside me. Bursting out, again and again. I can hardly see through all the tears. And then there's Vaughn in front of the car, holding his arms out.

I thrust my foot on the brake, but the car barrels toward him. I must have hit the accelerator accidentally. I jerk the wheel to the left too late.

His body makes a sickening thud against the metal and disappears beneath the car. The Porsche smashes into a parked car on the left side of the street. All I can see is his face, his expression right when the car hit him.

Everything turns silver-white. It's like when Julia died. I'm in a void that feels like death. I wish it were death. I've killed Vaughn. How is it possible this is happening again?

Someone is yelling at me. The car door is open. A middle-aged man holding a gun.

"I said get out!" he shouts. His gun is aimed at me. A woman standing behind him is talking urgently on a cell phone. She's giving instructions to 911.

I have to see Vaughn. But as I stumble out of the car, the man with the gun shouts, "Hands on your head! Hands up, I said!"

He holsters the gun and shoves me up against the car. He tells me he's a Chicago police officer who has the authority to arrest me, though he's off duty. He handcuffs me from behind, reading me my rights.

I'm not listening. All I want to hear is that Vaughn survived. But I can't see him. He's still lying in the street with three people bent over him.

"Is he okay?" I call.

Only one of the three looks at me, aiming a bitter stare before she turns back to Vaughn.

"Now you're concerned about him?" the cop says.

"I didn't hit him on purpose!"

"I saw it all, and so did my wife. The fight. Everything. You easily could have stopped in time."

"I tried! The car is stick shift. My foot was on the wrong pedal."

"Tell it to the judge."

A squad car arrives. And twenty or more people out of nowhere. They all stare at me as if I'm the evilest being on Earth.

How many times have I dreamed this? The whole world finally knowing what I've done and hating me for it? I've wanted this for a decade. To be punished, to pay for those awful things I did to Julia. Isn't that the real reason I haven't let myself live a normal life?

When the policeman pushes my head into the squad car, I know exactly how to duck down and slide in with my hands cuffed behind my back. I've done it a hundred times in my imagination.

26

TYLER WEBB

The damn light shines like a knife into my brain again.

"What's your name?" the man asks. "Sir, can you tell me your name?"

I think he's a paramedic. But he looks like Kaz. Same scruffy, wavy hair. Dark eyes, beard stubble, thin lips. I force my eyes open and stare at him. "Kaz?"

"Do you know where you are?" he asks.

"Chicago."

"And what's your name?"

"Tyler."

Kaz frowns and glances at a woman. She must be his girlfriend. From habit I know not to look directly at her. I've been careful around girls he likes since middle school. That was when girls started to be attracted to me—and me to them. Kaz hated how easy it was for me, and he'd get angry if I even talked to a girl who interested him. Junior year, he went berserk when he found out I'd helped Chelsea Wells after she passed out at one of our notorious neighborhood garage parties. I'd only walked her to her friend's house so she could sober up before her parents saw her, but Kaz punched me because he didn't believe I hadn't done something with her.

"Think hard and tell me your name," Kaz says.

Screw you, Kaz.

He's waiting for an answer.

"I'm Tyler Webb. And if you have anything for this pain, I'd much appreciate it."

"Working on that," the woman says.

I try to see what she's doing to my arm, but I can't turn my head. Am I in an ambulance? I'm tied down and can't move. What the hell are they doing to me? Why does my arm hurt so much?

"Get me out of this! Get me out!" I struggle to rise against the straps.

"Calm down," the woman says. "This will help."

The drug floods my brain fast. It's good stuff. Softness slips over me.

"Do you remember that telescope?" I ask Kaz.

"Telescope?" he says.

"The Celestron."

If Kaz answers, I can't hear him. I'm looking at the Celestron. As if I'm in the past and present at the same time. It's like I'm an airplane contrail in a starry sky, a thin ribbon of cloud stretched out over everything that's happened since that night I saw the telescope.

~

Kaz and I were walking back to his house after a night out. We didn't have a car because I couldn't afford one and Kaz's dad's was in the shop. We walked in silence between mounds of snow piled on the sidewalks. Kaz was stoned. I'd had only a few beers, and Kaz was angry that I didn't want to party as much lately. I dared not tell him the truth. I was tired of the feeling of being wasted. I was tired of friends who slept all day and partied all night. Tired of our neighborhood. Tired of Chicago. I was sick and tired of everything.

I was nineteen and going nowhere. Worse than nowhere. Kaz was getting into oxy and cocaine, and twice in recent months he'd broken into homes to fund his habit. Sometimes I thought I'd have been better off if I'd stayed at my father's house. But I'd be going nowhere there, too. My father had said it often enough: "You're a loser who's going nowhere. It's a good thing your mother can't see how bad you turned out."

I dug my hands deeper into my jacket pockets. I was cold because I had no gloves or hat, and I didn't have money to buy them. I lived with Kaz, sponging off his father for food and paying no rent, and I couldn't very well ask Mr. Kazmirski to buy me things. As was, the coat belonged to him.

I once watched a dragonfly eat a moth, chewing its body until all that remained was a crumble of papery wings. That was how I felt all the time, as if something were gnawing away at my innards, and some crucial part of me was already gone. Soon there would be too little of me left to escape.

Every day I tried to plan a way out. But Kaz would be difficult to escape. He was like the gatekeeper of hell, always pulling me down anytime I tried to crawl upward. Throughout middle and high school he'd ridiculed me for studying and getting decent grades, even for being liked by teachers, as if this were some major character flaw. He caused trouble in my relationships if he thought the girl was too nice. When I talked about getting a job, the next day he'd hand me a wad of money he'd weaseled out of one of his parents. After graduation, Kaz laughed at my idea of working to pay for English classes at the nearby community college. He said all that degree would get me was a job selling sunglasses at the mall.

I was thinking about where I might find a job when I saw the telescope. It caught my attention because the porch was lit up, the only bright windows at three in the morning. The telescope rested high on a tripod, and I could see the brand written on its side: CELESTRON.

I stopped in front of the house and stared at it. I imagined seeing stars, planets, galaxies.

Kaz noticed I wasn't walking with him. "What are you doing?" he asked irritably.

"I always wanted a big telescope like this."

He came to my side.

"I wonder how powerful it is. Imagine what you would see with it."

"Looks expensive," Kaz said.

I cursed myself for drawing his attention. Sure enough, he looked around to make sure no one was nearby and walked to the door.

"What are you doing?" I hissed. "Someone will see you!"

"Just looking." But he didn't just look. He tried the door handle, not worried about leaving prints because of his gloves.

I was relieved it was locked. I liked the woman who lived there. I walked past the house occasionally, and she always greeted me warmly. Twice I'd seen a girl in the driveway, probably her daughter.

Kaz was still looking at the telescope.

"Let's go, I'm cold," I said.

"Babyass," he muttered.

Since third grade he'd called me *Babyass* anytime I behaved in a way he perceived as weak. I hated it but never let on. That would only make him say it more.

Kaz peered in at the cardboard cartons piled around the telescope. "Looks like they're moving. There could be good stuff in those boxes."

There was no **FOR SALE** sign, but I wondered about the boxes. The last few times I'd passed the brick house with green shutters, I'd noticed it didn't look as nice as it used to. No one had mowed or weeded, and when winter came, the front walk wasn't shoveled. I knew those weren't good signs. I hoped the lady wasn't sick.

"Let's go," I called to Kaz.

He walked away from the front door, calculation glinting in his eyes. I knew what he was scheming but dared not forbid it. Kaz didn't take kindly to being told what to do. Instead, I said, "A really nice woman lives here. She has a little girl."

The next day I applied for jobs around the neighborhood. I don't know why that was when I finally started working on my escape. Maybe it was how the Christmas lights made me feel, that sad feeling of wanting things I'd never had. Maybe it was wishing I had enough money to buy gloves and a warm coat. Sometimes I think it was the telescope. During the half minute I'd imagined seeing galaxies, the emptiness diminished a little.

I was determined to get away from Kaz. If I earned enough money to buy a car, I would go to New York City to look for work and maybe one day enroll for college classes.

I got a job three days later. A woman who owned a flower shop needed extra help with deliveries during the holidays. She said she might hire me after Christmas if I was diligent and punctual. Diligence and punctuality—my father had trained me well in those areas at least.

I liked delivering flowers. In cold weather someone was required to meet the delivery person at the door, and I enjoyed seeing how people reacted. One woman even wept with happiness. Being part of something positive in people's lives felt foreign in a good way. Even the smell of the work lifted me. A tropical, sweet-spicy aroma permeated the florist's shop and lingered on my clothes when I returned to the musty basement.

My friends teased me. Kaz called me *Daisy*, and they all started doing it. That was when I decided to get a second job to make money faster. Plus, if I got an evening job, my sleep schedule would be opposite Kaz's.

I'd had the florist job for a week when I saw the telescope again. I walked into the basement after delivering flowers and found it next to the couch where I slept. Kaz had put a tattered red bow on it. I stared at it, my stomach sick, as Kaz came out of his bedroom. "Merry Christmas early, bro," he said.

"You didn't."

"I did. And you wouldn't believe all the good stuff I found in that house. Come look."

Stacked all around his room were boxes he'd taken from the house, apparently in his father's van. A flat-screen TV, two laptops, a Nikon camera, boxes of silverware, even a food processor. I thought of the nice woman coming home and finding it all gone, her jewelry boxes emptied of all those pretty things that had sentimental value.

I stared at a crate of vinyl records. He'd even taken their old albums.

Kaz saw me looking at them. He flipped through the albums so I could see the titles. The Beatles, the Rolling Stones, the Who. "These are original," he said. "I think they might be worth something."

I was too shocked and disgusted to say anything. And afraid. Criticizing Kaz never went well.

"We'll split the money it makes," he said. "But keep the telescope."

"I don't want the money—or the telescope."

"Why not? You earned your share when you showed it to me. I'd never have noticed it."

"I didn't show you the telescope so you could steal it. You know I was only looking at it."

"You're involved whether you like it or not, Tyler. You cased that house."

"I did not!" I shouted. "If you get arrested and try to involve me, I'll tell them the truth!"

He shoved me against the wall. I had two inches on Kaz, but as always, I went limp when I saw the threat in his gaze, pitiless, as if he were a taunted wild animal.

"I went to a lot of trouble to get you that telescope."

He paused, as if waiting for me to thank him. But I couldn't. I wouldn't even if he tried to beat it out of me.

"I went to the house this morning at ten o'clock," he said. "Where were you?"

I had been asleep at ten because I didn't start work until noon. I'd stayed up late looking at information about New York City, dreaming about what I'd do when I got there.

"You cased the house, and you can't prove you weren't there," Kaz said. "You're involved. Got that?"

When I didn't answer, he squeezed me harder.

"Yes," I said.

"We'll split fifty-fifty. You can sell the telescope if you want." As he released me, he added, "And now you can quit that stupid job."

He shrugged on his coat. "Don't say a fucking word about this to anyone. It didn't go good at the house this morning."

My stomach dropped. "What do you mean, *It didn't go good?*"

I saw something that might be fear in his eyes. Panic. I'd never seen him look like that.

"Like I said, I went to a lot of trouble for you. We can't sell this stuff for a while. Wipe the computers right away. Tonight." He took a handgun out of his drawer.

I numbly tried to process what I was seeing. I'd had no idea Kaz owned a gun. But I wasn't surprised.

"Did you hear me? I said wipe the computers."

"I will."

He slipped the gun into his jacket pocket. "I'll be gone for a while. I need to get rid of this."

What he'd done finally sank in. "Oh my god," I said, slumping against the wall.

"Fucking Babyass," he muttered on his way out.

I slid down to the floor. He'd killed someone. The nice woman. The little girl. Maybe both.

I pulled my phone out and searched for news of a crime in our neighborhood. I found it within seconds: a woman murdered during a burglary that morning. I sat in shock for a long time.

Kaz was a murderer. I lived with a murderer.

The girl. The news hadn't said anything about her. She would have been at school when it happened. She was okay.

No, she wasn't okay. She would have found the body when she got home. It would ruin her for life. I knew very well how the worst moments of a person's life stayed inside them like a terminal disease.

Who would take care of her now? Twice I'd seen another woman at the house. I hoped she was a relative who could take the girl in.

I pulled the two laptops out of the boxes. One was a few years old, the other new. I turned on the new one. The screensaver popped on, a picture of the little girl surrounded by blooming peonies.

I felt sick. I focused on getting into the computer. It wasn't protected by a password. Even if it had been, I knew how to get around it. I'd learned from a guy I used to game with. That was how Kaz knew I could wipe the computers.

I checked to see who owned the computer. Nikki Mays. The news hadn't said the name of the victim, and probably that wouldn't be reported until tomorrow or later. I opened one of several photo folders. All pictures of the girl. I discovered her name was Riley. "Riley's First Grade Play," "Riley's Eighth Birthday," "Riley in the Garden." The girl had pretty eyes, catlike and an unusual color of light brown.

I scrolled through the photos of what looked like an idyllic life. Picnics, zoo, beach, birthday parties. I think I projected myself into every one of those photographs, imagining what it would feel like to remember a childhood like that.

Then I noticed something about her eyes in one of the photographs. She was little, only about six, and she was holding a baby goat. Her eyes were deep down sad, her smile only for the person who'd taken the photograph. I looked through more photos and felt certain I wasn't imagining it. I recognized myself in her eyes. She couldn't hide the pain. Why did she look sad when she lived in that nice house with someone who clearly loved her? Had something awful happened to her father?

I combed more photos looking for a father. In one file I discovered a few unlabeled photos of the other woman I'd seen at the house, the one with dyed-blonde hair. She had to be Riley's mother. They had similar eyes.

If the blonde was Riley's mother, who was the friendly dark-haired woman who'd greeted me in the front yard? Maybe Riley had two moms. I found only a few photographs of the dark-haired woman, and none were labeled.

I opened a folder labeled NIKKI'S BOOKS. Inside were four files titled "Book I," "Book II," "Book III," and "Book IV." I opened "Book I." There were three title ideas at the top, followed by a dedication: *With love to Riley.*

I looked at the other three. All had the same dedication.

Nikki Mays was a writer who'd dedicated her books to her only child. I'd erased the poor kid's happy life when I drew Kaz's attention to the telescope, and now I would delete the last vestiges of her mother. If Kaz had killed Nikki Mays, the books would be the last words Nikki ever spoke to her daughter.

I read the first paragraph of one of the books. It was fiction, and I was surprised by how good it was. Nikki Mays had a way with words.

That decided it. I wouldn't erase the books. Not yet. First, I'd find out who Kaz killed. If it was Nikki Mays, maybe I could send the books to Riley. I'd send them to her anonymously when she was old enough to read them.

I had to get the laptops out of there. I had to get *myself* out of there.

I shut down the computer and stuffed it into a duffel bag. I added the other laptop and covered them with as much clothing as I could fit. My heart pounded so hard it hurt. If Kaz caught me stealing from him, he might kill me. Even if he got arrested for the murder, one of his friends would kill me. No one would give a damn if my body floated up in Lake Michigan.

I had to get out of Chicago. And that meant I needed enough money for a bus ticket to New York and a few days of food and motel.

But what if I didn't find a job right away? I needed a backup plan. I entered Kaz's room and dug around in the boxes. At the bottom of one, I found the jewelry: two old platinum diamond rings, diamond earrings and rings, amethyst and pearl jewelry, and a ring in a fancy box that looked like the real deal—emerald and diamonds.

I took the emerald ring and left the rest. I opened the drawer where Kaz kept cash he bullied out of his dad and slid $250 into my pocket. I'd taken only that, one ring, and two laptops that were worth almost nothing. I was well within the 50 percent of profits Kaz promised. Even so, he would never forgive me for taking from him without asking. But mostly he'd be in a rage about me leaving—especially when he'd just committed murder. He would think I was going to betray him.

I needed a ride to the bus station, and I knew only one person I could trust. Paige and I had been together when I was a senior, but we'd drifted apart the summer after I graduated. She was still in her senior year, and I guess I wanted to put high school far behind me. Kaz hated her, mostly because she and I used to spend a lot of time together. After Paige and I broke up, we remained friends, but she and Kaz still despised each other. "You need to get away from that psycho," she'd say. "He's gonna kill someone someday."

I looked around the bleak basement for the last time. At first, it had felt like a refuge. But it turned out to be as dangerous as my father's house. I'd exchanged one tormentor for another. Had I chosen Kaz because I felt I deserved to be punished? Because my father said I'd killed my mother?

Thinking of my mother reminded me of the necklace. I opened my top drawer and pulled out the little silver box still hidden in the toddler socks. I made sure the key was inside before I pushed the socks into the duffel bag.

The last thing I looked at was the telescope with a red bow. Kaz's gift. A gift that cost a life.

I hurried out and got far from Kaz's house before I texted Paige. She came to pick me up immediately. "What's going on?" she asked as I jumped into the car.

"I need to get out of Chicago. Would you drive me to the bus station?"

"Tyler! Shit!" She glanced at me as she drove. "Kaz?"

"Yes. But don't ask. I can't say anything."

After a few seconds, she whispered, "Oh my god . . ."

"What?"

"Did you and Kaz kill that woman, the one who was murdered near Kaz's house?"

"Come on, you know me better than that."

"I do. I know you wouldn't have. But Kaz would, and when you're with him, you're—"

"I had nothing to do with it." I cringed. I was the sole reason the murder had happened. "Do you know anything about the murder?"

"Everyone's talking about it on Facebook. Haven't you seen?"

"I've been at work. Who was it?"

"Her name was Nikki Mays. She has a little girl."

There it was. Riley had lost her mother because of me.

"The poor kid found her," Paige said. "And it's so sad because her aunt died last August. Now she's an orphan."

I opened the window and let a shock of cold air hit my face. My eyes teared from the frigid wind, but I wanted them to be real tears. In the blur of city lights, I saw a little girl in a police station. I saw the horror she witnessed. I saw the words in each of her mother's books: *With love to Riley.*

I closed my eyes, relishing the sting of the biting wind on my skin. I promised myself Riley Mays would see those books someday.

27
RILEY

A jail cell is a good place to think. Actually, it's a horrible place for anything, but it's a situation that forces introspection.

Not at first. When I was put in here, I was in shock. My brain couldn't process everything that had happened in the last hour. I shut down except for the rote replies I gave the police.

But at least I knew Vaughn hadn't died. A police officer who was tired of me asking told me Vaughn was alive and on his way to the emergency room. That helped clear a little of the fog.

My thoughts didn't start to sharpen until a woman who'd been weeping continuously was taken out of another cell. I supposed someone had posted bail for her, and that made me wonder whether Alec and Sachi would be able to get me out without a bail hearing. When I called them from the police station, they said they were coming right away, but they wouldn't arrive for at least four more hours.

Without the woman's crying, the numbness of shock diminished. But the thud of Vaughn's body against the car and the horror in his face kept replaying in my thoughts. I used Sachi's meditation methods, and as my mind cleared, I tried to process why I was sitting in a cell when Vaughn had protected a murderer and stolen my aunt's books.

For hours I've been going over everything he confessed. It all makes sense now. Even why I was attracted to him in the first place.

He has no idea how alike we are.

I sort through it all again. He's told me the truth. He would have no reason to hold anything back when he was admitting serious crimes. It was a huge risk. He'll lose everything if I report the murder, robbery, and plagiarism. Everything. His fame. His money. His reputation. His freedom. He'll be in prison for a very long time.

He knew that and he still told me. Does this mean all those emotions I felt in him were real? I know mine were.

Are those feelings erased now? Do I hate him? I should. Any normal person would.

But I'm not normal. I'm as screwed up as him. A liar. A bad person who pretends to be good.

No, in some ways I'm a much worse person. I have no right to hold him accountable for protecting Kaz when I also lied for a murderer and even took part in the crime. Vaughn lies to strangers about being the author of Julia's books; I lie to the people who unfailingly love and trust me. I sensed Vaughn came back to tell me something important, yet I silenced him, imagining I was superior because I could hold in my sins.

I stare at the bars of my cell. I belong in here. Maybe I'll finally tell everyone why.

I close my eyes and go to the Sea of Clouds. I try to find Julia in the vaporous pastel swirls, but I can't see her. That's for the best. I wouldn't want her to know about this mess. I wonder what she'd think about Vaughn pretending to be the author of her books.

I remember visiting a neighborhood bookstore with her and asking if she would ever sell her books there.

"No, my books are just for me."

"Why?" I asked.

"Getting published is very difficult, and I don't have time for that."

"I bet they're really good. Better than all those books on that bestseller table."

She laughed, hugging me tight.

The knock of the lock startles me back to reality. A police officer opens my cell.

"Are my cousins here?"

"Come with me," she says.

I follow her into the police station. I'm stunned and relieved to see Vaughn looking well on the other side of the counter. Clustered around him are Sachi, Alec, Kiran, and Colton. Colton is as much a surprise as Vaughn. He must have driven down separately from Madison. I wish Alec and Sachi hadn't told him what I did. But I understand why they would. This is a family crisis, and Colton is family.

I can't look at Vaughn's fraught expression. The tears spilling out of my eyes are for my family. No one stops me from going to them, and they engulf me in tight embraces and the smell of home. Kiran is crying, his arms wrapped around my waist. I crouch down and look into his soulful eyes. "Everything is okay. Don't be afraid."

"What happened? Why are you in jail?"

"I'm not, you see?" I kiss his hot wet cheek. "It was just a misunderstanding."

I stand and look at Vaughn to see his reaction. When our eyes meet, it's as if we're simultaneously complete strangers and deeply intimate. He appears exhausted, his face darkened with shadows beneath his eyes. His left arm is in a cast, and he has a scabbed cheek and two bandages on his forehead. He's wearing the same clothing he had on earlier, and there's blood dripped all over the shirt. He obviously came straight from the hospital, and I wonder how he got released so fast. He must have called Sachi and asked her to bring him here.

"You're certain you don't want to press charges?" an officer asks Vaughn.

"I'm certain," he says, his eyes on mine.

The officer accepts without comment. I sense there'd been discussion between the police and Vaughn before I was brought out. Several of the surrounding officers are gawking at him. They must know he's a famous author.

"What happened to your arm?" I ask.

"Broken radius."

"I'm sorry."

"It was my fault for upsetting you. And I could tell you didn't know how to use the stick shift and clutch."

Colton has had a nearly continuous glower on Vaughn. He wraps his arm around my shoulders and says, "Let's go home. You can ride with me."

I imagine doing that, walking away from Vaughn forever and getting in a car with Colton, or with Alec, Sachi, and Kiran. I imagine the silence in the car, everything I can't tell them muting me for five hours, then for days, years, decades. All these new things I can't say piled on top of everything I already couldn't say.

Colton tugs on my shirt. "Come on."

Vaughn assumes I'm leaving and he'll never see me again. "Riley . . ." He glances at my family. "I never meant to hurt you. I will never forgive myself." He barely manages the next words as he tries to swallow a sob. "I'm sorry. I'm so sorry . . ."

I'm so sorry.

How many times have I said those words to Julia? Day after day, year after year.

It will never end. It can only get worse. I see that now.

I pull away from Colton. Can I do this? Can I?

If I don't do it now, while I'm in this place, I know I never will. *I will never forgive myself.*

For the first time in my life, I use those words to strengthen rather than weaken myself. I walk over to the officer who asked Vaughn if he wanted to press charges. "I want to report a crime."

He sighs and glances at Vaughn. "I think this matter is settled. Why don't you go home and get some rest?"

"Let's go, Riley," Alec says.

"No. I have to do this." I don't know the person who said that. She's as much a stranger to me as the people behind the desk. "I need a private room," I tell the officer.

"I don't understand," he says.

I don't want to say too much in front of Kiran, but I have to say enough for the officer to take me seriously. "It's an unsolved crime."

My family is looking at me as if I've lost all reason. Vaughn is pale, seems about to faint—or run away. He'd better not.

"Please take us to a room where I can speak privately."

Another sigh. But the officer nods.

I take Kiran by the shoulders. "I want you to wait out here. In that chair. Will you do that for me?"

"Why?"

"Because I have to talk about adult things."

"What things?"

"I said they're adult. It's okay. You're safe in here." I guide him to the chair and kiss his cheek. "Thank you, Kiran."

I turn to Vaughn. "I want you to come with us."

"Riley . . ."

"Don't say anything!"

I can't explain. Not now. I turn away from him and get the group moving.

"What is this? What are you doing?" Colton whispers.

I can't answer. I'm shaking so hard I don't know if I can do it.

At the door to an interrogation room, the officer says, "I want to warn you that falsely reporting a crime is a crime." He still thinks this is about the fight between Vaughn and me.

"It's a murder, and I know it's not a false crime."

I think he sees how scared I am, because his expression turns serious. He leaves and returns with a person he introduces as Detective Moore. I pull Vaughn aside. His hand is cold and sweaty. "Don't be afraid," I whisper.

"Don't be afraid?" he says in an incredulous tone. "You're about to—"

"Be quiet! I told you not to say anything!"

Detective Moore is near the door, staring suspiciously at us. I have no choice but to go in the room without explaining to Vaughn. He sits with my family, watching me with bewilderment.

"Where did the crime take place?" Moore asks.

"Chicago, this precinct," I say in a shaky voice.

"And the victim's name?"

The tears start.

I look at Vaughn. If he could do it, I can.

"Julia Mays. My aunt. Her death was called an accident or suicide. But it wasn't either."

Sachi, Alec, and Colton look as stunned as Vaughn.

"My mother killed her, and I lied to cover it up. I want to confess. I want to tell you everything that happened."

"When was this?" Moore asks.

I have no trouble giving the day of the week, the date and year, and the approximate time of death. That night is stamped into me like the imprint of one of Kiran's fossils.

Sachi stands. "You were hurt by everything that happened, and you were only eleven. You had nothing to do with Julia's death. It was an accident."

"Sit down and listen."

"Riley, don't do this to yourself. You know you didn't—"

"Sachi, please . . . please sit down."

She sits and Alec grabs her hand. They look about to cry. Tears already magnify Colton's bright-blue eyes. Vaughn looks at me more with wonder than sorrow. Now he gets it. Now he knows why we could never stop what happened between us. As soon as we met, we felt the pull of each other's darkness. Creatures as aberrant as us need to know how to recognize our kind from the subtlest of signals.

I sit across from Moore and the other officer. They still look unconvinced that I have a real crime to report. They'll believe me once they hear it all.

"My mother, Nikki Mays, brought me to my aunt's house when I was five. She found out her father left the house to both her and her sister when he died. Nikki wanted the money for her half of the house, but Julia refused to sell. So we stayed. I think Nikki figured her sister wouldn't put up with her for very long. She thought Julia would rather sell the house than live with all the problems her sister brought into her life—including me."

The detectives still seem dubious about my confession, or are they irritated? It's late, and they don't want to deal with this. I look down at my hands knotted on the table to avoid their eyes.

"But Julia didn't see me as a problem. After a while, she became like my mom. Nikki hated that but used it to get things from Julia. She'd threaten to leave with me if Julia didn't give her money. Nikki used drugs and drank and refused to get a job. I know Julia wanted to make her leave, but she didn't because she loved me . . ."

My hands blur. "And I loved her. My mother never forgave me for loving Julia. She had to punish me." I look up at Moore. "I think she plotted killing Julia for years. But first she had to make sure she would inherit the house."

"How did she kill Julia?" he asks.

"They'd been fighting more than usual—about where I would go for middle school. My mother won the fight even though I agreed with Julia about where to go to school. That summer I stopped talking to Nikki. And I finally told her the truth. I told her I hated her."

"You think your mother killed your aunt because of that?" Moore asks.

"I know she did. I saw it."

"What happened?"

"They were fighting like always. In the kitchen. Fighting about me."

I don't think I can say it. I'm afraid I'm going to vomit.

"Go on," Moore says.

"All of a sudden Nikki smashed an iron pan on Julia's head. Her head hit the counter and then the floor when she fell. Nikki freaked out. She said she hadn't meant to do it. I kept saying to call an ambulance, but Nikki said Julia was dead. She put her fingers on Julia's neck and said there was no pulse."

Sachi, Alec, and Colton have tears streaming down their cheeks. Vaughn isn't crying. Our gazes meet for a moment, and I feel an intimacy between us, more intense than when we made love. How strange and sad is that?

I have to look away, so I stare at my hands again. "Nikki said it was my fault she'd killed her sister. Because I made her and Julia fight all the time. She said I'd be taken away from her if the police found out. I would be put in a foster home, and she would go to jail . . ."

The officers are listening with rapt attention.

"But later I figured out she was lying. Julia wasn't dead. Nikki only wanted me to think she was so she could finish what she'd planned. She made me help her put Julia in the trunk of the car. I was in shock, I think, because I don't remember much about any of what happened until we got to the lake."

"Lake Michigan?" Moore asks.

"No, a place where Julia liked to go stargazing. It was a gravel pit lake. Private. People weren't supposed to go there, but her boyfriend was a construction engineer who showed her how to get in. They would go swimming there. She used to take me sometimes, except she didn't let me swim. She said it was too deep and dangerous."

"Where was Julia's boyfriend when all of this happened?" Moore asks.

"He died in an accident at work before I came to live with Julia."

"What did your mother do at the lake?"

"She left the engine running and opened all the windows. She put Julia in the driver's seat with her purse next to her and her binoculars in her lap. The binoculars were to make it look like she was there for the stars. August twelfth was the best night of the Perseid meteor shower. That was all part of the plan. Because Julia went there during meteor showers."

I can't stop the sobs that erupt from me, from the underworld of that night that's roiled in me for ten years. Alec gets up to help me, but I wave him back.

"Nikki . . . she put the car in drive and barely got out in time before it started rolling toward the lake. That was when Julia woke up. She called my name. She said, 'Riley, help me.' I tried to get her out. I grabbed the door handle. But I saw I was going to fall over the edge with the car if I tried to open the door. So I let go. I let go and just stood there, watching the car sink into the black water. I wished I was with her. I wished I'd died with her."

Alec and Sachi lift me out of my chair. They wrap me tight in their arms.

"Jesus, what a story," Moore says to the other officer. "Go check the records on Julia Mays to verify all of this."

As the officer leaves, Moore asks Vaughn, "And where do you fit into all of this?"

He saw us whispering outside the door.

Vaughn says, "I'm . . . Riley and I are—"

"Vaughn and I are friends," I say, pushing out of Sachi's arms.

Moore looks to Vaughn for confirmation.

"We met in Wisconsin a few months ago," Vaughn says.

"The officer who witnessed your accident didn't describe it as a friendly kind of situation."

I respond for Vaughn again. "It was the first time I went back to Julia's house. I was upset. I tried to leave, but the stick shift confused me."

"Three witnesses say you argued," Moore says.

"Yes, we argued," Vaughn says, "but that doesn't mean we aren't friends."

"Let's focus on the murder of my cousin," Alec says. "Didn't forensics see the head injuries?"

"I can't say," Moore replies. "I was in a different precinct back then."

"They were suspicious of Nikki," I say, "but they had no proof that she'd done anything. She used me as her alibi. We told them we were at home watching a movie when Julia died. I was terrified and cried every time they questioned me, but they thought that was because I was upset about my aunt dying."

"How did you get home from the lake that night?" Moore asks.

"We walked for a long time. Then Nikki used a pay phone to call a man who dropped us off near Julia's house."

"The police didn't question him?" Moore asks.

"They never knew about him. And Nikki knew he wouldn't talk to the police even if he heard her sister died that night. He was into drugs."

"Is it possible he was involved in the burglary of your house and murder of your mother later that year?"

I try to cover my surprise that he knows about the murder. The police must have researched my background when they booked me. "Everyone Nikki knew could have been a suspect. After Julia died, more of her drug contacts came to the house. They might have cased the house while they were there."

The other officer returns. "So far everything she said checks out with what we have on file. Julia Mays was found drowned in her car four days after the date Riley says she was murdered. The head trauma could have happened as the car went down because it flipped over and she wasn't wearing a seat belt. There was no clear evidence to prove her death was a homicide. And Nikki Mays provided a journal that indicated Julia could be suicidal. She'd written about her suicidal thoughts after the death of her boyfriend."

"That was just more of Nikki's plan," I say. "She knew she could use that journal to make Julia appear suicidal. But Julia wrote those things a long time before, right after her fiancé died."

"What now?" Alec asks.

"We'll need to reopen the case," Moore says. "But for now you're free to go."

"You won't keep me here?" I ask.

The officer rises out of his chair. "Even if you'd confessed your part in this ten years ago, you wouldn't have been held responsible. You were as much a victim as your aunt was."

"I was the reason my mother murdered her. I lied to the police."

"You were a child who was coerced and threatened into lying. Your mother used your guilt and trauma to keep you quiet. What she did to you was a crime."

I know that's true. I've always known. But why does hearing a stranger say it make losing Julia hurt even more?

The dark water I've kept inside surges. I can't hold it back anymore. It rushes into the room with a roar, erasing everyone and everything like a night tsunami.

Riley, help me!

I grab her hand. Stars tumble as we plunge. I hold on. Not once in the thousand nights we've fallen have I let her go.

28

VAUGHN

Colton tries to support Riley as she slumps to the floor. She's sobbing in violent, heartrending gasps. I rush over and wrap my uncasted arm around her back. Colton does the same from the other side, and together we lift her to her feet.

She needs to get outside. They had her locked in a damn jail cell. When Sachi told me at the hospital, I demanded the doctors release me. They said I couldn't leave so soon after the concussion, but I ignored their warnings and left.

"Let's get her out of here," I tell Colton.

Alec and Sachi get Kiran on our way out. Everyone on the sidewalk stares at us. Riley is using her feet, but she looks as if she's trapped in a nightmare. The force of her crying is like nothing I've ever seen. It's more like she's been poisoned and her body is trying to expel it.

Kiran starts crying again. "What's wrong with Riley? Dad, tell me! What's wrong?"

"She's upset about something," Alec says in a quavering voice.

Kiran's sobs bring Riley back. She abruptly stops crying, pushes Colton and me away, and pulls Kiran into an embrace. "Everything is okay. I'm all right." She wipes away Kiran's tears. "Here are our cars. You and I will ride together. Let's go, okay?"

Let's go. Her words jolt me. *Let's go.* That means I'll never see her again. I feel like I've been slammed by another car.

She turns to me. "Do you still have the hotel room reserved? My family has been on the road for five hours, and they need to rest."

"I can handle driving," Colton says.

"No, you all look exhausted. I don't want to risk it, especially at night."

"I agree," Sachi says.

"Do you think they'll have rooms at this time of night?" Alec asks.

"I'm Vaughn Orr. They'll have rooms."

I'm stunned when Riley manages a soft laugh.

"You know it's true."

"I know," she says. "The lesser god."

Lesser, indeed. We exchange a long look. I don't see the hatred I saw in her eyes at Julia's house. Where has it gone?

No, I won't let myself hope. Hope led me to the confession that brought about this mess.

"You never did tell me where we were staying," she says.

"It was supposed to be a surprise. The Drake Hotel."

"Oh, the Drake," Alec says.

"You've been there?"

"I looked inside the lobby once. Never stayed there."

"It's an old, fancy hotel," I tell Kiran. "Good place for a family that loves antique stores."

Kiran attempts a smile but can't make it look real.

"I'll pay for the rooms, of course," I tell the family, and they're too spent to resist.

We have to split up for the drive. I'd be best at city driving, but I dare not with the cast and the influence of pain medications. We decide that Colton and I will drive together, and the family will follow in the other car. Being alone with Colton will be no joy ride. He's been barely civil since the family met me at the hospital.

Colton doesn't speak initially. I can tell the bear whisperer, as Riley calls him, is nervous about driving in Chicago. At a long stoplight he finally asks the question I've been expecting. "What happened to cause all this?" When I don't immediately respond, he says, "That policeman said you and Riley had a fight."

"It's complicated."

"Why did you go to her old house? Was that your idea?"

"It was hers."

"Why go to the place where her mother was murdered?" he asks, his tone rife with blame.

"She said she wanted to see it again because she never had a chance to say goodbye."

"What was the fight about?"

"I can't talk about this right now. And you'd better keep your attention on the road."

"I've known Riley a long time. She would never get so upset that she'd run someone over with a car. What did you do?"

"Get in the left lane and turn left at the next light."

The directions become complex, and he doesn't ask more.

I've arranged valet parking, and I'm sure they'll allow another car. I thought we'd be arriving in the Porsche. The concierge stares at our two old sedans as we pull up, and it doesn't help that I'm beat up and wearing dirty, bloody clothes.

I tell him who I am and that there's been a car accident. My name and a few large bills make the check-in process move fast as the Mays family looks around the lobby of the Drake with wonder.

The luxurious room I'd reserved for Riley and me feels wrong in this radically new situation. Instead, I get three regular rooms near each other. The family says we can make do with two, but I see no benefit in deferring to their frugality when they need good rest.

The staff expresses great concern about my injuries. As always, this fawning attention makes me uncomfortable. I doubt Tyler Webb would get a free bottle of champagne delivered to his room if he arrived looking this disheveled.

When we find our rooms, there's awkwardness about who's going where. Riley disentangles our knot when she tells her family she needs to speak to me alone. None of them contests this, not even Colton.

My heart throbs as I push open the door.

Riley walks ahead and looks around the room. When the door closes, she turns to me. "I'm sorry you thought I was turning you in. But I had no way to tell you what I was doing without it looking suspicious. And I knew if I left the police station, I'd never do it."

"I can't believe you're apologizing to me."

She just stands there staring at me. I'm struck by how different she looks. Gaunt, diminished, as if the part of her tied to her secrets fell away when she told the truth. But the word *diminished* isn't right, because she also seems more vivid in a way I can't define. Standing before me is Riley Mays. The true Riley Mays.

"Why are you looking at me like that?" she asks.

"How am I looking at you?"

"Like I'm someone you don't know."

"You sort of are someone I don't know. And I'm someone you don't know."

She doesn't disagree.

"Riley . . . what your mother did was . . . there are no words. Nothing I say could possibly be enough, but I'm sorry you went through that. Thank god for Sachi and Alec."

"I know. I'm sorry you never had anyone like them to get you away from your father."

I don't want to talk about my father. I've had enough time to put him behind me. But she's dealing with fresh pain. I can't imagine how she's bearing it so well. I have an overwhelming urge to hold her, but

I'm no longer her lover, the guy who came out of the stone. I've crushed her soul—on top of everything else she's suffered. I need to get Vaughn Orr away from her.

"Is there anything I can do for you before I go? Ask anything and it's yours."

"You're leaving?"

"I'll take a taxi to another hotel and pay the bill on my way out. Call me if you or your family need anything."

I walk to the door, no last look at her. It already hurts too much.

"Vaughn, stop."

I pause.

"Would you please look at me?"

I turn around but keep my hand on the door.

"You can't walk away from this. I said I wanted to come in here to talk, and I meant it."

"What more can we say?"

"A lot more. Get back in here. You said ask anything, and this is what I'm asking."

My momentary relief is replaced by a constriction in my chest. She'll ask me to do what anyone would. She'll insist I confess my involvement in her mother's murder and come clean about stealing the books.

My life is over. I numb myself to prepare for it, a skill I learned living with my father.

She looks into my eyes. "Hey, come on, we can do this. Don't be afraid."

"What do you want to talk about?"

"Damn you. Stop shutting down on me."

She heard the coldness in my tone. But I can't help it. Once I enter this state, the dissociation locks in like a downloaded program.

"I need you to be here, Vaughn . . . or whatever your name is. What is your real name?"

"Vaughn Orr."

She exhales softly. "Okay, we'll deal with that later. Sit down. You don't look good."

I sit on the foot of the mattress. She pulls a desk chair in front of me. I'm surprised when she leans forward and takes my cold hands in hers. "Come back to me, Vaughn. I know what you're doing. I've done it all my life, too."

Tears burn my eyes.

"Okay, good. I can see you again." She presses on my hands, and I think she's also trying to stifle tears.

"You should hate me. You *did* hate me. I saw it when you ran away today."

"I was in shock," she says. "All those lies you told me . . . it hurt. It hurt bad. But while I was in jail, I had time to think."

"Thinking about it can't change what I did."

"It can't."

The coldness floods me again. "Then what are we talking about? You brought me here to say you can't forgive me?"

"If I can't forgive you, how will I ever forgive myself?"

"You weren't responsible for what happened to Julia. But I was with Nikki."

"No, you weren't. Kaz did it."

"Pointing out the telescope to him was stupid. I should have known it would tempt him."

"I've been thinking about that."

"What?"

"That looking at the telescope made so many things happen. What did you think when you saw it? Was it about money?"

"It had nothing to do with its value. I was wondering what you could see with it. I always wanted to look at galaxies and planets and things like that."

She looks about to cry again.

"I'm sorry it was the telescope of all things that led to the murder. I know how attached you were to it."

"There's no use imagining what might have been. It's all in the past. All we can change is the future."

The future. I'm afraid to ask what she means by that. And she still hasn't said anything about the books.

"Even if you can overlook my failure to report the murder . . . what about the books? It's disgusting what I did. You must hate me for that, at least."

"Disgusting . . ." She contemplates the word.

"It was wrong."

"It was. Of course it was."

I'm struck with a wave of relief, the same feeling I had when she rammed me with the car. I've been waiting—*wanting*—to be punished for publishing the books all these years. And who better to deliver the sentence than Riley? I want her to say, "You're right. I can't forgive you for taking credit for Julia's books."

I give her time to say it. I've waited for years. I can wait another minute.

"I've been trying to imagine what Julia would think about you publishing her books under your name. I've thought about it so much, I feel like she's right here with me . . . with us." After a pause she says, "Those words you used—*disgusting* and *hate*—they weren't words in Julia's vocabulary. I can't recall her ever saying she hated something or someone."

"She might if she knew me."

"She'd say you shouldn't have put your name on her books, but she wouldn't hate you for it." She sits back in her chair, studying me. "You said ask anything of you . . ."

Here it comes. She wants me to confess my sins to the world. Why do people think confessions miraculously scrub a soul clean? All it does is spread the shame to more people. Julia's readers love her books. To confess to them would spoil the beauty of her stories.

"If Julia were here, she would want to talk to you about what you did. She'd want to hear the whole story. And that's what I want. Tell me everything that happened with the books. I was upset when you tried to tell me, and I need you to explain it better. You said you saw the books when Kaz told you to erase the computers?"

"I didn't know who he'd killed at your house. When he left to dispose of the gun, I turned on a laptop to try to find a name and identify the people I'd seen at your house."

"Who had you seen? When?"

"Mostly Julia. I sometimes walked down that block and she always said hello."

"Oh my god."

"I saw you, too. And a few times I saw Nikki."

"Did I see you?"

I shake my head. "Both times you were playing in the driveway."

"This is so weird!"

"I know. Imagine my shock when I arrived at the farm and saw you grown up."

"I saw how you stared at me."

"I knew you saw. I wanted to turn around and run away. But I had no gas in my car."

"On purpose."

"Yes."

"Go back to the books. Why would you even open them?"

"When I was looking at the computer, I saw the pictures of you, and I was sick about you losing your mother. But I didn't know that for sure yet. I only knew the blonde woman in the pictures must be your mother because you had similar eyes. I opened the folder named NIKKI'S BOOKS because I was trying to sort out your family. When I saw they were all dedicated to you, I decided not to wipe the computers. I had to find out if Nikki was your mother—and who Kaz killed—before I did anything with the laptop."

"Why would any of that matter to you?"

"Isn't it obvious?"

"No, tell me."

"I thought those books were your mother's last words to you." I take the key out of my shirt. "My father once made me throw this key into the garbage. I think my mother hid it in my drawer for me . . . before she left. It was all I had of her because my father got rid of everything, even photographs. I don't even know what she looked like. If I hadn't been able to get her necklace out of the garbage that night . . . if he'd been watching to make sure I didn't . . ." I cover the key with my hand, suddenly insecure about mentioning it. "There's not really any comparison. Books are so much more."

"There is a comparison. I'm sorry for what he did."

I nod, tucking the key inside my shirt.

"I feel better knowing that's why you kept the books. Did you read any of them that night?"

"I didn't have time to do anything but pack a bag. I had to get the computers out of Kaz's sight, and to do that I had to leave Chicago. I was afraid he'd kill me if I took the laptops. I lived in fear of Kaz and his friends finding me for years. It's part of the reason I changed my name and kept a low profile. But by the time the first book came out, Kaz was in jail. It was such a relief to find that out."

Riley sits back in her chair, staring at me.

"What?"

"You risked your life to save the books."

"It wasn't as brave as it sounds. I was reacting. I was scared and hardly thinking straight. All I wanted to do was get away from Kaz."

"But through all that you kept the books safe. You really wanted to give them to me?"

"I really did. That was one of my first thoughts. When my friend drove me to the bus station, she told me details about the murder. That's when I found out your mother was the victim—and I thought the laptop was hers. That's when I decided to keep the books safe for you."

"And with all that going on, you got on a bus and went to New York City."

"It was quite a night. But I'm sure that night was worse for you."

"It was a bad night. But I hardly remember it. I went to the moon and stayed there."

"I thought about you all night on the bus."

We go quiet and look at each other.

"You must have been scared when you got to a city you didn't know," she says. "Did you have any money?"

"A little." I consider glossing over this part. But I want her to know the whole truth.

"I took something Kaz stole from your house. It turned out to be very valuable when I pawned it. It kept me fed and in a cheap motel until I found a job."

"What was it?"

"An emerald and diamond ring."

Her eyes widen. "That was the engagement ring Julia's fiancé gave her a few months before he died."

"I owe my life to that ring. I don't know what I would have done without it."

"I can't believe this."

"I'm sorry. I thought you should know the truth."

"It's okay. I'm glad I know. It makes it so much better!"

"Makes *what* better?"

"Everything. Don't you see? How the universe was working so hard to bring us to this moment?"

My god. That is so like something one of Julia's characters would say. I see what living with Julia was like. The magic. Riley's got it, and she doesn't even realize.

"Tell me the rest," she says. "When did you read Julia's books?"

"I read the first one in my motel room the day after I arrived in New York. *Book I*. And from the first page I was pulled in. I knew it was good. My best subject in school was English."

"Which book was it?"

"The third published, *The Feather and the Heart*. I quickly read the other three, and I couldn't believe how compelling they were. I had a bad book hangover—but that hangover felt a hell of a lot better than when I hung out with my friends."

She smiles. It's such a relief to tell someone. To finally talk about the true author's talent.

"After reading, I couldn't have destroyed them—even if I weren't saving them for you. But keeping stolen computers is dangerous. There were two laptops, and both had the books on them."

"I remember when she got the new laptop. She used a picture of me for the screensaver."

"I saw it."

"With the peonies?"

"Yes." I won't tell her how devastated I felt when I saw the photograph. I have no right to talk about my emotional state when she's dealing with far worse.

"When I earned enough money to get a cheap laptop, I copied the books and destroyed the two stolen laptops."

Now comes the worst part. But she told me to tell her everything.

"Once the books were on my computer, I started to feel more and more possessive of them. Julia's characters are so raw and real, so flawed but capable of redemption—they become part of you even after you're done reading. It's the same with how she creates plot. Her beginnings are like inviting spells, and once you're inside, you're involved, really involved. All that love and heartbreak and bitterness and beauty. I felt emotions I'd never known I had in me. It was like I had four entire worlds in my possession."

Riley looks too emotional to respond.

"I read each book several times. I was . . . it was like I was obsessed with them. I thought about them all the time—when I was walking around the city or working as a dishwasher. That job was boring, and the books gave me something to think about hour after hour. Julia is a genius with setting, describing just enough to make a scene vivid and give it the perfect mood. On my days off, I visited every place in the city she mentioned so I could experience the story more realistically."

"The books were a refuge."

I think about how living in the books made me feel during those first rough months in New York. "You're right. They were a way I could escape my constant fears about Kaz and my future. I'd have to say the books saved me as much as the ring those first months."

"I was living on the moon; you were living in the books. Julia created refuges for us both."

"I suppose that's true."

"How did you go from being obsessed to publishing?"

"You can imagine how one might lead to the other."

She nods.

"But it was still about you . . . at least it was when I first got the idea."

"That doesn't make sense. You took the laptops to save the stories for me. You thought they were my mother's last words to me. If you got one published—"

"I know. It didn't make sense. This is when everything started to get morally muddled. I was obsessed with the books, and I was obsessed with you—with fixing the damage Kaz and I did to your life. But in all honesty, I wanted someone to read one of those books. I wanted someone to feel how I did when I read it. I had to see if I was right about how good the writing was, and I admit there was a lot of egotism in what I did."

She waits for more explanation.

"You were only twelve when I got the idea to publish. I felt certain you were too young to understand the power of the books. I admit, the main reason I published was the fear that you never would. I envisioned your shock when the books arrived at your house. I imagined the pain they dredged up when you read them. And for some reason, I always saw you storing them away in a box for the rest of your life."

"I wonder if I would have."

"Now that I know you studied writing, I think you might have gotten them published. That was part of the reason I was shocked when Sachi said you were a writer. At that moment, I felt I'd made an even bigger mistake than I thought."

"Why did you ask to read my journal?"

"Several reasons. I was curious to know if you had your mother's talent. Also—I know this will sound wrong—I wanted to experience your side of the murder. All these years I've agonized over what I did to you when I drew Kaz to the telescope. I've wondered how much that moment wrecked your life."

"You were so sure I'd write about the murder?"

"That's what I wanted to see, because you said you were supposed to write about an important life event. But there was another reason I wanted to see the journal, maybe my main motivation."

"What?"

"I had to see how good you were. If you were a bad writer, I'd have felt better about not giving the books to you. You need at least some skill with writing to get published."

"Julia told me it was too difficult to even try."

"Not when you write like she did."

Riley smiles. "Tell me how you did it."

"The idea had been creeping up on me, but I started to act on it when I was browsing in a used bookstore. I was thumbing through all these novels, thinking how much better the books on my computer were. Then right in front of me is a manual about how to get published."

"It was a sign."

"I thought so. After reading the guide, I became more obsessed with getting one of the novels published than with the books themselves. And I confess . . . you faded from my thoughts at that time. I think I pushed you and the guilt away to make it easier to do what I wanted."

I gaze down at the blue cast, rubbing my fingers over its plastered gauze. "Pushing you away to get that first book published was the biggest mistake of my life." I look up at her. "It started a cycle of guilt that's been eating me alive for years. I'm sorry, Riley. I can't explain it any more than this. It was wrong and I expect no forgiveness."

"You expect none, or you want none? Maybe you'd rather keep hating on yourself."

I think she sees I'm surprised by her insight. "Remember, I'm something of an expert on guilt, too," she says. "It hurts to be forgiven when you've lived with guilt for as long as we have. I feel like a vital artery inside me is bleeding out."

I so badly want to hold her. Am I imagining she looks like she's fighting the same urge?

"Tell me more about how you got the books published," she says. "Was it easier or more difficult than you'd imagined?"

"Well . . . neither. I was too busy at that time to think much about it. I was waiting tables at night and taking writing classes during the day. During free time, I looked up agents and publishers, studied vocabulary, and read fiction that was similar to the books. I spent a lot of time researching everything that was mentioned in the books."

"The Sea of Clouds. And John Keats and *Endymion*."

"Yes. But the most difficult part by far came after I signed with an agent and the book was picked up by a publisher. I wasn't prepared for the editing process. I worked with a professional editor, and sometimes she asked me to rewrite scenes or write new ones. That was agonizing because I could never write as well as Julia. I'm grateful I had a good editor who helped me get through it."

"Weren't you afraid to publish them?"

"They were written from both male and female perspectives and took place in Chicago, New York, and other places I might have visited. I was pretty sure I could pull it off."

"But what if I'd read the books or Julia had told me about them? I'd have recognized *When Leaves Let Go* and *A Box of Broken Stars* when I read them."

"Not just you. What if she'd asked beta readers or friends to read them? That fear caused many sleepless nights. But after reading her notes, I had a feeling she hadn't shown them to anyone."

"It was a much bigger risk than being accused of plagiarism. If someone had known the books were Julia's, you'd have been tied to the burglary and murder."

"Now you understand the fears that have tormented me all these years. I've often wished I never published that first book."

"Yet you did. Your desire to see the books appreciated was a higher power that conquered your fears."

"Don't make it sound noble. Publishing the books was one hundred percent wrong. The only saving grace is that the books lived on after the burglary. It's almost a miracle that I happened upon them and didn't erase them."

Riley abruptly stands and strides to the window. She stares out at the city lights.

I walk over to her. "Are you okay?"

"How can you say the only saving grace is that the books survived—especially after everything that happened today?"

"Everything that happened today was more pain I caused when I published the books."

She's shaking her head. "I see it as so much more than pain. It's *almost a miracle*, like you said, that I finally let go of what happened to Julia. I don't think I'd ever have done it if you hadn't found the courage to tell me about the burglary and the books."

She returns her gaze to the bright city, her eyes reflecting a thousand lights. "It's the books," she says softly. "The books are the key to everything."

"What do you mean?"

She turns to me. "Why did we tell the truth? Why are we even together in this room right now? Because of Julia's books. Like you said before, they became part of you. And that means *she* became part of you. Her characters and stories. Her thoughts and emotions. She inspired you to put your past behind and start a new life. To get jobs, take writing classes—even to work hard at getting the books published. Don't you see? It was the books, Julia herself, who urged you to give her stories to the world."

"I wish I could believe that."

"Then believe it. I used to think it was Kiran's magic that brought you to the farm, but now I think it was Julia's." Smiling she adds, "Maybe they're 'in cahoots,' as Colton would say."

"I went to the farm mostly to figure out how to give you the money. I was sick with guilt, and I thought that would somehow make me feel better."

I cringe when I think of my initial, patronizing assumptions about her family.

"I went there to give you money, and I found a family that needed nothing. All of you gave me so much more than I could have given you."

Her smile is knowing, as if to say this is also part of the magic. But I'm not feeling anything magical. Talking about her family has reminded me of where I stand. Her family is just down the hall, and they know nothing of my crimes.

I don't know why I felt hopeful about Riley and me. She has a beautiful family, and I have dangerous secrets. Merging our lives isn't possible.

"Riley . . . thank you for giving me a chance to explain. But I should go now. Do you want to talk about the money now or after you've had a chance to think about it?"

"What about the money?"

"I made a mess of giving you the books, but at least you know the truth now, and I can give you the royalties. But transferring the money will be difficult to explain to your family—we'll have to figure out how without raising suspicion. It's millions, Riley. I lived well enough to play the part of a successful author, but I mostly used the money to make more. I invested it, and it's done very well."

"Do you honestly think that's what I want from you?"

"It's all I have to give."

She looks as crushed by my words as I felt saying them.

"Is it all?" she asks. "Today you said your feelings for me were real. Were you lying?"

"My feelings for you have been truer than anything in my life."

"Okay. Do you think we can try starting over?"

Hope has always been painful for me, but this is the worst it's ever been. "There's no way we can start over. Surely you see that. Your family will—"

"Leave my family out of it."

"We can't leave them out—and I wouldn't want you to."

"So, other than your worries about them, you would want to start over?"

"You know you can't leave them out of this."

"Just answer me."

"Yes."

We stand many feet apart, looking at each other. I feel more like we've negotiated a house sale than rekindled a romance. I don't see how it can work. The lies she'll tell her family will create increasing resentment, and no relationship can withstand that. My secrets are dark beasts that consume everything around me. Not one woman or friendship in my past has survived them.

"You know what you need?"

"What?"

"You need that cast signed."

This non sequitur is unexpected. She must feel as overwhelmed as I do.

"I'll get a Sharpie," she says, heading for the door.

"Where?"

"Alec. Field biologists tend to carry them."

"Tell your family they can order room service and put it on the bill."

"They'll have eaten in the car. Sachi always packs food for a trip."

"They left in a hurry."

"I know, but she still would. And Colton probably grabbed a burger when they stopped for gas. Anyway, I'm sure Kiran is nearly asleep. He looked exhausted."

She returns a minute later, holding up a Sharpie. "I told you. Alec had one in his briefcase. They said they ate sandwiches Sachi packed, and Colton got fast food when they stopped for gas. They're all in their pajamas. Kiran is already in bed."

I'm impressed that every prediction was true. It must be comforting to feel that familiar and secure about your family.

She sits next to me on the bed, gently takes my cast in her hands and writes: *Now we're even. Riley.* "You said I could pay you back for spilling the beer on me. Do you remember—at the Blind Wolf?"

"Of course. You take your paybacks very seriously, don't you?" I stare at the words, *Now we're even.* It means much more than the payback of a broken arm.

She touches the Sharpie's tip next to her name. She draws a little heart and colors it in with the black ink.

I can't take my eyes off the heart.

"Your turn," she says, handing the pen to me.

"People don't usually sign their own cast, do they?"

She holds my gaze. "I want the Vaughn imposter who came out of the magic stone to sign it."

That can't happen, and now she knows why.

"Come on . . . what's his name?"

"I never say that name. For good reason. It's too dangerous."

She caps the pen. "You said we could try starting over, right?"

"Yes, but—"

"I can't be with you unless you agree to one condition."

I knew this was coming. The damn soul cleansing.

"You have to tell my family everything. Not Kiran, of course—"

"I can't do that!"

"You have to. Can you imagine us trying to hide a secret this big?"

"I'll go to jail. There won't be any *us*."

"They won't tell anyone."

"Even if they don't, they won't want anything to do with me when they find out."

"I guarantee they will."

"Tell them about the books, too?"

"Yes."

I get up, pace to the window. "Jesus, Riley! And Colton? He hates me. He might tell the police."

"I know Colton's heart, and he won't."

How can she ask this of me? It's cruel to make this a requirement of our future together when she knows how reckless it is to tell anyone. I'm an accomplice to a murder and burglary. I'm possibly the most shameful plagiarist in American literary history.

She walks over to me. "I think it will be good to finally let go of it—to just a few people. It hurts at first, but now I feel like my whole life is starting over. I want you to feel that. We can start over together."

"I did let it go. I told you. And it's a miracle you don't hate me. But to expect three more people to forgive what I did? Other people aren't like you, Riley."

"My family isn't *other people*. You can feel safe with them. You need this. *We* need this or we won't survive. We can't hide who you are from my family. Don't you see that?"

"Of course I see it. That's why I said this can't work."

"It can work!"

She doesn't understand. *Now we're even* will never be true of us. Her secrets were different from mine. Telling hers freed her. Telling mine would put me in prison, not to mention make a grand mess of her life.

"You can't do it?"

"Riley . . ."

"This is the only way I can be with you. Now that I'm out from under that weight, I won't do it again . . . the lies, the guilt. I can't take any more."

"I know."

Another agonizing moment of truth. But she means it. I either tell her family or I lose her. I try to imagine the future without her. My bleak existence before I met her, a world without a scrap of magic.

My heart races as I take the pen from her hand. I feel more like I'm skydiving than signing a cast. I pull off the pen cap with my teeth and lift my left arm to write on the cast. Above the little black heart she drew next to her name, I draw another heart, upside down from hers. I color it black to match. Next to it, I sign, *Tyler*.

"Tyler? Really?"

I push the pen into the cap and pull it out of my mouth. "Really."

"What's your whole name?"

"Tyler Ryan Webb."

"You have a middle name."

"Yes."

"*Webb*," she says, studying my face to see how it fits.

"Too boring to be an author name, don't you think?"

"I've never found anything about you boring."

"Same for me with you."

She strokes her finger on the hearts we drew. "Two dark hearts. I like that." She takes my hand and tugs me to my feet. "You know what I'm wondering?"

"What?"

"Would a first kiss with Tyler be as good as the one with Vaughn?"

"It would be tough to beat the Vaughn kiss, coyotes, moon, and all."

"I guess so."

"But I'm willing to give it a try."

"Yeah?"

"Yeah." I can't wait any longer. I grasp her with my good arm and pull her against my body. She holds me tight. No coyotes or moonlight, but the kiss is infinitely better because I don't feel guilty about it.

She makes a thoughtful face. "You know, I think Tyler Webb kisses better than Vaughn Orr."

"No he doesn't."

"I think I could maybe go for this Tyler guy."

"Okay, I have a condition, too. You have to call me Vaughn."

"I might want to call you Tyler sometimes."

"Nope."

"How about we negotiate this further after you talk to my family?"

I nuzzle her cheek. "How about we negotiate now and let your family get some sleep?"

"Do you really think Alec and Sachi are tired after all this? They're waiting for me to talk to them about what happened. Colton is, too."

"Oh god." I let go of her and plop onto the chair.

"Don't you dare back out on me."

"You know . . . I think I'm dreading this more than telling you. Sachi likes me. She's the only mother-like person I've ever known, and I can't bear for her to think poorly of me."

Riley places her hands softly on the sides of my face. "I know it's hard for you, but you need to trust my family."

"Not Colton."

"Yes, Colton. Especially Colton. He might act a little bristly at first, but he's a super softy inside. He'll come around."

I'm not seeing it.

She delicately strokes her finger under one of my eyes. "You're tired and you must be in pain. We need to do this before you can't."

"You've been through worse today."

"I hit you with a car."

"I hit you with the metaphorical equivalent of a car."

"Okay," she says, "so we both need rest. Let that be our incentive to get this over with."

"Sleep is our incentive?"

"Sleep and a bath. You can't get that cast wet. You'll need help."

I wrap my arms around her. "This is sounding more like incentive."

She leans down and kisses me. "You don't know the meaning of the word, Mr. Orr."

29
RILEY

I've never seen Vaughn sleep so deeply. Even in a hotel room bed, he makes me think of Endymion sleeping under a spell when Selene came to make love to him in the night.

I wonder if all people experience this emotion as they watch a lover in the peace of slumber. The sensation fills me, thick and sweet, like honey poured into a pitcher. When did the first human feel this? I imagine an early hominid, a creature that looks more ape than human, staring down at her sleeping partner this way. Whenever or however it happened, I'm in awe of the magic in our double helix that brings about this mysterious emotion.

I'm trying not to doubt my genes. I don't know why I thought I had to be like Nikki. I'm more like Julia and her father. And Alec and Sachi. I'm no longer afraid to believe I have good in me. And I'm not afraid to believe Vaughn is good despite some bad things he's done.

The night I was released from jail, Vaughn told Alec, Sachi, and Colton everything. Alec and Sachi immediately forgave him. I knew they would. Colton was more reserved. He didn't say he forgave him, but he's not as tough on Vaughn as he used to be. I saw how his expression softened when Vaughn described how his father hurt him.

I trace one finger over the raspy stubble below Vaughn's cheekbone. He said his father sometimes woke him from sleep for no reason other than to berate and beat him. I stroke his forehead, wishing I could erase those memories.

He opens his eyes, lunar gray, flecked with yellow. He smiles sleepily and says, "Hello, love." He often says that, as if greeting both me and the newness of love.

He's never said he loves me. And I haven't either. But I think this feeling must be love.

"I'm sorry I woke you," I say, "but we have to get ready for the Annunciation."

This is what we've been calling the book event. The Annunciation of a Lesser God.

We're all going. Vaughn insisted on buying clothes for my family because they hadn't brought anything nice to wear when they left Wisconsin. We took Kiran to four stores before he found a dress he liked. He loved it so much he wore it out of the shop and to bed that night. We could hardly get the dress off him to send it out to be cleaned and pressed yesterday.

Vaughn pulls me down to the bed. "I have to be anointed first."

"We just did."

"We'd better do it again to make sure we're up to divine standards."

"We have to be there in an hour and a half."

But there's no stopping him now. Or me. The cast on his arm doesn't slow us down one bit.

Later, while we dress, I ask, "Have you figured out how you're going to explain me being Riley?"

"I'll tell them the truth. I recently met you in Wisconsin. I can even say we joked about the coincidence of your name."

"What if they ask about the Riley in your book dedications?"

"I've been asked before, and I've never answered. But that just led to more speculation."

"What will you say now?"

"I met someone named Riley in New York when I first arrived, someone who inspired my books but who prefers to remain anonymous. That's the truth, too. I met eleven-year-old Riley in those photographs on the stolen laptop."

I help him pull his specially tailored white dress shirt over his cast. "I assume you got rid of all those photos?"

"Of course." He looks into my eyes. "It wasn't easy to do that—to erase your whole childhood. Destroying those photographs felt worse than publishing the books."

I focus on buttoning his shirt to keep from crying. "Remember what we said. No more guilt."

"It'll take a while."

"I know. Me too."

I straighten his collar. "I'm scared about tonight. I'm afraid someone is going to piece this all together."

"We need to get as much as possible out in the open right away. If we're secretive, people will dig."

"They will anyway. I wish we'd canceled this thing."

"I know how you feel. This is how I've lived since the first book was published. Always lying. Always afraid of being found out. Forbidding myself friendships, too scared to let a woman get close to me."

I kiss his lips. "We've got that last one covered."

"Damn right," he says, kissing me again.

After I help him put on his jacket, he looks in the mirror and holds up his bulging arm. Same as his shirt, the gray jacket was tailored to cover his cast. "Is this as noticeable as I think it is? I look like one of those beach crabs that has one big claw and one little one."

"Those are called fiddler crabs, and they use the big claw to fight off competing males and attract females. You should see it as a good thing."

"You find it attractive?"

"Only if you successfully fight off competing males."

288

"I'll do my best."

Kiran knocks on our door. We know it's him because he always keeps knocking until we open the door.

"Looking good, Kiran," Vaughn says as he lets him in.

"You're gorgeous," I tell him.

"I know." He stands at our full-length mirror to look at himself in the dress. The silky fabric is deep lavender, similar to the periwinkle color of his bedroom walls, and it's printed with impressionistic white shell shapes. He couldn't have found a more perfect dress. I think he must feel secure in it, as if he's wrapped in his room at home. He's wearing his favorite glittery gym shoes, though Vaughn told him he could buy any new shoes he wanted.

The shoes were mine when I was a little older than him. I refused to throw them out when I outgrew them. I was like that with all my favorite clothing. I guess Kiran and I have the same collector genes. It must be from the Mays side.

I remember the day Julia bought those shoes for me. I was thrilled, because glittered technicolor shoes were popular with some of the girls in the third grade. Julia said, "These are too cool, Riley! They look like actual magic."

I loved her so much for saying that. I was walking in magic, in Julia's magic, whenever I wore those shoes.

Sachi, Alec, and Colton enter our room. Sachi looks beautiful in a simple, cream-color dress. She's wearing my favorite of her glasses, the turquoise and indigo frames. Alec and Colton look hip in the slim-fitting suit jackets and pants they chose with Vaughn's help. They aren't wearing ties because the dress code is *casually elegant*, an oxymoron Vaughn had to explain. He said my simple green cocktail dress is perfect for the event.

"I have something really cool for you, Kiran," Vaughn says.

Kiran turns away from the mirror and looks at the large gear resting in Vaughn's palm.

"It's from inside a grandfather clock that was made in the eighteen fifties. Have you ever seen a grandfather clock?"

"Lots of times," Kiran says. "But I never took one apart."

"Go on, take it," Vaughn says.

Kiran reverently takes the gear into his hands and says thank you.

"Where did you get it?" I ask.

"I asked around and had it sent over from a shop that specializes in old clocks. I've always wanted to give him a grandfather clock to take apart, but I guess one gear will have to be next best for now."

"Thank you," Sachi says. "That's a very thoughtful gift."

"I have to provide some compensation for making him go to this boring book thing."

"Boring?" Alec says in a wry tone.

Colton grins, but he's as nervous as the rest of us about all the lying we have to do.

Vaughn has arranged a limousine to take us to the book party. We don't say much during the ride over. We're all nervous, aware of the danger of exposing our secrets to the world.

Kiran turns the clock gear in his hands, rubbing it as if trying to conjure his magic. He seems troubled by it. It's larger than any clock gear he's seen, and he's never had a gear from a clock he didn't dismantle himself. Vaughn meant well, but he doesn't understand how particular Kiran is about his clocks and fossils.

Our limousine pulls to the curb in front of a two-story art gallery that's owned by Tommi Singh, a close friend of Vaughn's literary agent. The venue was originally a trendy bookstore owned by Tommi's husband, but the event quickly outgrew the store as word spread that Vaughn Orr would be in Chicago to sign books for the first time since he'd left his hometown. Tommi and her husband decided to hold an evening party at the art gallery to accommodate more people. No doubt they also saw it as an opportunity to sell art.

Before we get out of the limousine, Vaughn says, "Just to give you all a heads-up, there will be a few people from the press here."

"How did they find out?" Alec asks.

"My agent and publisher got the film studio involved—to promote the movie that's coming out next year. It's probably an idea my agent and Tommi cooked up. I think Tommi got funding for this event from my publisher and the film studio."

"They should have asked you if you wanted media here before they did that," I say.

"I'm okay with it. I have something to say, and I want the media to run with it."

"What are you going to say?"

"You'll see." He smiles, but I can tell it's only a cover.

"Vaughn . . . just don't say anything, okay? Let's keep a low profile."

He kisses my cheek. "Try not to be afraid. Let's all think of Julia tonight. This is really her night, isn't it?"

Sachi and I become teary, thinking of Julia.

We've arrived a little late, and the gallery is already crowded. My family enters the party in a tight cluster, like a school of minnows navigating the dangers of an unfamiliar sea.

We're introduced to Tommi and her husband, Paul, who's selling all four of Vaughn's novels from stacks on tables. Vaughn is surprised when his agent, Mel, walks up to him, grinning. "You knew I'd have to fly out here and see you do this," she says.

"I thought you came to see me," Tommi says with mock affront to her friend.

"I'm well aware that you two have been scheming this event for years," Vaughn says.

His voice and manner are different. He's more like the slick Vaughn who came to our farm last February.

"How's the arm?" Mel asks.

"Good," he replies.

"Classy way to get run over," Mel says. "I hear it was a really nice Porsche."

I cringe when Mel glances at me, guessing I'm the one who did it. Vaughn and I had hoped the story wouldn't go public, but it came out in an article that said Vaughn Orr's girlfriend accidentally hit him with a car.

"Good thing it wasn't a garbage truck," Vaughn says. "Imagine what that would do to my image. Let me introduce you to Riley and her family."

I can tell Mel is intrigued by my family. But her gaze keeps returning to me.

"She's not the Riley in the dedications," Vaughn says to preempt her question.

"Tommi told me," Mel says, "but what an odd coincidence."

"Life is stranger than fiction," he says. "If you'll all excuse me, I want to show Sachi something."

"It's over there," Tommi says to Vaughn, gesturing at the other side of the gallery.

Vaughn leads us through the room, constantly replying to the people who greet him. When we arrive in front of the painting, he looks at Sachi to see her reaction. It's *Man, Asleep*, the painting Vaughn bought from her.

Sachi is speechless.

"I had it sent from Brooklyn," Vaughn says. "I hope you don't mind. It's not for sale, of course."

"I've had many offers," Tommi says, appearing behind us. "I looked up your work online, Sachi. I'd love to talk to you about it and maybe bring in a few more paintings."

"You rascal!" Sachi says to Vaughn.

"I am. But even rascals know talent when they see it."

"It's one of your best skills," Sachi says.

Alec, Colton, and I grin as Sachi and Vaughn embrace.

We leave Sachi to discuss her art with Tommi. The rest of us get drinks before Vaughn sits down to sign books and talk with readers. Alec, Colton, Kiran, and I browse the lower and upper levels of the gallery. I like many of the paintings. Some are surreal like Sachi's. I think her art would fit well here.

Kiran stays close. He still has the clock gear in his hands, and he often rubs his hands over it. Sachi offered to put it in her purse, but he wanted to keep it.

Tommi clinks a bottle opener against her wineglass to quiet the crowd. The voices drop to a hum, and she says, "Thank you, everyone, for coming to honor Vaughn Orr, one of Chicago's most celebrated writers." Looking at Vaughn, she says, "This guy has written four best-selling novels, with two movie adaptations, and he isn't thirty yet. Can you believe that?"

The crowd applauds. I know Vaughn well enough to see how uncomfortable he is. He told me that concealing his fear from his father was good training for hiding his anxiety in situations like this.

Tommi continues, "If you didn't catch that reference to two movies, *A Box of Broken Stars* will be a major motion picture coming out next year."

The crowd applauds again.

Tommi holds up her glass of wine and says, "Thank you, Vaughn, for letting Chicago bestow the admiration you deserve. We're all so proud of our gifted hometown author!"

"Hear! Hear!" many say, raising their glasses.

Vaughn smiles humbly as everyone toasts him. A woman from the press snaps photographs of him. Vaughn looks at me as he walks over to Tommi. I think he's going to say whatever it is he wants *the media to run with*. I can't imagine what he would want the world to know.

"Thank you, Tommi, for hosting me in your beautiful gallery tonight. And many thanks to Paul, who apparently is my number-one fan in Chicago. I think his bookstore sells more copies of my books than Amazon."

"Working on that," Paul says, and everyone laughs.

Looking at Mel, Vaughn says, "I'd also like to thank my agent, Melanie Dagesse. She pulled my first manuscript out of her slush pile eight years ago and has championed my writing ever since. Thank you, Mel, for being the best agent I could imagine." Vaughn raises his wineglass toward her.

Mel beams and holds up her glass to Vaughn as everyone applauds.

Vaughn glances at me as he takes a sip of his wine. "Tonight many of you have asked about my next book. I haven't answered because there is no next book."

The crowd murmurs. A few fans even call out in protest.

"I've decided to take a break from writing to work on something new. Recently, a Wisconsin biologist showed me something that sort of woke me up. He showed me a white snowshoe hare living in a brown forest in February."

Alec and I look at Colton, flushed from neck to ear tips.

"This February was the warmest on record in North America," Vaughn says, "and a white rabbit doesn't do so well in a world without snow. Predators get them. If you're wondering what on earth I'm talking about, look it up. In recent years, snowshoe hares have disappeared from much of Wisconsin."

After a pause he says, "Maybe this all sounds foolish to some of you, but you know, I think it's more foolish to ignore what's happening on our planet."

Many in the audience clap as Vaughn continues. "That's why I've decided to put my creative energy into saving our home. For the foreseeable future, I'll work on creating a foundation that funds research to help slow global climate change."

The same people cheer and hoot. The rest in the crowd look stunned.

Vaughn holds up his drink. "Now, if you aren't all too annoyed with me, I'd like to toast everyone who came out to honor me tonight. Thank you to the best readers any author could ask for." Most applaud, but many people look like they're trying to make sense of a book signing at which the author says he's not writing more books.

"Well, that was unexpected," Alec says.

"Was it?" Sachi says with a knowing smile.

Vaughn is sieged by people asking questions, but he excuses himself and pushes toward me. "What do you think? It was your idea, by the way. Remember that first day in Sachi's studio?"

"I remember. Is this really something you want to do?"

"Yes. And I want you, Alec, and Colton to help me—if you'd like to be involved. I want to dedicate the foundation to Julia. We could call it the Julia Mays Foundation."

He sees I'm trying not to cry in front of all the staring people. He takes my hand and leads me outside. On the sidewalk, he pulls the decorative square out of his jacket pocket and dabs it beneath my eyes. "Polyester. Useless. Gone are the days when a guy could be of assistance with an absorbent cotton hankie."

I take the square out of his hand and tuck it back into his pocket. "Your assistance is just fine. And I love your idea—the Julia Mays Foundation. It's beautiful."

I pull him close for a kiss. People flow around us.

Vaughn tucks me into his chest. "I think this can work, this future I'm imagining. I could never see the future before I met you. It was just dark. But now I see so much it makes me dizzy."

I pull out of his arms. "What do you see?"

"I see us setting up this foundation. I see the money Julia's stories made going to a cause she might have invested in herself. I see me buying the seventy acres next to your land—because you told me the owner might sell it soon. I see us having an organic garden that's even bigger than Sachi's—"

"Wait . . . what is this *us*?"

He grins. "I can't divulge *everything* I've seen yet. There has to be some suspense in a story to keep it interesting."

"Could you really live like that? A simple life in the country? No fancy house, car, whiskey . . . ?"

"I'm tired of all that. It never brought me any real pleasure. But there might be the occasional bottle of excellent whiskey . . ."

"Will you be able to afford that without more books to sell and investing in the foundation?"

"I may not be a writer but turns out I'm good at managing money. And I've lived prudently. I didn't travel, or buy expensive jewelry, cars, and clothes. I didn't frequent fancy restaurants or clubs, and I own one ordinary house. I was a white rabbit trying to blend into a brown world."

Alec often says one little moth transformed his whole future. And of course that changed mine. Maybe one snowshoe hare will change many lives.

He holds my hand. "What about you? Do you see a different future for yourself than you used to?"

"It's not different. It's the same dream I've had since I lived with Julia."

"What dream?"

"I don't know if I'm ready to talk about it."

"Come on, tell me!"

"Don't get all excited . . ."

"Okay, enough suspense."

"I always wanted to be like Julia. To see the magic in everything and somehow transcribe it into words."

"A writer? You want to write fiction?"

"I never told anyone, not even her. A few teachers said they were impressed with my writing, but I had to keep it secret from my mother.

She would have used it against me and ruined it like she always did. Anything I wrote I ripped into tiny shreds so she wouldn't find it."

He holds me. "Oh god. I'm sorry. But now nothing is stopping you, right? The wall is gone." He steps back, grinning. "I knew it! I've known since that day we talked at the creek."

"I told you not to get excited."

"I can't help it!"

"Don't tell anyone."

"I won't. But . . . this is so great!"

"We'll see about that. Vaughn Orr will be a tough act to follow."

"Not me. Julia. And that won't be a tough act to follow. All you have to do is follow her example. Embody her love and magic. You do it so well, Riley, so much better than you know."

He's made me cry again. He holds me close. The city around us feels so big, but in a bright, inviting way. I've never felt like this before, as if anything I can imagine is possible.

The wail of a siren a few blocks over pulls us out of our reverie. "We'd better go. Your fans are watching us."

He glances at the people in the gallery windows. "I'd rather go back to the hotel. You look so great in that dress—it's difficult to control myself."

"Thank you, and you can wait. Think of it as added suspense to the story."

He tries to give me a long kiss, but I keep it short. "Go on. Get your fans excited about your new future."

When we enter the gallery, he's surrounded by people talking about his foundation idea. His excitement is contagious. I believe I'm seeing the real Tyler Webb, the man who would have developed from a bright child if he'd been loved instead of beaten and belittled.

I leave Vaughn to his fans and head to the bar for a glass of wine. Vaughn's agent sees me in line and comes over.

"Well, that was quite an announcement," she says.

"Yes. It's exciting, isn't it?"

She brushes a shiny auburn tress off her shoulder. "Honestly, no. I'd be more excited to hear he's working on his next book."

"I can understand that."

"I'm not too worried. He'll settle down once he gets through this rough spot."

Rough spot? Doesn't she see how happy Vaughn looks?

Mel studies me, possibly sees I disagree with her. "A writer like him, a person with that much emotion locked inside him . . . he has to write to be happy, Riley."

I suddenly understand the pressure Vaughn's felt since the last book was published. And here I am thinking of becoming a writer.

"Of course I sympathize with his concerns for the Earth," Mel says. "We're making a real mess of our planet. But Vaughn's fears about that would be best expressed if he wrote them. That's his skill and how he can make the most impact."

I think she wants me to use my influence to get him writing again.

She gives me a pointed look. "His talent is like none I've ever encountered."

"Maybe he has other talents that will surprise us."

She has no response as I step up to the bar and order a glass of chardonnay. I'm relieved when she drifts into the crowd.

I don't see Vaughn anywhere. His suit jacket is draped over his empty chair. I wander around looking for Alec and Colton, and I spot them coming out of one of the gallery alcoves. Alec heads toward me, his hand wrapped around Kiran's. He isn't smiling like usual. Colton doesn't look like he's having fun either, but I expected that. He'd rather be in front of a campfire with his girlfriend right now.

"Everything okay?" I ask.

"Colton and I are going to take Kiran back to the hotel," Alec says.

"Really, so soon?"

"Kiran's tired," Colton says.

"I'm not tired!" Kiran says.

Something's upset him. He looks near tears.

"What happened?" I ask Alec and Colton.

"He was alone for a little while," Alec says. "He left the bathroom before Colton and I did, and he'd disappeared into the crowd when we came out. He was upset when we found him, but he won't tell us why."

Sachi joins our family huddle.

I crouch and ask Kiran, "What happened, Kee? Did you get scared when you thought you were lost?"

He shakes his head, but tears drip.

"Please tell me what's wrong."

"Vaughn . . . ," he says.

I peer around, looking for Vaughn. His jacket is still on the chair at the book-signing table. "What about him?"

Kiran looks at his clock gear and rubs his hands on it, as if to extract some magic that will make him feel better.

"What happened with Vaughn? Do you know where he is?"

"He's with that bad man," Kiran says, his teary gaze on the gear.

"What bad man?"

"The one . . . the one who said mean things about me."

"Who said mean things?"

A tear plops onto the clock gear. "Vaughn shouldn't have gone with that bad man."

I glance up at my family, and the looks on their faces suggest they're thinking what I am. Vaughn may have gotten into a fight with whoever it was.

"Where did Vaughn go with the man?" I ask Kiran.

Kiran rubs the tear into the metal gear with his forefinger. He looks at me, his somber gaze beyond his eight years. It reminds me of the day he said he'd put the mantel clock gear on the table for me. "I think something bad is going to happen, Riley."

A sense of dread hits like a specter. I feel it in my bones: Vaughn is in danger. He wouldn't have left his book party for this long.

"Please tell me where he is."

"You shouldn't go," he says tearfully. "Something bad is going to happen."

"But we have to help Vaughn, don't we?"

He nods slowly.

"Where did he go with the man? Which door?"

"The white door."

I look around. The front door is glass. The back door is white.

I say quietly to my family, "I think Vaughn got in a fight with someone who insulted Kiran."

"So do I," Colton says, his face red with rage, "and let me at him."

Alec says to Sachi, "Wait here with Kiran." He adds, "You too, Riley."

"Can we not do the men-take-charge thing right now? I need to know Vaughn's okay." I stride toward the white door, Alec and Colton following.

"No!" Kiran wails. "Mom, stop them!"

Alec, Colton, and I turn around.

Kiran runs to us, his face flushed and wet. He holds up the gear. "I have to put this on my table. It has to be with the fossils. Don't go there until I fix it!"

"Home is too far away for that," Alec says. "We're just going to make sure Vaughn is okay."

"It's not okay! You can't go. Dad, don't!"

People are staring at him. Sachi takes his hand. "We'll get some fresh air. Go find Vaughn."

She leads Kiran away, and we walk to the white door and enter the stairwell. Alec opens the door to the alley and peers up and down. "Not here," he says.

I jog up the stairs. The door to the roof is half-open. I hear Vaughn's voice. I can tell he's trying to keep his tone down but detect no signs of a fight.

Colton is about to push past me. I grab his jacket to hold him back. "They aren't fighting," I whisper. "We should let him handle it on his own."

But I won't leave until I'm certain he isn't in trouble. What Kiran said has unsettled me.

While Vaughn and the man continue talking, I quietly step out the door into shadows. The roof isn't lit, but the surrounding city glow provides enough light to see dark shapes of heating and air-conditioning machinery. Vaughn is easy to see in his white dress shirt. He's talking to a shorter man about twenty yards to my right, near the roof edge.

I didn't hear what Vaughn said, but the other man says in reply, "You're so full of shit, Tyler!"

Alec and Colton sidle up to me, listening.

"I've told you everything," Vaughn says. "If you don't want to believe it, I guess that's your problem." He turns away from the man, as if to walk to the stairs.

"You're the one with a problem," the other man says. "A very big problem."

"Why don't you come downstairs and have a beer?" Vaughn says.

"Are you sure you want me to go down there and talk to all those people?" the man says, a clear threat in his tone. "I know I'm right. I figured it out."

Vaughn turns to him. "How do you figure it, Kaz? Tell me how you made the leap from me being a writer to I must have stolen the books."

My heart thuds. Alec and Colton look at me with wide eyes. We know who the man is. He's the one who killed Nikki: John Kazmirski.

30
Vaughn

I hope Kaz can't sense my panic.

"You have a lot of time to figure things out when you're in prison," Kaz says. "It's funny. Sometimes they let you go to the library, like, to *improve* yourself."

He grunts a sarcastic sound. "The books in prison are all old crap people donate. And one day I pick up this book called *The Sound of Absence*, and there you are on the cover. Tyler fucking Webb! This nobody Babyass who never said one word to me when he left Chicago. And now he's a bestselling author with the douchiest pen name I ever heard? I mean, it killed me. And I said to myself, you're going to find Vaughn Orifice when you get out of prison, and you're going to get back what he took without asking. We were bros since third grade, but you stole from me when you ghosted. You owe me big, Tyler."

"I told you I'll pay you back for what I took. It gave me a fresh start, and you deserve the same. Let's go somewhere and work out how much I owe you."

"I can have a fresh start and become a famous author?"

"You can do whatever you want."

"Okay, I'm a felon who can't get a job, can't so much as pick my nose without going back to prison, but I can do anything I want."

Prison has made him bitter on top of being unstable. It's a dangerous mix.

He comes closer. He's high on something and drunk, his gait uneven. "So, like I said, I had a lot of time to think about this Vaughn Orifice shit. And I'm trying to put two and two together, but it's not adding up to four. You weren't any genius in school. You were a suck-up all the teachers loved, but you weren't some brilliant writer of bestselling books. And one day I was thinking about that girl everyone was going on about because she was an orphan. Her name was Riley, same as the dedication in *The Sound of Absence*. That's when I put it together with those two laptops you took. I always wondered why you took two crappy laptops instead of more jewelry. I don't think I had to be too much of a genius to figure out you stole the books."

"This is your evidence? Some ridiculous scenario you concocted in prison?"

"It's not ridiculous, and you know it."

I shouldn't have tried talking to him. I should have fought him for what he said about Kiran and his beautiful dress. I feel sick every time I remember the look on Kiran's face. Kaz deserved to be pummeled for that.

Maybe I didn't punch him because I'm still afraid of him. He's a good fighter, and his temper fuels his fists. But tonight he's so stoned I might be able to take him—if not for the cast on my arm.

"So you're okay with me telling the media?" Kaz says.

"You're willing to incriminate yourself to do that?"

"Who said I'd have to incriminate myself? All it takes is an anonymous tip, and they start digging."

It's all over. With that last sentence, Kaz has erased my future. And Riley's, and her family's. Even Julia's. There will be no Julia Mays Foundation. Why does evil always win?

Kaz laughs at my silence. "I have you by the balls, and you know it. I think a million for starters? Does that sound about right?"

I don't know what to do. Should I let him blackmail me? The biggest problem is the money isn't mine. It belongs to the Mays family. I can't believe I've unleashed Kaz on them. Again. And I know from experience that Kaz is never satiated.

"How much do you have in the bank?" Kaz asks. "I hear you just sold another movie."

The sound of crunching gravel catches my attention. Damn it. Riley! She has no idea of the danger she's walking into.

"Hey," I say, trying to keep my voice from shaking. "Were you looking for me? I'll be down in a minute. Go back to the party."

She walks straight toward Kaz. "He owes you nothing. You betrayed him the day you killed Nikki Mays and threatened to implicate him. He had every right to ghost you."

She's been listening. She knows he's extorting me.

"Jesus Christ, you told her?" Kaz says to me.

"I know everything," Riley says. "I also know there were no books on the computers you took."

"Oh really? And how do you know that?"

"Because I'm the daughter of the woman who owned the computers."

"Wait . . . wait . . . what kind of a mind fuck is this? You're Riley?"

He must not have seen the news article about her hitting me with the car.

"I saw you kissing her outside," he says to me. "Your girl is the daughter of that skanky woman with the telescope? Seriously? How did that happen?"

"Get the hell out of here!" Riley shouts, rushing at him.

She stopped just short of making contact, but he backed away, startled by her fury, and his drunkenness caused him to stumble a little. That slight sign of weakness triggers his rage. I see it in his eyes and the tautness of his muscles. I've watched it happen many times.

"Don't get into this, Riley," I warn. "Please go downstairs."

"I'll go downstairs when John Kazmirski leaves."

"She's hot, Tyler, in more ways than one," Kaz says.

"I told you to go!" Riley says. "You have no right to be at this celebration. You were never *bros* with him, and you know it. You dragged him down. You wanted him to be like you—but he was too good. And too smart. You knew back then, and you know it now. He *is* brilliant. Of course he wrote those books!"

Kaz lunges and grabs her into a stranglehold from behind before I can do anything. When I try to intervene, he pulls a gun out of his jacket pocket and presses it to her temple. "What you gonna do, Tyler?"

"Let her go!" Alec bellows.

Alec and Colton rush out of the darkness, and Kaz swings the gun at them. I turn around, pushing them back. "Stop, he has a gun on Riley!"

"Put away the gun, coward," Colton growls. "Let her go, and it's you and me one-on-one."

This is no bear whisperer. Colton's the bear. Alec and I can hardly hold him back.

None of them understand Kaz's instability, and I can only imagine it's worse since he was in prison. He could shoot at any moment. He's done it before.

"One more step and she's dead," Kaz says to Colton. He squeezes Riley's neck and presses the gun to her temple.

Colton looks like an enraged animal about to spring.

"Who is this ginger guy?" Kaz asks.

When I don't reply, Colton says, "I'm the one who's going to kill you first chance I get!"

"Okay. Got that." My legs go weak when Kaz points the gun at Alec. "And who are you?"

"I'm Riley's father. I became her guardian when you killed my cousin."

"Jesus Christ, Tyler! You have a really fucking big mouth!"

"Yes, he's been honest with the people he cares about," Alec says.

Kaz snorts.

"But he has no intention of telling anyone else, for obvious reasons," Alec says. "None of us have thus far, and we won't in the future. Release Riley and we'll all go our separate ways."

"Did he tell you about the books?" Kaz asks.

"We heard your accusation," Alec replies, "and that's all it is: something you've made up to extort him."

"Wrong. If you're not lying, he lied to you. He's not the great guy you think he is. He was the one who cased your cousin's house."

"He did not!" Colton says. "You're the only one responsible for that burglary and murder!"

Alec puts his arm out to quiet Colton. He takes a step toward Kaz. "This can't go anywhere, and you know it. If you try to blackmail him, you'll incriminate yourself, and you committed a murder. There's no sense to this."

"There is sense to it. Like you said, it's blackmail." He tightens his arm on Riley's neck. "And his squeeze arrived just in time to make it easier to squeeze a few million out of him."

He presses hard on Riley, and she starts to struggle because she can't breathe.

I can't bear it. Her pain erases all caution. I rush at him, Alec and Colton with me, but we stop when the gun aims at us.

"Let her breathe!" Alec shouts.

"I will when Mr. Orifice tells me the truth about the books."

He crushes harder, and Riley makes a horrible choking sound.

Colton and I exchange a glance. We're going to jump him, but Kaz sees it and takes aim at my torso. "I won't mind doing more time for shooting you, Tyler. I've dreamed of putting a bullet in your belly every day since you stole my stuff and ran off like a little rat."

Before his last word, he's falling backward. Riley has her leg wrapped around his and yanks it out from under him. She shoves her elbows into him as Colton, Alec, and I leap forward. Kaz and Riley topple backward onto the ground. Riley is perched on top of Kaz when the gun goes off.

"Riley!" I shout. I grab Kaz's hand with my right one and twist it away from Riley. The gun fires again, thankfully missing all of us. I thrust the cast into Kaz's face. The blow stuns him, and I pull Riley from his grasp.

Kaz is on his feet, battling Colton for the gun. When Alec, Riley, and I try to help, Colton yells, "Get her back! Vaughn, get her out of here!"

"No!" Riley screams. She's trying to help Colton. Alec and I pull her back as the gun fires. Then again. I'm not hit, but surely someone was. We were in a tight clump when both shots fired.

Colton stumbles backward with the gun as Kaz slumps to the ground. Colton sets the safety on the gun.

"Who has a phone?" Alec asks. "Call 911!"

None of us has a phone. Mine is in my jacket downstairs, and Alec and Colton aren't ones to be wedded to their phones. Riley left hers behind because she didn't want to carry a purse. Only Sachi and I brought phones.

"Medics won't do him any good," Colton says in a strangely calm tone. "It was a heart shot, or near to it."

Riley starts sobbing. Alec envelops her in his arms as I kneel next to Kaz. He isn't dead yet. He's staring at me, his bloody lips trying to work.

"Oh god. Kaz!" I'm crying, and I swear he's trying to call me Babyass as he dies.

Colton puts his fingers on Kaz's neck to verify. "Yep." He looks around. "Everyone else okay? Riley? Alec?"

"We're okay," Alec says shakily.

I stand, wiping my hands down my wet face as Alec takes off his suit jacket and lays it over Kaz's face. Riley holds me tight. "I'm sorry," she says. "I'm so sorry."

"For what? I'm the one who put you all in danger."

"Not you," Colton says. "It was him. Now I see what you were up against with this guy. No wonder you had to sneak away."

"Did you hear the whole conversation?" I ask.

"We were listening for a while," he replies. "Riley came out to stop you from blabbing about the books. She made Alec and me stay back because she didn't want Kaz to feel threatened." He exhales a soft laugh. "Turns out she's more threatening than all three of us would've been." He sits down in the gravel. "By the way, Riley, good move with the tanglefoot. You're a fighter. I always knew you were."

"I really think we need to call 911," Alec says. "We have to report this."

"Alec?" Sachi calls from the stairwell door.

"Dad, where are you?" Kiran shouts frantically.

"We're okay," Alec calls.

"Damn," Colton says. "I don't want Kiran to see the dead guy."

Riley, Alec, and I stand in front of the body, trying to block it. Sachi throws her hand over her mouth when she sees Kaz. Kiran doesn't seem to notice. He walks straight to me and extends the clock gear with a solemn expression.

"You're giving it back?"

"I have to," he says. "It messed up everything."

I take the gear from his hand.

"I have to be the one to take it out of the clock—so I know where it fits."

"I'm sorry. I'll let you handle the magic from now on, okay?"

"Okay."

Sachi and Alec are whispering, Alec filling her in on what happened. "But what are we going to do?" she says. "How will we explain this?"

"You won't explain anything," I say. "I'm going to tell the police everything."

"What?" Riley says. "You can't do that!"

"I won't entangle you all in my lies. You could be put in jail."

"We'll tell the truth, minus a few details," Alec says. "This man was clearly mentally ill, and he came here to start trouble with you."

"You only need to say he's an acquaintance from your past who was jealous of your success," Riley says. "That was obvious, too. And he was drunk. I smelled it on him."

"He was more than drunk," I say.

"That means they'll find drugs in his body, and that will prove he had reason to behave irrationally. All we leave out is the extortion. It will be easy."

"Believe me, it's not as easy as you think."

"Vaughn, why would you do this now when we've come so far?" Sachi says. "When we all care about you and want you with us?"

"And why would you ruin Julia's books for all those people who love them?" Riley says.

"And what about the Julia Mays Foundation?" Alec says.

I remember the day Colton said, "That family is the love of my life, Vaughn. Don't mess with them." Now I get it. If I weren't still in shock from seeing Kaz die, I think their compassion would have me sobbing.

"You aren't going to blab anything," Colton says to me.

This surprises me. "Your vote is with the family?"

"Of course it is." He sounds strange. He's the only one of us who's seated, and he's hunched over with his arms hugged close to his body. "Promise me right now you won't tell about the books and all that."

"What's wrong with you? Are you hurt?"

"Yeah. That's why you're gonna promise me. I didn't take a damn bullet for you so you could ruin everything."

"Oh my god!" Riley cries. She drops to her knees next to Colton.

Sachi is crying, too, trying to press the buttons for 911. Alec takes the phone from her and puts the call through.

Colton feebly swats away Riley's and Sachi's attempts to open his suit jacket. "Vaughn, I'm serious," he says breathlessly. "Don't let that creep wreck our family. If you do something stupid and go to jail, you'll break Riley's heart. Promise me you'll always be here for her. Promise me I didn't do this for nothing."

"Colton . . . I'm—"

"I'm about to pass out. Would you just say it?"

"Okay, I promise."

"Keep your cool when the cops get here. Don't mess up my family, Vaughn."

"I won't. I know how to lie. You know I do."

He snorts a little laugh. "Okay, good." He puts one hand in the gravel, trying to control his body as he attempts to lie down, but instead he slumps to the ground.

"Oh my god, look at all this blood!" Sachi gasps.

"Colton, no! Stay with us!" Riley cries.

Kiran kneels on Colton's other side, tears streaming.

Riley puts her hands on Colton's cheeks. "Please try, please!" She kisses his cheek. "Don't you dare leave me!"

He opens his eyes and smiles. "I ain't goin' nowhere, Riley."

She sobs with relief. "You better not!"

His eyes close again.

"Colton?" she says. "Colton?"

"I'm not going . . . ," he mumbles. "Just tired. I love you, Riley."

The keen of sirens grows louder.

31

RILEY

Kiran selected our clothing for the memorial service. He wants us in vintage white. He chose white because that's what people wear at Hindu funerals. Kiran has studied religions with Sachi, and he knows many ancestors on his mother's side were Hindus and most were Christian on his father's side. He said he chose white over black because it's *prettier and happier.*

I sit on the porch swing, settling the box of ashes in my lap. The rest of the family is finishing lunch, but I feel too sick to eat. Just the thought of saying goodbye for the last time is already tearing my heart out.

I hear car tires crunching gravel. I set the ashes on the bench to greet Colton as he parks his car next to Vaughn's. We hug tight, so much tighter since the night in Chicago. I add a kiss to his cheek before we part, and he grins. "If I'd known I could get kisses from you just by taking a bullet, I'd have done it much sooner."

"You shouldn't joke about that night. I thought I'd never see you again."

"It's not my fault you didn't believe me. I said I wasn't going anywhere, and I meant it."

He insists hunting from an early age made him familiar with bullet wounds, and he knew how long he could wait before an ambulance was called. He wanted the family to plan their story before his injury distracted us. And he needed to make sure Vaughn didn't incriminate himself. He said he'd never seen me happier than I'd been during our days at the Drake, and he wanted me to stay that way. Nothing like *I took a bullet for you* to get Vaughn to comply.

The promise Vaughn made to Colton worked. It saved Vaughn, Julia's books, and the Julia Mays Foundation. In many ways, it saved all of us.

There is no better being on Earth than Colton Reed. I know that with certainty now. Just thinking about what he did that night still makes me cry.

He notes my tears, his chicory-flower eyes brimming with concern. "Well darn. I'm sorry, Riley. I won't joke about it anymore."

"It's okay. Keep joking about it. I need to remember to lighten up—especially today."

He wraps his arm around me and walks me to the porch. "You'll feel better when you give her back to the Earth. I know you will. It's time to let her go."

I start tearing up again. We nestle into the porch swing, his arm wrapped around me. He pushes his feet on the wood planks to gently swing us.

"There's lunch inside," I tell him.

"Nah, I ate. I'd rather be here."

He keeps us softly swaying. I hold the white box against my chest. The moment—his embrace, the warm June day, the gentle weight of Julia's ashes in my arms, the voices of Vaughn and my family drifting from the kitchen out the open windows—is almost unbearably poignant.

Vaughn comes out through the screen door. Colton gets up and they embrace. They usually do if they haven't seen each other for a while.

Colton takes in Vaughn's white tuxedo. "Well look at you. Now you really are a white rabbit."

"If the tux fits," Vaughn says. "And it was a bargain, only five dollars."

Finding cheap used suits for Alec and Vaughn was easy because white isn't a popular suit color. Alec's suit is eighties-style and Vaughn's tux looks like it's from the seventies. Sachi and I are wearing vintage wedding dresses. Kiran has always been drawn to old wedding dresses, and he didn't mind that Sachi shortened them so we could move more easily.

"How'd it go with the doctor today?" Vaughn asks Colton.

"I'm as good as new." He adds, "Better than new. Leigh says the bullet scar is sexy." He winks at Vaughn. "I owe you for that."

Alec and Sachi laugh as they come onto the porch and hug Colton.

Kiran does the same, then frowns as he surveys Colton's white T-shirt and cargo shorts. "I said to wear *vintage* white," he says.

"It's the best I could do," Colton says. "And it is vintage. These shorts are horribly out of fashion now."

Kiran smiles. "I'm wearing your favorite outfit."

Kiran's wearing clothing we had in the house, and it's quite a contrast to our formal wear. The belted sixties-era shirtdress with matching white vinyl go-go boots is one of his favorite outfits for dress-up lunches. Colton always says it's his favorite look for Kiran.

"In that outfit, you're an impossible act to follow," Colton says. "I'm glad I didn't spend long on mine."

"Are you hungry?" Sachi asks.

"I'm good." Colton looks at me. "I think we should get on with the ashes. Riley doesn't need more waiting."

I receive sympathetic looks from each of them.

"I'm okay. But Colton is right. Let's walk over."

Vaughn holds my hand, the box of ashes in my other. I'm finally going to do it. And I have no doubts.

Nikki's ashes were scattered a few weeks ago. Sachi didn't want them in the attic after she found out what Nikki did. She asked if I minded her dispersing my mother's remains, and I was grateful for the offer. She's kept the location secret from all of us. She told me it's a pretty place and she said a prayer.

Vaughn tightens his hold on my hand as we walk up the hill toward the tree. All these years the perfect place for Julia's ashes was right here in front of me, but I couldn't see it.

My family waits in considerate silence. When I'm ready, Vaughn helps support the box with his cast as I untwist the tie on the plastic bag. I caress the Julia moondust for the last time, thinking of all the times I've talked to the ashes, hugged the carton to my chest, cried all over the cardboard.

Now I have Julia's books to touch. All four are on the shelf where I kept the ashes.

"I won't give a speech or anything like that. To get an idea of who Julia was, read her books. And I don't have anything more to say to Julia. I've said everything I've wanted to say to her for ten years."

I take a handful of the ashes into my hand. "Sachi, would you say a prayer while I scatter them?"

"I will, my love."

She softly recites poetic words, a mix of her own spirituality and the many beliefs she grew up with. Her way with prayer is earthy and inclusive, perfect for Julia.

I sprinkle the first handful of ashes around the oak trunk I lean against when I read novels and schoolbooks. I read the last of Julia's books in this shade two weeks ago. I scatter ashes over the grass where Sachi painted the watercolor of me. I walk in a circle around the tree, casting more of the cherished powder over the ground where Kiran and I have held tea parties and pretended we're explorers on a distant planet. I save the last Julia moondust for the grassy earth where Vaughn and I first made love beneath the moon, at the outer reaches of the oak's branches. I turn the empty box upside down and tap the side, releasing fine dust into the breeze. It floats away in little clouds, and I wonder how far it will drift.

Goodbye, Julia. I love you.

Already the ashes I scattered into the grass are mostly invisible, assimilated into the earth.

Julia holds a palm of earth out to me. "There are bits of stars in this soil, Riley."

The perfect place for her.

"Riley, look." Vaughn is pointing at the sky.

The moon. A daylight moon, blue and white, lucent, one of the most wondrous sights from Earth. Yet so few people notice it.

My family steps out from under the tree to look at it. "I like the moon in the day," Kiran says. "The oceans are blue, like when you painted the water into them."

"I like that, too."

Sachi hugs and kisses me, then Alec and Colton. Kiran wraps his arms around my waist. "I love you, Riley."

"I love you, too, Kee."

Vaughn stands apart, looking at me, his eyes expressing more than words could ever say.

"Take your time," Sachi says. "We'll have dessert when you get back."

I give her the box as they depart.

Vaughn bundles me into his arms. His warmth and smell are comforting.

"Does it hurt?" he asks.

"Yes. But I like her being free in this place more than it hurts."

We hold each other. Chimney swifts twitter over the field. Oak leaves whisper their soft poetry. An approaching storm's thunder rumbles.

I pull out of his arms to watch the advance of black clouds. "It'll rain soon. The ashes will wash into the soil."

He touches my cheek, sympathy in his gaze.

"It's okay. She would like that. She always did like summer storms."

He smiles. Yet always there is that sadness in his expression. I know it will never leave him. His past can't be mended in the same way as mine. He knows the world would scorn him if they knew what he did. How difficult it must be to live with that. Sometimes, when I look in his eyes, I feel as if my heart is breaking. But in the same moment it starts again, renewed and stronger. Like Kiran's heart at the moment of his birth.

I pull him close and kiss him. The kind that stretches time and space.

I used to think the darkness inside Vaughn and me was what drew us together. Now I believe it was light. Julia's light. From the moment we met, we recognized what we'd each learned from Julia, and nothing could stop us from being attracted to all that beauty.

"I want to tell you something," he says.

I wonder why his voice trembles.

"I love you," he says, but his eyes change, like a window being shuttered. Saying it has frightened him. "I've never said that to anyone. Not once. It took me a long time to even figure out if it was love. But I think it is."

"It is love. I've been afraid to say it, too."

His gray eyes open all their passion and wonder to me again.

I smooth back a wave of hair that has drifted over his eye. "I think I've loved you since that night on the pier when I held your hand."

His eyes brighten more. "I felt that, too. Was that love we were feeling?"

"I don't know. It was something real if we both felt it."

"Magic," he says.

"It had to be."

We kiss again. Thunder rumbles closer, and the sky darkens. He makes shivers ripple over my skin, nuzzling beneath my ear. "I want to stay here and make love in the storm," he says.

"Sounds dangerous."

"It always will be for us."

"You know I can handle that."

"Yes, I know."

"We'd better go before it pours. We're expected for dessert."

He nibbles my neck. "I prefer salt at the moment."

He's difficult to resist. Especially when he looks so good in a tuxedo, his farm-tanned face and wind-tousled dark hair all the more striking in contrast to the formal, white jacket. I reluctantly pull away from his kisses and tug his hand. "Come on. Kiran and Sachi made my favorite dessert to cheer me up."

"Haven't I cheered you up?"

"You have. Much more than pecan pie ever could."

As we descend the hill, he asks, "Will you still want to make love here?"

"Her ashes make this hill more precious to me. Making love could only get better."

"I'm glad to hear that."

Butterflies and moths scatter out of flowers in our wake.

"How's the book going?" he asks.

"Good. And no, you can't see it yet."

"Just a peek?"

"No."

The house is in sight when the first raindrops fall. We run, laughing, as the downpour begins. The rest of the family is seated on the front porch, smiling when we run up the stairs holding hands.

"You look like people in pictures and movies who just got married," Kiran says.

"I guess we do in these clothes," Vaughn says.

"And because you look so happy." He gazes curiously at Vaughn. "Do you want to marry Riley?"

Vaughn and I exchange amused glances. We've only just found the courage to say we love each other.

"I want you to get married," Kiran says. "And I get to choose your clothes."

Everyone laughs.

"Do you think Riley would say yes if I asked her?" Vaughn asks Kiran.

"Why can't she ask you? Maybe I'll help her pick out a pretty ring for you."

Vaughn grins. "You'd like that, wouldn't you?"

"I would. I know a store that sells the best vintage rings. I like the amethyst and diamond ones."

"This is sounding better and better. Here . . ." Vaughn pulls off his watch and hands it to him.

"Really? I can take it apart?"

He nods. "Put in a good word with the universe for me."

Kiran runs into the house, screen door banging. His go-go boots clatter up the wooden stairs. Sachi, Alec, and Colton are all grins.

I look at the pale band the Rolex left on Vaughn's tanned wrist. "I can't believe you did that. Isn't that an expensive watch?"

"It was, but it's too beat up to be worth anything now. I bought it after the first book, and I've never felt I deserved it. It only makes me feel bad when I look at it."

"I'm sorry."

"Don't be. I'm glad it makes someone happy. And maybe it'll make some good magic."

"Watch out. His magic is pretty powerful."

"I know. That's why I gave it to him."

My family sees how we're looking at each other. "We'll get the pies ready," Sachi says as they enter the house.

Vaughn holds my hands. Rain drips down his hair and beads on his eyelashes. "Will you get down on one knee when you ask me?"

"I'm sure I can think of something more interesting than that."

"Such as . . . ?"

"We'll be sitting on the hill watching the moon rise. As Alec begins playing 'Hallelujah' on his trumpet, a cloud of luna moths will float down bearing an amethyst and diamond ring on their wings."

"I like it."

"If the magic Kiran makes is especially good, a pack of coyotes will sing a chorus with the trumpet. A few snowshoe hares may somehow be involved, but that remains to be seen."

"I'm really looking forward to this."

I wrap my arms around him. "Will you say yes?"

He pulls me closer. "How can I know my answer before the watch is taken apart?"

"Come on, you know Julia always writes happy endings."

ACKNOWLEDGMENTS

Thank you to my readers, especially my friends on Instagram, for your encouragement as I worked on this story during difficult pandemic months.

Much appreciation to my agent, Carly Watters, for your support and help when I decided to rewrite this manuscript.

Huge thanks to editors Alicia Clancy and Laura Chasen for all you've done to improve this story.

Thank you to everyone at P.S. Literary Agency and Lake Union Publishing for helping bring my books to the world.

Many thanks to Dr. Dave Steadman for paleontological advice.

More thanks to Dr. Akito Kawahara for help with details of moth natural history.

Last, another round of appreciation for my husband, Scott, who's always there to help with a writing crisis, even at three in the morning.

ABOUT THE AUTHOR

Photo © 2021 Scott K. Robinson

Glendy Vanderah is the *Wall Street Journal, Washington Post,* and Amazon Charts bestselling author of *Where the Forest Meets the Stars* and *The Light Through the Leaves.* Glendy worked as an endangered-bird specialist in Illinois before she became a writer. Originally from Chicago, she now lives in rural Florida with her husband and as many birds, butterflies, and wildflowers as she can lure to her land. For more information, visit www.glendyvanderah.com.